The
Price of Greed

The Displacers Series

Book 4

Simon Brading

First published 2017

This edition published 2025

Cover design by Andrėja Dikšaitytė

www.forgottenscriptorium.com

ISBN: 978-1-917470-53-7

JJH.

PROLOGUE

Peru, 1914

Cordoba's research had been correct - the entrance was pristine, untouched by human hand in centuries, covered with vegetation and dirt from the landslide that had hidden any sign that it had ever existed.

It had taken him weeks to dig around the doorway, clearing away enough earth for him to be able to squeeze through. It could have been done much quicker, but he hadn't wanted to bring in anyone here to help him; secrecy was paramount, especially here in the jungles of Peru where the remnants of the local tribes jealously guarded their territories. This way, if he found what he thought was inside, he would be able to grab it and disappear without anyone ever knowing he had been there, until he published his research, of course, and then fame would finally be his.

Fame.

It had never been his goal to become famous, he had only ever been a scholar, but that was before that American, Hiram Bingham, *such a stupid name*, came along and made everything so distastefully newsworthy. The man was nothing more than a glorified tourist. Bingham had just waltzed in and the locals had taken one look at his stupid grin and annoyingly perfect white teeth and taken him on a tour of the local ruins, probably for the promise of gold.

He wouldn't have minded, but they happened to be the very same ruins that he himself had spent years of research locating and was about to catalogue. He had trekked up the mountain, watching every step he took to make sure he didn't step on anything, just to find the useless gringo kicking the dirt off his boots against a priceless Incan carving while the natives dug the statues out of the ground with pickaxes. It was all he could do to stop himself from strangling the man then and there, instead he had just turned around and walked back down the mountain.

Bingham was back there now, thankfully with a full team of archaeologists who would hopefully stop him from doing any more damage. The idiotic amateur still didn't have any idea what he was dealing with and he wasn't about to enlighten him; the American could do his own work.

That had been 1911 and Cordoba had spent the last three years doing research, chasing rumours, mapping the trails through the jungle, following paths that hadn't been trod in centuries and extrapolating the likely places where ancient cities and temples would have been.

It had been a stroke of luck to find a reference to this particular place in a carving from Cusco. Years ago it had been mistranslated and discarded as useless by "experts," but for him it had been the last piece of a puzzle finally falling into place, leading him here, to what could be the most important find of his career.

He bent down and peered into the shallow hole that he'd painstakingly opened into the depths of the hill.

The hill had actually been a pyramidal temple until a landslide from the nearby mountain had covered it and the settlements around it - it had only been a thin layer of mud, just a few feet thick, but according to his research it had been enough for the superstitious locals to see it as a sign of the displeasure of the gods and they had moved away, which caused the surrounding trails to become unused and forgotten, the forest overgrown and wild.

Cordoba could smell the staleness of the air coming from the hole and was encouraged; if it was that bad it meant nobody had been inside for many years, but, more importantly, it was also far more likely that whatever was hidden away in the pyramid would be well preserved.

He took his pocket watch out and wrote the time down in his journal along with the entry *broke through mud wall*, then sat down against a nearby stone and pulled his hat low over his eyes for a snooze - he would wait an hour before going in; he didn't want to suffocate.

Almost exactly an hour later he woke. He checked his watch again and noted the time in his journal once more, writing the entry *attempting ingress* next to it. He liked to keep fastidious records; in his line of work you never know when the notes you made were going to become part of history.

He went to the hole and took another breath of the air. It still smelled of must and damp, but it was cleaner, fresher, and more breathable. Ideally he would want to wait longer before going in, just to make sure, but he wasn't feeling very patient; he'd been overshadowed for too long and it was time to grab the spotlight.

He lit a lantern and went in.

He'd been precisely right in the orientation of his digging and the hole opened up directly into the antechamber of the temple itself.

It wasn't very big, but he hadn't expected it to be; the nearby villages and trade routes hadn't been important or large enough to warrant a large temple. What made this one special, and infinitely valuable, though, was that it had been buried and abandoned and had lain undiscovered so anything that had been inside when it was in use would still be there and not looted, which would make it unique, almost in the whole world.

He trod carefully, looking around avidly, taking in the details.

There was evidence everywhere of the people who had worshipped there. Rotted baskets, scattered goods, rusted tools and animal bones showed the offerings that had been brought to the temple the day of the landslide and abandoned in the rush to leave. It was an incredible find and the insights it would provide into Incan life would be remarkable, but that was work for the future and wasn't what he was there for - what he was really looking to find that day would be further into the temple, where only the priests were allowed to go.

Picking his way across the room he made his way towards the back, where a small door led towards the inner sanctum, and there he stopped.

That was where the traps would start.

He scanned the walls and the floor, swiftly identifying a few simple trips and switches; all standard stuff and easily avoided. He was still too close to the public areas of the temple for there to be anything too elaborate yet; that would come soon, in those rooms where the priests would have had elaborate rituals and movements to perform when they entered, movements that would have seemed mystical to the uninitiated, but had simply been the way to avoid the hidden dangers.

The further he moved into the temple, the better preserved it was; closed doors had sealed rooms and kept away much of the moisture of the damp earth that had covered it for centuries. The light from his lantern revealed carvings and paintings on the walls that looked almost as fresh as the day they had been made, priceless religious ornaments standing on pedestals, unique examples of ceremonial robes and hats hanging on dummies, even chests along the wall in one room that undoubtedly contained precious metal and stone offerings - the temple was filled with a veritable treasure trove, an archaeologist's dream, but still none of it was the prize he sought.

Cordoba was looking for something much more impressive to carry with him to the outside world, something to show off when he applied for funding to come back with a proper team (like that idiot, Bingham, who had somehow persuaded Yale University and National Geographic to give him money) and if the layout of this temple was anything like that of similar ones that had been documented in Peru then there should be one last chamber ahead.

That was where he would find the idol.

He put his shoulder against the massive door that safeguarded the Sanctum Sanctorum of the temple and pushed, stumbling and almost falling as the door swung open easily, soundlessly, its mechanism as fresh and well-balanced as it had been the day it the temple had been buried.

A breath of air came out of the room as the seal was broken. It wasn't fresh, but somehow it smelt of incense, not of musty earth or decay.

He lifted his lantern and looked through the doorway.

The room was glowing and for a second he thought that, impossibly, there was a light source inside the room, but he realised that it was just the reflection from his own lantern; the walls were almost completely covered in gold, stamped with figures and writing. This chamber alone would provide a lifetime of study and might well provide answers to many of the mysteries of the ancient civilisations of the Americas, but that also was a task for another day and, much as he wanted to spend hours looking around, he forced himself to concentrate on his goal - there, on a small dais in the centre of the otherwise empty room, was the idol.

It was just a head, only about a foot high and gold, but, unlike the walls, which were just reflecting the light from his lantern, it seemed to shine with a light of its own that came from within it. It was an almost mystical moment as he stared at it; he could almost feel its eyes piercing his soul, its stern expression judging his very existence.

He shuddered and tore his gaze from it with difficulty to look around the door frame and at the floor in front of him. He immediately spotted several possible pressure plates and various tiny levers that would set off traps. The walls nearby were dotted with little holes, which he knew from experience held minuscule darts that would be set off if he made the wrong step. There were also a few very obvious traps around the idol - he could make out a couple of them from where he stood and he would deal with them when he got to it, along with the not so obvious ones that would undoubtedly be there.

Usually the traps in a temple this old would have failed long ago; the wires and cords that they used would have rotted and decayed and the poison on the darts would have lost its potency, but this temple was so well preserved that he couldn't rely on that to be true and he would have to take especial care.

He took his watch out again and once more noted the time in his diary alongside the entry *entered the inner chamber.*

He replaced his watch and diary in his pockets, making sure that they were secured and wouldn't spill out and set something off, then took his first cautious step forwards.

It took him almost half an hour to cross the room, stopping and scouring the floor for traps before he moved his feet. Several times he had to backtrack and look for an alternate route when he found his way completely blocked, but finally he made it to the dais and felt safe enough to lift his eyes and gaze upon his prize.

'Cordoba Fernández? You're *right* on time.'

The voice came from right next to him and he barely managed to stop himself staggering backwards in surprise as he came face to face with a man standing behind the dais, casually leaning on it.

'What...? Who...?'

'My name is Larry Croft and I'm the world's laziest tomb raider.'

'You're what?'

'Oh, never mind.' The man waved away the question. 'I don't know why I even bother, people aren't going to get pop culture references from almost a century after their time, now, are they?'

Cordoba gave him a blank stare then looked around, expecting to see some sign of where the man had come from. There was nothing. 'How did you get here?'

'Magic!'

'Really?'

The man laughed, mockingly. 'No! Of course not!'

Cordoba's tongue involuntarily wet his lips as the man reached out and gently touched the idol. He watched nervously as a long thin finger caressed the hair that had been lovingly carved into it, each individual strand clearly discernible, the dirty and bitten nail an insult to the purity of the statue.

He wanted nothing more than to slap the hand away, but that might have set off the pressure plate that the idol was resting on and there was no way of knowing what that would set off. Perhaps the ceiling would fall, or the floor collapse into a pit - although those were rather stupid and destructive measures that would have meant having to build a whole new temple every time someone made a mistake while cleaning and were best suited to the pulps that seemed so popular these days with weak-minded idiots.

His train of thought was cut off abruptly as the man moved his hand down to cup the idol under its chin. He still didn't move it, though, (even though he certainly spoke like a fool, he didn't seem to be one) so there was still a chance to warn him about the trap. However, before he could do so, the man spoke again.

'You know, I'm sorry to deprive you of the sole reason for your presence in the history books, but I assure you that it is for a *very* good cause.'

Cordoba watched as the bizarre looking young man closed his eyes in concentration. He opened his mouth to ask what he was doing, but...

He shook his head, suddenly feeling a little disorientated.

He looked around the room, positive that he had heard something, but it was empty. He shrugged and turned his eyes back to the dais in front of him.

He blinked.

Wasn't there supposed to be something there?

And what was that rumbling noise?

Quentin opened his eyes and looked down at the large reference book that was propped open on his lap: "Peru and the Incas". The description of renowned Spanish archaeologist Enrique "Cordoba" Fernández's discovery and subsequent excavation of an extensive and remarkably well preserved tomb complex in the Peruvian jungle, along with the incredibly precise and extremely helpful excerpt from Cordoba's own journal, had been replaced by a two page aerial photo of the Nazca lines.

He snapped the book closed with a chuckle, then laid it to one side, placing the surprisingly heavy golden head on top of it.

He opened his laptop and connected to Skype. He waited impatiently for a few minutes, but eventually received the incoming call that he had been expecting.

There was no image, just voice: the Master's voice.

'Did you get it?'

'Yes, sir.' Quentin picked up the idol and held it in front of the camera briefly. He grinned.

'Good. That will be all.'

'Sir!' Quentin called out, trying to prevent the Master from disconnecting. There was silence for a few seconds and he thought that his boss had gone, but then there was a crackling noise and the voice returned.

'What is it, Mr Price? I am very busy.'

'Well, sir.' Quentin frowned as the noise came over the speakers again. It was annoying, but it wasn't static because the connection was always perfect. 'It's all very well and good for me to go back and retrieve things like this, and don't get me wrong, I don't mind doing it, but... well it's not as if we don't already have funds, and, um, I think my talents could be better put to use on more important ventures.'

'We can never have enough "funds", Mr Price, and besides, we have to replenish what was lost in that police raid last month. As for giving you something important to do - we know that the damn Elders can sense changes before we make them and the Vives boy seems to be able to handle you easily enough, so we are going to have to take a different approach.'

There was another pause accompanied by crunching noises this time.

'As I told you before, I will take care of things for now - I am working on something big and, be assured, you will have your part to play in that. Be patient, Mr Price. Once Andrew is dead the Displacers will fall apart and we will be able to take over. Also, do not forget that Sam Vives is not the one that the prophecies speak about; that person is still out there and there is still a chance to turn them to our side. If we manage to do that then there will be nothing to stop us!'

Quentin stared at the blank screen as the sound of Masters laughter rang out, but then it was abruptly cut off as the call disconnected.

His mind was in turmoil; there were so many questions, so many scenarios going around in his head. What would happen to him when the Master found whoever the prophecies talked about? Would he still have a place in the Illuminati? Would the Master even let him live after all of his failures?

He remained staring at the screen, distracted. He reached out almost automatically for the crisps he had been eating before he Displaced.

He popped one in his mouth and started chewing, then froze as he realised what the noises he'd been hearing in the background were - it was highly significant and a mark of the Master's lack of respect and consideration for Quentin that he had been eating crisps while talking to him. It did not bode well for his future.

All because of that bloody Vives kid.

CHAPTER 1
SCHOOL OF HARD KNOCKS

Greece, 487BC

"He's not the Messiah, he's a very naughty boy!"

Thanks to Rachel's joking around, the line from the Monty Python film was what came to Sam every time he thought back to the announcement that Philip had made at the Displacer's Christmas dinner.

And, thanks to the momentary distraction as his mind wandered back to the party, he was now lying on the dirt floor of the courtyard, groaning in pain in front of the large audience who had come to watch him and his fellow students fight.

'Sam isn't the chosen one!'

Philip had burst in to the dining room and, unable to contain himself, had just blurted the information out without so much as a greeting or a by your leave, interrupting Sam just as he was about to tell the gathered Society about his Displacement to Victorian London with Rachel.

When all eyes turned from him to the old man, a relieved Sam took the opportunity to slide back into his chair, hoping that his report would be forgotten and he wouldn't have to address the members after all.

Philip was the Society's expert on all things ancient Egyptian and had just that day, after months of careful work, managed to read the scroll that Sam had brought back from a previous journey into the past.

The Displacers had expected that the scroll would give them confirmation that Sam was the one that was spoken about in the prophecies, the one who was destined to save them all, but in just five words Philip had dashed all their hopes.

After his initial outburst, Philip had looked around, noticing the shocked faces of the members and realised how devastating his statement had to have been for them. He deflated and apologised profusely before going to take his place at the table, moving with far more dignity than he had when he had flung open the doors and made his entrance.

Every face at the table followed him as he pulled out his chair and sat.

He licked his lips nervously as he looked around the group and when he tried to talk his voice came out as a croak. He sipped at the wine that was hastily poured for him, then cleared his throat.

'First of all I'd like to apologise…'

James, Sam's Grandfather and the senior Elder, waved his hands and interrupted. 'There is no need to apologise, Philip. Please, just get to the point. What did the scroll say, exactly, and is your reading of it open to further interpretation?'

Philip shook his head. 'I'm afraid not; the translation is unequivocal. Lisa can corroborate. I'm afraid that the inevitable conclusion is that Sam is not the one that the prophecies talk about.'

Heads turned briefly to Lisa, who had worked with Philip on the restoration and translation of the scroll. She confirmed his statement with a nod and there were groans from all around the table; they hadn't wanted to believe it, they had wanted there to be some room to manoeuvre so that they could keep clinging to their hope that they had found the answer to their worsening problems in Sam.

'However, far from taking all merit away from Sam, the scroll adds more information to the existing Prophecy. I can now say with absolute confidence that, while he is not the *main* subject of the Prophecy, he still has a far greater role in it than any normal Displacer could possibly have.'

'Explain, please, Philip. And please, be succinct.' This came from Andrew who was the leader of the Displacers and Sam's uncle.

There were chuckles as Philip spluttered in protest, but they weren't unkind and he soon nodded in acknowledgement of the validity of Andrew's request - self-awareness was a side-effect of a Displacer's very long life and he himself knew very well how he could go on, especially about a subject of which he was enthusiastic, and the Prophecy was very definitely one of those subjects.

'Perhaps I should first read what the Prophecy has to say?'

Andrew nodded. 'That might be a good start, thank you.'

As Philip pulled a piece of paper from his pocket and put on his reading glasses, Sam watched from his place near the end of the table as dozens of people unconsciously leaned forward to hear the old man speak. He looked around, finding almost universal expressions of shock on all of their faces, tainted with a sliver of hope at the news that the Prophecy might not be as simple as they'd though, but there was one member showing quite a different emotion - a smirk was twisting the corner of the mouth of Ralph Price, the father of Sam's nemesis, Quentin, and the one-time rival to Andrew for leadership of the "Honourable Society of Displacers". He was the only one at the table that didn't seem to be taking the news in the slightest bit badly, in fact he seemed to be enjoying himself immensely. Sam filed the information away for later as Philip started to read.

'"The time will come when agencies will work against *Thoth*, and, in that time of need, will come forth the *Diviner* to pave the way forwards. But it will not be until the *Changer* ascends that the balance of fate will truly tip and the world will plunge into eternal darkness or be lifted into grace."' Philip finished and looked up from the paper. 'The only part of that which is perhaps open to debate are the names of the two parties mentioned, the "Changer" and "Diviner". There are various possible translations for each, but I have chosen the ones that best fit the context and the other scraps of the Prophecy that we already have.'

There was a long silence as the group digested the information.

Surprisingly, in the presence of so many intellectuals and great minds, it was Rachel that broke the silence. 'I'm really hoping that you didn't just call Sam divine, because his head is big enough already as it is.'

There was quite some laughter at that and, through his embarrassment, Sam noticed his grandfather smile and nod at Rachel. His heart swelled as he realised that she had deliberately made a flippant comment to break the tension that was threatening to swamp the room and spoil their celebration dinner. It was so like Rachel to deflect attention on herself and take it away from others who couldn't defend themselves.

James tapped his knife against his glass and stood up, forestalling any other comments. 'I suggest that we leave the debating on Sam's godlike status until after we have finished the wonderful meal that

Richard had prepared us. I for one do not want my dinner to get cold; I have enough problems with my digestion these days as it is!'

Shouts of approval rang out around the table and Richard, whose restaurant had provided the food, left to go and organise the next course.

Andrew called Sam and Rachel's attention, and they leaned in close to him over the noise. 'After what you two just did, the pressure should be off for a while and I can probably do without you for a couple of months. Why don't you take a break and plan something fun for your next Displacement together?'

He smiled at them, then turned away to follow the other conversations going on.

Rachel smiled across the table at Sam. 'I've got some *wonderful* places to take you!'

'Great, I need a break! I want to have some fun!' Sam smiled wistfully. 'A beach would be nice. I can just see it now: some sun, a few massages... anything to take my mind off of all this stress for a while!'

The one thing that the Displacement *hadn't* been was fun; the training they had come for had been brutal, violent and single-minded in its purpose.

Rachel had a long list of times and places that she wanted to go to when she had the chance; she was obsessed with martial arts and physical training, and at the very top of that list was ancient Sparta - she wanted to go through the *Agoge*, the training that a young Spartan man went through.

When they had Displaced they had appeared at the edge of a grass field and Sam had immediately seen the young men and women exercising nearby.

They were all nude.

He had instantly turned a bright red and his mouth had dropped open.

They were all so lithe, so good looking...

He didn't feel Rachel's hand slip from his, but he did feel it when she slapped his arse as hard as she could.

'Ow!' He rubbed himself and found that he was actually in pain; the slap had stung much more than it should have. Which was explained when he looked down and found that he was just as naked as everybody else. 'Oh...'

If anything he went even redder and moved to cover himself.

Rachel laughed. 'Sam, this is Sparta, of course everybody exercises naked! What did you expect? Under Armour under the armour?' She looked him up and down and grinned her lopsided grin. 'Anyway, you shouldn't worry; you have nothing to be ashamed of.'

She ran away, her beautiful blue eyes sparkling with amusement and her blonde hair flowing behind her, to join the young men and it was only then that he saw that she was just as uncovered as everybody else.

He could have stood there watching her all day, if it hadn't been for the shout in his ear and the stick hitting him in the back of the legs which instantly drove all lustful thoughts from his mind.

'You! Get moving and join the rest before I make you regret it!'

He looked up into the furious eyes of a huge man in bright armour and yelped as he was struck again.

He ran awkwardly across the grass to join Rachel and the other young men in their training, pursued all the way by the man and his flailing stick.

The days from then on had been filled with such intense training that he didn't often get a chance to appreciate Rachel's body as he would have liked, but the short times he was able to catch his breath and watch her were moments that he knew he would remember for the rest of his life.

To start with, Sam had been puzzled as to why they were letting Rachel exercise with the young men and not telling her to go with the girls, but he soon realised that it was a Displacer thing; she had wanted to train with the boys and the Displacement had fortunately obliged, placing her in the time-line as a boy. He remembered his first Displacement and the way he had seen Quentin as a weedy young man while everybody else had seen a tough pirate. The same thing had happened to him - everyone had seen him as a handsome (probably) captain and not a fifteen year old kid; when you Displaced you arrived in the past not as yourself, but as someone that would fit into the time-line so, while he saw Rachel as she was in the real world, everybody else saw her and knew her as a young man who was already taking part in the training.

It had been essential that she arrived as a male because, while the young women did go through some training, it was nowhere near as extensive and strenuous as what the men went through, and of course Rachel had wanted to do the tougher training. It did, however, make things somewhat complicated between the two of them; they had to be careful how much they were together and couldn't be as close as they had been during their previous Displacements - in Victorian London they had lived happily as husband and wife, but in Sparta that wasn't possible. In fact their situation reminded Sam of their trip to Okinawa to train with Master Hamato. It had been their first long Displacement together and they had trained for years, side by side, fighting each other and learning together - it hadn't been until the very last day, the very last hours before they had come home, that they had finally given in to their attraction for each other.

They had come to love and care for each other over years spent together in the past, so it was understandably frustrating for them to have to restrain themselves once more.

Fortunately they were almost always far too tired to even think about anything romantic; the conditions they were living under were inhumane, with the constant exercise, hunger and pain that young Spartans were subjected to, and Sam often wondered why he was even there, it was so bad. But then he took one look at Rachel and he knew exactly why.

They had come at the height of Sparta's military might, only a few years before the battle of Thermopylae, when the training that was given to the young men was at its most strenuous and there had been times when even Rachel had been close to giving up because, while their previous training gave the two of them an advantage when it came to fighting, there was no way they could match the sense of purpose that the other students had due to their upbringing; their whole culture was based around their ability to fight and they approached it as if their survival depended on it, which it did. So, the other youths were able to put up with incredible levels of abuse that, as Rachel commented, would have "broken an SAS sergeant".

The only thing that had stopped them from going home several times had been each other; they valued these times together so highly that they were willing to struggle through anything and they knew that they would come out the other side stronger than ever.

'Really, Sam, that was bloody awful!'

Rachel's chiding insult brought him out of his thoughts and back to himself and the "fun" Displacement she had brought them on. It was only one of many such jibes, and worse, that rang out around the courtyard as everybody watching his match, students, teachers and onlookers alike, called out their derision at his incompetence - it was traditional for an audience to hurl abuse at a fighter who did badly; it was the Spartan way of spurring him to greater efforts.

Sam was furious at himself for his mistake; failure was not an option, failure meant never becoming a citizen or gaining acceptance into society.

He flushed in humiliation as he picked up his long stave and struggled to his feet.

However, his shame wasn't just for the insults, but also because he was naked in front of all those people - he'd become somewhat accustomed to not wearing anything while exercising over the two years they had been there and it had actually been quite liberating, but he wasn't usually the centre of attention like he was at that moment; his was the only fight taking place so everybody was watching it. Also, since they had been getting closer and closer to their final test there had been more and more people observing them every day. And of course the young girls who trained with them were there all the time now, watching the boys with obvious interest as they strove to become men. It all served to make him suddenly conscious of how exposed he was.

Sam hid his pain, burying it deeply, and turned to face the young man who had thrown him to the floor.

Normally he wouldn't have a problem defeating this opponent; he had done so many times before, but that had made him complacent and his thoughts had wandered back to the present-day and what awaited him there - he'd been distracted, only briefly, but enough for the man to put him on his back.

Sam was barely upright before his opponent attacked again, coming at him with a straightforward attack, nothing complicated, and Sam blocked it with ease and stepped out to give himself room to retaliate.

He stumbled slightly; the blow that had knocked him off his feet had hit his calf muscle and it was weak beneath him now, putting him off balance. He compensated for his weakness automatically, shifting weight onto his good side, but overplayed his vulnerability, making it look like he was an easy target, then, as his opponent came in for what he thought was an easy finishing blow, he thrust with his staff.

It was a simple blow, but it had been completely unexpected and it took the boy directly in the solar plexus, instantly knocking his breath from him and sending him to the ground, choking and squirming.

The bout wasn't over until the teacher said it was, so Sam followed through with a circular swing, aiming for the back of the boy's head, just as he would on the battlefield.

'Stop!'

The shout came just in time and, with reflexes honed over two years of training, Sam halted the blow inches from its target.

He withdrew, receiving the silence that was all the congratulations he was going to get from the onlookers.

Failure was punished harshly, but a victory was not something to be celebrated, it was simply *expected*.

That night, Sam and Rachel sat side by side looking up at the multitude of stars overhead, wrapped in the red cloaks that were their only item of clothing and leaning back on the step of the rough wooden hut on the edge of the forest away from everyone else, where the boys lived.

The next day was their final test. They would be awarded their citizenship if they passed it, the reason they had come, and they were desperately trying to grab as much time together as they could before they had to head back to the present; a present where they were separated by hundreds of miles, Sam in Barcelona and Rachel in London.

Even with that distance between them, they had coordinated their arrival perfectly, arriving hand in hand as if they had been in physical contact before they had Displaced - it was another clear indication of how special Sam was as a Displacer, even if he wasn't the one the Prophecy talked about.

Sam hadn't known whether to be relieved or disappointed at the revelation. He had liked everyone thinking that he was the one who was going to save them all; it had made him feel special, but at the same time he was glad that there wasn't so much pressure on him anymore. He still had to work towards foiling Quentin and the Illuminati, but now everybody knew that there was someone else who was going to bring about the change they had all been waiting for not all their eggs were in his basket, so to speak.

Sam chuckled. 'I tell you one thing, I don't think I'm ever going to be hung up on being naked again. I might even start going to the nudist beaches at home in Spain.'

Rachel grinned. 'You'd better wait for me before you do that; I don't want to miss it!'

'Haven't you got sick of seeing me naked? It's all day, every day!'

'Of course not. Why? Are you sick of seeing me?'

'No way!'

'Well then.'

Sam rubbed his arm just above his elbow where he had a cut from sword practice a couple of days earlier - they had been using real weapons for a year, in preparation for entering the army immediately on graduation, and accidents happened. 'Although, if I'm going to walk around naked I'm not sure how I'll explain all these new scars...'

Rachel grinned and ran her finger along the roughly-stitched cut. 'Yeah, I'm afraid you've finally baptised that pristine, baby-soft white skin of yours.'

Any injury or scar they got in the past would follow them back home, even though they reverted to the bodies they had when they Displaced. It meant that there were some Displacers, more unfortunate than others, who were covered in scars and Andrew was one of them - when he had been training Sam they had gone to the beach one day and Sam had been shocked to see just how many scars his uncle had collected in his years of service.

Sam shrugged. 'It had to happen sooner or later, I suppose. I just hope I can hide them from my mum; I don't want her stressing.'

'Well, you're not going to walk around naked at home, so you should be OK.' Rachel turned onto her side and looked at him. 'I'm going to miss you. I might not see you again for months unless we Displace together again.'

Sam grimaced. 'Andrew said he wants me to start saving my Displacements again, just in case. He says that until we find the real "chosen one" I'm the best they've got. I think his words actually were "you'll have to do". He only let me come on this one because I told him I would throw a tantrum if he didn't.'

Rachel guffawed. 'You? Throw a tantrum?'

'Yes. I've been getting lessons from an expert.'

'Violeta?'

Sam nodded.

Rachel laughed. 'She's growing up so fast.'

'I think the word is "precocious."'

'You're just worried that she'll surpass your brilliant achievements one day.'

'What achievements?'

She leaned over and kissed him briefly on the lips, before lying back down again. 'You won me, didn't you? That's no small feat.'

Sam smiled back at her. Much as he wanted to reach out and pull her to him he knew he couldn't; if they were seen it would mean a lot of trouble and they had come through far too much to risk it now.

'Anyway,' said Rachel. 'I hope your loss of prudishness isn't going to be the only thing you take away with you from your time here.'

'Well, I'm certainly not going to be so unfamiliar with pain. That beating I got in London at the hands of the Twins seems more like a few lovetaps now.'

Rachel winced. 'It has kind of put things into perspective, right?'

'Yeah.'

Rachel laid back again and they looked up at the stars in silence for a while.

'Are you worried about the trials tomorrow?' she asked.

'Yes. A lot.' Sam was completely serious; the final test was going to be the hardest thing either of them had ever done, the toughest and probably the most painful experience of their lives. What he didn't tell her was that he wasn't so much worried for himself, but for her; some of the worst times that he'd been through over the last two years here weren't when he'd been in pain, or tired, or hungry, they had been when he'd had to watch her suffering - seeing her getting hurt day after day had been horrific and there were many times that he would have begged her to go home with him, but he hadn't, because he knew that it was what she wanted to do.

'I love you.'

The words were out of his mouth before his brain caught up. He couldn't believe that he'd said it, the first time ever, but at the same time he knew that it was true and he stared up at the stars in wonder.

The answer came softly after a few seconds. 'I love you too.'

He felt a hard, calloused hand find its way into his and together they let the night surround them as they waited sleeplessly for the day to come.

CHAPTER 2
GRADUATION

The six boys in the graduation class drew straws to see in which order they would fight. Sam was relieved when Rachel picked the longest straw of all because it meant she would go last and he didn't want to watch her being beaten before he fought; it would be too distracting - he'd spend his whole fight wanting to go to her. He himself picked the third shortest and he was happy with that as well; he would have the chance to watch how the two boys in front of him did, but he wouldn't have enough time to get too nervous.

The trials were taking place in the main amphitheatre in front of the entire population of the city - there were thousands of people there to see their success or failure and, as always, the boys would fight naked; they wouldn't be given armour or clothes until they were men. None of that was what was making Sam nervous, though, rather it was the hundred warriors standing in mass ranks at the side of the arena waiting for them that was doing that.

Rumours of an army massing in the far east had caused the Spartan leadership both to intensify its training and also to focus on fighting against superior numbers. The trial for the young men for the last few years had therefore been changed to suit that new philosophy and was brutal in the extreme.

Each boy would face increasing numbers of foes, the warriors from the regular army. They would face one, then, if they defeated that warrior they would be confronted by two, then three, and so on. The purpose of the trial was not so much to see if the boys could defeat these battle-hardened warriors, it was more a test of how much punishment they could take and remain standing, remain fighting.

No boy had ever beaten more than two.

A couple had died.

The boys filed into the arena in the order in which they would fight and lined up, each of them carrying the long wooden stave that simulated the spears they would use in battle.

Sam spared a quick glance in Rachel's direction, but her gaze was fixed ahead and he saw that she was already in the battle mindset that she could fall into so easily. It was something that she had learned before she had even met him, something that was still beyond him, and he hoped it would be enough to see her safely through the day.

There was no delay, no fanfare, no announcement before the trial began, the first boy was just called forwards and thrust straight into his fight.

The soldiers weren't using the same staves as the boys were, instead they were using short wooden poles, like swords. At first Sam was puzzled as to why, but after the boy had been hit several times, he realised that the lighter sticks were doing a lot less damage than the long staffs would have done and, instead of breaking bones, they were just bruising and incapacitating.

There were different rules for the boys and the soldiers to match their different weapons. The boys' staffs were heavy enough to break bones, so the soldiers were wearing leather armour which would completely negate any damage, but not the pain of strikes. However, if a boy landed what would be a killing blow from a real weapon, then the soldier was considered to be eliminated. There were no eliminating blows for the boys, though; the soldiers were free to hit them as many times as it took to force them to surrender. Or completely incapacitate them.

The first boy did creditably well. Even though he didn't manage to defeat his opponent, he managed to stay on his feet and keep fighting despite taking dozens of hard blows that would have felled just about anyone that Sam had ever known, including, he had to admit, himself a couple of years ago. He was only defeated after a particularly strong blow to the side of his head knocked him unconscious.

The crowd stood in respectful silence as the boy was dragged from the arena to where there were doctors waiting to treat their wounds.

The next boy did better. He managed to defeat the first soldier, but in doing so took a vicious blow to his right forearm which broke it with a loud snap that could be clearly heard from where Sam was standing.

The two soldiers who stepped up to replace their companion showed no compassion. They attacked simultaneously, raining blows on the boy as he tried to ward them off ineffectually with only one arm. Even so, he lasted almost a minute more before collapsing to the ground, battered and bruised.

And just like that it was Sam's turn.

He strode forward without hesitation to face the soldier who was already waiting for him.

He was big, much bigger than Sam, but he wasn't as muscled as Sam had been expecting. When Rachel had told him that she wanted to go to Sparta he had watched *300* again, and this man looked nothing like the inflated actors in that film - this man was lean, fit and looked *dangerous*, not *pretty*.

There was no bow, no greeting, no handshake, just like there had been no preamble to the trials, they just started fighting as soon as they got within range.

Sam had the advantage of reach, but the warrior had greater experience and tried to take that away from him - the only way a sword could beat a spear under these condition was if the sword-user got in close and the warrior immediately moved to do so. It was a move that he had obviously practised thousands of times, but Sam knew it as well and didn't let him. He swung the stave at the man's legs, trying to take them from under him and the man only just managed to parry the swing and step back out of range.

At this point, in any other fight Sam had ever had, there would be a moment of assessing or circling where the two of them would eye each other and plan, but that wasn't the Spartan way and a battle couldn't be fought like that; if you took a break in a pitched battle you would die. The warrior immediately looked to move back in, but Sam didn't give him the chance. He thrust out, forcing the man to lean back from the point of the stave and then when the man went to knock it away he reversed the blow, bringing the bottom end up and into the man's genitals. The warrior's eyes crossed slightly as the strike penetrated the armour enough to cause him quite some distress, but he immediately began to recover and Sam knew that he would be able to continue fighting in moments, so he instantly reversed his weapon again to push it hard into the man's chest; a killing blow.

It had been deceptively easy; these men were extremely experienced, professional soldiers, but they had been trained to fight in a line of battle - they couldn't hope to stand against the training that

Sam had received at the hands of Master Hamato in how to fight individual opponents.

Even through his pain and wavering consciousness the man retained enough awareness to know that he had been beaten. He straightened as much as he could and walked away with all the dignity he could muster to rejoin the ranks of soldiers, an impressive feat in itself.

His place was immediately taken by two more men, who ran forward side by side.

Their coordinated attack spoke of years of fighting side by side and Sam was instantly forced to retreat. As he desperately parried and spun away from their initial attacks he briefly reflected that maybe he shouldn't have beaten the first warrior so quickly because now he would find it harder to defeat these two; they wouldn't underestimate him like the first man had and would probably go harder on him for having defeated their companion. Then again, the object of this exercise wasn't for him to beat his opponents - he would never be able to do so, there were a hundred lined up to face him if needed - the object was to see how he handled defeat and continued fighting through pain. It was a test of will.

He grinned as he beat back the warriors, taking the initiative from them with carefully placed strikes, then moving quickly around them to place one of them in front of the other so that they couldn't flank him - if he was going to go down, he was going to go down fighting and take as many of them with him as he could.

His feet moved in a blur, kicking up dust from the hard ground as he pressed the nearest man back, forcing him into his companion, never letting them separate and confront him together. It was a tactic that he had been able to use against his fellow students successfully several times, except when one of them was Rachel; she knew him too well and always found a way around his tricks.

Unfortunately, these men weren't as easily foiled either. Instead of tangling themselves together, fighting to get within range of him, the man at the back stepped forwards and put his left hand on the other one's shoulder and began to move with him, as one. Although they couldn't attack him from different directions this way they were much more effective than just a single person.

Sam took several blows to the arms and shoulders due to the unexpected turn of events, but thankfully they were only glancing blows and weren't nearly enough to disable him or do any lasting damage, however, they were painful nonetheless and too many of them would disable him just as much as a heavier blow would.

He hadn't been idle while he had been taking punishment, though; he had been watching the men closely, gauging their responses to his stimulus and finally he worked out the solution to his problem. The men worked well as a team, but they had fallen into a pattern very quickly: the one at the front always parried Sam's attacks leaving the man at the rear free to counterattack, but it wasn't instantaneous, there was always a delay between parry and riposte, and that was what gave the victory to Sam.

He let the two men fall firmly into a pattern of parry and riposte, letting them get in a few more hits to make them complacent, then suddenly changed everything - he let the first man parry him and used the force of it to spin in place and was therefore not where the second man expected him to be, but behind both of them.

They were slow to react and by the time they did Sam had landed killing blows on them both in quick succession.

There was no surprise or disappointment, no offence on the men's faces. There wasn't even any respect at his outmanoeuvring them, they just turned and went back to the massed soldiers.

Three men now charged forward, immediately pressing their attack, just like the others had, not allowing Sam to get his breath back for an instant.

If two opponents had been hard to deal with, three was impossible and Sam was forced to retreat constantly, working hard to defend himself from every direction and getting in some shots every so often whenever he saw an opening.

He knew it was an impressive display, but it wasn't nearly *Spartan* enough and he smiled, resigning himself to what he knew was coming.

It was time to show them what he was made of.

He went on the offensive with a growl.

He took the first man by surprise and swept his feet out from under him, but before he could plant a killing blow his stave was blocked by a sword from the side. Almost simultaneously the third man hit him hard across the back, making him stiffen involuntarily.

That was all the opening the men needed. The one on the ground was able to roll and come back to his feet and then they were on all sides of him.

Blows fell from every angle and Sam whirled and spun, blocking several and striking back, but there were too many and they landed on every part of his body.

He felt himself weakening slowly, but he knew that he could continue for hours more if necessary.

The blow to his head put paid to that notion. His vision clouded and he lost focus. He could no longer see well enough to react to the attacks as they came and his swings became more and more random as he tried to block the non-existent swords his confused mind put in front of him.

The men showed no mercy and continued to rain strikes on him.

He didn't notice when he sank to his knees and the stave slipped from his hands; in his mind he was still fighting.

He blinked and found himself lying on the side of the arena with four other boys, in the care of the doctors. He counted the boys again, slow to realise what it meant to have four of his companions with him, until a familiar shout rang in his ears and his awareness shot into sharp focus.

Rachel!

He struggled to his elbows, ignoring the sudden dizziness and encroaching black to look out across the arena.

He thought he was still disorientated for a moment, seeing double, but he soon realised that he was in fact seeing four men around Rachel.

She was moving faster than he had ever seen her move, but even so, he could tell she was hurt. Blood streamed from her nose onto her chest, she was obviously favouring her right side because her left foot was barely touching the ground and he could see that her left hand was holding the stave awkwardly; it looked like at least one of her fingers was broken if not more. She was still fighting, though, and he knew that this was why he had worried so much about her; she would never give up, never give in to the pain and they would have to incapacitate her totally before she would stop.

Sam forced himself to watch silently, although he wanted nothing more to shout out, to stop it and get them to leave her alone; this was what she had wanted, this was why they were here.

He had had his turn, and now it was hers.

It didn't take long.

The men connected with their weapons more and more and she recovered more and more slowly from each blow. The strike that hit her already hurt left leg was the final straw and she went down on one knee, unable to stand on it.

Even so, she didn't scream or cry out, she just kept fighting, whirling her stave like a baton over her head, but it wasn't enough and she was hard pressed to keep up with them. She rolled on the floor to avoid an attack, a final desperate measure, but it failed. She came up against the legs of one of the men, making him fall, but the others surrounded her and their swords rose and fell, over and over.

Until suddenly they stopped and the men backed off leaving the broken form of Rachel lying motionless on the ground.

That was all Sam saw before he willingly slipped into welcoming darkness.

Sam opened his eyes and looked up into Rachel's bruised and swollen, but smiling face. She was leaning over him from the bed next to his and he realised that they were lying on straw mattresses and, despite his innumerable aches and pains, he was more comfortable than he had been since his arrival - in the hut their beds had been made of reeds that they had to pull from the river themselves, a task that was tiring in the extreme and that ripped unprepared hands to shreds, so they had often had only a very thin coating between them and the hard floor.

He reached up to touch the side of her face, smiling back at her. 'Thank god you've still got all your teeth.'

She laughed. 'After all this, my looks are what is important to you?'

'Of course, why else would I be going out with an older woman?'

Rachel was a year and almost fifteen years older than Sam because of the extra years she had been Displacing and she had had much more experience than him when they had first started seeing each other romantically.

'So, you'll no longer love me when I hit two hundred? I'm offended!'

Sam laughed, but then groaned as a sharp pain shot through his ribs. He put a hand to his side and instead of skin found a tunic on top of bandages. He looked down at it in wonder. 'I'm wearing clothes… I have clothes!'

'Yeah, I'm not liking this new look, I much prefer your old fashion sense.'

She looked at him and there was tenderness and love in her eyes.

'I wish I could kiss you right now.' Sam whispered, looking around for the first time, hoping that they were alone.

Unfortunately, they weren't. They were in a long stone building with whitewashed walls and there were dozens of beds set out in two parallel rows. On the nearby beds were the four other boys that they had been training with, each in a different state of consciousness and injury and further down the room there were warriors moving around.

They were in the barracks with the soldiers and there was only one reason they would be there.

Rachel saw the realisation hit him. She grinned and pointed down.

Lying on the floor between their two mattresses were two short swords. Real ones, well made and sharp, not the rough, slightly dulled ones they'd been training with.

'We did it? We've been accepted in the army?'

'Yes, we're men now.'

Sam couldn't help but laugh again and once more the pain in his ribs shot through him. 'Ow, that really hurts.'

'Yeah, you've got a couple cracked ribs apparently, nothing serious, but it'll hurt for you to do exercise for a while.'

'How long has it been?'

'I was only out for a day, but you've been unconscious for two; apparently you've got a nice concussion. Apart from that and the ribs you're fine, though, nothing substantial. In fact I don't know why you didn't keep fighting...'

'Ha, ha, very funny. What about you, how are you?'

'I've got about a thousand bruises and a couple of broken fingers, it hurt like hell when they straightened them and I almost passed out, but apart from that I got off fairly easy.' She jerked a thumb at the boy next to them and Sam recognised the boy who had fought like a lion and taken a bad beating. 'Dismas there got a broken arm and nose and hasn't woken up yet. If you were worried about my teeth you should see what's happened to his nose; it would put you off me for good.'

She grinned at him, but he swallowed and looked away, fighting back the very unspartan-like tears that were threatening to come. 'I was so worried about you. I didn't want you to go through with it, I wanted to stop you and drag you back to the present.'

'I know, darling. Don't think I didn't feel the same way about you some of the time.'

'Then why did we stay?'

'Because this was something that we had to do; after this, nothing will be able to hurt us ever again. Anything that Quentin does to us, anything that we come across in our Displacements, will pale in comparison to this experience.' She reached out and put a hand gently on his shoulder 'And we did it together. It doesn't matter what happens to us from now on; nobody can take this from us.'

Sam turned to face her, ignoring the pain in his ribs as he twisted his body. 'Are you still upset about what happened in Victorian London?'

She nodded. 'I almost lost you, Sam. I don't know what I would do if something happened to you.'

Sam opened his mouth to reply, but she pointed her finger at his face to stop him. 'And don't you dare say that nothing is going to happen to you; we both know how dangerous Displacing is already without having someone trying to kill you all the time.'

'OK, then, I promise that I won't go anywhere without you. That way we can look after each other. Deal?'

'It's a deal. But…' Suddenly she went quiet and looked towards the door, her mouth open wide and what she had been saying completely forgotten.

'What?' Sam turned to see what she was staring at and froze in shock as well.

Walking down the aisle between the two rows of beds was a warrior. He was wearing the same tunic and bright red cloak as everybody else and wasn't a particularly imposing or powerful figure, but somehow Sam just knew who it was.

'That's…' Sam asked.

Rachel nodded and her voice croaked in wonder. 'Yes.' King Leonidas had come to visit his soldiers.

'But he looks so ordinary, not at all like Gerard Butler.'

Rachel waved him to silence. 'Shh! Don't make me laugh! I want to savour this moment.'

Sam watched the man as he moved towards them. He may not have looked any different to anyone else, but there was something about him, an aura surrounding him. Or maybe it was because they could see the weight of his responsibilities painted clearly in the lines on his face; there was a solemnity and sadness to him that made him stand out from the regular soldiers.

They noticed that none of the warriors paid much attention to him as he strode past them, they neither saluted nor acknowledged his presence beyond a word of greeting if he chanced to look in their direction. The King nodded in reply to them all, but didn't stop to talk and Sam and Rachel realised with a start that he was coming towards the end of the barracks where they were laying.

They separated, Rachel moving back into the middle of her own mattress and Sam struggling to sit up a bit straighter on his.

The King glanced briefly at the boys around them, but his eyes quickly settled on Sam and Rachel.

He stopped and stood at the end of their beds, looking down at them. They began to struggle to get to their feet, but he waved at them to stay as they were.

'There are troubled times ahead. We are in danger of being wiped out by forces beyond our control, but I watched you two fight yesterday and thought that, if two men such as you can come up through our training, then maybe there is hope for us, maybe we can survive the storm that is coming.' He smiled briefly, but it didn't last.

'Our society does not allow us to be rewarded for good work and we don't ask for it, but I thought that you deserved some kind of acknowledgement of how well you did yesterday, so I am giving you these as a token of my esteem.'

Leonidas pulled two thin golden torques from within his tunic and held them out, one in each of his large hands.

'You have your king's permission to wear these with pride and if you should ever need anything, you need merely present yourselves to me and I will do all that is within my power and the bounds of honour to aid you.'

He knelt between the two mattresses and with his own hands fixed the rings around their necks where they hung loosely. They were much heavier than they looked and Sam felt the weight of the metal pressing painfully against a bruise on his collar bone. He said nothing, though; such a petty inconvenience was insignificant compared to the honour they were being given and it was less than nothing for a Spartan.

Once he was done, the King stood up. He looked down at them and nodded. 'Work hard, work diligently and in a few years we shall see if you fulfil your promise and are judged worthy to join my personal guard.'

Without another word he strode back the way he had come, his cloak billowing behind him.

They watched him until he left the hut, then turned and gave each other a sad look; there was nothing they could do to prevent the tragic, yet glorious, fate of the man who had just put his hope for the future in their hands.

Sam opened his eyes to meet Rachel's beautiful blue ones. Unfortunately they were being projected on the monitor of the computer in Andrew's flat in Barcelona and their owner was hundreds of miles away in another country.

He withdrew his hand from the golden band around his neck and saw Rachel do the same. He then carefully laid aside the sword that was clutched tightly in his other. The only way to take something or bring it back from a Displacement was to physically hold it in your hands, and neither of them had wanted to lose their souvenirs from this one; they had gone through too much to get them.

He sat back in the chair and winced; his ribs hurt more in the present than they had in the past - his body wasn't as hardened to resist here. 'How are you feeling? How are those fingers?'

Rachel held her hand up in front of her camera and turned it back and forward. Her broken fingers were covered with yellowing bruises. 'Well, they're straight, but they hurt like hell.'

They had been given a week to recover before taking up their duties in the army and had spent the whole week together, walking in the hills around the city built on the Eurotas river. They had finally found some time to be alone and had taken full advantage of it; they weren't going to let the pain they were in stop them from doing that. The week hadn't been enough time for their wounds and injuries to fully heal, but it was as long as they'd had before they had to leave.

'Get Andrew or James to take you to the hospital, please?'

'I'll be fine!'

'Rachel, please! We're not in Sparta anymore, there's no reason to tough it out, there's no reason to pretend that we don't feel the pain and these bodies aren't as used to punishment as the ones we just left. I'm in agony here, so I can't imagine how you are feeling!'

Rachel chuckled and shrugged. 'Speak for yourself - I've been keeping up with my training regimen, my body is just as hard as it was there.'

'Let's not start talking about things like that, I'm frustrated enough as it is…'

'Don't worry, we'll see each other again at Easter. That's only two months away.'

Sam groaned. 'I can't take it! Not only are you half a continent away, but I'm stuck going to school while you get to be at Displacer Central every day.'

As always they had left their real lives completely behind when they Displaced. It was something that Rachel had insisted on since Okinawa - when they were in the past, they were *there* and all talk of home was forbidden. It was only now that they were catching up on what had been happening in the present and it was another quirk of Displacing that the events of the present were always as fresh in their minds as if they hadn't been gone for years.

'It's not all that great working for Andrew, you know, especially now that I'm having to chaperone Miss Stuck-up Birch around all the time.'

Sam laughed. 'How is that going? Is she giving us anything we can use?'

Diana Birch, a beautiful red-headed agent for the Illuminati, who they'd last seen holding Sam captive in Victorian London, had turned up on Rachel's doorstep on the third of January and the young Displacer had understandably been shocked. When Diana had recovered her senses from the punch that had been Rachel's natural reaction, she explained that she had been thinking about her time with Sam and had decided to turn over a new leaf and be a double agent for them. Rachel had taken her offer to James and Andrew and they had leapt at the chance, tasking Rachel with being the liaison between them and making her responsible for getting Diana to and from meetings with James in secrecy.

The woman had struck Sam as a bit unstable and possibly a bit disturbed when he'd met her, but the more he thought about his conversations with her, the more he had come to think that it might have been more a symptom of her circumstances than of her actual personality. Rachel on the other hand wasn't convinced; as far as she was concerned, Diana was crazy and dangerous and couldn't be trusted, but she reluctantly agreed that the Illuminati might be of some use to them and so far she had been.

'Actually, yes. She gave us the address of one of the places where the Illuminati store their stolen loot and James used his connections to get the place raided by the police. It wasn't a big haul; apparently it's only one of their smaller caches, but there were artworks and stuff that were on lists of stolen items dating back almost a hundred years and the police confiscated the lot. She says it's the only cache that she knows about, but that there are probably a couple more in London. However, she also said that Quentin boasted one time that they keep the greater part of their stolen assets and most valuable items in bank vaults in Switzerland, which means they won't be hit particularly hard by this.'

'What about their plans? Has she been able to tell us anything about them that's been worth all this effort?'

The seizure of the cache was a small victory, but material things like that weren't what they most wanted from her; the most important thing that she would be able to do for them was to inform them of the Master's plans. They were hopeful that she would be on Quentin's team again when they next had a major operation and would be able to give them advance warning so that Sam wouldn't have to go in blind again - the last time they had faced up against Quentin's gang, they had been very lucky to stop them, in fact Sam had been captured and beaten and would've been killed if it hadn't been for Diana's intervention and the timely arrival of Rachel with the police. They didn't particularly want to have to rely on their luck again.

Rachel shrugged. 'I dunno much about that side of things; she only meets with James and they spend all of their time locked in a safe house in Chelsea. I have no idea what it is they talk about and I haven't bothered to ask; I can't stand being around her and it's all I can do not to strangle her when I'm sneaking her around, I certainly don't want to strike up a conversation. But your grandad is pretty damn excited by what she's telling him, so it must be useful.'

'That's good. It seems I was right about her after all.'

'I wouldn't count those chickens quite yet; beyond the raid we haven't seen any firm results from her intel; she's given us nothing that will help us sort out the time-line.'

'The results will come, I'm sure of it. Did she know what Quentin was trying to get into the attic for, back in Victorian London?'

'She didn't even know that he'd tried! So, no, we have no idea what he was looking for. James has got a few of the Elders looking through the inventory trying to find some clue as to what he was after, but so far they have a list of a couple of hundred items which isn't particularly helpful.'

'I don't envy them that job.'

'Yeah, especially seeing as what he was looking for might not have even been there in the first place; he could have been searching for something he wasn't sure we had.'

Sam groaned. 'When did this all become so complicated?'

'About the time you joined us.'

'Oh, ha ha...'

'Well, it's true! It was simple before because we had almost no way to fight back. Since you arrived we have a lot more options and there is suddenly so much we can do to stop them. The only trouble is we're having to devote a lot of our resources to following every lead, like the info you and I brought back at Christmas, and other projects are starting to suffer as a result.'

'Well, maybe that's what they wanted...'

'I don't know. Quentin doesn't strike me as clever enough to have done it just to waste our time. But still, whether it's a dead end or not, James wants us to investigate every clue, no matter how small. He says it's vital to be able to anticipate the Illuminati's next move.'

'I can understand that.' Sam nodded. 'And what about Andrew? What's he been doing? I haven't had a chance to talk to him since Christmas, he's been too busy with this new plan of his.'

'I haven't seen much of him either; he's locked away in one of the bedrooms here at HQ with John every day and only comes out for meals. They're working on some grand plan to take away a large portion of the Illuminati's riches apparently, although he won't tell anybody how. He's got this light in his eyes at the moment, like he's some kind of religious maniac.'

'I hope he's not planning something for me; I need a break…'

Sam stopped as Rachel glanced away from the camera and chuckled. 'Speak of the devil.'

The smiling face of Sam's uncle came into view as he leaned over Rachel to peer into the camera.

'Hi, Sam! Did you have fun in Sparta?'

'Well…'

Andrew laughed and waved away the question. 'I'm sure I'll hear all about it later, but for now no more selfish Displacements please, either of you; I might need you to do a job sometime - we're a bit short staffed right now seeing as both John and I have to save ourselves.'

'About that, what…?'

Andrew didn't let Sam finish his question. 'You're coming over for the Easter holidays, right?'

'Yes, but only for a few days, the schools here don't…'

'Good, good, I want you here standing by. Just in case.'

'Just in case of what?'

'You'll see!' Andrew grinned. 'So, did you get the book? Sorry, I meant to give it to you in person, but with one thing after another it just slipped my mind.'

Yes, James gave it to me before I left, thanks. I haven't had time to…'

'Right, well I must get back to it, I'm afraid. Thanks for the chat and I'm looking forward to seeing you again soon!' Andrew grinned and waved then moved out of range of the camera.

Sam blinked, not quite sure what had just happened.

On the monitor Rachel watched Andrew go, then turned back to Sam and gave him a shrug as if to say "told you so."

Sam frowned. 'Has he been like that since Christmas?'

'Pretty much.'

'Are we sure he's not on happy pills or something?'

Rachel chuckled. 'If I was cooped up with John every day, I would certainly need *something*, but I think your uncle is just excited about whatever it is they're planning.'

'Any idea what it is?'

'None whatsoever.'

'I guess they'll tell us when they're ready.'

'I suppose. What's that book that Andrew was talking about?'

'It's just more experiments by Everett Lloyd.'

'Great... Sounds fascinating...'

Sam nodded. 'Actually it is. For me anyway.'

'OK, each to his own, I suppose. You're going to be an Elder before you're even a real Displacer.'

'What do you mean? Of course I'm a real Displacer!'

Rachel grinned cheekily. 'Actually you're not; you're still counted as an apprentice until you've been Displacing as a member for a year in the present day. I passed that ages ago so, in fact, I outrank you!'

Sam laughed. 'There you go, thinking you're better than me just because I'm not the chosen one anymore!'

'Not *just* because of that...' She winked. 'Anyway, think yourself lucky; fifty years ago you would have had to have gone through a whole training regime and written exams. You would have done your first Displacements shadowing one of the older members... you could have gone on some adventures with John! Wouldn't that have been nice?'

Sam cringed at the thought of sharing years in the past with the annoyingly nerdy John. It wasn't that he didn't like nerds, he was a bit of one himself, it was just that John wouldn't *shut up* about the computer games he played, or the comics he read, or the movies he watched. There were no other topics of conversation with the man and he always managed to make everything come back around to them. John's main frustration with being a Displacer, which he never stopped reminding them of, was that he couldn't use his powers to be a nerd; almost everything he was interested in had been invented within his lifetime which meant he couldn't go to see it happen.

'I keep forgetting that the "Honourable Society of Displacers" is a lot more archaic and old than you and Andrew made it seem when you were teaching me.'

'You're welcome!'

They shared a smile, but Sam's quickly faded when he saw the clock in the corner of the screen. He sighed. 'I guess I'll see you in a few months, unless we get to Displace together before then.'

Rachel shook her head. 'There not much chance of that; you heard Andrew.'

'Yeah…'

They were both reluctant to sign off, but unfortunately Sam had to go; his parents were expecting him home for dinner. He sighed, then put on a stern, commanding face. 'Get yourself to a hospital, Spartan!'

Rachel laughed. 'Yeah, as if you'd have been promoted higher than me there either.'

They looked into each other's eyes for a last few moments.

Sam smiled. 'Goodbye, my love.'

'Bye, Sam. I love you.'

Sam reached out and terminated the call.

He sat back in his chair, staring at the screen. It took a little effort, but eventually he forced the thoughts of Rachel from his mind and made himself shut down the computer. He stood up and looked around, making sure that everything was shut down properly, turned off the router and left the room.

He walked down the corridor towards the front door, but stopped as something caught his eye: there was one door in Andrew's flat that he had never seen open, one room that he'd never been inside. Despite the fact that Andrew lived alone and the only visitors he had were Sam, Rachel and occasionally Sam's mother it was always locked.

Sam had always wondered what was so valuable or secret that it needed to be kept behind its own locked door. Perhaps it was some top secret Displacer thing - maybe Andrew had some of the things that were usually kept in the attic at Displacer Headquarters in the room.

He tried the handle, but as always the door was locked and he mentally shrugged; if Andrew wanted him to know what was in there he would tell him in his own time.

He gave the flat one more quick check, then left.

It was only when he was walking towards home, down Barcelona streets that were unusually warm for February, that he realised he was still carrying his sword and had the golden torque around his neck. He tutted and turned back around, tucking the sword under his coat as best as he could to hide it from passersby; he had to leave these particular souvenirs in Andrew's flat so his mum didn't find them and have a fit.

CHAPTER 3
PLANS AND BETRAYALS

Rachel sat in the computer room of Displacer Headquarters, staring into nothing; it was a strange feeling to be without Sam suddenly, to be wrenched from him and placed hundreds of miles away without any chance of physical contact. Every other journey they had been on they had had physical contact to ensure that they got to the same place, but this time had been different. It was amazing that they had been able to end up in the same place at the same time and, even though Andrew would probably say that it was because of Sam being so special, she knew in her heart that it was more because they were so attuned to each other - there was some kind of connection between them that went far beyond the bond that had formed from having trained and fought together for so many years.

She shook her head and reached out to turn off the computer then winced; somehow she had forgotten about her fingers and she looked at them, gently pressing the area around where they had been broken. They hurt, but she found that she could easily deal with the pain. If it wasn't for the fact that she had actual broken bones that could shift and not heal properly then she probably wouldn't have bothered doing anything about them, but, annoyingly, Sam was right; she needed to go and have them splinted. First she had a job to do, though.

She finished with the computer, then left the room and went downstairs. She made sure there was nobody watching her then took the wooden plaque with her name on it off of the pegs declaring her "in" and walked out onto the snow-covered street, heading towards the safe house where James and Diana were cloistered together.

She didn't head directly towards her destination, but took several random turns, each time checking for anyone that was tailing her. It was all part of the craft that Jacques had taught her and Sam in France and it was those skills that, along with the fact that she already knew about Diana, had gotten her assigned to getting her to and from the house in secret: how to lose a police tail was exactly the same as how you would lose the trail of any other nefarious characters that might be following you.

Or any of your colleagues who were poking their noses in where they weren't wanted.

It was all very cloak and dagger, but it had paid off at least once; Ralph had gotten suspicious that there was something secret being kept from him and had tried to follow her. She had seen him immediately because he hadn't been at all proficient at staying unseen and had led him on a wild-goose chase around much of London. She let him follow her around for an hour before exaggeratedly looking around and making it obvious that she was slipping into an alleyway. She lifted a sewer grate and then hid behind some nearby bins to watch as Ralph had obligingly "followed her" down into the filth. It had been all she could do not to laugh when he had turned up at Displacer Headquarters a few hours later in new clothes and stinking of bleach.

The safe house James had rented in a false name was about a mile away, in the heart of Chelsea and was a nondescript two-storey house, just one in a long row of identical, attached buildings. It was very small compared to Displacer Headquarters, but it was more than enough for James and Diana to meet in comfort, and its anonymity served its covert purpose well.

Rachel took one last circuit around the block just in case before finally approaching the house. She got to the door just in time to have it burst open in her face and winced as James knocked into her as he rushed past, his bony elbow unerringly finding one of her many bruises.

'Oops, sorry Rachel.'

'James…'

'Sorry, can't chat, no time! Important stuff! Take care of Diana would you?'

He rushed on without even looking at her, not noticing the small wounds that covered her exposed skin, and disappeared around the corner, heading directly towards Headquarters. She shook her head;

she really didn't know why she bothered being careful if James was just going to rush in a straight line from one place to the other.

'It looks like you had fun in Greece.'

Rachel turned to find Diana standing in the shadows of the doorway that James had just vacated at such speed.

She was dressed elegantly, as always, in clothes that didn't quite suit the times they were living in. She wore a dark green velvet dress with a lacy white shirt beneath it that, to Rachel's mind at least, made her look like she was an extra from "Penny Dreadful" or some such period drama, although thankfully she didn't have a bustle. Despite being an unusual style choice she managed to pull it off incredibly well and Rachel always felt extremely dowdy next to her, especially in the jeans and baggy jumper she habitually wore.

'It was OK.' She shrugged and then winced as yet another injury made itself felt.

Diana's smile disappeared instantly and her brow furrowed in concern. 'Did Sam get hurt? Is he alright?'

'He's fine, a few bruises is all. And I'm fine too, thank you for asking.'

'I'm glad. Please tell him I asked.'

'Yeah, right. Come on, the coast is clear, let's get you home and out of my hair.'

Diana came out of the house and Rachel pulled the door closed behind her.

They walked through snow which was fresher and cleaner there in the backstreets than it had been on the busy Grosvenor Place, Diana daintily picking her way along the pavement in her calf-high heeled boots while Rachel plodded along in her battered army ones, heading towards the main road where they would get a taxi for the first leg of the roundabout route they would take towards Diana's home.

'Aren't you cold? Didn't you have a coat this morning?'

Rachel only now realised that she hadn't bothered to grab her coat on leaving Headquarters and hadn't felt at all cold, despite the sub-zero temperatures.

She shrugged. 'I haven't been wearing any clothes at all for the last two years and I guess I'm not as sensitive to the cold right now.'

'You've been... Really?' Diana's eyes opened wide and then a slow smile crept across her face. 'And Sam... has he been wandering around like that as well? Because that's something I'd like to see, although I did get a little bit of a peek when he was our "guest" in London and he certainly looked impressive.' She winked. 'I'm assuming you two have, well, you know...'

Rachel looked at her with some distaste. 'Are you going to do the "wink wink nudge nudge" sketch from Python? Because I'd rather you didn't; I have enough of that kind of thing from one of our other members already.'

Diana blinked rapidly, fluttering enviously long eyelashes over ridiculously beautiful green eyes, her mouth opening in a shocked pout as she laid her hand on her chest. 'I wouldn't dream of it!'

'Good.' Rachel gave Diana a dark look, knowing full well that the red haired woman was just teasing her. She didn't like the idea of how close Diana had gotten to Sam in Victorian London; the woman had taken care of him when he was unconscious after beatings, seeing him vulnerable and probably without any clothes on. Rachel was jealous and she couldn't help it; Sam was the best thing that had ever happened to her and, although she trusted Sam to resist Diana's advances, she didn't want this traitorous but extremely good-looking woman showing any interest in him.

'Never you mind about Sam, just concentrate on redeeming yourself.'

The confident smile slipped slightly from the woman's face, but it was back almost instantly as she looked Rachel up and down. 'So, apart from the obvious cuts and bruises, I'm guessing you've got a fair few other injuries. I'm seeing a bit of a limp, probably a strained knee, and those fingers look like they were broken fairly recently.'

'What do you know of it?'

'I did a rotation as a nurse in the Crimean war under Florence Nightingale.'

Rachel stared at her, dumbstruck. 'Seriously? You did something to help other people?'

'This was back before Quentin's group found me - I had originally wanted to go into nursing before discovering I had a "higher calling" so to speak. It was my first Leap, sorry, *Displacement* and for a long time I thought it was a dream; I'd been reading about the war for history class and it mentioned the advances made in medicine and the role people like Florence Nightingale played in them. It was only when people started dying and I couldn't wake up that I realised that it was something else.'

'Then I guess you know what you're talking about and you've seen worse, so you know I'll survive.'

'You still need a doctor.'

'I'll be fine.'

'You won't be fine. Those fingers might heal badly if you leave them; judging from the bruising they're only a week old and that's far too soon to be out of splints.'

Rachel was impressed despite herself and a bit jealous again; one of the things she had always wanted to do during a Displacement was some proper medical training and it seemed Diana had beaten her to it.

'I'll take you home first.'

'Thank you, but that's not necessary. Besides, there are two hospitals right around the corner, let's get you to one of them and you can take me home afterwards.'

She shook her head. 'I can't turn up to a hospital looking like this; there will be too many questions. We have a doctor that we use. Just let me make a call.'

Rachel went to pull her phone out of the pocket of her jeans, but realised that she couldn't use her left hand to do so and ended up twisting to reach her right hand across her body. It was a struggle; her jeans were tight and the phone was one of those ridiculously big smartphones that Andrew had insisted she have, but in the end she got it out.

Diana smirked at her awkwardness and smiled seductively. 'You know, I could have helped if you'd asked.'

Rachel stared at her for long seconds, unable to tell if she was joking or not. It didn't matter, though; the woman already made her uncomfortable in so many ways that she didn't need that kind of tension as well. She shook her head in exasperation, then looked down at her phone and went through her contact list until she found the Society's doctor, "Asclepius", the ridiculously obvious codename that some Elder had assigned more than a century ago to the medical professionals that worked with them.

As expected, there was no answer machine message or indication that she had the right number, but as soon as the call connected she left a voice message. 'One, female, non life-threatening. Grade three.'

She hung up the phone and saw that Diana was watching her with the smirk still on her face. She stared at her coldly. 'I don't know what it's like in your organisation, but we take care of our people. There's a doctor on permanent standby to treat our members.'

The smile faded somewhat. 'Yeah, we don't have anything like that; we're left to fend for ourselves. Because we work in cells and don't have a central headquarters or organisation like you guys, we don't have the same kind of "health package" or support that you do. We don't even know who all of the other members are.'

'And you're more expendable.'

The smile completely disappeared and Diana looked away - she obviously didn't want to admit that Rachel was right; it would make everything she had done over the last few years a lie.

For some reason Rachel didn't feel particularly gratified at having wiped the smirk off the young woman's face. Her phone vibrated and she used the excuse to look away herself. 'He can see me now. Come on, it's not far from here.'

She stomped away along the road, not waiting for Diana to follow her.

The woman caught up after only a few steps, moving quickly and fluidly on the snow even in her highly impractical shoes. 'Want me to put your phone back in your pocket for you?'

She laughed daintily as Rachel growled at her.

Half an hour later they were in a taxi that was moving frustratingly slowly along the crowded, and now dark, London streets.

Rachel had been patched up quickly and efficiently by the doctor, a small bald man with round glasses who had obviously been retired for some years but still retained all his skills. Throughout it all Diana had stayed at her side and, while she hadn't openly expressed any concern over Rachel's well-being, her relief when she was pronounced fit and healthy was clear. It surprised the Displacer somewhat and she found herself begrudgingly opening up to her.

Usually they travelled in silence; Rachel always got the impression that Diana was tired out by James' questioning and didn't feel like talking much afterwards, especially not to her, but that day was different. Rachel didn't know if it was because James had rushed off early and the woman had energy left over, or whether her injury and the talk of Sam had loosened her tongue, but whatever the case, the floodgates were open. She wasn't entirely sure if she preferred the aloof Diana or the friendly one, but if the woman wanted to talk she wasn't going to stop her, she might get something out of her in an informal conversation that James might not.

Rachel sat on the backwards facing seat as they headed across Chelsea Bridge and past the power station, one of her favourite London landmarks. The plan was to get out a few streets from Clapham Junction train station and walk around the block a couple of times. They would separate there and Diana would get a train to

London Bridge, from where she would have another taxi ride to her house near Greenwich.

It was just one of a dozen routes that Rachel had mapped out and ready to use. Obviously it was much more important to make sure that Diana wasn't being followed on the journey in to meet James in the morning rather than the return journey, but in her experience it paid to be paranoid.

They were stuck in traffic at that moment, though; James' early departure meant that they were travelling in rush hour that day when usually they finished much later. It made Rachel's job a lot harder as it was understandably difficult to spot a tail when nobody was going anywhere, but it also meant that she had time and attention spare to talk to her charge.

'Seriously, though. Is Sam alright? I know he hasn't had the time to develop the skills that you have and if you look like *that...*'

There was real concern in Diana's voice and again Rachel didn't know how to take it. The jealousy briefly reared its head again, but it was also joined by a measure of gratitude and genuine surprise that Diana cared so much about people who had once been her enemies.

'Sam did very well, actually, and he got away with only a few cracked ribs and a concussion. He'll need to move carefully for a while, but he has no lasting injuries and should be able to hide them from his parents without too much problem.'

'Good. That's good.'

Diana went quiet and looked out of the window. It was slowly misting up and she began to draw meaningless patterns in the condensation.

Rachel could tell that she had something on her mind and waited patiently for her to talk, all the while scanning the nearby traffic.

When they came, the words from the young woman were almost too quiet to hear.

'You know how lucky you are, right?'

'Lucky with what? Sam?'

'Yes, with Sam. He's such a wonderful person, you're so lucky to have him and I can tell he loves you, but that's not the only reason. You're lucky to have your friends, your colleagues and you're lucky with the life you've been able to lead.' She swiped her hand across her doodles, completely obliterating them, almost angrily. 'When Quentin turned up at my door I thought that I was lucky. He promised me a life full of adventure and riches, away from my father and his...'

She stopped talking and dropped her head, as if she had suddenly realised what she was saying or who she was talking to. 'But I was wrong, so wrong...'

When next she looked up her eyes were shining with tears, but her face was calm as if her control over her emotions wasn't quite perfect and something was leaking past her barriers. Even that slight weakness was gone in a heartbeat, though, and she dabbed her eyes with a handkerchief from her sleeve before turning back to the window. The lights on the street gave her an orange glow that somehow made her even more beautiful.

'Quentin is very frightened of Sam, you know.'

'Really?'

'He fears him just as much as he hates him; he sees Sam as the only thing that is standing between him and success, the one obstacle that he *has* to overcome, but can't. The Master is furious with him for always losing to Sam, especially now that they know he's not the "Chosen One" that everyone keeps talking about. So angry that he's stopped Quentin from doing anything important - he sent him off get some little bit of treasure this month, which is one of the small jobs that are usually given to lower-ranked people like me or the Twins. Quentin's understandably quite annoyed and he blames Sam for what he sees as a demotion.'

'So, if Quentin's just doing scut work, does that mean there's nothing big planned?'

'There's something *very* big in the works, but Quentin doesn't know what it is. He told me that the Master is getting involved personally.'

'Quentin's not going to run the operation?'

Diana shrugged. 'He says he's going to have a role, but if the Master is going on the mission then Quentin's part in it might not be nearly as big as usual.'

'Any idea when he's planning it for?'

'No. But I get the impression that it won't be for a good few months.'

'And in the meantime, Quentin is just running around collecting things to swell the Illuminati's bank account.' Rachel chuckled, shaking her head. 'From what Sam has told me about him, he has an inflated sense of his own worth, so he must love that. But if you don't know anything about the Master's plan, why did James go racing off like that?'

'Because I told him that the Master has instructed Quentin to acquire some gold mines in South Africa. I don't know exactly when and where we're going yet, but if it's only going to give us more money, then it can't be very important in the grand scheme of things. However, it is a big enough deal to warrant taking me and the Twins, which is why I know about it. I also get the impression it's some kind of test to see if Quentin is worthy of being part of the Master's grand plan and he is desperate to succeed.'

'No wonder James was in a hurry.'

Diana nodded. 'Exactly. He said that he needed to "get the ball rolling" then mumbled something about needing to check his research before running off.'

'That sounds like James; he'll be working on every possibility, even though you're going to give us the details of the mission later. You know it'll probably be me and Sam who'll get sent to try to stop you guys, right?'

'I hope so; it would be nice to see him again.'

Rachel huffed. 'Yeah, it'll be a wonderful reunion. We can be like one big happy family, frolicking together in the past.'

Diana grinned at her. 'You know, you're pretty funny. I can see what Sam sees in you.'

Rachel stared at her, searching for some sign of sarcasm, but to her surprise it seemed like the young woman was being completely serious and again she found her opinion of the normally standoffish woman changing.

They had cleared the traffic now and were close to their destination, only a few blocks from the train station. She knocked on the cabby's window and gave him thirty pounds when it slid open. 'You can let us out here, thanks. Keep the change.'

The taxi pulled over to the curb and they stepped out into the dirty slush that was all that was left of the snow. It was even colder than before, now that it was fully dark and Diana pulled her coat about herself as Rachel led them into the residential streets. They headed indirectly towards the station, moving swiftly and taking several unpredictable turns. Each time they changed direction, Rachel would look discreetly behind them for tails, but there was never anybody and she hadn't really expected there to be; she didn't think that even Quentin was stupid enough to follow Diana to her house, after all he already knew where she lived.

It started to snow again, settling on the pavement and putting a fresh layer of clean white on top of the unpleasant grey.

'Oh, I keep meaning to ask - have you been able to find out for sure whether the Master has a spy in the Displacers or not? Because you weren't sure when we were in Victorian London.'

Diana shook her head. 'I haven't been able to confirm it a hundred percent, but James says that it's almost definite, judging by how quickly we found out about the translation of the Prophecy Sam brought back from Egypt.'

Rachel nodded; it made sense.

They reached a back street away from the busy main road and slowed down, strolling along for a few minutes in companionable silence, enjoying the sudden quiet and the softening of the harsh world caused by the steadily settling snow.

There was a buzz from Diana's handbag, accompanied by a few bars of discordant guitar music.

Rachel looked at her quizzically. '"Nancy Boy"?'

Diana look surprised. 'You recognised it?'

'Of course! Placebo is one of my favourite bands.'

'Mine too! Have you been to any of their concerts?'

'A few: in Brixton years ago and then last summer in Barcelona with Sam.'

'Aren't you a bit young to have seen them "years ago"?'

Rachel shrugged. 'I was always grown up for my age and my mother never seemed to care or even notice when I was gone.'

Diana chuckled. 'We might have actually gone to the same concerts then. That's pretty unbelievable.'

'Small world.'

'That was Quentin, by the way.'

Rachel raised an eyebrow. 'And you have "Nancy Boy" as his message tone?'

Diana grinned. 'Yes.'

'Does he know?'

'He doesn't have a clue.'

They laughed and Rachel glanced sideways out of the corner of her eye at Diana as they continued along the street. Despite the reservations she had about her, she was feeling more and more drawn to the surprising woman; she was not at all like she had expected, or wanted the world to see her as - she put out such a strong image that Rachel was only now starting to see for what it was: a façade that was there to protect her.

'So, do you play?

Rachel turned her head to look at Diana in surprise. 'What? Guitar, you mean? No. Why, do you?'

'Of course.' She laughed at Rachel's expression. 'Don't look so surprised! I had a rebellious phase too, hence the concerts.'

'No, it's not that, it's just, well, I thought you'd be more of a piano or a violin player.'

'Oh, I can play those too, but guitar is more fun.' Diana grinned at Rachel. 'You know, I'm pretty sure you're under the impression that I'm some kind of stuck up brat…'

'I actually used almost those exact same words with Sam earlier today.'

'Almost? I think I can guess which word was different!'

Diana laughed and Rachel was struck with how beautiful it sounded, especially seeing as it was based on genuine feelings for once. She smiled back. 'I bet you can. I don't mind admitting I was wrong though.'

The young woman's face turned suddenly sharp and forbidding and Rachel recoiled slightly. 'Don't start going all mushy on me, Rachel; I've done some bad things and it didn't take much persuading for me to do them. You don't know anything about me and you wouldn't want to be my friend. Trust me.'

She glared at Rachel for a few seconds, but then her face softened, saddened, and she looked down to pull her phone out of her bag. She unlocked it and raised an eyebrow as she read the message from Quentin. 'I have a meeting tomorrow to discuss the African mission. That's quite a bit sooner than I was expecting.'

'Why do you say that?'

'Well, he's only just come back from a trip to Peru and he won't be able to Displace again for another month.'

'Don't you usually plan missions this far ahead?'

'No, not really. Not us, anyway. The Master always draws up the most important plans and only sends them to Quentin a day or so before the trip; he's paranoid and doesn't like to give anybody the chance to betray us.'

'So, what does this meeting mean?'

'Probably nothing.' She shrugged. 'I guess Quentin just wants to get a head start.'

The station was in sight now, barely visible through the thickening snow and Rachel pulled Diana to a halt in the shelter of a bus stop.

'Well, if we assume that Quentin plans to leave as soon as he's able, we can assume we have a month to prepare before you go on the mission.'

Diana nodded. 'I'll find out more tomorrow and let you know when I can meet again to share the details.'

'Thank you.'

Diana started to leave, but she turned back to flash one last beautiful smile at Rachel. 'And for God's sake put a coat on; you're making me cold just looking at you.' She winked, then walked away and was swiftly swallowed in the gloom.

Rachel stayed where she was, scanning the few people that were still on foot in the streets for familiar faces that might have been following them and for suspicious behaviour, but there was nothing untoward.

She sat on the bench and ran through the strange encounter with Diana in her mind while she waited for the next bus to take her back over the river. Sam's original thought that there was something wrong with the young woman seemed to be spot on and the more she opened up the more questions there were - she got the impression that Diana desperately wanted acceptance and to have Rachel as a friend, but at the same time was pushing her away because she didn't want to get close to anybody.

The more she got to know her, the more Rachel wasn't sure if it was a good idea to depend on her intelligence; the beautiful redhead's mood seemed to swing willy-nilly from one end of the spectrum to the other. Who knew if it might get into her head to start turning the tables on them. If she wasn't already.

Rachel shivered and rubbed her arms, but she wasn't sure if it was the cold was finally getting to her or the thought of the damage Diana could do if she betrayed them.

Headquarters was unusually quiet when Rachel got back; normally in the evenings there were at least a half dozen people there, mostly Elders, who met up to eat and talk - it was hard for people who had lived for more than a century to find stimulating conversation elsewhere and there was a special kind of companionship that was found among Society members who had often spent many years together in the past. Tonight, though, because of the inclement weather, there were barely any plaques hanging on the wall in the entrance, just John's, Andrew's and James'. Rachel put her own up next to James' then went looking for the old man; she knew that he would want to hear about the conversation she'd had with Diana and the content of the text from Quentin.

James wasn't in the sitting room so she headed downstairs to the kitchen in the basement. She knew he wouldn't be upstairs with John and Andrew because they were keeping their work completely secret from the rest of the Society, much as James and Rachel were keeping Diana's apparent defection a secret. Andrew knew, of course, but nobody else even suspected that something was going on and as far as the other members (including John) were concerned, James and Rachel were working on a similar project to Andrew and John.

She found the Elder sitting at the table in the open kitchen area with a plate of food and a small crystal tumbler with a couple of inches of brown liquid in it.

He looked up as she came in and frowned at her bruises. 'Looks like you've been in the wars, do you want some painkiller?' He waved at the thin bottle on the table.

She smiled. 'Glenfiddich?'

James nodded. 'I'm sorry, it's only the regular vintage; Phillip and Ralph drank all the fifty-year-old over Christmas and it hasn't been stocked up again yet.'

Rachel grabbed a tumbler from the cupboard then pulled out the chair next to him. He poured her a couple of fingers while she sat down.

James smiled and lifted his glass at her. 'Your health.'

Rachel saluted him back. 'Aren't I a bit young for whisky?'

He laughed. 'I think we both know that you're well beyond the age to start drinking, even in the colonies. Just don't tell your mother.'

'No worries there.' She smiled and took a sip. The liquor was sour. It was definitely an acquired taste, one that she would have to work on a bit more before she could truly appreciate it. She held the liquid in her mouth, acclimatising herself, before swallowing and taking another sip.

He gestured at his plate of food. 'Richard left some good stuff in the fridge for us, I've got some beef bourguignon simmering on the cooker if you want some.'

Rachel didn't need telling twice and almost leaped out of her chair and across the room. She filled a plate with food, piling it up high and grabbing several bread rolls to go with it, then came back to the table. She shrugged at James' raised eyebrow. 'I feel like I haven't eaten in a couple of years; Sparta wasn't very big on feeding its recruits apparently.'

'I see you didn't exactly come through unscathed... uh... is...'

Rachel chuckled around a mouthful of food; why was it every time she got beaten up everyone asked about Sam before they worried about her? 'Sam's fine. He's got a few bruises, but nothing that I haven't given him each and every time I've kicked his arse while sparring.'

The relief on James' face made her shake her head. 'Sam's a big boy, James, he can take care of himself. And if something had happened to him don't you think it would have been the first thing I would have told you?'

'I guess so.' The old man sighed. 'It's just I can't wrap my head around how bloody accident prone that boy is, and what with this new revelation of him not being the one who was prophesied... It makes him seem even more vulnerable than I thought.'

'Don't worry about him; I've trained him well.' Rachel grinned and James just had to laugh.

'Well at least we know why his hair was turning white, now. I knew we shouldn't have introduced him to such a slave driver...'

'Oi! It's not my fault you gave me such a wimp to train and care for!'

They grinned at each other. Sam was a favourite subject of theirs and, while they often poked fun at him behind his back, they didn't mean it; they both knew how good he was at his job and they both loved him.

They ate in silence for a while; wanting to properly savour Richard's cooking.

Rachel took cautious sips at the whiskey while she spooned the stew into her mouth, but in the end poured herself a glass of water with an apologetic look at James.

Eventually they both finished and pushed their plates away. Rachel eyed the pot that was still keeping warm, but decided that she had eaten enough; it was late, she was exhausted and she didn't want to feel ill when she went to sleep. She did, however, decide to give the whiskey another go, now that she had a full stomach, and picked it up again.

She leaned back in her chair, relaxing as much as her mistreated body would let her, but frowned when she realised that James was watching her intently. 'What?'

'I just find it remarkable how much you and Sam suit each other, and how much you've grown together in such a short time.'

Rachel shifted uncomfortably in her seat, unused to being under such scrutiny - one of the reasons she liked being with Sam so much was because she could fade into the background and let him take the lead. Except, of course, when it came to the fighting.

One day John had laughed and called her a "support", comparing her to a character in one of the video games he played. It was a special type of character whose only purpose was to aid the more powerful characters - they did everything they could to help those characters stay alive, even up to the point of sacrificing themselves. Of all the rubbish that John had said to her over the years she'd known him, for some reason *that* had stuck in her mind and made the most sense to her.

James saw her discomfort and chuckled into his whiskey.

Rachel coloured slightly and took a big gulp of her own drink to cover, coughing as the fiery liquid burned her throat which provoked more gentle merriment from James. When she finally recovered she launched into a recounting of what Diana had told her on the trip to Clapham.

James immediately became serious and listened attentively to her. Even though she knew he had most likely already heard most of what she had to tell him, she said it all anyway, because he had instructed her to tell him everything that Diana said to her; there might be some detail that he had missed, or something insignificant on its own but that when combined with what he knew, might catch her in a lie. It wasn't until she told him about the text message from Quentin that he really looked interested, though, and she could almost see the cogs turning behind his eyes as he took in the information and worked out possibilities.

James really was the brains behind the Displacers. While everybody else contributed in their own ways, providing information and research, he was the only one who could really put all of it together and see the big picture. He was the only one that could pinpoint the threads that needed to be picked at to make a troubled time-line slip back into place. Or to cause an Illuminati plan to collapse into tatters.

They were extremely lucky to have him, especially now that they couldn't rely on Sam to miraculously save them. In fact, Rachel had suspected right from the start that Sam wouldn't be enough, that he would need to work with the Society as a whole, but especially his grandfather, if he was going to stop the world from slipping into an Illuminati-controlled nightmare of darkness and despair.

She finished her report and James nodded his thanks. 'I know that she rubs you up the wrong way, but it would be good for us all if you developed this new connection you have to her; who knows what she might tell a lovely young companion that she wouldn't an old fogey like me.'

'I'll try, but she can be *very* annoying.'

'I know, believe me. Just try to keep your temper in check; I'd rather you didn't beat her senseless until *after* I've finished with her.'

'Sorry. Can't promise anything.'

He laughed. 'Fair enough.' He set his glass down on the table and sat up, serious once more.

She did the same, knowing that it was time to leave the joking behind and get down to the real business.

'Since that little conversation you had with Diana in Victorian London I've been trying to track the Illuminati through time, but I wasn't able to do much more than follow the chain of rumours that thread through most of the world, from Bavaria to Rome, from the first banks to modern global corporations. It's a complete mess and it's become increasingly confused over the last few years with how much their legend is being used in what some people call "literature".'

Rachel hid a smile behind her hand; the whole Society was well aware of how James felt about modern writers and their "flights of fancy" as they put them - if you wanted to pick a fight with him all you needed was a few hours to spare and to mention the name Harry Potter.

'However, that has all changed with Diana's information and much of my conjecture has passed into the realm of fact. She has provided me with the names of the companies she has used as a front, both in the past and in the present and I have been looking at them in an attempt to find out how they were affected to suit the enemy. I'm hoping that we can find weak points to attack so that we can chip away at them piece by piece.'

'Is that what Andrew is working on?'

James nodded. 'Surprisingly, many of the stories about the Illuminati have proved to be true - for example, they did in fact have a hand in the Templars and their subsequent financial empire. So yes, that's what Andrew is looking at as a possible point at which we can strike, but you didn't hear it from me. I'd really like to be helping them with that; it's probably the most important missions we've planned for years, but I have no spare time because I'm stuck compiling all the information we've been getting from Diana - there's a hell of a lot of it and because we don't know who this damn spy is I can't take the chance of assigning anyone else to help me.'

He paused to refill both their glasses, taking another sip of his to wet his whistle, then continued.

'As to what she told me today, I spent the last hour or so looking into possible links between the companies that I have identified and the South African gold mines and as far as I can see there aren't any, which, I suppose, is why they have made that their next target. There was, however, a branch of one of their offshoots in Cape Town at the time of the gold rush and I think it is safe to assume that their plan will involve persuading mine owners to sign over part, or all, of their holdings to the personnel at that office. Probably by force.'

Rachel shook her head in wonder; it was astounding how much James had been able to accomplish in the short time since he had left Diana in her hands. It further reinforced her belief in him. 'That makes sense. And it sounds like something Quentin would come up with.'

'But any conjecture about their plans on my part can be only that. So, until Diana tells us exactly what they are going to do, I will go back to my work on tracing the Illuminati's corporate holdings.'

'Have you been able to identify who owns the corporations? Perhaps we can work out who the Master is from that.'

'Ooh, you clever girl! Not just a pretty face!' He laughed and she smiled, pleased with the complement even if it was rather out of date and mildly sexist. 'Yes, I did think of that, but I haven't been able to make much progress; the web of ownership is so complex that it just leads from one company to the next and never to an individual. I'm sure it's only a matter of time, though, and that would indeed be a giant leap forwards in eventually being able to bring down the whole house of cards.'

They had to cut short their conversation when footsteps sounded on the stairs and Anne, one of their few American members, appeared around the corner.

She paused in the doorway and smiled at them. 'I thought I heard voices down here.'

She was wearing a long, expensive-looking dark blue dress and had her brown hair done up into an elaborate confection at the back of her head. Once again Rachel was reminded of how shabby her own clothes made her look when compared to what seemed like all of the women around her. She easily managed to console herself, however, with the knowledge that she could take any of them in a fight.

James called out in greeting. 'Anne!'

'Evening, James.' She nodded respectfully at the Elder and then looked at Rachel and raised an eyebrow. 'Rachel, I see you've been on another of your interesting trips. Did Sam survive?'

Rachel scowled, but James just laughed. 'Are you back for long?'

'Just a flying visit, I'm afraid. Enough time for some business and for Andrew to take me to dinner. We have reservations at Richard's place in half an hour, have you seen him?'

'He hasn't come out of his meeting with John yet.

'Oh, well, I suppose Richard will keep the table open for us.' She eyed the bottle of whiskey in front of James. 'Do you mind?'

'Not at all, help yourself.'

She went over to the kitchen cupboards to grab a glass and Rachel saw with some satisfaction that she had picked the wrong kind for whiskey; behind her perfect make-up, perfect clothing, perfect figure and perfectly groomed hair the woman wasn't perfect after all.

Anne poured herself a small glass and sat down with a sigh. She reached under the table to take off her shoes. 'I hate wearing high heels, but I wanted to look good for Andrew tonight; I have no idea when I'm going to be able to come back to London again.'

'Are things busy, then?'

'You have no idea. We're moving headquarters to a bigger building in Dallas and it's utter chaos; I have to organise all these inauguration parties with a ton of politicians. The President is invited, but I'm really hoping he declines because I *do not* want to deal with that hassle!' She took a big gulp of her whiskey and smacked her lips in a very un-ladylike fashion.

Anne was an event manager at a large multi-national corporation. She ran the department that organised the parties, conferences, ceremonies and such. Her people made sure that any function that needed catering, or special equipment, or furniture, or anything beyond what was used for the normal 9 to 5 life of an office, went smoothly. This didn't just include big parties, it meant everything, down to tiny things like making sure that a projector was available for a presentation or water was on the table for a board meeting. While she was based in New York, the company owned buildings in various major cities in the States as well as Europe, which meant she was often in London and used the opportunity to pop in to Headquarters whenever possible.

She and Andrew had started a bit of a romance about a year ago and it had been awkward for quite a while, with the two of them not quite ever saying what they meant or wanted and with matters complicated further by the fact that Andrew had never really gotten over the death of his wife, Susan. Finally, over the Christmas period and to the relief of everybody in the Society, the romance had turned into something more substantial and they were now "courting" as James liked to say. John, as always, had another word for it, but, of course, it wasn't particularly polite.

'Anne?'

Andrew's question came floating down to them from the hallway above and Anne lifted her voice to shout up to him without moving from her seat at the table. 'Down here, darling!'

After a few seconds Andrew came bounding into the room. He smiled broadly and went straight over to kiss Anne on the cheek.

James and Rachel shared an amused grin at how demurely he was acting.

His boyfriend duties done, Andrew nodded in greeting at Rachel and James, but then he turned his attention right back to Anne and looked down at the glass in her hand.

'You've started already, I see.'

'Just a little something to warm me up. It is far too cold outside for a dress like this, I should be wearing ski pants and my Uggs.'

'And no doubt Richard would still let you in, dress code be damned! Speaking of which, we should be going; we're never going to be able to get a taxi in this weather as it is.'

He offered Anne his hand and she allowed him to help her out of her chair, then smiled at Rachel and James. 'Well, it was nice to see you both again. I'm sorry I couldn't stay longer.'

James waved away her words. 'Nonsense. Go. Eat, drink, and be young. We can catch up any time.'

Anne left the room and started up the stairs, but Andrew lingered. 'Everything all right, James? Anything I should know?'

'Everything is in hand, just concentrate on your mission.'

Andrew nodded and then frowned at Rachel. 'You look terrible. Is…'

'Yes, Sam is fine!' Rachel interrupted him with an exasperated shout. 'Why is it everybody thinks about Sam every time I get hurt? Why can't you people just be concerned for me for once?'

Andrew grinned. 'It's because we know what a bad influence you are on him, I guess.'

He ducked as a bread roll flew at his head and ran out the door as another one followed closely behind. He called back to them from the stairs, safely around the corner. 'Goodnight!'

When the sounds of Andrew climbing the stairs had faded, Rachel turned to James and lowered her voice. 'You're not sharing what you learn from Diana even with him?'

'We called it compartmentalisation during the war: both of us only know what we need to know.'

'I understand keeping Diana a secret from the rest of the members, but it's a little extreme not to talk to Andrew about what she's giving us, isn't it?'

James shrugged. 'Yes, of course, but this is the way it has to be done until we're ready to make our move, or until we find this damn spy.

You don't share information with *anyone*, even with those people who are beyond suspicion. That way they can't let anything slip by accident.'

'What if she says something that Andrew could use?'

'I know what he's working on and I'll let him know if I find out anything that's relevant, don't worry, but I have to weigh the benefit of telling something to Andrew with the possible loss of Diana as a source if somebody realises where it came from.'

'OK, this is just whole levels of paranoia beyond what I've ever been able to cope with...'

'Welcome to the war.' James raised his glass to her with a sigh.

She looked at him in shock. 'Is that what you think this is?'

He put his glass down and stared at her, all pretence at humour gone. 'Don't you?'

'Well... I guess I'm not sure.'

'You *have* to be sure.' His face turned hard and it was that more than his tone of voice that sent a chill through her; she had never seen him with anything except a kind or jovial expression on his face, even when things weren't going well.

'This is a war, Rachel, and the sooner you get that into your head the better. They will not bat an eyelid at killing any one of us, or worse, make it so that we never lived. They are trying to conquer the world and have already amassed an empire that puts those of Rome, Alexander, Hitler or even Soviet Russia to shame. Just because they don't have a flag or an army on the march doesn't make them any less a conquering force.'

Rachel blinked; she had never really thought of it in quite those terms. Displacing was fun, even more so now that she could do it with Sam, and she had always treated it as a kind of game, albeit a dangerous one. Under James' intense stare she now realised how childish that outlook was and was ashamed at her naivety. However, before she could say anything, his face fell and the stern expression was replaced by one of such extreme sorrow that she couldn't even come close to comprehending.

'Unfortunately, like most wars, it is being fought by the young while the old are forced to stay behind and watch, often sending them to their deaths. We have suffered too much already, you just have to look in the sitting room to see that, and there is no end in sight, especially after the tidings we had at Christmas.'

The old man fell silent and stared into his glass.

Rachel watched him gently swirling his drink and tried to imagine the things he had witnessed, the sorrows he had lived through, all the people that he'd had to say goodbye to. Not just in the past or among the Displacers either: he'd fought in a World War and seen friends killed in front of him, been through horrors that she couldn't even comprehend. Then, to make matters worse, he'd had to carry those memories with him during a life that had been extended immensely due to the quirks of time travel. It was saddening in the extreme, yet hugely inspiring that he still managed to keep his smile most of the time.

'Wotcha!' They both jumped when John appeared in the doorway as if from nowhere. Neither of them had heard him coming - for such a big nerd he moved quietly. 'Oooh, whiskey! Gimme!'

He picked up Anne's discarded glass and inspected it briefly. Rachel clearly saw red lipstick on the rim, but John just shrugged and filled it almost to the brim before taking a big gulp.

He wheezed, then coughed, thumping himself on the chest before smiling. 'Ahhh! That hit the spot!' He looked from James to Rachel and back. 'So, what are we talking about? Why so serious?'

'Rachel was just telling me how tired she was after her Displacement today. We were about to leave actually.'

'That's a shame; it's going so well upstairs that I feel like celebrating, you know? I hope your secret project is going as well as ours is!' John winked, inviting James to comment.

The Elder didn't rise to the bait though, he just smiled, humouring the man. 'I have no idea what you're talking about.'

John laughed and tapped the side of his nose. 'Of course you don't!'

When John tipped his head back to swallow more whiskey James gave Rachel a scathing look and inclined his head towards the exit.

Rachel took the hint and stood up. She faked a yawn, but then staggered slightly as her head swam; she was a lot more tired than she realised - the conversation with James had been keeping her awake and alert, but now that it was time to go her exhaustion hit her hard. The whiskey didn't exactly help either.

'You alright there, love?' John looked her up and down appraisingly and she suppressed a shudder. She didn't know what she disliked more, the way he was looking at her or his calling her "love", a word that she was just getting used to Sam using, but she forced a smile.

'Just a little bit of post-Displacement exhaustion. I really should go before I'm too tired to get home.'

James looked concerned. 'Why don't you stay here tonight?'

'Wish I could, but my mum's expecting me and she'll freak out if I don't come home. Again.'

'Alright, then. Be careful, though, it's getting worse out there all the time.'

'I'll catch the Underground, I'll be fine.'

'I can accompany you if you want?' John offered.

She was somewhat surprised; it was more consideration than she would expect from him. 'Um, no thanks, I'll be fine.'

'Fair enough. Well, goodnight then.' John saluted her with his glass.

She gave him a small smile, then nodded at the Elder. 'Goodnight, James. I'll keep you appraised.'

'Thank you. Take care.'

She gave him a smile a much larger smile than the one John had gotten, then climbed up to the hallway. She took her name plate off the peg and went out, then turned straight around and went back in for her jacket, before finally started her long trek home.

Diana made sure that the door was locked securely and the alarm was on before taking her coat and shoes into the bathroom to dry. Her flat was empty and silent, as it always was, and she walked through it into the kitchen without putting any of the lights on. She never put them on unless she needed them; she enjoyed the darkness.

She put on the kettle and used the soft blue light from it to prepare a chamomile tea. While she was waiting for the water to boil she scrolled through the music on her phone, selecting her playlist of the more mellow songs by Placebo and sent it to her music system.

The soft sounds of "Follow the Cops Back Home" filled the flat.

She went to the window and looked out at the night.

She lived alone in a fairly recent development on the Thames, just west of Greenwich and only a short walk from the Cutty Sark. Her flat was right in front of the river and she could usually see the colourful lights of Canary Wharf, but tonight her view was blocked by the thickly falling snow and she could barely make out the water sluggishly flowing towards the sea. It was an expensive home in an exclusive development and she had decorated it with elegant furnishings to suit her own taste.

One thing that could be said about working for the Illuminati was that it paid well; the Master made sure that they were well compensated when they carried out his orders successfully and she had been on several lucrative missions before Sam had come onto the scene. Since then, though, it had seemingly been one disaster after another, but Quentin had gotten the major part of the blame for those defeats. He had tried to pin the failures of both the Egypt and Jack the Ripper missions on her, but the Master had seen through him and besides, as the group leader, he was ultimately responsible anyway. She hadn't received any rewards for those missions, but neither had she been punished like Quentin had.

She smiled as she remembered the day they had gone on their mission in Victorian London. The Master tried to be present, if only electronically, whenever they went on important missions and had been watching via Skype, so Quentin had been forced to tell him of their failure immediately on their return.

The Master had been quietly furious and had ordered the Twins to beat Quentin, which they had done all too willingly. It had only been a few blows to the stomach, nothing like what Sam had received from them, but it had been enough to have Quentin vomiting all over his own carpet and expensive Italian sofa. She had been sure that she would receive the same treatment, but had been spared - despite his vindictiveness the Master wasn't one to lash out without reason; he knew it was far more of an incentive to do well if you knew you would only be punished if you failed.

It was a harsh system, but it had seemed fair to her. Until she had met Sam and Rachel and found out that there was another way.

She knew exactly what the girl thought of her and she didn't blame her; she had been an agent of the Illuminati too long and they had tried to kill Sam on various occasions - it was too much to forgive easily, but even so, she had really come to value the time she spent with Rachel. The silly roundabout routes she insisted on taking for "security" should have annoyed her, but instead she found herself wishing for the journey to be as long as possible so that they could have more time together.

Of course, Rachel didn't know that her precautions were completely unnecessary and she wasn't about to enlighten her, but if Quentin or the Master ever even suspected her covert activities then she would be dead. There would be a visit from the Twins and that would be that. It had happened before: an example had been made of an older member of the Illuminati, a contemporary of the Master and one of the few people who had actually known his true identity. Some said that the Master was just covering his tracks, but she knew that the victim had been having second thoughts; he had been the leader of her group before Quentin had been recruited and had said as much to her.

The Twins were the Master's enforcers and advisers on criminal matters and they were very good at what they did. They had taken lessons from the best, Leaping to work with Capone and various mafias from around the world, as well as many of the London-based criminals like the Krays and other mobsters. They knew the ins and outs of the criminal underworld like the back of their hands and had enough contacts in the present day crime syndicates to allow the Illuminati to act almost with impunity. Making her body disappear would be the simplest of tasks for them and no matter how friendly she had been with them, they wouldn't think twice if the Master told them to kill her - they were incredibly loyal to him; he had personally pulled them out of juvenile detention. That little tidbit also meant they were two of the very few people who knew who he really was, but she was absolutely positive they would never tell anyone, not even under torture.

"Follow the Cops Back Home" gave way to "Burger Queen" and the kettle clicked off. She turned from the window and went back to the kitchen.

After she poured the water she unlocked her phone and pressed a few buttons, but then froze, her finger hovering over the green call button, not quite sure what she was doing.

She was sorely tempted to make the call, to ring him and confess everything, to beg for forgiveness and confess her feelings. She desperately wanted to make it all right again, to go back to a time when things had been so much simpler, but she knew that she couldn't; there was too much still to be done before that could be even a remote possibility.

She snarled suddenly, angry at herself for her weakness at a time when she would need every ounce of her strength to survive and with a swipe she got rid of Sam's telephone number, the number that she had stolen from James' telephone when he was out of the room making one of the many cups of tea they drank to get through the tough days. Instead, she consoled herself by calling up an image from the memory card as she walked back across the room to the window, the steaming mug in hand.

It was a surveillance photo that the Master had distributed to all his agents. It had been taken the year before in Barcelona and was of Sam and Rachel as they walked hand in hand down a street in the bright summer sunlight. They looked happy and carefree. It was almost like a scene from a romantic comedy or something equally saccharine and hopeful and was very different from the dark world that was all Diana had ever known.

She hadn't told Rachel why she liked Placebo, for the same reason she would never tell her about the dozens of photos of her and Sam she had on her phone; Quentin had reported following Rachel and Sam to a concert in Barcelona and she had been curious. She had listened to a couple of albums and had grown to like it, not only because the music itself was good, but because it made her feel closer to them somehow, closer to the people she truly wanted to be like.

As she sipped her drink she zoomed in on Sam's smiling, innocent face and smiled as she thought of the kiss they had shared.

Rachel closed the door behind her as quietly as she could and leaned her forehead against it. From behind her she could hear the blaring of the television and the laughter of two people - her mum was watching some reality show or other at full blast. Rachel hoped that she hadn't heard her come in, but the volume went down just a little and her mother called out.

'Is that you, Rachel?'

She pushed off the door and forced a smile as she looked into the sitting room. Her mother was on the sofa leaning up against her boyfriend, the latest in a long line of them. She forgot this one's name - Brian or Barry or something. 'Yeah, Mum.'

'Grab us a couple of beers from the fridge, willya?'

'OK.' She went into the kitchen and took a couple of cans from a fridge that was empty except for beer, ketchup and what looked like leftovers from the Indian place around the corner. She took the cans back to the sitting room and handed them over.

'Cheers, darlin'!'

The man, William she remembered now, her mother called him Bill, gave her a lewd look and she shuddered. Her mother didn't notice, though; she had her eyes glued to the TV and didn't even look as she reached out a hand for the beer.

'Thanks, love. You have a good day?'

'Yeah. I'm going to bed now, alright? I'm a bit tired.'

'OK, g'night then.'

Rachel ignored the wink from Bill and walked out. Her body felt heavier than it ever had and she barely made it up the stairs and into her room before her energy completely gave out. She locked the door, a precaution that she had put in place years ago to dissuade the occasional nighttime visits from one of her mother's previous suitors, then fell face first onto her bed.

She desperately wanted to just go to sleep, but instead she groaned and rolled over; there was something she needed more than rest right now.

She pulled out her phone, opened WhatsApp to make a call. While she waited, she gazed around at the photos that were plastered on her walls of her and Sam taken over summer in Barcelona and Christmas in London. In pride of place over her bed was the poster that Sam had bought her at the Placebo concert they'd gone to in the Palau Sant Jordi and she smiled and looked up at it as the call connected, her exhaustion momentarily forgotten.

'Hey, Sam...'

CHAPTER 4
THOUGHTS

Rachel had deliberately chosen Saturday afternoon for their Displacement to Sparta because it would give Sam a couple of days rest before going back to school on Monday.

He needed every minute of it.

He went straight back home after leaving Andrew's flat and joined his family in the sitting room. He yawned his way through a film then dinner, but as soon as he had helped to clear up after eating he went to his room and fell unconscious on his bed.

The call from Rachel woke him up with a start. He'd been expecting her call and hoping for it, but hadn't known if she'd be able to in the end; he knew how busy she was and had been sure she would be just as exhausted as him. More so because she had to work as soon as she got back.

'Hey, you! How did Diana behave today? Did you have to slap her around again?'

'Not this time.'

'Shame.'

Rachel laughed. 'It is, a bit, although I must say she's growing on me... Like a fungus.'

Sam chuckled. 'I told you she wasn't as bad as you thought she was. She's just had a rough time of it.'

'And she's pretty damaged.'

'That too.' Sam yawned and heard Rachel do the same on the other end. He laughed. 'Hey, I didn't know yawning was contagious over the phone as well!'

'I'm exhausted.'

'Me too... I guess we should both get some sleep.'

'Yeah, I suppose. I'll have to tell you about Diana's newest revelations tomorrow.'

'OK, just tell me one thing, though.'

'What?'

'Tell me that you love me again.'

'I love you, Sam.'

He smiled to himself. 'I can't get enough of hearing you say that. I love you too, Rachel. Goodnight.'

'Goodnight, darling.'

Sam was barely able to switch his phone off before his eyes closed by themselves and he fell into the deep sleep that was caused by Displacement exhaustion.

He woke up only when his mother shouted through his door at him to "stop being so lazy and lay the table for lunch!"

He had slept for almost fifteen hours, but, even though lately it took him less time to recover from Displacing than it had at first - the first time he had Displaced he had slept almost two days when he had arrived in the past and just as long on his return - it still felt like it was barely enough.

Yawning, he pulled on some clothes and staggered out of his bedroom, then wandered down the hall to the kitchen, grabbed some cutlery and took it into the dining room. Violeta was busily drawing pictures at the table, but he didn't bother moving her, he just worked around her.

His mother appeared and stood in the doorway looking at him disapprovingly. She tutted and walked over to him and he suddenly realised that he hadn't done anything to cover his injuries. He frantically searched his brain for excuses and waited for the inevitable questioning about what he'd been up to, but instead she just wet her finger and rubbed at one of the bruises on his cheek.

'Really, Sam, I would have thought by your age you would have learned to wash your face properly.'

'Aw, Mum!' He pulled away from her, turning his head so that she wouldn't see that her rubbing wasn't doing anything. He also wanted her to stop because, frankly, it hurt.

Violeta laughed. 'Yeah, wash your face, Sam!'

Sam grinned down at her and she gave him a knowing look, which surprised him somewhat, before she went back to her drawing. He looked over her shoulder at her pictures. She was actually very good for her age; most of the things she drew were recognisable, and her latest effort was no exception - it very clearly depicted four men walking across a road. It was a strange subject for a child of eight and not Violeta's usual type of thing; she was more into horses, dogs and rainbows.

'What's that you're drawing, Violeta?'

'The Beatles!'

'Really? How do you know about the Beatles?'

'Your father's been listening to his old records with her...' Sam's mother shook her head, but smiled as she left the room, going back to the kitchen.

Violeta handed Sam her drawing. The four men were crossing a crude depiction of a zebra crossing and he realised that it was Violeta's take on the Abbey Road photo, but she had drawn it from a different angle, as if they were walking away from them and not across the page. It was an impressive feat of imagination for one so young.

'Hey, sleepy head!'

Sam handed the unfinished drawing back to Violeta before smiling at his father. 'Hi, Dad.'

'Nice to see you up and about so early.'

'Ha ha...' Sam's father, although Spanish, had apparently taken sarcasm lessons from his English wife quite early on in their relationship. However, while he made an effort, it still didn't come as naturally as it did to people like Rachel and Andrew, who had been born with their tongues firmly planted in their cheeks.

'OK, everybody up the table, please! Violeta, come on, put your stuff away. Sam, go get the vegetables, please.'

Sam's mother came back in carrying lunch, the full Sunday roast that she insisted on doing every week, whether it was winter or forty degrees outside. Today, Sam was looking forward to it immensely; he was starving after Displacing the day before - time travel used up an immense amount of energy, and the sandwiches for dinner the night before hadn't come close to satisfying him.

In the end Sam ate almost four portions, although he tried to make it look like he had eaten less; he had learned the hard way that if he ate too much his mother would start to look at him strangely and he didn't want to give her yet another reason to think there was something up with him. She wasn't a hypochondriac or an obsessive mother, but if he gave her too many things to think about, like sleeping all day, eating too much, and strange bruises turning up on his body, then she would likely take him to the doctor's, and then there would be all sorts of questions that he couldn't answer.

After lunch he went back to his room to write his report on Sparta while it was still fresh in mind. He sent a copy of it to the secure Displacer's email account and saved his own on a pen drive that he kept hidden with some of his more innocuous souvenirs in a box under his bed.

He could very easily have gone back to bed, but again, that might have made his mother suspicious, so instead he left his door open so that his parents could see him being normal and did the homework that he had been set for the weekend.

Sam's attitude towards school had changed a lot over the past year. He'd always been unhappy at school, having been bullied since almost his first day, and his work had suffered as a result, but since he'd started Displacing, Rafa Sánchez, his own personal bully, was no longer a problem; he had been completely neutralised when Sam had learnt martial arts with Rachel - one little demonstration of his newfound prowess had caused the cowardly bully to stop picking on him for good and Sam now watched him closely whenever he could, trying to make sure that he didn't find another poor unfortunate to target. So far it seemed to be working.

Fencing had also become a lot more rewarding again, but only because he had completely changed his focus. He had enjoyed fencing for many years and had worked incredibly hard to get onto the team, trying to become one of the best. However, when he had first started Displacing and studying martial arts with Rachel, he had suddenly become so much better than everybody else because of the advantage his years of training gave him. While he was sure that most children his age, most people, in fact, would love to be in his situation, Sam was smart enough and mature enough to realise that it wasn't fair to everybody else. The way he saw it was that if he had no competition, then it just wasn't fun and there was no point in even taking part if right from the start he knew that he was going to win, no matter what the other person did.

He had almost given up and walked out of his first fencing class after Displacing to Okinawa, but fortunately he was brought to the realisation that it was just as fulfilling to pass on his knowledge and skills to others as it was to compete himself, so he became an unofficial coach to the team. He assisted the actual coach and the teachers whenever he could and complemented their training, all but taking over the teaching of the new recruits, which allowed them to spend more time with the team.

There were, however, some team members who had come to him every class, pleading for him to teach them personally and initially he was reluctant to agree because he hadn't wanted to step on any toes, but the team coach quickly said it was fine with him.

One of those team members was Marc, the twelve-year-old boy who had initially been singled out by Rafa as his new target for abuse once he realised he could no longer touch Sam. Sam had immediately prevented that from happening and taken the small boy under his wing. Marc had made great strides and had come in the top ten of the Barcelona novice tournament after only a few short months of training. It hadn't been all due to Sam, of course, because the boy's enthusiasm and talent had a lot to do with it, but he liked to think that at least some of the credit was down to his lessons.

With his focus turning away from fencing Sam tried going to various martial arts classes, thinking that he might be able to learn something, or at least have someone to spar with in Rachel's absence, and he did test classes at various dojos in Barcelona. He ran into the same problem as he had with Fencing, though: classes were either run by someone who was less experienced than he was, or who wasn't willing to treat him as an adult, even after he demonstrated his skill. So, for the time being at least, Sam had resigned himself to doing his own training and only sparring with Rachel during Displacements and holidays - it was a wholly unsatisfactory state of affairs, and his skills were going to suffer, but there was no helping it.

Despite his problems arranging his extra-curricular activities, school itself became much less of a chore; he was finding it easier to concentrate in classes and was getting better marks in most of his subjects. Andrew told him that it was a sign that he was finally developing the patience that came to every Displacer, but Rachel insisted that it was a consequence of the discipline he'd learned in martial arts.

Sam, however, knew differently; while both were probably true to a certain extent, there was another, even more important, reason behind it - he had finally turned sixteen in the present and, if he wanted, he could leave school at the end of the year, but *only* if he passed his exams.

It was strong motivation.

Rachel was seventeen and had left school the previous year and Sam was desperate to do the same so that he would have the freedom to spend more time with her. He also wanted to start working full time for the Displacers as soon as possible.

He had discussed the possibility of leaving school at the end of the year with his parents and, while they weren't at all keen on the idea, they hadn't dismissed it out of hand. They wanted him to go to university, of course, but they seemed to be open to the idea that it might not happen and they could also see the current climate and knew that a university degree didn't necessarily mean much anymore.

Of course, Sam knew better than them that his education wasn't going to come in a traditional manner; it was going to come at the hands of experience - they didn't realise that their son was no longer the sixteen year-old boy that he appeared to be: Sam had been to war; he had dealt with murderers and been tortured; friends had been killed in front of him and then miraculously resurrected; he had learned about colleagues and relatives that had died while Displacing and because of that had never existed; he had lived and loved for years in the past.

They would never know any of that, and he could never tell them.

So, he played along and lived a life that increasingly seemed like a lie to him, all the while planning to leave it behind as soon as possible.

Sam checked the time on his computer. He had run out of homework to do and there were still a couple of hours to go until he'd arranged to talk to Rachel. He sat back in his chair and looked around for something to do.

Weekends were a particularly hard time for Sam. His schoolwork no longer occupied as much of his time as it had before and he had a fair amount of free time, but not much to do with it; Rachel was busier than ever, either working or with her mother, helping with shopping and housework and such, which meant she could only Skype in the evenings and both James and Andrew were busy with their secret Displacer business and couldn't talk to him.

More often than not he ended up just going on long training runs in the hills by himself on Saturday and Sunday mornings, keeping himself in shape and burning the time with something that was at least half-way productive. Today, though, after his recent Displacement, he was far too tired to go for a run.

His eyes were drawn towards a pile of books on the shelf above his head and the leather-bound, hand-written volume that was stashed there. Beyond a quick glance when he'd first gotten home after Christmas he hadn't had much time to look at it and he decided that it was as good a time as any.

He got up and stood in the doorway, trying to hear what the rest of his family were doing. It sounded like Violeta had gone back to her drawing and his parents were having a coffee in the sitting room, reading the newspapers - something they did after lunch every Sunday.

Satisfied that he wouldn't be disturbed for a while he closed the door and pulled the book from its hiding place. It was the final volume of the diaries written by Everett Lloyd, accounts of his attempts to find the limits of Displacing, that his grandfather had lent him over Christmas.

The book was the same size as the others but where those had been bound in brown leather these were black and, while the others dealt with experiments that Lloyd had actually performed, this one contained accounts of purely theoretical experiments that naturally occurred to an inquisitive mind, but that *could not*, or *should not* be carried out. Neither did it follow a logical progression like the others, instead it was a kind of rambling treatise that went from one thought to another, seemingly at random. It presented a different approach to the theories and practises of Displacing than what was traditionally taught and Andrew hoped that the fresh perspective would finally inspire Sam and lead him to understand his powers a bit better. He had told Sam that Lloyd took his thinking to extremes in this final diary, pushing the limits of what was known and delving into the realms of possibilities and sometimes even beyond acceptability, which was probably why James hadn't given this book to Sam originally; it was forbidden thinking.

Sam's enemies and detractors often said that he had only managed to achieve what he had out of sheer luck, which would run out eventually, but he knew different; he did things because he instinctively felt they were *right* - he couldn't explain it and he couldn't say how he knew what to do, but he just did. Andrew was also slowly coming to realise how different Sam was, that he was something apart from the rules that normal Displacers acted under and that if he tried to make his nephew stay within the bounds of what was generally accepted as being possible then he would be restricting him unnecessary. This was his first attempt to help Sam "think outside the box".

The book turned out to be almost a philosophical treatise and, as he read, Sam found it fascinating and headache-inducing in equal parts.

Thought Experiment the first.
It is an accepted fact that if one of us dies in the past we disappear from the time-line as if we never existed.
What would happen, though, if one of us is killed in our own time-line by a Displacer from our future?
The usual rules of Displacing would suggest that when the future Displacer returned to his time then the present Displacer would return to life. However, we have often observed that there are special rules for us that do not necessarily follow what we would expect, and it is quite possible that we would prove to be a tragic exception.

Whenever time travel was discussed among normal people, that is to say outside of Displacer circles, a very common theme, or desire, was the ability to travel back in time to kill someone like Hitler, someone who had caused suffering to so many people. It was also a very common topic of debate among the Displacers as well. The prevailing argument at the moment was that you wouldn't be changing the circumstances that *created* a person like him and it was more than likely that someone else would just step up and take his place. And nobody knew whether that person wouldn't be worse.

This was discussed in great depth at the start of the black book; apparently it had been just as hot a topic more than a century before, and was naturally the first thing that Lloyd tackled. It wasn't Hitler he mentioned, of course, because it had been written in 1875, it was Genghis Khan, but the reference was applicable. Sam quickly skipped over it, though; thanks to long evenings listening to Elders at Headquarters he was more than familiar with just about every angle of the argument.

Next, Lloyd debated why the Elders never sensed that the time-line needed protection before the start of written history and put forward the theory that the time-line was more fixed because there were less people creating less important events. He then went on to expand on the idea of deliberately going back far enough to affect major changes on the entirety of humanity, for example: giving fire to cavemen millions of years before they eventually got it.

Would the world we live in be changed into some technically advanced marvel? Would we even still be here, or would humanity have long ago annihilated itself with vastly superior weaponry in its seemingly insatiable need to make war?

Both outcomes inevitably lead to the same paradox that continually rears its head in those cases where sweeping changes are made in history; if we ourselves are changed by our actions, or cease to exist, then how could we have made the changes in the first place?

Most of the rest of the book was taken up by increasingly complicated discussions of the multifarious paradoxes that were associated with time travel.

The typical paradoxes that everybody knew about involved things like going back in time and killing your grandfather: if you did that you would cease to exist and if you ceased to exist then you couldn't kill your grandfather and if you couldn't kill your grandfather... and so on. Lloyd's thought experiments not only dealt with those, but also with the rules of Displacing themselves - you could, of course, go back in time and kill your grandfather but, because it was direct involvement in the time-line, then the change would revert back as soon as you left.

Thought experiment the twelfth.

What would occur if one Displaced with one's own father and then conspired to kill him whilst you were both in the past?

The first and most obvious extrapolation is that the father would cease to exist in the minds of the world, but not among the society.

Two outcomes are therefore possible - the son continues to exist or ceases to do so.

If he ceases to exist then we are left with the paradox of who it was that killed the father.

If the son continues to exist, however, then we are left with the question of why. Is it because the perceptions of the Society members override those of the world at large? Or is the time-line protecting itself?

We have suspected for some while now that the time-line is elastic: it will always attempt to find some way to snap back to its original form, unless it is stretched too far. Which begs the question: what would happen if the time-line were stretched too far? And what monumental change would be needed in order to do so?

(A further, perhaps more frivolous, but possibly more important question now presents itself to me: who would the world at large see as the father of the son, once the father is gone?)

Sam finally snapped the book closed and sighed in exasperation; he just couldn't wrap his head around most of it and Everett Lloyd's lack of clear direction in his writing was frustrating. Far from clearing things up, the book was just making them worse, and it was giving him a headache as well. Andrew's intentions had been good and it was all very interesting, but it wasn't really helping.

There was one thing that he'd read that had instantly seemed to make sense to Sam, though. One phrase that had leapt off of the page. That had resounded with him like a *truth* hidden amongst all the conjecture.

Or is the time-line protecting itself?

The prophecy he'd brought back from the Egyptian temple had said that someone called the "Diviner", who everybody now believed was Sam, would come at a time of need to help "Thoth", who, among many other things, was the Egyptian god responsible for regulating time and of conserving balance. While Sam didn't believe that he was here to help an actual god, could it be that there was some agent, some force guiding him? Had someone or some*thing* given the Displacers their powers and the instinct to protect the time-line?

The Society members insisted that it was just luck that he always turned up in a time-line as exactly who and where he needed to be in order to foil Quentin, but what if it wasn't? What if it was the *time-line itself* doing what it needed to survive?

He resolved to ask James if there was anything in the archives about his theory; perhaps there would be answers there.

Sam took a deep breath and was just about to open the book again to search for any other references of time's elasticity or ability to protect itself when his phone beeped and a WhatsApp message popped up. It was from Rachel and simply read "Skype?"

He smiled, put down the book in relief, and opened his laptop.

CHAPTER 5
LAST CHANCE

The thick wooden door of Quentin's luxury penthouse apartment opened to reveal a huge hulking brute of a woman, more than six foot tall with dark brown hair. Diana was surprised to see she was wearing a long black dress rather than her usual tracksuit. She was even more surprised to see that it looked good on her.

'Hi, Tessa. How are you?'

'Dandy.' The woman's voice was deep and both she and her brother had thick Liverpudlian accents that made them barely intelligible.

'Good! I like your dress, by the way; it suits you.' Diana smiled up at her then glanced into the apartment towards where the sound of voices was coming from. 'So... What kind of mood is he in?'

Tessa just rolled her eyes in reply. Neither of the Twins spoke very much and it seemed that wasn't going to change any time soon.

Diana chuckled and went to move past her, but the big woman put a large hand on her shoulder to hold her back momentarily.

'Got a visitor. Bigwig. Be careful.'

There was a genuine look of worry on Tessa's face, something so unusual that it gave Diana pause and she looked up at the woman quizzically, but Tessa wasn't saying anything more so she just kept walking; she would find out what was wrong soon enough.

The sitting room had been tidied up since she had last been there and no longer had its "nerd with too much money and no taste" look. The dozens of little statuettes from films and games were gone, the posters were off the walls, the table that Quentin had fallen through after being hit by Tristan had been replaced, and he had also cleaned the carpets, removing the blood that had poured from his nose after a blow from Tessa.

Quentin himself was standing by the window, looking into the night towards the Houses of Parliament just down the river. With what he was paid by the Illuminati he could have afforded an apartment anywhere in London, but he had chosen one with a view of the country's seat of power. Diana suspected he believed that one day he would be able to occupy a place in one of the two houses, at least as a Lord, if not as a Minister, or even Prime Minister; his ambition knew no bounds and with how things had been going over the last few years, it wasn't beyond the bounds of possibility. She was actually quite surprised that he hadn't chosen a home that looked out at Buckingham Palace, but that would have placed him too close to the Displacers for comfort.

Usually at these meetings she wouldn't take her eyes off Quentin, watching him closely for signs of dangerous mood swings, but tonight her attention was drawn elsewhere.

Lounging on the sofa was someone new, someone who looked far too comfortable for it to be the first time he was in this flat. He was in his early twenties, thin, wiry, with dark hair and pale skin and he exuded a kind of power and confidence that only a position of superiority imparted and in that respect he looked a lot like Quentin usually did.

He looked like trouble.

'You're late,' snapped Quentin, turning from the window to glare at her.

'I'm right on time, actually,' Diana replied without taking her eyes off of the newcomer. She smiled at him. 'I don't believe we've had the pleasure...?'

'This is Grant Davis. Grant, meet Diana Birch. Diana is in great part the reason for the supposed necessity of your presence here.'

The young man locked eyes with Diana. There was an uncomfortable moment as he just stared at her coldly and then his mouth twisted into a smile. It didn't quite make it to his eyes, though, and it was far more disturbing than the stare had been. 'Nonsense, Quentin, as you have been told, *you* are ultimately responsible for the success or failure of your team. Do you need another reminder of that?'

Out of the corner of her eye she saw Quentin seething in fury, his fists clenching and unclenching and she had to work hard not to smile at his discomfort.

Davis didn't break eye contact with Diana while he spoke and he winked at her before standing up. 'Grant Davis. How do you do?' His good manners were somewhat spoiled when he wiped his hand on his trouser leg before offering it to her, but she smiled at him nonetheless and shook the hand briefly, hiding her disgust at its clamminess.

'Pleased to meet you.'

'I'm the leader of one of the Master's better teams. He's asked me to be here to keep an eye on Quentin and make sure this operation goes off without a hitch.' He shot a pointed look at Quentin. 'He doesn't like leaving things like this in the hands of people he doesn't fully trust.'

Quentin snarled. 'Well, now that the pleasantries are over and done with, perhaps we can begin?'

Davis smiled at him. 'Of course, you *are* the boss here, after all.' He sat back down on the sofa, once again lounging indolently.

Quentin nodded and started away from the window.

'For now.'

Quentin's step faltered slightly at Davis' words, but he recovered quickly and took a seat in an armchair facing the sofa.

Diana sat down. She didn't particularly want to sit next to either of the men so she chose a chair that was equidistant to them both and as much out of their eyelines as possible.

Tristan came out of the bathroom still doing up his trousers. He muttered 'Dodgy curry,' then joined his sister by the door.

Quentin eyed the big man with distaste, but didn't say anything, he just rapped on the table with his knuckles.

'As you all know, the Master has given us our next target: the gold mines in South Africa. We are to do with them what was done with the diamond mines, that is to say, gain as large a share in them as possible. The Master is extremely busy right now so he has placed his full confidence in me to come up with a suitable plan.'

Davis coughed slightly at the words "full confidence", but otherwise refrained from commenting.

'This is a very complex undertaking and there are certain pieces that have to be moved into place before we can proceed with the objective, so we are going to carry this out in two parts. The mission itself will take place two months from now, but we will also Leap in a month's time to prepare the way.'

Diana put up a hand and waited for him to notice her; she had learned from long experience that he expected his subordinates to act just that, subordinate. It didn't stop her from shooting a look at Davis as if to say "see what he makes us do?" though.

'Yes, Diana?'

'Why is this going to be hard? Can't we just go in and get someone to claim the land before anyone else?'

Quentin shook his head. 'That is not an option, unfortunately; apparently the Society have already fixed the time-line in the years leading up to the find.'

'How do we know? Has someone tried?'

'No, but the Master found out that little fact from the Society's records.'

Davis laughed, not missing an opportunity to rub what he saw as Quentin's incompetence in his face. 'Why don't you do what you should have done at the start and inform us of everything that the Master told you when he gave you this mission? Maybe then your team will be on the same page and won't have to ask unnecessary questions.'

Quentin glared at Davis and Diana could see the murderous hatred behind his eyes. Not many people were brave, or stupid, enough to provoke Quentin and those that did usually didn't survive - the only exception to date was Sam, in fact. She wondered if the Master had told Davis exactly how dangerous, how irrational, and how cruel Quentin could be.

She almost guffawed when Davis waved a hand at Quentin in dismissal.

'Yes, yes. We all know how much you want to kill me right now, it's pathetically predictable. It's such a shame you can't; the Master has given strict instructions, has he not? Now, *tell us* what the Master said.'

Quentin growled, barely managing to control his temper and started his report, spitting the words out between clenched teeth. 'The local time-line is fixed from before the time that gold was first discovered in 1852, all the way to 1886, when the last claims were made on newly discovered deposits. There is no way we can influence any of that. The earliest that we can go is 1890, which makes our job all but impossible.'

Davis sighed. 'If it was an impossible job, Mr Price, then the Master would not be sending someone to do it. You don't think the Master would give you this mission if he hadn't already done a study of its feasibility, do you?'

'Or, *Mr Davis*, it could be that I am being set up to fail, so that I can be replaced.'

Davis didn't confirm or deny Quentin's implied question, he just crossed his arms and smiled knowingly.

Diana looked back and forth from one team leader to the other. She was enjoying herself immensely, watching the battle of wills between the two of them. Davis was as stubborn and belligerent as Quentin and he was obviously used to getting his own way. Despite being on enemy ground, he was in the position of power here and he knew it. Quentin, however, didn't seem to have gotten the message yet and was still trying to fight a battle that he couldn't possibly win.

At the moment they were just glaring at each other, so she took her eyes off of them for a second and glanced at the Twins. They were standing together near the door back into the hallway, covering the only access point like guards. They looked bored and Tristan was actually cleaning his fingernails with a wicked looking switchblade. Diana shook her head; the big siblings may have looked like stereotypically brainless thugs, but they weren't nearly as thick as they appeared; they were actually extremely intelligent and remarkably cunning and were perfectly capable of helping with the planning, but Quentin always treated them as merely brawn and didn't ever allow them to take part in the decision making, hence they had fallen into the habit of fading into the background while Diana and Quentin discussed what to do. It had gotten to the point where they barely even listened during the meetings, instead just waiting for their instructions.

In the end it was Quentin who backed down first and he leaned forward to pick his drink off the coffee table, which gave him the perfect excuse to break eye contact. He took a big gulp of coke, then slammed the empty can back down, taking his frustration out on it, rather ineffectually, before continuing.

'Right, so, as I was saying before I was so rudely interrupted, we will carry out the mission itself in two months. The first month we will spend doing research. I want to know everything about South Africa in the late nineteenth century: what was shipped to Cape Town and Johannesburg, who was there, what links our corporation has to anybody in the area. I want to know everything about the changes of ownership of the mines, I want to know what the land itself looked like in the 1890's, and so on and so forth. To that effect: I will remain here in London and go to the British Library, Lloyd's, the National Archive, the Public Record Office, and wherever else occurs to me. In the meantime, Diana, you're flying to South Africa; I want you in the offices of the gold companies digging up records. I've already had some fake credentials made up for you; you'll be going undercover as a researcher from the University of London. I also want you to go to museums to look through the Joburg records and such. Tessa will go with you and Tristan will stay here with me.'

Davis raised an eyebrow. 'And me?'

'You can go to hell for all I care.'

'Now now, don't forget I have final approval for the mission - if I don't like what I see you don't go. And if you don't go...' He left the sentence unfinished, letting the implied threat hang.

'Fine. You can stay here and trawl the Internet for anything relevant and help me collate the data as it comes in. Unless, of course, you have a way of getting into Displacer Headquarters and lifting their records?'

Davis snorted in derision at the idea.

Quentin smiled coldly at him. 'I didn't think so.' He took a small pile of envelopes from the coffee table and flicked through them. 'These are your instructions.' He gave one to Diana, then waved the other two at the Twins before chucking them in their general direction. The envelopes went nowhere near them, but the Twins moved to pick them up from the floor without any sign of complaint.

'Diana, Tessa, your envelopes contain university identities and open-ended round-trip airline tickets for tomorrow at 6am from Heathrow.' He grinned. 'Economy, I'm afraid; you are supposed to be poor academics after all.'

While he spoke, Diana opened her thick packet. Inside were electronic airline tickets in her name, along with about a dozen sheets of A4 paper covered with printed writing. It was going to take her a while to get through it all, but she snarled when she saw that he wasn't joking about the economy class tickets.

'In there you'll also find the name of our contact in the history department at London University who will be able to provide you with a reference if necessary. I suggest you familiarise yourselves with the details tonight and if you find any gaps or have any questions then call me. You have three weeks to get the job done and report back, so that we can go on the preparation trip and I expect daily updates. Any questions?'

He looked around the group, passing quickly over the Twins.

Davis just smirked and looked away out of the window.

When he glanced at her, Diana just shook her head. She fully expected there to be some flaw with the plan, there always was, even if it was the Master's plan, but without first reading through the contents of the envelope she couldn't know what it would be.

'Well, much as I'd love to have you all stay for dinner...' He trailed off, staring at them.

Diana took the hint and stood. Quentin wasn't big on niceties and frankly she was glad; she had no desire to socialise with him. It was bad enough having to work with the despicable man.

She went over to where the Twins were standing. 'Tessa, we need to arrange a time to meet tomorrow. Shall we share a taxi?'

The big woman considered briefly, then nodded.

Diana smiled. 'Good, I'll send you the details later when I've worked it all out.'

Tessa smiled back at her.

'See you tomorrow, then.' With a last look towards Quentin, who was now flicking through his phone, Diana turned to leave.

She walked out of the apartment, went to the lift and pressed the button, then glanced up, slightly startled as a shadow appeared next to her, reflected in the polished metal of the lift doors.

It was Davis, but he didn't look at her, he just stood silently, waiting for the lift.

There was a ping and the doors opened.

They went in. Diana pressed the button for the ground floor and the doors closed.

As soon as they started moving Davis turned to face her.

'Be online and connected to Skype tonight at nine.'

Diana looked at him and raised an eyebrow. 'Why?'

The lift pinged and the doors opened, revealing the lobby.

'Just do it.'

He strode out of the lift and into the night, leaving Diana behind, wondering what was so secret that Davis couldn't just speak to her right then, face to face.

At nine Diana was sitting in a chair in her dark dining room with her laptop open on the table in front of her, online as she'd been instructed and sipping a cup of tea as she waited.

There was a ping and a pop-up message from the Skype program.

User: Steelman66 would like to connect.

Diana shrugged and clicked *accept*.

Immediately, there was an incoming call. She accepted it and the chat window opened, but the video wasn't working for the other person. She leaned forward, frowning, looking for the problem.

'Davis? I can't see you, can you see me?'

'I'm sorry, Miss Birch, but this isn't Grant Davis.'

The voice that came through her speakers had been electronically altered - it was the Master.

Diana swallowed. She found that she was sweating suddenly; this was first time she was talking to him alone, every other time she had been part of a group using Quentin's computer. She forced a smile and sat back in the chair, trying not to seem nervous; just because she couldn't see him, didn't mean that the Master couldn't see her - her webcam was on even if his wasn't.

'I am sorry for the subterfuge, but I thought that it was time that we had a little chat, privately, without Mr Price's knowledge. I hope you don't mind.'

'Of course not, sir.'

'Thank you.'

There was a short silence and Diana used the time to take another sip of her tea, trying to calm her nerves.

'I have been watching you very closely, Miss Birch.'

She barely managed not to choke on her drink and put it down on the table while she composed herself.

'Really, sir? May I ask why?'

'Of course. I have been watching you because, despite your misfortune in being assigned to Quentin Price's team, you have long stood out as one of my more... *competent* agents.'

'Thank you, sir.' She told herself to relax. Some nervousness would be understandable, but it wouldn't do to appear like she had a guilty conscience and she had nothing to fear; if the Master knew about what she was doing behind his back then there wouldn't be any call to confront her about it, there would just be a quiet visit from one of the Twins.

'I understand that it was mostly due to your initiative that the Vives boy was captured in London and, despite Mr Price's protests to the contrary, I know that it was *his* fault and not yours that he ultimately survived.'

The Master fell silent, as if expecting Diana to confirm his supposition, but she didn't rise to the bait and he continued.

'Whatever the case, I wanted you to know that I have noticed your exemplary work and as soon as a position as team leader becomes available then it will be you who will fill it.'

'Are we expanding our ranks, then, sir?'

'Yes. I am hopeful that we may have some new recruits soon, but that is not the only way that a position may become vacant - we have yet to see whether Mr Price can achieve anything, even when given the proper motivation.'

Diana had nothing to say to that. It would certainly serve the interests of the Displacers if she were higher placed in the Master's organisation, but even so, she didn't want to be taking the place of someone who had been killed for failing one too many times. To her surprise, not even Quentin.

'Having said that, I will be very upset if you do anything to deliberately sabotage this operation and it will count heavily against you. The quickest way to gain the promotion you deserve is to stay firmly in my good books.'

'Understood, sir.' She nodded but it felt strange to do so; there was no way of knowing if the person on the other end was watching her or not, or whether it was in fact a "sir" or "madam" she was talking to - the altered voice was male, but it could just as easily be a woman, or a child on the other end of the call.

'Good. Then there is no more to be said. Goodnight and good luck with your mission.'

'Thank you, sir.'

'Oh, and you should put the lights on more often, Miss Birch; it's not good for your eyes to sit in the dark all the time.'

The connection clicked off.

A chill went through Diana and her eyes shot to the windows.

She looked out into the night, searching; was the Master having her watched? Were Rachel's precautions warranted after all?

She closed the lid on the laptop, sending it to sleep and making sure the webcam was off, then went over to the window and pulled the curtains closed for the first time ever.

She pulled out her phone then navigated to her WhatsApp conversation with Rachel to inform her of the meeting with Quentin, but paused, unsure about what she should say about her conversation with the Master - whether she should inform Rachel of his offer, or the fact that he might indeed be having her watched.

In the end she decided against telling Rachel anything that she wasn't sure about; it was better not to send her into a panic and make her start taking insane precautions instead of simply irritating ones.

She bent over the small screen and typed.

Won't be able to meet for a while. Doing research for mission and am flying to South Africa tomorrow AM. Exploratory journey to 1880 in one month, no changes in time-line planned. Main mission to take place in two months to ?1887? Will send final details when they become available.

She sent the message then erased the conversation history. Rachel's number was already listed under "plumber", but it was best to take as many precautions as she could, just in case.

She settled back into the sofa and tried to relax, but found that she couldn't.

She all but leapt up and ran from room to room, switching all of the lights on; suddenly the darkness in her flat didn't feel so comfortable or safe.

CHAPTER 6
SYMPOSIUM

On average a Displacer could travel into the past once a month. Some were ready to travel again in slightly less time than that, while others couldn't Displace more than once every five weeks or so. Sam was a very special case: he was capable of Displacing every two weeks. Unfortunately, he had been instructed not to do so by Andrew and James unless it was an emergency, because of the incredible strain it placed on his body.

Almost exactly two weeks after the trip to Sparta, Sam woke up knowing that he was ready to Displace again and this brought with it an almost unbearable desire to do so; travelling in time was almost addictive and he always felt antsy when he knew that he could, but wasn't allowed to.

It was another two, very frustrating, weeks before he finally received a message from James.

You busy? As soon as you can, go to Andrew's flat. I have a job for you.

It had been a month since Sam had heard anything from a Displacer other than Rachel and he had a huge smile on his face as he eagerly sent his reply and hurriedly threw on some jogging clothes. It was Saturday morning and there was no problem with telling his parents that he was going out for a run.

He sprinted all the way and let himself in less than three minutes later, barely out of breath, but froze just inside the door; the flat wasn't empty, there were voices coming from the sitting room.

Sam's eyes alighted on the Spartan sword that he had left next to the entrance in the umbrella stand. He pulled it out as silently as he could and then stalked down the hallway towards the intruders. He moved in a crouch with the weapon held ready in front of him, just as he'd been taught more than two thousand years before.

He only got a few steps, though, before one of the voices, a gentle male one, called out. 'For god's sake Sam, don't you recognise your own girlfriend's voice?'

Sam straightened and lowered the sword, placing it to one side against the wall. Rather sheepishly he went into the sitting room.

Sitting in the armchairs on either side of the coffee table and grinning at him were Rachel and James.

'Surprise!' Rachel jumped up and ran to him, jumping into his arms and giving him a lip-bruising kiss.

When they finally came up for air, they sat down on the sofa together and Sam looked at his grandfather, who had been watching them with a big grin and no embarrassment whatsoever. 'What are you doing here? Shouldn't you be meeting with Diana?'

'She's busy planning Quentin's next mission with him and she can't meet because right now she's in South Africa. They have a Displacement in a few days, but Diana says it's just a preparatory trip and that the real mission will take place in just over a month from now, sometime in April.'

'OK, so, what? Are you sending us back to spoil their preparations?'

James smiled. 'Nope, Ralph is going to get off his lazy arse and take care of some preparation of our own, then you two will deal with Quentin's main mission in a month when Diana gives us the exact date.'

Sam grinned and looked at Rachel. 'Where do you want to go? I was thinking that maybe...'

'Hold your horses!' James cut Sam off with a laugh. 'Just because you're not going on a mission doesn't mean that we haven't got something for you to do!'

'Oh... alright.'

'And don't look so glum; this will be fun and it's very important, one of the most important Displacements you'll ever go on actually. It's only a short trip, nice and easy, and you'll be going together. Then, when you get back, you'll have the whole weekend to yourselves.'

Sam smiled. 'OK, what do you want us to do, then?'

'Well, it's about time you both went to *Symposium*.' James leaned forward in his armchair and smiled, looking back and forth from one of them to the other.

They could see he was expecting them to know what he was talking about, but neither of them did and he frowned. 'Really? Rachel, I expect this kind of ignorance from Sam...'

'Hey!'

'... but not from you.'

Rachel shrugged. 'Sorry, James, I have no idea what you're talking about.'

James sighed and sat back, shaking his head. 'The youth of today...' He reached into the inside pocket of his suit jacket and drew out two white envelopes. 'Here, one each.'

Sam took them from him. He handed one to Rachel and kept the other. The envelope was roughly four inches by three, heavy and made of a very thick and creamy paper. There was no name on it, but on the back was a thin red wax seal, cracked and broken with age, but still intact. The wax was imprinted with the crest of the Society and it almost seemed like sacrilege to break it, but he did.

Inside was a card.

You are cordially invited to a meeting of friends.
The Symposium.
Price Manor.
August 1st 1712 at 9am sharp.

Sam turned the card over. On the back were numbers, a latitude and a longitude, and then a very short physical description of the place itself, a manor house in the middle of England.

As he read the words he felt them settle into him and when he finished he realised that he had the destination fixed in his mind already. The card was remarkable; in very few words it managed to give a very precise reference for a Displacer, something that usually took more than a page of writing. Someone very clever had written it.

James saw Sam's expression. 'Good, isn't it?'

'It's incredible! But what is "Symposium" exactly? Apart from another incredibly cringeworthy name.'

'Good question, and sorry, but I'm going to give you the long and boring answer, so get comfortable.'

The two young Displacers laughed, but nonetheless snuggled closer together.

'The Honourable Society of Displacers, of which we are members, was officially founded in the early nineteenth century. Before then it had been a kind of unofficial club for about fifty years, but it wasn't until 1825 that there were enough members for them to actually consider it worth trying to formalise it as an actual group. One of the first things that the early Displacers realised was that they had a unique opportunity to preserve the knowledge of each of their members, so they created Symposium.

'Symposium is the one place in time where *every* Displacer has gone.

'They chose August in 1712 because it is what we consider to be a boring date: nothing of particular note happened that year and it is as stable as a time is ever going to get, so it doesn't matter that not a single Displacer is available to work in that month. They also knew that a certain manor house belonging to a certain Lord Price's family would be sitting empty for the whole of that month. The place is huge, it has more than a hundred bedrooms so it's perfect for the job.'

'So what do we do? Turn up and stay in a country house for a month?'

'No, because that would defeat the object of the Symposium - it is there so that, if you have need to do so, you can go and ask the past members for their knowledge. If you stayed the whole month then you wouldn't be able to go back, would you?'

Sam coloured. 'I guess not.'

'So, what you're going to do now is go for twenty-four hours, which will establish your presence there. Every time you go back in the future you will use that card for reference, so keep it safe, and it will automatically take you to the exact same place and time that you left, which will "update" your persona, so to speak, with what you have experienced and learnt since you were last there. Traditionally, one of, if not *the* last, Displacement that someone does before they go through the Transition and become an Elder is to return to Symposium and stay for the rest of the month in order to provide the greatest access to them for subsequent generations.

'Unfortunately, the knowledge that we accumulate as Elders can't ever be taken, but this is the best that we can do. And besides, Elders like to write, so nothing much is lost from us.'

'So, you're there, then Grandad?' Sam grinned. 'I'll get to meet you as you were, what, fifty years ago?'

James snorted. 'Cheeky bugger! How old do you think I am? It was only... um, well, forty-eight years ago...'

Both Rachel and Sam laughed and James joined in.

James stopped laughing suddenly and put on a serious face. 'When nine hundred years old you reach, look as good, you will not, hmm?'

Sam and Rachel's mouths flopped open and they looked at him in shock.

'Grandad, did you just make a *Star Wars* joke?!?'

'*Empire Strikes Back*, actually.' James tutted and shook his head.

Sam shook his head in wonder. 'Wow.'

James grinned. 'You see what I did there? It wasn't at all gratuitous, because, you know, I'm like *really* old because I'm an Elder and I've spent so many years in the past and everything.'

Rachel leaned forward and spoke quietly 'James, you're spoiling it now. You're not supposed to explain the culture reference; it's the same as explaining a joke.'

James' face fell and he looked down at the table, chagrined. 'Oh... Right.'

'It *was* really cool though, Grandad.'

The Elder brightened up again immediately, almost too easily, and Sam wondered if the old man had been playing with them all the time.

'Thank you, lad! Alright, so, last thing before you go: you will be expected to give the entire society an update at dinner so make sure you have something ready. This is serious. Talk about the Illuminati, talk about the prophecy you brought back. *Do not* be shy and hide the fact that you are special, Sam; that is information that is needed by everybody, and if anybody there has anything to add then they can only do so if they have all the facts.

There was something bothering Sam, though. 'I have a question.'

Rachel rolled her eyes and looked at him. 'Is it a stupid one, Sam?'

'Of course not!' He grinned at her. 'When do I ever ask stupid questions?'

James chuckled and shook his head. 'Ask away, Sam.'

'Well, the way you tell it, everybody who is a Displacer is already there, so if we go there too, then who is left to come and ask *us* questions if anything happens to us?'

James actually looked surprised when he considered the question. 'Maybe you're not as stupid as you look after all, boy!'

Sam beamed. 'Gee, thanks, Grandad!'

Rachel laughed at their clowning.

'Well, there's a simple answer to that: we only send someone to Symposium when there is a newer Displacer behind them, that way there is always someone who can use the invitation to go and ask any urgent questions of the entire Society, including the newer members.

Normally that would mean Rachel would have gone when you joined, but she's been too busy. You are going now because we have a new member just joining.'

'Really?'

'Yes. I'll introduce you at a later date.'

Sam shared a glance with Rachel, but she just shrugged. 'Don't look at me. I didn't know.'

'Anyway.' James reached around the side of his armchair, pulled out a large paper bag and put it on the coffee table. 'Sam, go and put this on; you can't go to Symposium looking like that.'

'Why not? Won't I be dressed appropriately when I get there? Like I always am?'

James shook his head and Rachel rolled her eyes at the Elder. 'I told you he wouldn't work it out.'

'I know, I'll pay up later.'

Rachel turned on the sofa to face Sam. 'We're going into the past, yes, but everybody that has an invitation is a Displacer, who...'

Sam thought about it for a second and then suddenly realised what he was missing. 'Who will see us as we really are in our present.'

'Bingo! Give that man a cigar!' James laughed. 'He got it in the end, so I guess that means I don't have to pay up, right?'

'In your dreams, oh wise and ancient Elder, sir!'

James laughed again and Sam smiled; his grandfather was a wonderful person who had been through a lot of sorrow in his life and it was great to see him happy.

'You didn't think I'd dress like this just because I'm seeing you, did you?' Rachel stood up and showed off her dress, which was a lot nicer than anything he had ever seen her wear before, in the present at least; usually they both wore jeans or a tracksuit - clothes to work in - but her dress was long and black, tight around the body before flaring out into loose skirts, made of some kind of soft velvety material that made Sam want to reach out and stroke it...

Rachel seemed to read his mind. 'No touching! I don't want your grubby hands making this dirty before I've had a chance to show it off! Now go on, get changed so we can Displace already!'

'OK, OK!' Sam stood up and grabbed the bag. Inside were several boxes, all black and without names on them. He shrugged and left the room.

The boxes contained a very expensive suit from a top London store and when Sam came back into the room Rachel whistled, impressed.

'You never looked that good, even when we were in full Victorian dress clothes.'

Sam blushed slightly and tugged at the sleeves of his jacket. The suit was a dark grey, three-piece suit and he had a stiff-collared white shirt underneath. He felt foolish, but the admiring look on Rachel's face made everything better.

She walked around him, squeezing his bum sneakily when she passed behind him. 'Nice...'

James nodded in appreciation. 'Finally got you in some decent clothes, didn't I, lad?'

'Thank you, Grandad, this is actually pretty nice.'

The Elder laughed. 'Pretty nice? I should damn well hope so, the amount they charged me for that; I could've made one for a couple of quid in my day! My hands aren't what they used to be, though.' He eyed the cut of the suit appraisingly. 'It looks like I got the size right. I haven't lost my eye for that, at least.'

Sam turned to Rachel and grinned as he gave her a small bow. 'Well, then, shall we go, madam?'

'I believe we shall, young sir!' She curtseyed back at him.

They sat back down on the sofa again.

'Are you going to lead or shall I?' asked Sam.

'Actually,' James interrupted. 'I'd like it if Sam took the lead if that's alright; I've never been around him when he has and I'd like to feel what it's like first-hand.'

Sam was surprised. 'You can do that?'

James gave him a scathing look. 'I'm an Elder, boy, not dead - just because I can't Displace, doesn't mean I can't still feel the energy others use.'

'Oh.'

Rachel laughed. 'That's fine with me, James! You're in for a bit of a shock.' She looked at Sam. 'You all set?'

'Ready when you are.'

'Hang on a sec! Almost forgot...' James reached into yet another bag and pulled out two bottles of wine. He handed one to each of them. 'It's tradition to take something to Symposium, and if I remember correctly there is a distinct lack of decent booze on the first day.'

They laughed and grabbed one of the bottles each.

Sam nodded at Rachel and she closed her eyes to start Preparing.

Sam reached for her, feeling her energy building. When it was just right he closed his eyes and...

Sam opened his eyes to find himself standing on a carefully manicured lawn in front of a huge mansion, surrounded by a huge crowd.

There were a bewildering array of costumes and hairstyles displayed on the people around them. Two hundred years of style were represented, ranging from sombre Edwardian dress, to military uniforms, to elaborate ball gowns, to a couple of very colourful people wearing tie-dyed shirts and flares. They were all carrying something in their hands and Sam was surprised to see that a couple of the bigger men carried entire animals - he and Rachel had to move out of the way of one such man, who was proving to be a menace as he walked through the crowd, a massive deer complete with sharp-looking antlers on his shoulders.

Sam realised that many of the people were doing the same thing as he was: looking around as if it they had just arrived and it was the first time they were there. It was puzzling in the extreme; all these people were from the past, so surely the only ones that were coming for the first time were Rachel and him...

Rachel saw Sam's confused look and tutted. 'I'll explain it to you later, for now just pay attention!' She jerked her chin towards the house.

'Excuse me! Hello?'

Sam looked up to find that a man had climbed up the grand steps of the mansion and was standing in front of the doors facing them.

The man was very elegantly dressed in a dark blue tailed jacket and white breeches and was leaning on a cane as he waved a top hat over his head to catch their attention. He waited until he was sure that he had everyone's attention before he spoke again.

'Hello everyone and welcome to Symposium. For those of you who don't know me I am Victor Price, your host. Before we make our way inside for the festivities would the newcomer please identify themselves?'

'Come on, that's us.' Rachel tugged on Sam's hand. 'Over here!' she called out, waving her hand as she led him through the crowd, which obligingly made way for them.

Price beckoned for them to join him. 'Come up here next to me, please.'

They stood on the steps next to him where everybody could see them.

He clapped his hands in delight. 'There's two of you! Wonderful! Firstly, do you have urgent business?'

Rachel shook her head and answered for the both of them. 'No. This is just a normal establishing visit.'

'Good! Then introduce yourselves please.'

'Rachel Evans and Sam Vives, from the twenty-first century.'

'My word! It's the twenty-first century already, is it? How time does fly!' Laughter rang out among the listeners and Price leaned in to whisper to them. 'That joke never gets old.' He winked before turning to the crowd of people. 'Rachel Evans and Sam Vives. Can anyone vouch for them?'

A hand shot up among the crowd and a familiar voice cried out. 'Yes! I can!'

There was a disturbance in the gathering as two people made their way up to the front: Andrew, accompanied by a woman, who Sam recognised with a shock was Susan, his aunt.

Andrew wasn't quite as old as he was in the present, so Sam surmised that he hadn't "updated" for some time, Susan, however, was much younger, about as young as she had been when Rachel had taken him to see them at Wembley stadium in 1966; she had obviously died before she had been able to come back.

Susan had been killed on a Displacement, which meant that she had ceased to exist in the eyes of the world at large. Her own sister, Sam's mother, didn't even know that she had ever had a sibling. It was the greatest tragedy that could befall a Displacer, something that had happened far too often over their long history and the sitting room back at Headquarters was filled with the portraits of those who had "never existed" as they called them.

'Sam! So I *was* right about you!' Andrew bounded up the steps and shook Sam's hand vigorously before turning to Victor Price. 'This is my nephew, Sam.' He stopped as he saw Rachel for the first time. 'My god, Rachel? Is that really you? Why, you've grown!' He looked back and forth from Sam to Rachel. 'Are you two...? Bloody hell, I wish I would update myself more often!'

There was a wave of laughter from the crowd at that and Sam groaned inwardly; it seemed that even Society members almost two hundred years dead appreciated Displacer humour.

Price smiled broadly at them. 'Well! It looks like we have two new members! Wonderful! Come on, let's get you registered and then we can all go to breakfast!'

He turned and pushed open the large doors.

Sam and Rachel followed him and were in turn followed by Andrew, Susan and the rest of the Displacers. Sam looked over his shoulder and watched with amusement as the crowd began to sort itself out; it seemed that, even here, the mainly British Displacers were going to form an orderly queue. They went back to their conversations as they moved forward, but did so quietly, respectfully and Sam chuckled briefly as he imagined what the scene would have been like if the Displacers had been Spanish; it would have been very different indeed and not nearly as quiet.

His musings were cut short and his mouth flopped open as they went through the large double doors and into the main entrance of the house.

The hall that they stepped into was massive. It looked like it could easily have housed Displacer Headquarters in it... with room to spare for a double decker bus. The floor was almost entirely white marble, which was lovely and cool after the warm summer morning outside, while the walls were a light beige colour and liberally scattered with paintings. Two marble staircases wound up against the walls on either side, leading to the upper floors and underneath them on each side were open double doors leading to what looked like a ballroom and a dining room. Opposite the entrance, about fifty metres away, Sam could see large glass doors opening out onto more gardens at the back of the house.

There was a large book set out ready on a wooden table in the middle of the hall and it was there that Victor Price led them. He opened the book to the first page and gestured to it. 'If you would, please, sign your names and put your details.'

Sam smiled at Rachel. 'Ladies first.'

'Why, thank you, kind sir!' She picked up the feather quill that served as the pen and dipped it in the ink on the desk before bending over the book and filling in her name on the blank page.

Thankfully, Sam had used a quill pen enough times in Victorian London that he knew how to use it and managed to sign the book without dripping ink everywhere or otherwise disgracing himself.

'Splendid! Now, do you want one room or two?'

Sam and Rachel shared a glance before answering together. 'One, please, Lord Price.'

'Wonderful, you can have the Master bedroom.'

Sam frowned. 'Uh... Isn't that already taken?'

The man raised an eyebrow and looked sideways at Rachel. He smiled, not unkindly. 'He hasn't quite gotten how this works yet, has he?'

Rachel sighed and shook her head. 'You don't know the half of it, my lord.'

Price winked at her before addressing Sam. 'Everyone gets the Master bedroom, Mr Vives. Come on, I'll show you where it is while everybody else signs in. And please, call me Victor!'

Sam moved aside as Susan took his place in front of the book and he eyed the queue that wound its way across the hall, down the steps and out onto the lawn. The Displacers, more than two hundred of them by the look of it, would take ages to sign the book and he was suddenly very glad that they had been the first to sign it. Although... He blinked as another thought came to him: all these people had come here before them, so why were they signing the book again? And how was it that Rachel and he were the very first ones to sign it?

He shook his head and cleared his mind; just like with the experiments in the black book, such thoughts only served to give him a headache and didn't make anything any clearer.

They followed Victor to the staircase on the left side of the room and started climbing. It was about thirty stairs up to the landing where there was a small balcony overlooking the entrance and Sam paused there to look down at the people. He frowned suddenly as he saw someone in the crowd that he recognised.

He tugged on Rachel's arm and she followed where he was pointing. 'Rachel, isn't that...?'

'Quentin. Of course he's here. And so are James, Richard, Philip, Lisa and all of the other Displacers that you've met. You can't tell me you missed John walking around in ripped jeans and an X-Files t-shirt!'

She turned to follow Victor, who had gone on without them, but Sam lingered, looking down at Quentin; the man being here was bothering him and it wasn't just that he was Sam's enemy, there was something else that he couldn't quite put his finger on.

'Come on, Sam!'

When Sam looked up, Rachel and Victor were about fifty metres down the corridor, about to turn a corner and he was in danger of being left behind - he really didn't want to risk getting lost in the huge mansion, which would certainly add to his legend as one of the most clueless Displacers ever, so he hurried after them, walking quickly, but not running because he didn't want to wrinkle his new suit. He followed them around several twists and turns and up a small flight of stairs, but lost sight of them when the corridor branched off in several directions. The house was even bigger than it had seemed from the outside and he wondered why the owner of the house had hidden his bedroom so far into the maze of corridors.

He was about to call out when Rachel's head poked around a corner a few metres away.

'Keep up, Sam!' She poked her tongue out at him then disappeared again.

He laughed and forgot about his worry for his suit as he jogged down the corridor, catching up with them just as Victor opened a large door and showed Rachel into their bedroom.

It was a huge room with the biggest bed that Sam had ever seen and if their host had turned around in that moment and told them that they were going to share the room with ten of the other Displacers because they were overcrowded he would have believed him. Opposite the door were large windows that looked out towards the back of the house and he could see trees and grass and miles of rolling hills stretching off into the distance. It was incredibly picturesque and it was finally clear to him why the bedroom had been situated as it was.

'There's water in the jug over there if you want to freshen up, some nightclothes in the wardrobe, and a chamber pot beneath the bed. I'm sorry, you'll have to empty it yourselves; there are no servants, of course.'

Rachel smiled at him. 'I think we'll be able to manage, thank you.'

'Great! Do you think you can make it back to the dining room from here?' He eyed Sam a little bit sceptically and Sam wondered how people got such a bad opinion of him so quickly.

Rachel looked at Sam. 'Don't worry, Lord Price, Victor, I won't let him get lost.'

'See you at breakfast when you're ready, then!'

The man nodded to them and left, closing the door.

'Lord Price? A relation of Ralph's?'

'Of course. You really need to read some Displacer history - Victor Price was the founding leader of the Displacers and a hereditary peer. He was the one who provided the Society with a headquarters and enough funds to set us up for the last two hundred years. This is his family's seat.'

'Which is how he knew it would be empty, I suppose; his family records would have told him.'

'Exactly.' She grinned at him. 'See, you're catching on!'

'I just don't get how this is even possible. I mean, for a start why do we get this bedroom?'

Rachel groaned. 'Just when I thought you were finally getting it, you go and say something like that.'

'What? As far as I can see, this whole setup doesn't obey the rules you've all been trying to drill into me. It feels right to me somehow, but my brain is just telling me that this shouldn't be possible.'

She considered for a second, looking at him appraisingly. Finally she took a deep breath and nodded. 'Alright, I'll give you that. But only because I love you, OK?'

Sam smiled. 'Fine with me.'

'I can't quite explain it myself, actually...'

'Hah!'

'...but, it's something about us all using the same invitation and arriving at the exact same time. It's an exception that has been specifically created and exploited to create a unique set of circumstances. If you want to understand it properly you should ask an Elder about it sometime... if you have several days to spare.'

'I think I'm good, thanks.'

Rachel laughed. 'I thought you might say that!' She walked up to him and put her arms around his waist. He had grown taller than her in the last year, but she was wearing heels and he once again had to tilt his head back to kiss her.

After a few seconds she took a step back and looked him up and down. 'You look very handsome, Mr Vives, and I'd really like to drag you to that big bed over there.' She pulled him forward gently by his suit lapels and kissed him again before pulling back from his reaching grasp. 'But I'm hungry, so let's go and get breakfast!'

She grabbed his hand and dragged him out of the room and together they hurried back the way they had come.

Breakfast was an extremely eclectic affair; dozens of the Displacers had volunteered as cooks and each had made something from their own time, using what had been brought and the stores that they had found in the larder. Lord Price had plans to send parties out to the neighbouring farms and villages to buy more supplies, but for breakfast they had to make do with what they had.

It proved to be more than sufficient as the cooks laid out about fifty different dishes on the sideboard, ranging from simple breads to complex latticed pastries and of course there were also the obligatory ingredients for an "English breakfast" including what looked like a whole pig's worth of bacon and dozens of eggs.

Sam was about to ask Rachel whether the Lord whose manor it was in the time-line wouldn't notice that they had eaten him out of house and home, but stopped himself just in time; eating was about as direct an interference in the time-line as you could get and as soon as they left the larders and pantries would be restocked to how they were before they'd arrived.

They had debated on the walk down from their room whether they should look for people that they knew and sit with them, but both of them had immediately realised that this was a unique opportunity and they should take full advantage of it by talking to as many people as they could, so they filled a couple of huge plates from the buffet and found themselves room at one of the huge tables that filled the dining room. They squeezed in between a man with dark, greying hair and a thin moustache, wearing a green nineteenth century army uniform and a large pink woman, wearing a huge and equally pink dress which stuck out a couple of feet either side of her chair because of the dozens of petticoats underneath it and while Sam turned to engage with the man, Rachel did the same to the woman.

'Good morning, sir, my name is Sam Vives.'

'Good morning, young man, Albert Fidwick at your service.' The man nodded in greeting and Sam got the impression that he would have clicked his heels together if he had been standing.

Sam eyed his uniform, it was extremely familiar and gave him a perfect starting point for the conversation. 'Would I be right in saying that you are a colonel in the 95th rifle regiment?'

'Why, yes! However did you recognise it? I was led to believe that uniforms like mine died out a full century before your birth.'

Sam wasn't about to tell him that he had become interested in the rifle regiments after watching the *Sharpe* series on TV - the man was wearing almost the same uniform as Sean Bean did. 'From books.' It wasn't exactly lying to tell him that, after all, the TV series had been based on the books. 'I have an interest in military history and the rifle regiment in particular. Tell me, sir, did you fight in the peninsular war?'

'I did, indeed.' The smile faded slightly from the man's face as he thought back to what had obviously been difficult times, but he was still enthusiastic as he launched into a recounting of the campaign.

Sam listened with interest. If he didn't speak to anyone else in his 24 hours at Symposium it would still have been worth it just to hear the man speak about his experiences. He had even been at Waterloo!

Rachel in the meantime wasn't having such an interesting time. The pink woman turned out to be obsessed with women's fashions and insisted on talking about the time she spent as one of Marie Antoinette's closest friends at Versailles. During the course of the breakfast she managed to describe in intricate detail every single one of the almost thirty different dresses that she had worn to balls during that Displacement. When Rachel finally got a word in edgewise to ask her what her mission had been, the woman looked astounded and offended at the same time.

'Mission? What mission? I was there for the *dresses*, girl! What could be more important?'

Rachel was quite glad when the woman pushed her chair back and left in a huff, realising that her audience wasn't quite as appreciative as she'd thought.

Her place was taken almost immediately by Victor, who called Sam's attention away from the soldier so that he could talk to them both. 'At lunch I'll call upon you to inform us of what has been happening in your present day and if there's anything particularly interesting we'll probably spend the rest of the day discussing it. Do you think you have something stimulating enough to keep our interest for that long?'

Rachel and Sam looked at each other and laughed before Rachel nodded and answered for them both. 'Yes, my Lord, I think that we do.'

'Wonderful! Well, lunch is in three hours, at one sharp, please feel free to wander to your heart's content until then. I recommend the maze, but, uh, just stay with Miss Evans, please, Sam; we wouldn't want you getting lost and missing all the fun.'

Sam flushed with embarrassment, but nodded with a smile. He didn't mind these people gently poking fun at him; he knew that at heart they were all good people and they didn't mean anything by it.

Victor stood and moved on to another group, continuing with his role as host. Nobody filled the chair he vacated, so Sam took pity on Rachel and introduced him to the soldier, Fidwick, and they spent the rest of the breakfast talking animatedly. Sam actually began to feel a bit left out at one point because Rachel turned out to know a lot more about military matters and tactics than he did. She and Fidwick even started to move plates, glasses and condiments about the table as they replayed aspects of the battle of Vitoria, which had been instrumental in forcing Napoleon out of Spain. Sam didn't mind too much; he was enjoying himself immensely as he watched Rachel drawing information out of Fidwick, who informed them that he himself was a student of tactics, having Displaced to study with, among others, Julius Caesar and Alexander.

They could have spent all day talking to the man, but after about an hour he stood up and regretfully announced an end.

'Much as I would like to continue this discussion, Miss Evans, Master Vives, I must beg your pardon and excuse myself from your presence; it is your first time at Symposium and you should not be spending all of your valuable time with just the one person. I suggest that you investigate the maze, as Lord Price suggested, and then search out others whose knowledge will better benefit you. If you wish, however, I would be more than happy to speak to you further on your subsequent visits, but for now: welcome to Symposium and good fortune.'

Sam stood to shake his hand, Rachel allowed him to kiss hers and then, with a small bow, he marched off across the room to where a small group of men in military uniforms had congregated.

'Glad you came?'

Sam looked at Rachel and grinned. 'Oh, yes! I didn't think you knew so much about military stuff; I thought that was my area of interest.'

'Don't you remember whose idea it was to watch the Sharpe series? Besides, it goes with the whole martial arts thing; the clue is in the name: you know - "martial" arts.'

'I just think you should have kept talking to that woman instead of butting in like that; I'm sure we'll be able find Quentin's weakness by analysing his fashion sense.'

Rachel laughed. 'You mean, so that I didn't make you look bad and less of a man in front of the nice soldier?'

Sam bowed his head and pretended to sulk. 'Yeah...'

She punched him on the shoulder. 'Come on, stop being silly and let's go see what all the fuss is with this maze.'

'OK!' He grinned, instantly changing his facial expression; clowning for her.

Hand in hand they left the dining room and headed out into the gardens.

The sun was higher in the sky and it was hotter now, so Sam took his jacket off and slung it over his shoulder as they strolled down a path between rose bushes in the direction of the maze.

'I guess we should decide what we're going to talk about at lunch.'

'I was thinking that you should tell them about Quentin and the Prophecy, while I tell them about Diana and the Illuminati.'

'What will Quentin do? And what will the members do when they find out that one of their own is working against us?'

'I...' Rachel stopped and considered. 'Actually, I'm not sure, although theoretically nothing should happen; they can't kick him out because he's already here and it's not as if he's spying on us either - the Quentin who's here is a version from before he joined the Illuminati. Come to think of it, we might actually be able to question him and see what he knows, find out whether this version of him has been approached by anyone to betray us yet.'

'That would be a big help, but I'm pretty sure it would be the kind of thing Andrew would have sent someone to do already.'

She shrugged. 'He might not have. It won't hurt to try, anyway.'

They paused at the entrance of the maze, which was marked by an ornately carved stone arch, depicting what looked like fawns and satyrs frolicking in the forest.

Sam grinned at Rachel. 'Bet you I can get lost before you.'

Rachel laughed. 'That's not a bet I'm going to take, besides, I'd rather lose myself with you.'

She wrapped her arm around him and together they walked into the cool shadows of the maze.

CHAPTER 7
PLAYING FOR TIME

The maze was fun, but others had had the same idea and they hadn't been alone, so after about half an hour they wandered back to the house where they were greeted by a sight that made them very glad that they had.

The various soldiers were warming up on the lawn, preparing to duel, thinking that it would be fun to have a bit of a fight before lunch. Quite a few of them had been carrying their swords as part of their uniforms, but apparently they had also found the current Lord's armoury and had raided it for any other blades that might be used.

Rachel and Sam shared a grin, then simultaneously hurried forward.

They found Fidwick among the men warming up.

'Colonel! I don't suppose we could join in?'

He glanced at them in surprise, his eyes widening as he took in Sam's civilian suit, then widening further when he realised that Rachel intended to fight as well. 'Well, I... It's just that... a woman...'

Rachel raised an eyebrow. 'Are you frightened of losing to a woman, colonel?'

The men around them had all stopped warming up by now and were watching the exchange with some interest. Fidwick realised and looked around nervously.

He recovered quickly. 'Of course not, madam. I was just trying to protect my fellow officers here from being disgraced when they lose to you.'

There were jeers and laughs at that.

Rachel smiled and looked round at them. 'Well, at least you know your places. Will you let me play if I promise to go easy on you all?'

Fidwick leaned in and spoke quietly so that only she and Sam could hear. 'Are you sure, madam? We are fighting to first blood. There may be accidents...'

'I am no stranger to blood, Colonel Fidwick, and I don't have accidents.'

The colonel nodded 'Very well then.' He looked over the crowd and raised his voice. 'Mr Chapman! We have two more to add to the lists, Master Vives and Mistress Evans. Place one in each group if you please!'

'Yes, sir!' A thin man wearing small round spectacles and a Victorian suit was standing on the back steps of the mansion. He was using the dark grey stone wall of the mansion as a chalkboard to note the names of the participants and he added Sam and Rachel to the lists, placing them in separate groups, which meant that they wouldn't have to face each other unless they both got to the final. Once done the man turned back to address the fighters. 'We will begin in five minutes, gentlemen! Oh, uh, and lady.' He flushed slightly and gave Rachel a small bow which she returned with a laugh.

Fidwick shook his head and smiled wryly at them. 'Good luck to you both, and please, try to take care. I suggest you find yourselves a weapon and familiarise yourselves with it.'

'Thank you, colonel.'

He nodded to them both and stepped away to continue limbering up with his fellows.

Sam and Rachel walked over to inspect the pile of weapons.

Rachel immediately picked up a rapier and gave it a few practice swishes. 'That's nice! They don't make swords like they used to.'

Sam looked at what was left. It was fairly slim pickings and many of them were highly inappropriate for a duel - he saw what looked like a twelfth century broadsword, a Turkish scimitar and a huge two-handed Scottish claymore among the other more mundane duelling swords. He was mildly disappointed; he would have liked to have used a katana and shown the soldiers what could really be done by someone with a sword, but he realised that in 1712 the western world barely knew that Japan existed and they wouldn't have any of their weapons yet. In the end he settled for a rapier, much like Rachel's, but with a basket hilt instead of the cross guard that Rachel's had. It was superbly balanced and when he hefted it made him feel like one of the three musketeers.

'Do you know how to fight, Sam?'

He looked up to find Andrew on the steps above him, looking down at him with concern.

'Oh, I've had a few fencing lessons, Uncle.'

Out of the corner of his eye he just managed to catch Rachel's smirk.

Andrew sighed. 'Oh well, I guess you have to learn the hard way... What about you, Rachel? Please tell me you can use a sword better than this joker?'

'How hard can it be, you just stab with the pointy end, right?' Rachel hefted the sword in a tight fist and jerked it straight up into the air a couple of times.

Sam had to fight hard not to laugh out loud as Andrew's face went white. He decided to take pity on him. 'Don't worry, Uncle Andrew, we know what we're doing.'

They went back down the steps to join the rest of the fighters.

Sam took his jacket off and started to unbutton his shirt; he didn't want to get it dirty or bloody and intended to fight bare-chested like many of the other soldiers were doing.

Rachel looked down at her own long black dress.

She looked back up and grinned at Sam. 'Do you think it would give me an unfair advantage if I fought like we did in Sparta?'

Sam barked with laughter. 'I think you would give at least a few people a heart attack.' He nodded towards the spectators who were starting to gather on the steps above them. There were many ladies there, the pink woman among them.

'Shame.' She did a few twists and bends, testing out the range of movement her dress allowed her. She shrugged and just slipped out of her shoes. 'This will have to do, then.'

'Ladies and Gentlemen, your attention please!' They looked up as Chapman called out from the top of the steps.

The onlookers and participants went quiet and looked at him expectantly.

'The tournament is to be a simple elimination contest, with the loser going out and the winner proceeding to the next round. Each duel is to be fought to first blood, with honour, and the use of excessive force will be penalised. Please remember that your opponent is your brother...' He paused with a grimace and looked at Rachel. 'Uh... or sister.' There were some good-natured catcalls from the audience and he raised his voice over the top of them. 'So try not to do too much damage; we don't want to spoil lunch!' He gave them all a big smile then read the names off of the wall for the first bouts.

Since there was only a little over an hour until lunch, several fights were taking place at the same time in different parts of the lawn. Sam and Rachel weren't taking part until the second round, so they had some time to watch their rivals.

Most of the swordwork on display was fairly rudimentary, not much more than Sam had seen demonstrated by professional fencers. Despite the fact that most swords used in the armed forces were edged weapons, which were little more than metal clubs, everybody was using duelling swords, where it was the point that did damage. The closest modern day equivalent for the technique and swords on display was probably the epée, which was Sam's favourite sword type and he smiled confidently as he surveyed the competition.

'We should be able to take most of these guys. What do you think? Do you see anyone good, Rachel?'

Rachel didn't answer, she was caught up in one of the fights, and Sam followed her gaze curiously.

Fidwick was duelling a younger man, dressed in a blue navy lieutenant's uniform. Fidwick was barechested, like Sam, except for a pair of black braces that went over his shoulders and a white handkerchief wrapped around the upper part of his sword arm.

Sam watched them, wondering why Rachel was so interested. They looked perfectly ordinary to him and he was about to dismiss them, but paused when he looked closer and realised that he had been missing something.

At first glance the two men looked evenly matched, and Sam was sure that most people watching would have that opinion, but he had been trained to be observant of an opponent and there were things that he could see that someone who hadn't spent years doing martial arts wouldn't notice.

The colonel's technique seemed simple, basic, but it was deceptively so; he wasn't showing a lack of skill, instead he was demonstrating a superiority that was surprising in its economy and effectiveness. There was no energy wasted, no extra effort in his strikes and parries, and the naval man's attacks missed by scant millimetres each time, but missed nonetheless.

There was something strangely familiar about the way he moved, but Sam just couldn't place it.

By contrast the lieutenant was putting unnecessary force into his thrusts. It was quite obvious he was used to a different type of sword, most likely some kind of cutlass like Sam had used in Port Royal, and there was nothing particularly subtle about that kind of weapon. Fidwick's minimalist technique was having the opposite effect on the lieutenant, who was becoming more and more imprecise as the bout went on and in the end it was easy enough for Fidwick to take advantage of an overextension on the naval man's part to flick the point of his sword against his opponent's ear.

The naval lieutenant put a hand to the side of his head and it came away bloody. He smiled and bowed. 'Good match, sir!'

Fidwick came to attention and gave him a nod. 'Thank you, well fought, sir!'

The crowd applauded each fight as it finished and Chapman made notes on the wall as the results were given to him.

Rachel was up in the next round of fights, but Sam wasn't, so he accompanied her to where her opponent, a large and hairy, shirtless man wearing a kilt and a tam o' shanter, was waiting. It was the man who had walked through the crowd when they'd arrived, carrying the large stag on his shoulders without a thought of whose eye he could take out with its antlers.

Typically, when he saw who he would be fighting he laughed, flexing giant muscles. 'C'mon then, lassie! Let's see wotcher got!'

Rachel turned to Sam and rolled her eyes, but he just shook his head and smiled wryly. 'Try not to hurt his pride *too* much, please, darling.'

'I can't promise anything.'

She stepped forward and stood a few metres in front of the big Scotsman. She tilted her head and looked at him sideways. 'You know, you should be on a box of porridge...'

'Whassat mean?'

'Oh, nothing, sorry.'

At the umpire's signal they saluted, then the big man fell into a ready stance, his feet spread wide and bent slightly, his duelling sword tiny in his huge hand.

To Sam it was obvious just from the way he was standing that he would spring to the attack as soon as the order was given and he was fairly sure that Rachel knew it too. He looked at the girl he loved and sighed; she was just standing facing the Scotsman, her left hand on her hip and her sword hanging relaxed from her limp right hand as if it were a handbag or something.

The umpire looked at her nervously. 'Miss Evans, are you ready?'

'Yes, thank you!' She turned her head to smile cheerfully at him, but didn't otherwise move.

The umpire swallowed visibly and his voice squeaked as he spoke. 'Uh... fight?'

It was barely audible, but it was enough for the Scotsman and he charged ahead with a bellow.

Rachel watched him coming, the smile still on her face.

At the last second she stepped to the side and his sword passed inches from her nose, followed closely by the man himself. As he went by she flicked her right hand, then turned to look at the umpire.

'My bout I think.'

The Scotsman turned, still brandishing his sword. 'Wha? Nae! She didnae touch me!'

'First blood goes to Miss Evans!' The umpire declared, his relief that he hadn't had to preside over the death of a young girl at the hands of an experienced soldier palpable.

'Wha'? Ye cannae be seri...?' He stopped speaking as Rachel pointed a finger at his leg.

A trickle of blood was running down his leg from a minuscule scratch on the back of his knee, staining his white socks.

'Gah! 'Tis but a scratch!'

'But it is sufficient to give Miss Evans the victory,' said the umpire. 'I'm sorry Hamish.'

'Nae matter!' The man's glare instantly turned to one of the largest most genial smiles Rachel had ever seen. 'I know when I'm beaten, I just didnae think it would be at the hands of the prettiest wee lassie I'd ever seen! If yer weren't tekken I'd ask yer to dance wi me!'

He walked forward, holding out a huge hand and Rachel shook it.

'Well done, lassie, well done indeed.'

'Thank you, sir.'

The big man walked away, shaking his head, but grinning, to be received by the good-natured laughter of his friends and fellow soldiers. As Rachel walked back over to where Sam was waiting for her, she smiled as she heard him speaking to them in a voice that was only slightly less than a roar. 'You just wait till she comes up against you Sassenachs! She'll rip yer apart!'

Sam shook his head, feigning disappointment. 'That was boring. Impressive, but boring.'

'I thought you wanted me to go easy on him?'

'Yes. But I also wanted to see you fight. I like watching you fight!'

'You can't have everything, Sam. Make up your mind!'

He opened his mouth to reply, but before he could say anything smart they heard his name being called. They made their way over to an umpire, who was waving to catch his attention.

'Mr Vives, may I introduce Terence Walters, captain, Royal Marines. Captain Walters, Samuel Vives.'

Sam shook hands with his opponent, who turned out to be a wiry man with dusky blonde hair wearing a loose white shirt over white breeches and a pair of the shiniest boots Sam had ever seen.

'How do you do, Captain Walters?'

'Pleased to meet you, sir!' Walters glanced around Sam and looked at Rachel warily. 'I do hope you are not as proficient as your companion. Remarkable display, Miss Evans.'

She nodded in thanks for his complement. 'Thank you, captain, and no, Sam is not nearly as good as I am.'

'That's a relief!'

The umpire stepped in, reluctantly interrupting them. 'Gentlemen, we should get started. If you please?'

The captain nodded. 'Of course, Berty!'

While the captain went to prepare himself, Sam turned to Rachel.

'Why did you tell him that?'

'Because it's true.'

'It is not!'

'Please remind me: how many Spartans did you take down, exactly?'

'That was different, that just proved that you're more pig-headed, or maybe hard-headed than I am, not that you're better with a sword.'

'Well, then, Mr Vives, sir, you will just have to get to the final and prove yourself, won't you?' She gave him a mocking curtsy and bobbed her head.

'You can count on it!' Sam grinned and bowed back at her before stepping forward to face his opponent.

He took a deep breath and put Rachel out of his mind, searching for the serenity and peace that Master Hamato had taught him to find. A bare second later the world around him faded out until all that was left was the umpire and the marine captain.

He lifted his sword in salute and watched the captain do the same, taking note of the slightly imprecise path that the blade took up and down, the slight weakness of the middle finger of his sword hand which was likely an old wound, detected the slight quiver of the man's upper lip, betraying his nerves, and observed that he was watching his opponent's blade rather than his eyes. He registered those and a hundred more details in the time it took for his sword to come up to his face and then swish back to his side.

'Begin!' His job done, the umpire stepped back and faded from Sam's vision. Now all that existed to him was the man in front of him, the enemy.

Sam defeated the captain with ease and then did the same to his next three opponents, each time barely breaking a sweat.

Rachel didn't quite humiliate her challengers as much as she had the Scotsman, but it was close, and each time she won there was a huge cheer from Hamish and his friends, all of whom had become ardent admirers of hers and a kind of unofficial cheerleading section.

It took only half an hour to whittle down the competition until there were just four fighters left: Sam, Rachel, Colonel Fidwick and a small, but dangerous-looking man called Harlon Kettle, one of the few Americans present at Symposium. Both men were excellent swordsmen, but while Sam respected and admired Fidwick's talent, Kettle scared him. And it would be Rachel who would have to face him.

While Fidwick had won all of his bouts with masterful precision, Kettle had been rather more brutish and direct, but just as effective even so. He reminded Sam of the gunfighters in films; he had the same intense, unblinking stare and focus. It was very intimidating and he had given two of his opponents fairly serious but thankfully not life-threatening injuries, each time seeming to revel in the pain that he had given the other person. He had been called out by the umpires several times for not respecting the rules, but in each case he had pleaded that his lack of experience made his strikes imprecise. It was a clear lie that had nonetheless been accepted and he had easily made it to the semi-finals.

Seeing as there were only three bouts left, they were going to fight them one at a time in front of the steps of the mansion. By this time almost all of the Displacers had made their way out to watch and there was quite a lot of good-natured betting going on. Chapman had erased the names from the wall and was now using it to run a book and calculate the odds for each participant. Rachel was the clear favourite to take the tournament, which was no surprise to Sam, but it had proved to be something of a shock to everyone else, especially to the more over-dressed women in attendance, like the woman in pink, who came from a time before the suffragette movement and were used to the men being the ones who carried out the dangerous Displacements.

The remaining contestants stood at the foot of the lawn, waiting to begin. Kettle was swigging from a hip flask and glaring at anyone who glanced his way, while Fidwick was chatting to a couple of the umpires. Rachel and Sam stood together, slightly apart from the others, watching the crowd curiously. They had already spotted most of the current Displacers, including James, who, to Sam's shock and amusement, was only bald on top of his head, as well as Anne and Lisa, who both looked quite young; evidently, like Andrew, they hadn't updated their presence for a while. But, while it was an interesting exercise, they knew that they couldn't afford to be distracted for too long; they both had hard fights on their hands.

Sam grinned at Rachel. 'I'm loving this, can you tell?'

She stared at him and managed to keep a completely straight face as she said. 'No.'

He laughed. 'Seriously, though. While it's incredible to spar against you, it's great to be able to fight against so many different people.'

She smirked at him. 'Even though they're not presenting much of a challenge?'

'They haven't been much of one so far, that's true, but that doesn't mean I haven't learnt anything.' He nodded towards their next opponents. 'And I know that those two are going to teach us something.'

Rachel frowned as she looked at Kettle. 'I'm not sure what I'm going to learn from him.'

Sam sighed, turning serious and speaking softly. 'You've never been bullied, have you?'

'Only by my mother.'

He shook his head. 'That doesn't count; she's not really a bully. I'm talking about someone whose first thought in the morning and last thought before going to bed is who he can hurt and how. Someone who searches out a person's weakness and then exploits it over, and over, and over, until that person cracks. Someone who is happiest when others are suffering.' He jerked his chin at Kettle, who was sharpening his sword to a lethal point, even though the contest rules had specifically called upon restraint and respect. '*That* is a bully. He will do anything to win and he will cause as much damage as he can while he does it. To you.'

She looked at the man, evaluating him, trying to see what Sam saw in him. 'I wouldn't have thought the Displacers would have someone like that as a member. Everybody seems so, I don't know... reasonable.'

Sam shook his head. 'The talent for being a Displacer isn't limited to good people, so why shouldn't we have a bully like Kettle in the Society? I'm sure he had his uses and at least as a member he can be controlled. It would probably be quite interesting to look through the journals and find out what kind of jobs he carried out.'

'I guess. I don't like it, though.'

The umpires were starting to finish up their conversation and one of them was walking towards them.

Rachel was going to be fighting first and Sam leaned in to kiss her. 'Looks like you're up. Be careful, OK? I don't want to have to go home before lunch; I'm hungry.'

Rachel laughed. 'Thank you for your concern, I'll be fine.'

'Miss Evans? Are you ready?'

She nodded and smiled at the umpire. 'I am.'

She turned back to Sam and stroked his cheek. 'See you in a minute.' She turned and walked out into the middle of the lawn. She was still barefoot and her dress showed no sign whatsoever of the fights she'd had. She looked serene and beautiful, such a contrast to her opponent who seemed like not much more than a beast compared to her. Kettle had a thick moustache and was wearing a black vest over a white shirt and black trousers, his long black hair slicked down and tied back with a brown leather thong - he stood out like a sore thumb among the gentlemen and officers who had been fighting the duels, but then again, so did Rachel. He swished his sword back and forth in the air and glared at her, already starting his intimidation tactics.

Rachel just rolled her eyes and looked bored. She lifted her left hand up and inspected her fingernails as if she had nothing better to do.

'I hope Miss Evans gives that man a damn good hiding.'

Sam turned his head to see Colonel Fidwick standing beside him. 'I'm sure that she will.'

'Would you care to make a wager on it?'

'I'm sorry, I didn't bring any money.'

Fidwick laughed. 'Neither did anybody else!'

Sam frowned and looked at the other Displacers who were still placing bets on the fights. 'Then what is everybody gambling with?'

'Time, my dear fellow, we wager a certain amount of our time! What else? The winner has that time to ask questions, or may request that the loser recount a Displacement of particular interest. Frankly, our members don't mind whether they win or lose; either way they gain something from the interaction.'

'In that case, I accept your wager.'

'Excellent! Shall we say half an hour?'

Sam nodded. 'Half an hour it is.'

'This is one time I hope I lose.' Fidwick grinned widely before turning back to the combatants.

'Begin!' The umpire started the fight and backed away, but neither Rachel nor Kettle moved. They remained eyeing each other, swords held loosely at their sides.

Their audience watched, spellbound and silent, holding their breath.

After a few seconds Kettle smiled and slowly raised his sword. He saluted, almost ironically, then took up a fighting stance.

Rachel returned the salute, much more smartly, but didn't take up a preparatory stance, instead she just turned sideways to him, presenting him with her right side, leaving her sword pointed downwards.

Kettle slowly straightened out of his stance, still smiling, and started to move, taking steps around Rachel, circling her, watching her reactions.

She stayed were she was, but turned her body in order to keep her side to him.

After twenty seconds or so he stopped and planted his feet.

There was a moment of absolute stillness and then he leapt forwards.

The audience gasped as they went through a blistering series of parries and ripostes, with Kettle twisting his body and striking from various different angles, almost too fast to be seen.

Throughout it all Rachel just stood, still and impassive, her sword arm the only thing moving.

The attack was over in seconds.

A slow smile crept over Rachel's face as she watched Kettle fall back, panting slightly, the confident smile on his face faltering.

Sam was watching her closely, but even so he almost missed the instant when she decided to go on the attack; a slight flexing of her knees was the only indication and it was so minimal that he was positive that nobody else had seen it. Kettle certainly didn't.

She covered the distance to her opponent in an instant and her sword moved so fast that it was almost invisible.

Kettle staggered back, flailing about, desperately trying to parry a sword that was never where he thought it was.

Rachel pressed forwards, not allowing Kettle a chance to recover, forcing him back and back, keeping him on the retreat and his attention completely focussed on her whirling blade.

The audience scrambled to open a gap as they approached, thinking that they were going to pass through them, but Rachel had no intention of drawing the fight out or letting it be hidden among the crowd; she wanted everybody to see the bully's humiliation.

She went through a series of high attacks, making Kettle lift his sword to defend his head and then, when his attention was completely held, she ducked and leapt forwards. A quick tug on his ankle sent the man sprawling, sword flying from his hand as he landed heavily on his back. He recovered instantly and started to get up, but froze when Rachel put the tip of her sword against his nose.

'Do you yield?'

'I believe that the rules state that we fight until first blood, ma'am.' The man's voice was gentle and completely at odds with his appearance.

'Are you really going to make me cut you?'

The man considered for a second and then he completely took Rachel by surprise by jerking his head forwards, cutting a shallow scratch in his own cheek on her sword, causing a drop of blood to well up.

'Miss Evans is the victor!' the umpire called out to almost universal cheering.

Rachel held out her hand and after a moment's hesitation Kettle took it and allowed her to pull him up.

He looked at her, considering. 'You are the strangest woman I have ever met; you are stronger than most men I know and yet you hesitate to do what you know you need to do... I pray that one day that hesitancy does not get you or those you love killed.' He bowed to her. 'It has been an honour to lose at your hand, and I wish you luck in the final.' With that he spun on his heels and disappeared into the crowd.

Rachel watched him go a chill at his words passing through her, but she quickly shrugged it off and wandered over to where Sam was waiting with the colonel.

'Well?' She raised an eyebrow at them.

Sam looked thoughtful. 'You didn't do *too* badly, I suppose. What do you think, colonel?'

'I saw at least six openings that even a half-decent swordsman could have exploited to defeat her.'

'Only six?' Sam frowned. 'I counted eight.'

'I was only talking about the initial exchange, not the whole fight.'

'Oh. Sorry, I stopped watching; I was bored.'

'That's perfectly understandable, my dear chap.' Fidwick nodded sagely.

'So, in your opinion, he let her win?'

'Indubitably! It is the only possible conclusion.'

'I concur.'

'Ahem!' Rachel interrupted them and smiled sweetly at them. 'Gentlemen. Don't forget that one of you has to fight me next; I wouldn't want to have to cut off anything essential. By mistake, of course, seeing as I have such poor control of my sword.'

The two men exchanged a glance then started clapping gently.

'A masterful display!'

'Truly breathtaking!'

'You are a paragon among women fencers!'

'I am humbled to call you my girlfriend...'

Rachel's eyes flashed and she opened her mouth to answer back, but they were saved from her wrath by an umpire.

'Gentlemen, are you ready?'

'Yes!'

'I'm ready!'

They all but ran to the centre of the lawn, leaving a fuming Rachel behind, unable to bawl them out.

As they went to their places they looked over their shoulders at the girl who was now scowling at them with her hands on her hips.

'That was fun, but I think you are going to pay for that later, Mr Vives.'

'I know, colonel. I just couldn't resist, though. She is magnificent, isn't she?'

'Indeed. You are a very lucky man.'

They stopped in the middle of the lawn and faced each other.

'Don't go easy on me, Mr Vives; I have seen you holding back.'

'Then you must do the same, colonel, because I have noticed you doing the same.'

The colonel nodded and they stepped backwards. When they reached the appropriate distance they both drew themselves up and lifted their blades in unison, their hilts in front of their noses. They held the salute for a few seconds as they locked eyes and, at an unspoken signal, both blades swept down again and to the side, making identical, crisp swishing sounds, before coming back up again to the ready position.

Despite having had the same teachers as Rachel and never having trained with anybody else, Sam had a vastly different philosophy to her when it came to fighting; Rachel placed much of her focus on the "art" in "martial arts", hence her minimalist and intelligent approach to her bouts, while Sam was more focussed on the raw technique. It made for some interesting sparring sessions between them.

The umpire's call of "begin!" signalled them both to leap to the attack, and from the first exchange it was clear that they were evenly matched, with Fidwick's superior strength and experience compensated for by Sam's skill and speed.

In complete contrast to Rachel's match with Kettle, theirs was frenetic from the start. That duel had been fought and lost by Kettle before a single attack had been made, without him realising. This one took quite a bit longer.

The opening exchange was a quick series of attacks and counterattacks as each of them tested defences they already suspected would be impenetrable by ordinary measures, but which had to be tested nevertheless. Then, once they had gotten past that formality, the real fun began as the fight progressed quickly from what could possibly have been recognisable as a fencing match between two epée masters and into something far more eclectic and almost *Hollywood* in nature.

A thrust by the colonel was sidestepped by Sam, who used his turning motion to move behind the colonel, who then performed a quick and showy flip through the air to present his front once more, which Sam countered by rolling forwards under the colonel's sword and inside his reach, an attack which in turn was negated by a neat one-handed cartwheel.

The fight progressed like that, with the crowd gasping every couple of seconds as the fighters performed increasingly athletic and acrobatic feats, the duellists themselves grinning with almost insane abandon and reckless enjoyment.

Sam was having the time of his life; he thrived on a challenge and he had only ever found two people that could provide it for him. One of them was Master Hamato, who he had never been able to beat, and the other was standing a few metres away at the edge of the lawn. Here, at last, was a third, and he was revelling in being able to push himself and test the limits of his abilities with someone new and he'd already learnt six techniques to add to his repertoire in just this one fight. That feeling was still there at the back of his head, though, that somehow Fidwick's technique was familiar, and Sam decided to test something.

On the colonel's next attack, instead of parrying he stepped into the blow, letting it slip under his arm and clamping it in place.

Fidwick caught Sam's blade in turn, and looked at him in confusion. 'Why do that, if you know it's going to be a stalemate?'

'I just thought you might like to shake things up a bit.'

The puzzlement slowly left Fidwick's face and was replaced by eagerness.

Sam smiled and the two of them stepped apart, tossing their swords over their shoulders.

Before the weapons had even hit the ground they were throwing kicks and punches at each other.

Just as before, each attack was perfectly countered.

They moved back and forth across the lawn until they found themselves at the bottom of the steps only a few feet from the audience, who were completely enthralled by what seemed to many of them to be inhuman feats.

Both fighters stopped suddenly, each having the same thought at the same time.

They leapt for the stairs and the pile of swords that were still lying there.

Sam grabbed the broadsword while Fidwick picked up the huge claymore. Both swords were almost as long as the men themselves and incredibly heavy.

They sprinted back out into the centre of the grass, away from the bystanders, to give them room to swing.

Sam started laughing as he chopped his sword down towards the colonel's head, a swing that was as clumsy as the weapon itself and was easily sidestepped. He was then forced to leap back as the claymore came whistling in at him from the side, only just managing to block it with his own sword. There was a sound like a hammer striking and anvil as the two weapons met and the vibrations almost knocked the weapons out of their hands.

They took a few more swings at each other, blocking each blow with an almighty clang, but it wasn't as much fun as they'd thought it would be, and they soon threw the huge swords to one side, recovering their original weapons from where they were still sticking out of the lawn.

They immediately launched back into the duel, but once again there was no clear advantage for either of them.

The fight had only been going for a couple of minutes, but it had been at such a frenetic pace that both men were now breathing heavily and that counted against Sam more than Fidwick; due to the nature of

Displacing and its curious rules and loopholes Sam had travelled that day and his energy had already been sapped, whereas Fidwick had not.

It only took one slight slip by Sam on a suddenly unsteady leg to put him on the back foot, and once Fidwick had the advantage he didn't let go. In less than a dozen strokes the colonel had nicked the inside of Sam's wrist, drawing blood and giving him the victory.

Far from being disappointed, Sam was delighted to have had such a wonderful fight and he was looking forward to replaying it in his mind and hearing Rachel's analysis of it. Besides, he'd fought Rachel enough times and it would be much more rewarding to watch her going up against Fidwick.

He grinned at the colonel and, instead of offering his hand to be shaken, bowed to him in gratitude and respect, just as he would have done to Rachel or Master Hamato after a fight.

He was surprised when the colonel dropped his arms to the side and mirrored the gesture.

Sam gaped at him. 'Now I know why I recognise your way of moving, you studied with Master Hamato!'

Rachel appeared by his side, smirking. 'Surprise!'

He turned to her, astonished and slightly annoyed. 'You knew?'

'Of course I did; where do you think I found out about Master Hamato in the first place? From Colonel Fidwick's journals. You know, one of these days you should learn how to read, Sam.' She slapped him gently on the cheek. 'And if you hadn't been so sarcastic earlier, I might have warned you before the fight.'

Sam laughed. 'Honestly, I don't think it would have made a difference; I know when I am bettered, and even if I hadn't been tired from our Displacement I'm sure I would have lost eventually.'

The colonel nodded modestly. 'For one so young you are very talented, Mr Vives. You are not so far from me as you might think and I look forward to a rematch when you have had a chance to study more. Perhaps tomorrow?'

Sam blinked. 'Tomorrow? Isn't that a little soon? It'll take me years to learn enough...'

He stopped talking as Rachel's elbow dug into his ribs. 'Wow, Sam, you *really* need to get a refresher course on being a Displacer.'

'What? Why?' He thought from a second and then deflated; obviously "tomorrow" for the colonel meant in a day's time here at Symposium, but for Rachel and himself it could be decades in their own future before they came back. 'Oh.' He said quietly with a sheepish grin.

Fidwick laughed. 'Never mind, Mr Vives, it often takes Displacers years to get used to the rules. In fact,' the colonel winked at him. 'All too often a person's understanding of the rules is inversely proportional to their talent.'

'Ah.' Sam nodded, wisely. 'That explains Rachel being such a know-it-all, then. Oh, and by the way: you have to fight her now, so those comments you made earlier...'

Fidwick gulped and paled slightly as Rachel grinned evilly at him. 'Is it too late to forfeit?'

Rachel laughed cruelly. 'Yes, it is. Now come on, it's your turn to lose.'

And lose he did.

While it was true Rachel had the advantage of having seen Fidwick fight to the best of his abilities against Sam, she didn't need it. The same thing that allowed her to beat Sam more often than he beat her, allowed her to win against the colonel without much fuss. That wasn't to say that he didn't put up a good fight, but Rachel was just superior in every way; she was younger, fitter, smarter, and most importantly her instincts were among the best that even Master Hamato said he'd ever seen.

Every move that Fidwick tried, Rachel not only blocked, but had ready a perfect counter, so the colonel was at a disadvantage whatever he tried to do. He was constantly on the back foot, retreating in circles around the lawn while Rachel followed him, not hurrying or even expending much energy.

Rather than try something desperate or be humiliated further Fidwick eventually just stabbed his sword into the ground and threw his hands up. 'I surrender! I bow to your superiority.'

The crowd broke out into cheers and started collecting the bets that had been made.

Rachel grinned. She saluted Fidwick, then threw her sword so that it stuck into the ground next to his and shook the hand he offered.

Fidwick sighed. 'If we'd had a few like you and Sam in the rifles, Napoleon would have been a goner much sooner.' A slow smile crossed his face as he thought of something. 'Can you shoot? Now there's something I *have* to be able to beat you at!'

'Shoot what? Bow, pistol, rifle, dart gun... I'm sorry, you'll have to specify.'

Sam had joined them by now, buttoning up his shirt and carrying his jacket, and he laughed as Fidwick's face fell. 'Good luck trying to find anything physical you can beat Rachel at; she's obsessed with training.'

'Well, I shall have to rack my brains to think of something.'

Sam leaned in close to Fidwick and whispered loud enough that Rachel could still hear. 'Bowling. She's really, *really* bad at bowling.'

Rachel put on a mock angry face. 'Sam! Stop giving away my secrets!'

They all looked up as Chapman came down the stairs to them. He handed Rachel a sheet of paper with names written on it with a small bow. 'Your prize, my lady.'

'What's this?'

'Oh, that's right, you weren't there when prizes were discussed. You have won an hour of time from all of the contestants. That includes Mr Vives, of course.'

Rachel grinned at Sam. 'Oh, goody! Am I right in saying that I can ask for anything for that hour?'

Chapman nodded. 'Within the bounds of propriety, yes.'

'Propriety... Oh. That's a shame...'

Sam raised an eyebrow as she looked at him lasciviously, but thankfully they were interrupted before she could elaborate.

'Ladies and Gentlemen! Lunch is served!'

The call from Lord Price stalled any further conversation and the crowd started to stream indoors.

Rachel held her arms out on either side of her. 'I wish to be escorted to dinner!'

'Yes, ma'am!' Fidwick and Sam both grinned and then, arm in arm, the three of them went inside.

CHAPTER 8
REPLENISHING ENERGY

After lunch, Rachel and Sam told their fellow Displacers everything that had happened in the last couple of years. As James had requested, they left nothing out, talking about the Illuminati, Quentin's betrayal of the Displacers, and the new fragment of prophecy that Sam had brought back from Egypt.

As expected, none of the people there had anything to add to help them. Quentin was questioned briefly, but he pleaded ignorance of who had recruited him and didn't know of any of the Illuminati's plans.

After they had finished there were still a couple of hours until dinner, so everybody made their way to the huge ballroom. Some of the Displacers had brought musical instruments with them instead of food and, as was often the way with their kind, each of them turned out to be a virtuoso who would have been more than welcome in any symphonic orchestra in the world.

The afternoon was, therefore, filled with music and often a classical piece would lead into a more modern one as the musicians from different ages learnt and taught each other. For Sam, the most notable moment was when one of the hippies led the makeshift orchestra in a rendition of *Lucy In The Sky With Diamonds* while playing the guitar and singing along. He had to laugh at the faces of some of the musicians who, while they perfectly understood the music itself, were nonetheless completely bewildered by the lyrics.

Sam and Rachel split up for a while, mingling like Colonel Fidwick had advised them and accepting the invitations of various people to dance. At one point, Rachel strolled up to the big Scotsman, Hamish and asked him to dance, dragging him onto the floor despite his protestations. He turned out to be better than he looked, once he got past his embarrassment and loosened up, although he never quite lost the bright beetroot colour from his face during the whole time. He muttered his apologies to her, bowing and leaving as soon as the dance was finished, stalking off to return to his friends, who dutifully ribbed him for his embarrassment until he was laughing again.

Time passed far too quickly and very soon it was time for dinner. Once again the cooks had outdone themselves and there was an astounding array of dishes, quite a few of which they recognised as being specialities of Richard's, which begged the question as to whether he had learnt them from the chefs at Symposium, or vice versa.

During the meal there was an open invitation for any Displacer who wished to recount something or tell a tale, which didn't necessarily have to be based on their time travelling adventures, to do so and it turned out that storytelling was another thing that many Displacers were good at. It wasn't anything like the boring droning that most of the current Elders seemed to be so fond of and Sam found out later that there were a few Displacers who had made a point of studying with bards and minstrels and such, from times when stories and how to tell them were important.

In between orators, as he watched his fellows applaud the latest storyteller, Sam mused that there were far more ways of using his Displacements than he had imagined when he had first started and had made his to-do list - learning to fight had always been Rachel's main interest and perhaps he should be searching for his own.

Dinner finished, but the storytelling went on until late and nobody wanted to stop and make their way to bed, but in the end Lord Price had laughingly insisted that they do so. He rightly pointed out that there was a whole month to go and that they didn't want to burn themselves out right at the start.

Sam and Rachel walked hand in hand down the long corridors in a large group of Displacers, saying goodnight to each of them as they peeled off into their rooms, until they were the last ones left. They went into their own room and while Sam closed the door, Rachel placed the candle that she had been carrying on the bedside table, then came back and pulled him into a kiss.

'I kind of want to claim that hour right now...'

'You know that you don't have to; I'll already do anything you ask me to.'

'Mmm, yes, I do!' She kissed him again, but she felt some reluctance in him and pulled away, puzzled. 'What is it?'

'Nothing.'

'Come on, Sam, don't pull that "I'm a boy and I hide my feelings" crap; I know you too well and I can tell when something is wrong.'

'Alright, yeah. There are a few things bothering me.' He lifted a finger in warning as he saw her start to grin cheekily. 'And before you say anything it's got nothing to do with me not understanding the rules and how all this is possible.'

Rachel laughed. 'I wasn't going to say anything!'

'Yeah, right.' Sam smiled, but then he sighed. 'Let's get into bed first, then we can talk.'

'Sounds good to me!'

She turned and dug around in the wardrobe, eventually bringing out the nightclothes that Lord Price had told them were there. They were hideous: there was a frilly pink nightie for her and a long nightdress for him like the one he'd worn a couple of times in Victorian London. They both wrinkled their noses at them and then just took off their clothes and climbed into bed naked.

Rachel snuggled up to Sam and put her head on his chest. She waited, knowing that he needed no prompting from her to start speaking.

'Symposium saddens me.'

She pushed herself up onto her elbows and frowned down at him. 'Why?'

Sam was still trying to sort out his thoughts; he knew what he wanted to say, just not how to say it. 'Well, when we Displace we usually meet people who are going about their lives. We can interact with them and befriend them. Yes, when we leave they forget us, but they knew us for that time and if we ever go back they'll remember us again.'

'OK...'

'But this is different. All these people, all these wonderful companions of ours that we've met and befriended today, they're not in their own time-line and we're not in their lives, because all they are is the echoes they've left behind. They are never really going to know who we are.'

Rachel stroked his face. He looked so sorrowful and she wished that she could tell him that it was going to be alright, but it wasn't. 'Oh,

Sam, the people here knew that when they came and it doesn't matter; Symposium isn't about making friends or having a good time, Symposium is a tool. It's a resource. Its sole purpose, the purpose for which it was designed, is to provide future generations with access to the entire community at one time. That access is supposed to be used to learn. Having fun and getting to like these people, while expected and welcome, is only a side effect.'

Sam grimaced. 'I guess I already knew that, but it doesn't make it any easier.'

She lowered herself to kiss him and this time he returned it, but she could still feel him holding back. She pulled away gently, not annoyed, just curious. 'There's something more, isn't there?'

He sighed and nodded. 'I know that we don't usually talk about the real world when we're in the past, but we're only here for a day and I really need to discuss this with you while we're alone. Is that OK?'

'Of course.'

'Thank you.'

She gave him a quick peck and then sat up so that she could see his face better in the dim light of the candle.

Sam stared up at the ceiling as he spoke. 'You remember those experiments I told you about at Christmas? The ones in the two diaries by Everett Lloyd.'

'Yes...'

'And you remember that there was a third diary Andrew gave to me.

'Yes...'

'Well, it's filled with experiments that can't be carried out.'

'Can't? How?'

'Well, some of them are just impossible to do, but most of them shouldn't be done because they are just too, well, *dark* is the best word, I suppose.'

Rachel said nothing, again letting him sort out his thoughts.

'It's all pretty complicated stuff, theoretical experiments that I could barely follow or stuff that I would never dream of. There was one experiment in particular, though, which I keep going back to, which dealt with a Displacer travelling into the past with his father, who he then kills.'

'Sounds lovely.'

He chuckled. 'I know, right? Anyway, the diary goes through the various possible outcomes of doing that and the reasons why each of them could come about, but it wasn't the experiment itself that stuck in my head, it was something that Everett wrote in his conclusions: he asked whether, if the son doesn't cease to exist, then is it because the time-line is *protecting itself*.' He looked up at Rachel, finally meeting her eyes. 'Do you remember the Prophecy?'

'Of course I do. How could I not?'

'*In that time of need will come the Diviner to pave the way forwards.*' He quoted. 'That sounds to me as if I only exist as a response to the Illuminati, that the only reason that I can do what I do and feel when Quentin is going to change the time-line is because *something* has put me here to do just *that*. It would explain how I felt in Hyde Park that it was time to go. It would explain why I always seem to know what to do, *despite* not knowing any of the rules. It would also explain how I'm always in the right place at the right time - that something, whatever it is, is guiding me, putting me where I need to be and giving me the tools I need.'

'I don't think you're giving yourself the credit you deserve...'

'I don't *deserve* any credit!' He interrupted her and she recoiled at the anguish on his face. 'Can't you see? I only do these things because something chose *me* to be special. It could have been anyone, it could have been you! It *should* have been you! But instead it was me, *I* was chosen and I had no choice in the matter! This was *forced* upon me and I don't want it!'

He threw back the covers, leapt out of bed and started pacing up and down in the room, his hands pulling at his hair in frustration.

She watched him, aghast. She had never realised he'd been fighting with those kind of feelings; he had been just a boy when she'd first met him and she had watched him change and grow physically, but she was only now realising how much he had matured over the last year or so and how much he had changed mentally as well - he'd always been a serious boy, but this was something else entirely and she wondered how she'd missed it when his seriousness had turned into worry.

She slid over and out of the bed, catching him and pulling him to a halt. She drew him into her arms and held him tight as he started sobbing.

It took a few minutes, but eventually he stopped. She released him and he stepped back, wiping the tears from his eyes. 'I'm sorry, I guess I just hate the feeling that my life is not my own, that I'm being controlled or something. And I really don't feel like I'm up to the responsibility.'

'You know you're not alone in this, right? You have a whole group of people who love you and would do anything for you.'

He sighed. 'I know, and sometimes that makes it worse; you follow me blindly, thinking I know what I'm doing, but I don't.'

She laughed gently. 'Oh, we know full well you have no idea what you're doing! But that doesn't stop us from trusting you; we have faith in you, Sam, and we know you wouldn't let us down if you can possibly avoid it.'

For the first time in several long minutes the corners of Sam's lips twitched and moved upwards to form a smile.

Rachel returned the smile. 'Now, can we get back in bed, please? It's a bit cold standing around like this.'

Sam looked her up and down. 'Funny, that never seemed to bother you in Sparta.'

'OK, I lied, I'm not cold. I just want to get back in bed, alright?'

Sam laughed and stepped forward to hug her. 'Thank you. And I'm sorry to be such a downer sometimes.'

She tilted her head back to kiss him. 'It's going to take a lot more than this to make me stop loving you, now come on, we've only got one night together this Displacement, so let's make it count.'

He smiled at her and together they went back to bed.

It had been a long while before they had gotten to sleep, so they were both still unconscious when there was a knock at their door the following morning.

Lord Price poked his head into the room. 'It's almost nine o'clock and you need to be going; your twenty-four hours are up.' He smiled at their sleepy faces. 'I hope you've enjoyed yourselves and I think I speak for everyone when I say that we've certainly enjoyed you being here. Make sure you come back!'

'We've had a wonderful time, thank you.' Rachel smiled at him from under the blankets.

Yes! Thank you!' Added Sam sleepily.

'Excellent! Well, chop chop! Time to get back to your lives!'

With a last big grin, Victor left.

They got out of bed and slowly started getting dressed, reluctant to leave. It wasn't just that they had enjoyed themselves immensely, it had also been particularly special because they had been surrounded by people who knew what they were - it had been like a Society party, but taken to the extreme.

Finally they were ready and they stood in the middle of the room holding hands.

They smiled at each other and closed their eyes...

...to wake up back on the sofa in Andrew's flat.

'Wow, that was something.'

They both looked over to find James looking at Sam with wonder on his face.

Rachel smiled. 'I told you!'

The expression was quickly replaced by a frown, though.

'What? What's wrong, Grandad?'

'I'm not sure, I'll have to think about it, but...' He took a deep breath and then the frown cleared as he smiled at them. 'Well, I think it's time for tea! But first, I want to show you this.' He reached behind his chair and pulled out a book. It was a large, aged and worn, black leather-bound book.

He opened it carefully and placed it on the coffee table between them. There, on the first page were Sam and Rachel's signatures. It wasn't Susan's signature below theirs, though, it was Quentin's, and Sam only just stopped himself from asking why when he realised that it would once again just show how little he understood the rules of Displacing.

James closed the book gently and stood up. 'Right! Let's go! I need tea!'

He walked out of the door and Sam stood up to follow him, but stopped when he realised that Rachel was still staring at the book.

'What is it?'

Rachel looked up at him. 'How old would you say that Quentin was at Symposium?'

'I don't know... older than us maybe, but not quite as old as he is now.'

'And did you have a good look at his face?'

'I suppose...' Sam still wasn't sure what she was getting at.

'Did you see his scar?'

'Of course, it was there on his forehead, like it always...' He stopped suddenly. 'Oh. Shit.' Sam had given Quentin that scar in Port Royal, years after he had left the Displacers and started working for the Illuminati.

Rachel stood. 'Indeed. Come on, we have to tell James that Quentin has been going back to Symposium since he was kicked out of the Displacers.'

James was already down the road, standing on the corner of Plaça de Lesseps looking for a taxi to flag down, when they caught up with him.

When they told him about Quentin he frowned, but just shrugged. 'That's worrying, yes, but there's nothing much we can do about it, unfortunately; if he still has his invitation there is no way we can stop him going back.'

Sam wasn't willing to accept that; he couldn't bear the thought of his mortal enemy having free rein in such a special place. 'There must be something we can do, like warn the people at Symposium or something.'

James just gave him a look, then stepped off the pavement. He put his fingers to his mouth and blew the loudest whistle Sam had ever heard to attract a passing cab.

It was a fifteen minute ride to the old part of the city and James sat silently in the front of the taxi the whole way, staring into space, while Sam and Rachel sat in the back, holding hands and looking out of the windows at the world as it went past. More and more, the modern day looked grey and unappetising to them, as if the energy and joy were being sapped out of it. That feeling was more pronounced on days like these when they had just come back from such an enjoyable Displacement, but they could see the changes in the people around them as well; there was an unhappiness, a discontent in everyone, as if all hope had been taken from them. It was extremely reminiscent of how things had been in Victorian London due to Quentin's manipulation.

James remained quiet and lost in thought for the short walk from where the taxi had dropped them off down the tight back street in the Gothic quarter to the quiet little tea shop. It was such a contrast from how his grandfather had been just before they had gone to Symposium that Sam was starting to get worried.

He glanced at Rachel in concern and she squeezed his hand and shrugged; she was just as unsure as him about what was wrong.

James seemed to come to some conclusion just before they got to their destination, the frown dropping from his face and by the time they entered the shop, passing through the old fashioned glass door with a gently tinkling bell over the top, it had been replaced by a wide grin, a grin that the old gentleman immediately turned on the man standing behind the bar.

'Pere! Quant de temps? Com va això?'

The man looked like he was the same age as James and stood just as straight. If ever the phrase "cut from the same cloth" applied to two people it did to them. He had a clean white apron over a dark grey suit and wiped his hands on a cloth before coming around and shaking James' hand vigorously.

'Jaume! Benvinguts de nou! Com anem?'

'Bé, bé, gràcies! Us presento el meu net, Sam i la seva xicota Rachel.'

The man nodded at them. 'Bon dia, jovenets!'

Sam nodded at the man and smiled. 'Bon dia!'

Rachel just nodded and smiled; she obviously didn't have a clue what was being said and, as his grandfather exchanged some more pleasantries with the owner, Sam grinned and leaned in to whisper in her ear. 'Now you know how I felt in those first weeks when you and Andrew spoke English all the time.'

The man escorted them to a table in the corner by the window. 'Si us plau, seieu, seieu!' He pulled a chair out for Rachel and she gracefully sat and allowed him to push it in behind her.

James took his own seat and smiled up at the man. 'El de sempre, si us plau, Pere.'

'Molt bé! De seguida!' The man gave a small bow and hurried away to start preparing their food and drink.

James leaned over the table and spoke to them in a quiet voice. 'Pere is an old friend of mine, he was in one of the volunteer brigades in the war, stationed in Portsmouth. We got into a fight one night while I was on shore leave.' James laughed, remembering. 'He beat the crap out of me, even with my boxing skills. Anyway, the MP's arrested us and we ended up sharing a cell together. We've been good friends ever since.'

He leaned back in his chair and waved at the shop around them. 'He came back here after the war and opened up this place, modelling it after the tea shops he loved in the south of England.'

Sam took the opportunity to look around. It really did look like someone had picked up an old English tea shop and plunked it down in the middle of Barcelona; it was elegantly furnished and there was lace everywhere on the table cloths and the chair coverings. The walls were sparsely covered by newspaper clippings and old black and white photos. One of the photos hanging just over James' shoulder showed four people, two young men and two women. They were wearing bathing suits and sitting on a rocky beach, smiling happily up at the camera.

'Grandad, is that...?'

James turned to look at the photo. 'Yes. That's me, that's Jess, that's Pere and that's Lilly, his wife.' He sighed. 'Of course, it's just the two of us left now; Lilly passed away almost twenty years ago, about the same time Jess did.' He trailed off as he gently stroked a finger over the face of the woman who had been his wife for more than fifty years in the present and hundreds more throughout history.

'Anyway, we didn't come here to reminisce on my past, we came here to talk. And for the tea!'

Sam nodded. 'OK, so how is South Africa going?'

James waved a hand dismissively. 'Ralph went last week. He says that all preparations that can be made have been, but I don't want to talk about that.'

Sam sat back in surprise. 'What do you want to talk about then?'

James looked at him seriously. 'You. I want to talk about you.'

'Me?'

'Yes, you. I think we made a mistake when we were training you.'

Sam looked at him in shock. 'Really?' He turned to glare furiously at Rachel. 'I knew it!'

Rachel tutted, shook her head, then punched him on the arm.

James rapped his knuckles on the table to bring their attention back to him. 'Sam, this is serious, stop acting daft.'

Sam looked contrite as he rubbed his suddenly dead arm. 'Sorry, Grandad.'

'You were taught to put all your energy into Preparing, weren't you?'

'Of course.'

'Well, for a normal Displacer that's fine, because it's what they have to do, but you're special and you're using far more energy than you need to. I'm fairly sure that's why your hair went white; you've been brute forcing your Displacements, using dynamite to blast your way into the past when you could have just been slicing an opening with a scalpel. You're perfectly capable of Displacing every two weeks, but you use too much energy when you do it.' James shook his head and sighed, annoyed with himself. 'I should have realised this before.'

He reached out and grabbed the little container with the paper sugar packets and shook them out onto the table in front of him. 'Right, so, when we Displace we use huge amounts of energy.' He swept the sugar packets to one side. 'Which is why you feel so hungry and sleep for so long afterwards; your body goes into a kind of shock and has to recover.'

He started sliding the packets back, one at a time. 'A Displacer takes a month to "recharge", if you will, to restock all that energy before they are capable of Displacing again.'

When all the sugar was back in front of him he swept it to one side again.

'You recharge the energy at the same rate as everyone else.' He slid the packets back in front of him one by one, but he stopped when he had half of them in front of him. 'However, you don't need to use the same amount of energy as everyone else. You can easily Displace with half, which is why your body tells you that it's ready after two weeks. But, when your body tells you it's ready to Displace again you naturally try to use all of the energy that you usually do.'

He pointed at the sugar that was still to one side of the table.

'Ultimately, that means you're using energy that you hadn't recharged, and that deficit has to come from somewhere. I suspect that, if we had you checked out, we'd find other things wrong with you, probably in your internal organs - the kidneys seem to be particularly susceptible to our type of exhaustion. Tell me, have you had any difficulty going to the toilet?'

'Grandad!'

Rachel laughed behind her hand. 'So, what can Sam do about this?'

'Well, either he sticks to Displacing once a month or he learns to use less energy. I know which one of those options he'll prefer and frankly the Society would prefer it too, so hopefully we'll be able to help him with that this weekend, unless he's even more stubborn than I think he is. However, his body knows what it's doing, how much energy it needs, even if he doesn't, so it should just be a case of teaching Sam to listen to it.'

'And then I'll be able to Displace every two weeks again?'

'I'd still like you to leave it for a while longer; you need to make sure you've completely recovered from your previous overstress, but yes, if this works you should be able to go back to Displacing every two weeks.'

Sam grinned, but the smile quickly faded when he saw that Rachel wasn't looking as happy about the news as he thought she would and he quickly realised that it meant he would once again be travelling without her.

He put his hand on her arm and squeezed it gently. 'I promise not to have any adventures without you. How about I just use my extra Displacements for educational purposes or for Society business?'

Rachel brightened up considerably at that. 'That would be really nice of you, Sam, thank you, but you don't have to promise that.'

'Of course I do. Displacing isn't the same without you; I love you.'

Rachel smiled. 'I love you too.'

They leaned in to kiss, but were interrupted by the arrival of Pere, the owner, with a huge tray of tea and cakes.

To the astonishment of the shop owner, Sam and Rachel polished off all the cakes he had brought, and the second lot that James had laughingly ordered immediately afterwards.

When they finally finished, James paid the bill and they went to leave, but James didn't follow them, instead he waved them away. 'I'll be out in a sec; got something to do first.'

Sam and Rachel went outside onto the street and discreetly turned to watch.

Through the window they saw the old man go up to the bar where Pere poured four whiskeys. Each of the men downed one of them, leaving two on the bar. They exchanged some words and shook hands, smiling sadly at each other before separating.

James came bounding out of the shop. He clapped his hands together energetically and grinned. 'Right! I feel like a bit of a stroll! Let's go to the front - it'll be like a day at the seaside!'

They followed him as he strode quickly down the street in the direction of the sea.

They came out of the buildings in front of the old port where the all the millionaires' yachts were moored and James stopped short at the sight of the huge hotel jutting out into the water. 'When did they build that monstrosity?'

'A good few years ago, now, Grandad.'

James shook his head. 'Every time I come back they've done something to spoil another bit of the city. You'd have thought the town that produced Gaudí would know better.'

They crossed the road and the old man led them to an empty bench facing out over the water.

He slapped Sam on the thigh. 'Right then. Prepare for us please, Sam, just like you always do.'

Sam closed his eyes and did as he was told, sending the familiar tingling sensation, the energy, to every corner of his body until he was vibrating with power.

James gasped. 'Oh, god, that's incredible! I can't get enough of it; makes me feel young again.'

He basked in Sam's energy for a while, but eventually he shook his head and patted Sam on the leg again. 'Fine. That's enough, let it go.'

Sam relaxed and opened his eyes to find James sitting with his own eyes closed, clenching his fists, as if remembering the feeling. For a moment he thought he could detect sorrow on the old man's face, but it was instantly gone as he opened his eyes and smiled.

'I want you to try something for me. When you get to the point when the energy fills you I want you to pull it back, I want you to hold onto it, but try to deaden the vibration. See if you can hold onto that point where you can Displace, but withhold some of the energy.' He laughed and shook his head. 'I have no idea how to explain it properly, but I'm fairly confident you'll know it when you feel it.'

Sam closed his eyes and Prepared again. Usually at this point when he was Displacing he would reach out towards a destination and he would be there, but this time he reached out towards the vibration that he could feel shaking every molecule in his body. It was like trying to grasp one of the fishes in the river in Okinawa - at first they had just slipped through his hands, but then he had learned to anticipate, to squeeze and hold in just the right places so that you could...

He opened his eyes in frustration as the tingling sensation washed away. 'I lost it.'

'That's alright; it doesn't matter, you had it there for a second. You felt it too, right, Rachel?'

She nodded and smiled at Sam encouragingly. 'Definitely.'

James patted Sam on the leg again. 'You're still using far too much energy, but at least now we know it's possible.' He tutted. 'I really don't know how this didn't occur to one of us before.'

Rachel laughed. 'He's unique. We've never come across anyone like him before, so how would any of us know that we had to teach him any differently?'

James considered briefly then nodded in agreement. 'So, what did you do that time, Sam?'

Sam tried to put into words what had been just a feeling, pure instinct, and just like James he had no idea how to at first, but then something occurred to him and he chuckled. 'You know that old alarm clock you give us when we visit you in London, the big brass one with the bells on top that rings loudly enough to wake the whole house and makes the whole bedside table vibrate.'

James looked at him in puzzlement. 'Yes...'

'Well, when I get to the point where I'm about to Displace it's like that clock is ringing in my head, buzzing and jumping around. What I did was the same as if I'd taken the clock in my hands and put my fingers on the bells. The harder you press on them, the less noise it makes and the less it vibrates. It's still ringing, but it's not as loud and it's not as annoying.'

'That's...' James blinked in surprise. 'That's actually quite brilliant, Sam. I'm genuinely surprised at you and I'm truly sorry that it surprises me.'

Rachel sniffed and shrugged. 'He could have just said it was like putting a ringing mobile under a pillow.'

Sam laughed. 'Ah, but would James have understood that?'

'Hey! I'm not as out of touch as you might think!' James reached into his pocket. He brought out a mobile and displayed it proudly. It was one of the old Nokias that everybody joked lasted forever. His actually had.

He grinned when Sam and Rachel laughed. 'It's a joke - that smartphone Andrew insisted I got broke after a few months, so I've gone back to using this one until he gets me another one, so I'd appreciate it if you'd let me know if there are any alerts I should know about, Rachel.'

She nodded. 'OK, will do.'

'So, are we going to try again, Grandad?'

No, I think that's enough for today; you've already Displaced and I don't want you being too tired to work on it tomorrow. Now, go on, go away. Spend some time together. I'm going to have a wander around the city for a while. Don't forget you have to change back into your jogging clothes before you go home, though, Sam. I'll be at Andrew's whenever you can get away tomorrow morning.'

Rachel and Sam stood up.

James looked up at them and started reaching into his pocket as something occurred to him. 'Do you need some money for a taxi?'

Sam shook his head. 'We're fine, thanks, Grandad, I have a T10.'

'Good, because you almost cleaned me out with all the cakes you packed away between the two of you...' He smiled at them, all too happy that he had been able to treat them. 'See you tomorrow, Sam. Have fun you two!'

The first thing Sam did after they left James was ring his parents to tell them he had met some friends and ask them if he could stay out for lunch with them. They readily agreed - his parents were always pleased when he said he was doing things with friends; for a very long time nobody had wanted to be his friend when he was being bullied in case they got picked on too. However, even though he'd stopped being bullied when he'd started Displacing, the decade he'd spent in the past had made children his own age a lot less interesting to him and he still didn't have very many friends at school. That was fine with him, though; he had more than enough friends with Rachel and the Displacers.

He hung up the phone, then smiled at Rachel. 'So, what do you want to do?'

'It would be a shame to waste those lovely new clothes of yours, so why don't we go to lunch somewhere nice? Andrew's paying me more than enough, so it's my treat.'

'Really? Are you still hungry?'

'Always! Aren't you?'

'Of course!'

'Well, come on then, I know this nice little place in the back streets near the Tàpies museum that Andrew introduced me to. Metro's this way, right?'

Sam smiled as he let her drag him up the street towards the end of the Ramblas.

The next day Sam worked with James until he was completely exhausted, but they believed they had managed to considerably reduce the amount of energy that he would use on his next Displacement. He would only know for sure when he tried it, but if it was true it would mean a lot, both for Sam personally and the Displacers at as a whole.

Sam didn't think the weekend could get any better, but it did when Rachel received a message on Sunday afternoon.

They were in the sitting room, having afternoon tea and Sam was eating a good part of Andrew's biscuit stores, replacing the energy that he had expended in Preparing, when Rachel pulled out her phone and read the message. She grinned and looked up at James. 'Diana says that she can't meet up with me for a few more weeks; she's going to be in South Africa longer than she thought.'

James looked at her, curious about her sudden happiness. 'Are you smiling because you don't have to see her again? Or am I missing something?'

'Well, if Diana is AFK...'

'If Diana is what?'

'AFK. You know, not around? MIA?'

James huffed in annoyance. 'Then why didn't you just say that instead of just coming up with three letters at random?'

As Sam sniggered quietly, Rachel looked at the old man for a second, wondering if she should explain, but decided against it. 'If Diana isn't going to be in London, then there's no real point in my being there, so I could, maybe, stay here until Sam and I have to go to stop them.'

James shook his head. 'No, we need you back in London.'

Rachel's face fell and Sam reached out to grasp her hand.

They looked up as James laughed. 'Got you! Of course you can stay! Now, who wants more tea?'

The old man leaped out of his armchair and, still laughing, made his way towards the kitchen.

When he went home that night Sam told his parents that Rachel was going to be in Barcelona for work and they extended her an open invitation to come over whenever she wanted, as long as it didn't interfere with Sam's schoolwork.

It was going to be a good month.

CHAPTER 9
PLANS WITHIN PLANS

Diana hadn't had a particularly good month and the next one wasn't looking like it was going to be any better. It wasn't because her research was dull or never-ending, nor was it because the hotel she was staying in was far below her usual standards to fit in with her cover story. It was because Quentin was stressed, feeling immense pressure to succeed, which was only made worse by having Davis constantly watching over him, and insisted on micromanaging her every move. He was clearly terrified of failing in the mission and wanted updates after every single one of her meetings and sent Tessa to find her whenever she was even temporarily unreachable - she'd gone for a quiet drink one evening in a neighbouring bar, leaving her phone behind, thinking she was finished for the day, and had a rude surprise when Tessa burst into the bar, interrupting her just as she was getting to know an interesting group of businessmen and women. It had been a humiliating experience and she had been ashamed to show her face back there again, despite how hot some of the people there had been.

She hadn't had any specific instructions as to what to do with her monthly Displacement, so she just accompanied Tessa on her reconnaissance of the mines before the time that the gold was discovered. They wandered around the terrain, camping in a different place every night and hunting for food. Diana found it dull; she had nothing to do while Tessa familiarised herself with the ground and made the maps that Quentin wanted, so she came back early.

It was perhaps the most depressing Displacement she'd ever had, and she almost told Quentin exactly that, but caught herself just in time before she made that fatal error. She had unconsciously started calling it "Displacing" in her mind after she had started spending so much time with James and Rachel, but it was a habit she couldn't let herself fall into because it would give her away. She had to make sure she used the Illuminati word for a Displacement - a *Leap* - even in her thoughts.

After the Leap she went back to her research. As far as she was concerned she'd gotten as much information in her first week in South Africa as was needed, but Quentin wasn't satisfied. He was one of those people who thought that there was always something he was missing, one little gem of information that was going to provide the key to success. He had her searching archives and going to meeting after meeting with high-level executives in the gold companies and acting slutty so that she could wheedle out inside knowledge, right up until a couple of days before the Leap, when he finally called her home.

This time she upgraded herself to a business class ticket; there was no need to keep up the pretence anymore and she would need her rest if she was going to put up with Quentin's imbecility in person.

They met in Quentin's flat the day after she and Tessa got back. The entire sitting room was covered with papers and drawings and red string ran from one side of the room to the other. Diana had to laugh; it was like Quentin had watched a chapter of some detective show and decided that this kind of thing worked - what he didn't realise was that it was usually mentally disturbed people who did this, an ordered mind wouldn't have to.

Quentin himself was looking much the worse for wear; his greasy hair was messy and hadn't been cut since she'd last seen him, his clothes were mismatched, his complexion was pallid and there were bags under his eyes.

Davis, in sharp contrast, was looking relaxed and calm. He was sitting on the sofa in the same place he'd occupied the previous time and was sipping from a can of coke. He smiled and winked at her as she walked in, looking her up and down in a way that made her wish she had Rachel's fighting skills. She made no comment, though, and just smiled back before taking her seat in the same armchair as before.

Once again the Twins hovered in the background as everyone else discussed the plan and, despite the mess the room was in, it was clear enough and surprisingly simple, which annoyed Diana somewhat because it meant that 90% of the work that she'd done had been completely unnecessary, as she'd known it would be. She didn't resent Quentin too much for it, though; he thought and rightly so, that it was better to be thorough than have something unexpected kill him, or fail and have the Master kill him instead.

They would Leap to June of 1887, aiming for a small shanty town that Diana had found early on in the Johannesburg library. Tristan had Leapt to January of 1887 and riled up a group of Boers and they would be there waiting for them there. They would then use those Boers to bully the companies Quentin had identified as vulnerable, from the information he had gotten from Lloyd's of London and Diana had gotten from South Africa, hoping to frighten them into selling their holdings. Quentin had used his Leap the previous month to go to 1880 and had moved certain elements of Illuminati-owned companies, so that they would be in place to buy the holdings when they became available, making the Illuminati owners of a substantial percentage of the Johannesburg gold mines.

When he'd finished laying out the plan Quentin looked around the room. 'Any questions?'

When there weren't any, he continued. 'Well, I hope you're all rested because we're going tomorrow at twelve midday. I will give you further instructions when we get there.' He nodded, dismissing them all.

Diana had no desire to stay any longer than necessary so she immediately stood up and left.

Once more, Davis met her at the lift and again he didn't say anything until the doors were safely closed behind them.

'It looks like Price might come through.'

Diana nodded. 'It seems like a good plan.'

Davis barked with laughter. 'Any idiot can come up with a "good plan" for a job that's as simple as this one, but the effort that he's had to put into coming up with it doesn't exactly inspire confidence in his ability to handle anything more complicated at a later date.'

The lift doors pinged open and he gestured for her to exit first.

They walked across the lobby floor, the only sound the clicking of her heels on the tiled floor, and out onto the busy street. Davis turned to face her and leaned in to speak quietly into her ear.

'Whether the mission is a success or not, our unpredictable Mr Price might find himself discarded anyway.'

Diana pulled back and looked at him in shock. 'The Master would do that? Even if Quentin does what he's been told to do?'

'Sometimes even doing something right can get you into trouble.' He shrugged. 'Maybe the Master just thinks that it's time for some new blood.'

'New blood? Has the Master said anything to you about me?'

'Just that he has the utmost confidence in you and that he knows you will do the right thing when the time comes.'

She blinked. 'What does that mean?'

Davis just grinned enigmatically and walked away.

Diana watched until the man disappeared amongst the tourists and businessmen that crowded the street, then spun on her heels. She waved to the first taxi she saw and gave the driver her address as she settled into the back seat.

After her conversation with the Master on Skype she'd had a few doubts about betraying him; she had thought that, if she were promoted to a position of real power within the Illuminati, maybe she'd be able to influence them and change the way they worked, or at least make them less cold-blooded in the way that they carried out their plans. Also, she freely admitted that the increased funds she would receive as a team leader were extremely tempting.

However, now she saw that there was no real power within the Illuminati beyond that which the Master kept clutched in his vindictive hands and she wouldn't ever be allowed to change anything. And money certainly wasn't the most important thing in life, thanks to Sam and Rachel she knew that now.

Any doubts that she'd had about helping the Displacers disappeared and she pulled out her phone to give Rachel the details of the Leap, including the complete list of the companies they would be threatening.

The next day they assembled in Quentin's flat.

They clustered at one end of the dining room table, the chairs pushed together so that they could all sit down while holding hands for the Leap. Quentin's laptop set at the other end of the table: the Master was watching them.

Quentin insisted on guiding them, even though it was Tristan who had scouted out the Boer hideout and as Diana closed her eyes she thought it was just another symptom of Quentin's micromanagement, but...

...she realised that it wasn't as soon as she opened her mind and saw Table Mountain looming in the distance.

She frowned. 'We're in Cape Town... I thought...'

They were standing in front of a run-down one-storey wooden building at the edge of a city, a little way back from the waterfront, part of a long line of buildings that looked like dockside warehouses.

Quentin smirked. 'You're not here to think, Diana. You're here to obey my orders.'

He turned and went into the building.

Waiting inside were three men with long beards, Boers, wearing rough brown clothing, sitting around a table, chewing on sticks of dried meat and playing cards. There was a veritable armoury lying on a tarpaulin in the middle of the single large room among stacks of large sacks containing grain.

The Twins' faces lit up and they immediately went over to start checking the weapons, opening the breeches of shotguns and checking barrels and chambers.

In the meantime, Quentin had greeted the leader of the men and was receiving his report.

Diana hurried over to him to find out what was going on, but only caught the end of the conversation.

'... is still inside, but we haven't seen anyone else go in yet.' The Boer's voice was rough and gravelly and his English was heavily accented and hard to understand.

'Good, well, I'm sure they'll be here soon.'

The Boer nodded and left to rejoin his men.

Quentin smiled maliciously and turned to find Diana watching him. He laughed at the confused expression on her face. 'I suppose an explanation is in order. Come with me. You too Davis.'

He led them through the building to the other side which faced the water and pointed at another warehouse about a hundred yards down the front towards the sea. 'That building on the shore there was very recently purchased by "Harrow Shipping and Distribution", a subsidiary of a company owned by Sir Andrew Berry, cabinet minister, businessman and ancestor of the leader of our adversaries. It has been sitting empty for a few days, guarded only by a portly middle-aged clerk by the name of Stuart Watkins, who paid for it in bonds from the Bank of England shortly after he arrived on the steamer from London. It is the only building in the whole of South Africa that is owned by any of the companies that members of the Honourable Society of Dickheads have in their portfolio. So, that is where we will find our friends when they come, and that is where we will ambush and kill them before they can interfere with our plans.'

Diana's heart raced, but she hid her anxiety from him and frowned. 'That's a bit of a stretch, even for you. We have no idea if they're even coming to stop us.'

'Oh, did I forget to tell you that I saw my father talking to Sir Andrew in London when I Leapt back here to set this little deal up? Sorry, I guess I should have.' He laughed. 'Of course they'll be here. Even if I hadn't seen my father, you don't think that Vives boy would pass up the opportunity to come and play with me again, do you?'

Davis chuckled. 'Nicely done, Price. Maybe you aren't quite as hopeless as the Master thinks you are.'

Quentin scowled at the man, but before he could say something in reply there was a sound from overhead and they looked up to see a fourth Boer standing on the roof above them, keeping watch on the Displacers' warehouse.

Diana thought quickly. 'What about the plan? We're on a bit of a tight schedule, shouldn't we already be in Johannesburg?'

'That's why I have brought us here three months earlier than we had planned, so that we have time to set our little trap.'

She swallowed and looked out towards the warehouse.

She knew that the Displacers were coming; Rachel had said as much and knowing James he wouldn't let her information go to waste, but she truly hoped that they sent someone other than Rachel and Sam, or if it was them, that they didn't come anywhere near Cape Town.

CHAPTER 10
BEST LAID SCHEMES

Ralph and James flew to Barcelona a week before Diana had estimated the Illuminati would be carrying out their "Leap" so as to be in place in case they brought their schedule forward. Sam and Rachel still weren't sure if Ralph was the spy or not and for all they knew he was leading them into a trap, but when they confronted James about it, his grandfather had just shrugged and replied 'it's a necessary risk and there's nobody else available.' To make matters worse, despite James' rank as chief Elder, under Society rules he was relegated to the role of an observer and adviser. The old man took part in the discussions and helped as much as possible, but ultimately, since Ralph was the ranking Displacer and had already gone into the past to set things up, he was firmly in charge and any decisions were his to make.

In the end it wasn't so much Sam's doubts about Ralph that bothered him most, it was the fact that the man had immediately taken over Andrew's home as if it were his own, moving in to Andrew's bedroom, drinking his tea, eating his food and making a mess of the kitchen that Andrew would never have permitted. He also turned the dining room into a kind of war room, covering the walls with his research, which included not only details of the companies that owned gold mines at the time, but also the particulars of the "Harrow Shipping and Distribution Company" owned by Andrew's ancestor and namesake, Sir Andrew Berry, an agent of which Ralph had arranged to be moved into a specially purchased warehouse on the wharf of Cape Town. The agent would have letters of credit with which he would attempt to outbid Quentin on any mines that became available from the Illuminati's intimidation tactics, or with which they could possibly even hire mercenaries to counter him, depending on exactly what Quentin did.

Rachel immediately set about familiarising herself with Ralph's research, but Sam had school, which he reluctantly agreed he couldn't skip without causing trouble. He did what he could to memorise the information in the evenings and over the weekend, but he was having trouble holding on to it; somehow the task didn't sit right with him and he was finding it hard to concentrate on it. Neither did it help that Ralph was constantly watching him with a disapproving look, scrutinising everything that he did and berating him whenever he couldn't answer questions about the material. Sam managed to accept the man's criticism without complaint, but only because he knew how important the mission was. However, for the first time ever a Displacement was feeling more like an obligation than an adventure and he resolved to tell Andrew that he never wanted to work with the elder Price ever again.

Diana's message that she had been recalled from South Africa gave them a sense of expectancy and when she sent the final details of Quentin's plan the day before the "Leap" Ralph and James leapt into frantic action, analysing them and rushing to adjust what the Displacers were going to do accordingly.

When Sam got to Andrew's flat after school that evening he was slightly annoyed to find out that much of the information Ralph had made him memorise had been discarded as useless, but again, he said nothing. However, he couldn't remain silent when he read the contents of Diana's lengthy message. 'This is too simple, everything they've done so far had been far more complicated than this.'

Ralph laughed mockingly and shook his head in dismissal. 'That's because this is just a gold robbery. It's not important in the grand scheme of things. Both that and we know that my son planned it - he likes to pretend to be a genius but believe me, he's not.'

'I still think we're missing something...'

Ralph cut him off, annoyed. 'Nonsense! I know my own son and I know how to outwit him. I have a solid plan in place and we know all the details of his, I am confident that we will be able to stop him.'

Sam wasn't convinced and he shared a glance with Rachel, who just shrugged and turned back to her work.

Ralph insisted on doing last-minute research on the companies on Diana's list to see if there was anything they had missed. James trawled the Internet on Andrew's computer while Rachel used her laptop to dig up any information they might be able to use. Unfortunately, Sam had to leave early to be with his family, but he took a few names with him to look up on his own laptop at home. None of them found anything worthwhile and in the end all they really did was tire themselves out needlessly the night before the Displacement.

The day that they were due to Displace to South Africa was also a school day, but fortunately Quentin planned to go at twelve, which was one o'clock in Spain and Sam would be on his lunch break. He would have to hurry from school when his classes finished at twelve thirty, do the Displacement and then go straight back, but it was possible and he wouldn't have to do anything that would lead to awkward questions, like skip school entirely or pretend to be ill.

The only trouble was that Sam was delayed; his history teacher held him back after class to try to talk him out of leaving school at the end of the year and she was so enthusiastic and obviously cared so much about his future that he just couldn't bring himself to cut her off. He thanked her and made his excuses as soon as he could, promising to think about it, but he was still almost fifteen minutes behind schedule when he left school.

He had been continuously checking during classes throughout the morning to make sure that Quentin hadn't stolen a march on them and Displaced early, but it wasn't until he was walking to Andrew's flat that he got the same feeling that he'd gotten in Hyde Park at Christmas, like diving into the Eurotas in winter, and he suddenly knew that the Illuminati had gone. He instantly broke out into a sprint, almost knocking over an old lady carrying her shopping, and raced the last kilometre.

He rang the doorbell insistently and burst in when Rachel opened the door, dragging her after him into the sitting room where James and Ralph were waiting. 'He's there, we have to go! Now!'

Ralph looked disapprovingly at Sam. 'If some of us had been on time, then we wouldn't be in such a rush.' He looked sideways at James. 'I don't know why you all put so much store in this boy...'

The old man gave him a cold look and cut him off. 'Never mind that, right now you have a job to do, *Mr Price*.'

'I know that.' Ralph turned to glare at Sam and Rachel. 'Well? What are you waiting for? Sit down!'

They sat on the sofa, squeezing in uncomfortably close on either side of Ralph and linking hands with him; Ralph was going to be the one guiding them because he already knew exactly when and where they were going. They didn't like it, having someone else control their movements, but James had told them that was the way it had to be.

They had been given a precise date from Diana for when they were going to go back, but Ralph had decided they should Displace to a month earlier in order to give them time to prepare things for the Illuminati's arrival.

'Prepare!'

They looked at each other and rolled their eyes, stifling a laugh at Ralph's overbearing nature, but still closed their eyes and obeyed his command.

Cape Town, South Africa, 1887

They found themselves on a dirt road outside a row of wooden buildings, warehouses by the look of them, on the waterfront in Cape Town with the flat top of Table Mountain to one side of them and the sea to the other. It was late afternoon and the sun was still hot, but the shadows were lengthening, giving everything an added depth. It would have been quite picturesque if it weren't for the multitude of dock workers that jostled them as they went by on their way home and the smell of rotting fish that seemed to be coming from a nearby market that was closing up for the day.

Ralph let go of their hands and turned to confront them, his face stern. 'Right! I spent five years here last month setting this up. This is *my* mission and you're only here to support me, so do *not* get in my way. Just stay in the background and let me do all the talking.'

He walked past them and went into the warehouse.

They hung back for a second.

'This might still be a trap.' Sam expressed what they were both thinking.

'I know.' Rachel grinned. 'Let's go spring it and see what happens!'

Before he could stop her, she pushed the door open and went in.

Sam groaned, then followed.

Despite her seeming nonchalance, Rachel's attitude when she went into the warehouse was one of extreme caution. She motioned for Sam to move to the right as she moved to the left and they scanned their surroundings as Ralph walked confidently towards a small office at the back.

'Mr Watkins!'

After a few seconds the door to the office opened and a short man came out. He smiled nervously at Ralph, and gave an awkward little bow, wringing his hands. 'Lord Price! I wasn't expecting you so soon!'

Sam and Rachel relaxed slightly when they saw the man, who seemed to be some kind of clerk. He was wearing a dark suit with white pin stripes, had a gut that spoke of easy living and little exercise, and his scalp could be seen through his thinning hair. He really didn't look like the kind of person who would be involved in any kind of trap, except as the inept person who was comically falling into it.

The man looked towards the back of the warehouse where they could see the harbour through a large loading dock. 'Did a steamer come in today? I didn't...'

'Never mind that, I'm here now, aren't I? Do you have the letters of credit?'

'Yes, yes, of course!' The man hurried away to the office and came back in a few seconds holding a small leather case which he handed to Ralph, who opened it and started leafing through the papers inside.

Sam and Rachel looked over his shoulder as he flicked through them. There were a dozen or so pages, each of them embossed in gold.

They didn't have time to look any closer because the door to the street slammed open behind them and two scruffy-looking and bearded men burst in, brandishing rifles.

Sam and Rachel instantly turned to run out of the loading dock, but before they had gone even a single step they realised that the way was already blocked by seven people, darkly silhouetted against the light.

'I'm afraid there's no escape that way, Vives.'

Even though they couldn't make out who the seven were, the Displacers recognised the voice easy enough and as the figures strode forwards, the one in the middle became distinguishable as Quentin, who was grinning widely as he surveyed the four people trapped in the middle of the warehouse.

'Oh, this *is* a surprise! Not for me, obviously; I knew you were coming all along - I meant for you.'

The others revealed themselves to be two more roughly-dressed men, the huge Twins and Diana, as well as a dapper-looking young man who Sam didn't recognise. All of them were armed and they spread out to surround the smaller group.

Quentin sauntered forwards and stood in front of Ralph.

'Hello, father. Did you miss me?'

'You haven't seen me in years and that is the best you can come up with?' Ralph shook his head. 'Even now you are a disappointment.'

Quentin laughed. 'Really? Because from where I'm standing...'

The well-dressed young man stepped forward and interrupted him, exasperated. 'Oh for god's sake, Quentin. No wonder the Master is so disappointed with you! You talk when you should be acting.' He laughed. 'It's like you think you're a bond villain or something, well, I'm sorry to tell you this, but you're not, you're just a *joke.*'

'Stay out of this, Davis, I'll deal with you later.' Quentin growled at him out of the side of his mouth without taking his eyes off of his father.

'Not going to happen, Quentin; this is precisely why I'm here. You should not be the one who's trusted with the important missions, it should be me, and I intend to show the Master just how decisive and effective I can be.'

With that, he lifted his gun, a large pistol, and shot Ralph at almost point-blank range.

The force of the blast threw the Displacer backwards off his feet and to the floor, where he lay still.

There was silence for long seconds, then Quentin, who had been staring at the blossoming red stain on his father's chest, screamed and leapt at Davis.

The Twins laughed, watching with open delight as the two young men fell to the floor and started grappling.

That was the signal for all hell to break loose.

Rachel used the momentary distraction to spin and snatch the gun from the hands of the nearest man to her. She swung it and hit him on head the head with the butt, instantly knocking him unconscious, then reversed the gun to shoot two of the other bearded men.

Diana suddenly cried out and lifted her pistol. 'She's getting away!' She fired, but missed Rachel and hit the man behind her.

Rachel ducked involuntarily, but recovered quickly and leapt on the Twins, who were pulling themselves together and starting to lift their own rifles. She knocked the guns out of their hands with a downwards blow of the now-empty rifle across their wrists, then threw it in Tristan's face, stunning him and knocking him to his knees.

She backed away from them enough to scream at Sam over her shoulder. 'Get Ralph into the sea! NOW!'

She couldn't spare the time to look and see if he was doing as he was told because Tessa was now stalking towards her, a scowl on her face, and behind her Tristan was getting to his feet, equally angry.

The initial gunshot and the sight of the Displacer falling to the ground, spurting blood, stunned Sam for far too long, but then Rachel's shout spurred him back into action and he rushed to grab Ralph under the armpits and began to drag him towards the loading dock. The man groaned as Sam pulled him along and he saw that the shot had hit him in the stomach rather than the chest - it was a painful wound and would be fatal if left untended, but shouldn't kill him before he could get back to their time.

The water was less than twenty metres away, but it seemed like miles.

As he walked backwards, Sam managed to catch glimpses of Rachel fighting the Twins, but after almost tripping on a mooring ring he reluctantly realised he had to ignore her and concentrate on what he was doing - it was better that way anyway; the quicker he got Ralph home the better the man's chances would be and the quicker he would be able to help Rachel.

Finally he reached the edge of the dock and paused to glance over his shoulder. The sea was lapping against the wall a good few metres below, but seemed to be deep enough to cushion Ralph's fall.

'Sorry, Ralph, but this will have to do.'

He rolled Ralph off the edge of the dock.

There was a huge splash as the inert man hit the water, but Sam was already sprinting back to the warehouse and barely heard it.

It had been bright out in the sunshine and he was momentarily blinded as he ran back into the darkness of warehouse, but he blinked rapidly to make his eyes adjust quickly and assessed the situation without slowing.

He immediately dismissed the four bearded men; three of them looked dead and the other was obviously out of the fight. Diana was standing off to the side with Watkins, the clerk. Her gun was lowered at her side and she didn't look like she was going to join the fight on either side. Quentin and the strange man, Davis he had called him, were punching each other somewhat ineptly, while rolling around on the floor. It would have been laughable if Sam had been able to spare the time to watch, but he didn't, he had to give the last group his full attention - Rachel was staggering, barely staying on her feet as the Twins took it in turns to pummel her. She was scarcely conscious, blood streaming from her nose, one of her eyes swollen and closed. Her right arm hung loose at her side, twisted sickeningly, obviously broken, and she was limping as she tried to fend off the blows that rained on her from every direction.

It took barely two steps for Sam to take everything in and make a decision on how best to attack. He veered towards Rachel and accelerated, then leapt, his knee thrust out and aiming for Tessa's spine, his full bodyweight behind it.

It was a blow that would break the woman's back if it landed correctly and put her out of the fight. For the rest of her life.

If he'd stopped to think about what he was about to do to a fellow human being he might have hesitated, but all he could see was the blood on the face of the woman he loved, the pain she was in, and the rage took him.

Rachel hesitated.

She saw the man, Davis, step forwards and lift his gun, saw the eyes of the Boer covering her flicker towards him and knew that she could act.

But then she saw the gun was pointing at Ralph. Not Sam.

And she hesitated.

That hesitation might have cost Ralph his life, his very existence.

She wasn't going to make the same mistake twice.

While the sounds of the shot and Quentin's rather girlish scream were still reverberating around the empty space she disarmed the Boer nearest to her and knocked him out with his own gun, then shot two of his fellows with it. They were the first men she'd ever killed and, despite the fact that they would come back to life when she Displaced back home, she would still have to deal with the guilt. That was, if she survived; both Diana and the remaining Boer were lifting their guns towards her.

There was no way she could get to either of them before they shot, but the Illuminati was the closest of the two, so she put aside her feelings at the woman's betrayal and turned towards her, bracing herself for the coming pain and hoping that she would be able to carry on fighting afterwards and give Sam a chance to escape.

She caught the glint in the woman's eye and her warning shout just in time to twist out of the way as Diana took her shot.

If Rachel's reactions had been any worse the bullet would have hit her, but it whistled past with mere millimetres to spare and buried itself in the chest of the Boer.

The odds were getting better by the moment, but they were far from good because Tessa and Tristan still had to be dealt with.

Scant seconds had passed since Davis had shot Ralph and Quentin had leapt on him and the initial moment of surprise was fast wearing off. The Twins were recovering the focus they had lost, lifting their guns towards her and she knew with absolute certainty that she wouldn't be able to defeat them both by herself; they were too strong, but Sam was in shock, uselessly staring at Ralph's body on the floor. Despite all the training he'd had and probably because of his terrible experience in the First World War, he had never acclimatised to extreme violence.

Not like she had.

Despite knowing with absolute certainty that she was going to lose there was no longer any hesitation; she couldn't afford any. None of them could.

She closed the distance to the Twins in an instant. Disarming them had to be her first priority and she did so using the stolen rifle, bringing it down with all her strength and knocking the rifles out of their hands. She would have liked to at least break a couple of their fingers or a wrist, but beggars couldn't be choosers and she had to be satisfied with their cries of pain and the sound of the guns clattering to the ground, then the lovely crunch as she followed up by breaking Tristan's nose.

Sam told her later that she screamed at him to get Ralph to safety, but she didn't remember; her focus was already on her opponents, but she was aware on some level of Sam coming alive at last and bursting into motion. The wide trail of blood he left behind as he dragged Ralph away would normally have made her stomach turn, but at that moment it merely represented a hazard to be avoided lest she slip and lose her footing.

After the initial exchanges the fight itself was little more than a blur. Her instincts had quickly taken over and kept her alive, kept her on her feet despite the injuries, despite the punishment she was receiving. She knew that she had to buy time, knew that Sam would come back. He would save her, save them all. He always did. He would know what to do.

He just needed time.

Time... Perhaps it was because she'd taken one too many blows to the head, but she started laughing, even as she was hit over and over again; time was the one thing that Sam, that any Displacer, had in abundance, but at that moment hers was running out.

The fight quickly reached a point where she could no longer retaliate and all she could do was try to stop them from landing the blow that would finally put her on the ground and defeat her. She retreated over and over, hobbling backwards on legs that shouldn't have been able to support her weight, but the attacks still came, punishing, painful attacks that drove her mind into retreat, just as they did her body. Her training in Sparta was serving her well, but there was an added incentive now, beyond pride, beyond stubbornness: Sam.

The darkness had almost completely closed in on her, but something intruded and wouldn't let her slip into that blessed release - a familiar shape had appeared in the light coming in through the loading dock, as if from heaven, and it streaked toward her. Her feverish mind momentarily tried to fool her into thinking it was an angel, come to deliver her, but her eyes focused briefly and she realised it was Sam coming at last.

Their connection and understanding was such that she instantly knew what he was planning to do, saw his focus, saw his body tensing, readying. She knew what the blow would do to Tessa, but more importantly she knew what it would do to Sam later and she knew she couldn't let him do it.

She stepped to the side, as if to attack Tessa, making the huge woman rotate her body slightly in order to keep Rachel to her front. It was minimal, almost nothing, but it was enough to turn a potentially fatal attack into a merely dangerous one.

Sam's knee still hit the big woman in the back, but instead of snapping her spine it struck muscle.

Tessa dropped like a stone and lay still, her body instantly shutting off in shock.

As Tristan turned to face the new threat, Rachel seized the opportunity to give in and collapse to the floor. She retained her hold on consciousness by a thread, but she knew that there was no way she was going to be able to help Sam any longer.

Sam's fury initially drove Tristan back, overwhelming him, but the attacks lacked the power to seriously damage the brute and it didn't take long for the big man to recover and then it was Tristan's turn to use the indignation provided by a hurt loved one to fuel his attacks. He shrugged off Sam's ineffectual punches and was about to press his attack when there was another gunshot.

They froze and looked across the warehouse.

Blue smoke drifted slowly from the barrel of the revolver that Quentin was still pointing at the body on the ground at his feet and, as they watched in paralysed shock, blood began to seep from below Davis, spreading across the floor as his eyes stared sightlessly at the ceiling.

The gun dropped from Quentin's nerveless fingers and clattered on the ground as he fell to his knees next to the corpse, his mouth open and eyes wide in shock at what he'd done.

Tristan bellowed and Sam flinched, expecting an attack, but the man charged past him and ran to Tessa, only now noticing that his sister hadn't moved after Sam's attack. He shook her roughly, but got no response.

'She's not breathing!' The big man pulled the big woman into his arms as if she were a rag doll and barrelled out the loading dock, bawling her name all the while. There was an almighty splash as he jumped off the dock and then silence once again reined in the warehouse.

Sam hardly noticed; as soon as Tristan had ceased to be a threat he had rushed to Rachel. Not sure about whether Quentin would recover enough to attack again, he picked her up and struggled out, following in Tristan's footsteps. He staggered down the edge of the docks, along the water towards the fish market, until he came to an alleyway between two warehouses. He figured that they would be safe there for a while and he sat Rachel down against a few empty crates and knelt over her.

She was a mess, far worse than she had been after her graduation fight in Sparta; her breath was ragged, blood was oozing from her mouth, her obviously broken nose and one ear and her left eye was swollen completely shut.

Despite all that she managed to force a smile. 'I guess we know that Ralph isn't the traitor now, huh?'

The smile vanished as she was overcome by a fit of coughing and she gasped for breath, clutching at her ribs with her one good arm. The look of sheer agony on her face made Sam want to howl in impotence because there was absolutely nothing he could do to ease it.

She eventually stopped coughing and grinned up at him again, showing him her bloody teeth. 'Ow...'

Her eyes rolled back into her head and Sam grabbed her as she slid to one side, unconscious.

Sam held her for a long while, listening to her wheeze, struggling for breath, feeling her ribs scraping together as she did so. He knew what he had to do, but he didn't want to let go of her, however, when she started to stir, making noises of pain, he couldn't put it off any longer. He picked her up and looked around, quickly spotting a slipway a short distance away, further down the docks and stumbling towards it.

He lurched down the ramp, almost falling a few times, but eventually he made it to the water and waded in.

When the water was above his waist he kissed Rachel gently on the forehead, then slowly lowered her into the gentle waves.

He felt the energy filling her and then she was gone, her weight disappearing from his hands.

Sam could feel the tingling sensation in his legs and he wanted more than anything else to give into it and follow her home to make sure that she was alright, but he knew that he couldn't; he still had a job to do, his duty to fulfil, and besides, it didn't matter if he went home now or in several years' time, he would still get there at the exact same time that she did.

The decision made, he forced himself back into action. He stomped back up the ramp then ran back to the warehouse.

The scene that greeted him was quite different from the one that he'd left behind.

With Rachel gone, the two men she had killed were no longer dead, so all that was left were the bodies of the other one and Davis. Quentin had also disappeared, taking Diana with him and presumably the surviving Boers.

Diana was obviously still in the time-line because the man that she had shot was still there, but he needed to know if Quentin was there too and there was one easy way to do that.

He found the clerk huddled in a corner of his office behind a solid-looking wooden desk. 'They've gone now, you're safe, Mr Watkins!'

The man's head popped up when Sam called out and he looked around warily before answering. 'Oh, thank the Lord you're alright, Sir Sam!'

At the man's words Sam automatically fell into the "character" he had played in Victorian London over Christmas: Sir Sam Vives, the famous detective.

When he'd got home he'd researched some of the cases that had been attributed to Sir Sam and found that his persona was an amalgamation of several policemen and private sleuths, one of whom he'd undoubtedly pushed to one side, Displaced, when he'd taken on the Jack the Ripper case. Crime and detectives had been very popular in the Victorian press, it was the time of Sherlock Holmes after all, so Sir Sam was a lot better known in the past than he would have been in the present and his fame apparently even extended to South Africa.

He gave the clerk a confident smile. 'I'm fine, been through worse scrapes than this, I can tell you! Are you hurt?'

'Oh, gracious no! I got well out of the way as soon as the shooting started.' Watkins peered out of the window of the office towards the bodies. 'Did he get away?'

'Who?'

'The murderer you were looking for, uh, Quentin Price I think his name was.'

'Yes, he did, unfortunately. But don't worry, I'll catch him.'

The man flopped down in the chair. He took out a handkerchief and started to mop his brow.

Sam left him to it and wandered back out into the warehouse. Something didn't sit right with him about the ambush and, looking at the Boer on the ground, he knew exactly what it was: it was far too unlikely that Quentin would show up just as they arrived - not even Sam could be that precise when he was focusing on Quentin as a target for a Displacement. So, they must have arrived before them and been watching the warehouse, which meant that that they had to have been lurking somewhere nearby.

He left the bodies where they were - it wasn't as if they weren't going anywhere, although if they did it would be really good news - and ran back out of the loading dock and made his way around the side of the building and up the cluttered alleyway between it and the next. He reached the end and surveyed the street, easily staying in the shadows that were deepening as the sun slipped below the horizon.

The workers had mostly gone now, and the warehouses were silent and locked up, all except for one that had a soft light illuminating its windows. It was perfectly placed; not too far away, but not too close and it had a clear view of the entrance of the Displacer's warehouse.

Sam ran back down the alley to the water's edge and turned in the direction of the enemy hideout, racing along in the cover the buildings.

When he judged that he had gone far enough he turned down another alley and made his way back to the street, coming out on the other side of his target to the Displacer warehouse. A quick glance showed him no obvious lookouts so he sprinted across the street and made his way towards the building, hugging the walls. He stayed in cover as much as he could, using every ounce of the craft that Jacques had taught him and Rachel in France.

As he approached he could hear voices coming from within. One of them was raised in anger and was clearly recognisable as Quentin's.

Going round the side of the warehouse he found an open window and carefully peered through it.

Inside were Quentin, Diana and the three surviving Boers. The Boers were packing up dozens of guns into large bags and lugging them towards the back of the warehouse, while Quentin was pacing up and down in the middle of the room, shouting at Diana, who was just watching him go back and forth with her arms folded and a bored expression on her face. Far from trying to calm him, it looked like she was trying to antagonise him even more.

'I can't believe Davis did that. He's ruined the operation! The Twins have gone, that idiot is dead and we've lost one of our men.'

Diana shrugged. 'We should just call it a day, cut our losses...'

'No! We keep going. We can't go home like this! We still have the Boers and we can continue with the mission. We need to succeed.'

'No, *you* need to succeed.'

Quentin stopped pacing and the frantic, harried look vanished to be replaced by a coldly calculating stare. 'There's something you're not telling me, isn't there?'

Diana straightened from her insolent pose and dropped her arms slowly to her sides, her smirk fading. It was clear she knew she had made a mistake and she shrugged, smiling sweetly and trying to cover. 'I have my secrets. Everybody does. After all, we do belong to a secret society.'

The sharp sound of the slap shocked even Sam outside the window and the Boers paused momentarily in their packing to glance at the two, but went back to work almost immediately, trying to act as if nothing untoward had happened.

Diana reeled away from Quentin, putting her hand to her cheek, but he grabbed her by the shoulders and held her in place. 'What do you know?' He shook her roughly, hissing in her face and she squeezed her eyes shut as flecks of saliva hit her. 'Don't think I don't know that you and Davis were cooking something up behind my back!'

He released her and took a step back. He pulled the pistol that he had used to kill Davis out of the holster at his side and thrust it at her. It shook in his unsteady hand.

Sam could see Diana was terrified, but to her credit she still stood up to him. However, it was a very dangerous game she was playing and he knew that there was no way he could help her if Quentin decided to act.

'It wasn't Davis and I who were cooking something up, it was the *Master*.'

The pistol wavered and dropped a few inches before Quentin steadied it and brought it back up. 'And what? You were going to kill me here, then go home and then take my place, right?'

Diana shook her head slowly. 'No, the Master only told me that you were close to being removed from the Illuminati. I would only take your place if you failed.'

The pistol stopped shaking as Quentin prepared to shoot her.

She continued quickly, forcing the words out, seeing the burgeoning desperation in his eyes and willing him not to shoot. 'But he told me that if I did anything to stop you here then it would be me that would die, not you. He told me that I should do everything I could to make sure that you didn't fail, because there were other teams that I could take over if you succeeded and won his trust back. '

Quentin considered her words for long seconds before lowering the pistol to his side. He didn't holster it, though.

Diana dropped her hand from her face and, even from his vantage point, Sam could see the angry red mark that Quentin's blow had left. She took a couple of steps towards him, renewed confidence showing in her eyes and her posture.

'What Davis did *has* jeopardised the mission, I know, and if we went home now then we could blame him and we can tell the Master that his actions made the mission untenable. The Twins will back us up, I'm sure of it. We can also tell him about your brilliant plan to trap the Displacers, that it worked, but was ruined by Davis.'

She stopped a few feet from him and put her hands on her hips, giving Quentin one of her stunningly beautiful smiles. 'The Master knows me, he knows that I don't like you and wouldn't say that kind of thing to make you look good if it wasn't true.'

Quentin considered for a few seconds, then put the pistol away and smiled, an evil smile that Sam knew all too well.

'We're going to tell the Master all that, anyway, but we're going to do it *after* we've competed our mission.'

Diana's smile faded slightly. 'But...'

'Enough! I'm still in charge here, despite your machinations, and I say that we have no reason to abandon all the work I've done on this job. I will lead the Boers in their attacks on the gold mining companies, just as we had planned, while you...' he chuckled. 'You will use that devious mind of yours to keep an eye on our friend Vives. You will do everything you can to make sure he stays well out of the way.'

Diana stared at him for a few seconds, looking like she was going to object, but then nodded her agreement.

'Now, come on, get your gear together; we're leaving.'

Quentin turned away to speak to the leader of the Boers, so he missed the look of pure hatred that Diana gave him.

Sam didn't, though, and it stuck in his mind as he ran, retracing his steps back to the warehouse.

Watkins was still sitting in his office in the pool of light shed by a lantern on the desk. He had a glass of whiskey in his trembling hand and was taking small sips. He looked up with a start when Sam burst in and almost spilled the drink over himself.

'Did Lord Price tell you his plans?'

'Who?'

'Lord Price, the man...' Sam sighed and stopped himself. 'Never mind, why are you here?'

'I have orders from the company to be here. Our agents in Johannesburg insinuated that shares in some of the gold mines might soon become available and the company has requested that I be in position to take advantage of that. Although, why anybody would want to sell...'

Sam interrupted him. 'I need you to get ready to travel; we're going to Johannesburg. The men who attacked us are in a warehouse up the street preparing to leave and we have to follow them to make sure they don't accomplish their plans.'

'You want to follow the men who...' The man swallowed nervously. 'I am fully aware of your reputation, Sir Sam, but I don't think the company would want me...'

'The man I am looking for, the *murderer* who was here earlier, wasn't *just* looking for me, he was here for *you* as well. His activities are what are going to cause those people to sell their interests in the gold mines. The company knows this and sent me here to help you.'

Before they had Displaced, Ralph had made them memorise the names of the companies that Quentin was going to threaten and Sam wrote them down and handed the list to the nervous clerk.

'Here. These are the companies that are under threat. What can you tell me about them?'

The man read them through, his eyes flickering back and forth. 'These companies are all run by English South Africans, there's not a single Afrikaner-run company on this list.'

'So he's using racial tension to help him. Clever. Come on, pack your things, we don't have much time, we need to...'

Sam was cut off by shouting coming from out on the street and he hurriedly bent to blow out the lantern on the desk, plunging the office into darkness, then crept across the room and knelt down in the cover of the door jamb to look out into the warehouse. Men were streaming in through the main doors, moving slowly, spreading out and looking around.

'Oh god, not again!' Watkins immediately ducked back behind his desk.

The sun had gone down fully now and the space was completely dark except for the lanterns that the men had brought with them. The light didn't reach into the office, though, and for the moment Sam was hidden, but it wouldn't be long before they thought to check if there was anyone there.

There were about twenty of them, all armed, but Sam relaxed somewhat when he got a closer look at them and realised that it wasn't the Illuminati coming back with reinforcements to finish him off; unlike the Boers that had come with Quentin these men were wearing red uniform jackets and were clean-shaven. Shouts went up as they came across the two bodies and their behaviour immediately went from curious to aggressive.

The change in mood was troubling and he didn't particularly want to find out what happened if they found him hiding from them, so he decided to take a measure of control and reveal himself to them on his own terms.

He slipped out of the office and took a few steps into the middle of the room, putting his hands up in order to forestall any misunderstandings or mishaps.

'Excuse me!'

They shouted in alarm and rushed to surround him, bringing their rifles to bear.

'Hello, my name is Sam Vives...'

That was all he got out before he felt a sudden sharp jolt and the world twisted and fell into darkness.

CHAPTER 11
A GUEST AT HER MAJESTY'S PLEASURE

Light returned and brought with it a blinding pain. Sam lifted his hand to the back of his head, the source of the sharp piercing sensation, and found a bandage. It was soaked through and his hand came away with blood on it.

He sat up slowly and blinked his eyes, trying to focus. A wave of dizziness hit him and he almost passed out again, but he gritted his teeth and held on until eventually his vision cleared.

There wasn't much to see.

He was lying on a dirt floor in a tiny square room that was about three metres each side and whose only features were a wooden door opposite him, a metal bucket in the corner and a small window in the wall directly above him which was letting in a dull glow from outside.

He struggled onto his knees and pushed himself to his feet, but collapsed back, sliding down the wall as the world reeled around him. He barely managed to twist onto his side as he gagged and vomited - it seemed that his breakfast had accompanied him on the Displacement. When he finally managed to stop, he lay on his back and stared at a point on the ceiling until the room stopped spinning.

He didn't try to stand up again, he just got himself into a sitting position, shuffled a few feet away from the pool of vomit, then leaned back against the wall and closed his eyes.

He must have dozed off, because when he opened his eyes at the sound of keys in the door there was bright sunshine streaming through the window.

Sam struggled to his feet so as to be ready if an opportunity arose, but his vision swam and he bent over, clutching his stomach as nausea threatened to overtake him again. All thoughts of escape and of fighting his way out were instantly forgotten as he realised just how debilitated he was.

The door opened to reveal a man in a red jacket with gold stripes on the arms and blue trousers - an English army uniform. He was carrying a tray with a plate of food and a small metal cup.

'Awake at last are we?' He stopped just inside the door and looked Sam up and down, warily. 'Ooh, you don't look so good, son! Better sit back down before you do yourself a mischief.'

Sam straightened up and leaned back against the wall. The room spun once more at his renewed movement, but quickly settled as he held as still as possible. His legs were shaking and wouldn't hold his weight, though, so he took the man's advice and slid down into a sitting position.

He tried to speak, but found his throat dry and rasping. He eventually managed to croak out a few words. 'Why am I here?'

'You're under murder charges.'

'I'm innocent! My name...'

'Yeah, we know who you say you are, but we've got no way of knowing if you're telling the truth, do we now?'

The man stepped forwards and held the mug out to him.

Sam cautiously took a few sips of the water, soothing his throat. He coughed, but found that he could talk easier. 'Watkins. The clerk. He can tell you who I am.'

'He did, and that's the only reason you're not in front of a judge already. At his word we've sent for confirmation that you are who you say you are. It should only take a few weeks to get an answer from London.'

'Weeks? I can't wait weeks!'

If he was stuck in the cell for weeks then he might as well go home; even a few days might put him too far behind Quentin to stop him.

The man shrugged. 'Well, you're gonna have to.'

'But you don't understand! The man who killed those two men, he's planning an attack!'

'Sorry, but you're not going anywhere, matey. Eat, drink, and save your breath; you might need it for your trial.'

The man carefully bent down to put the tray on the floor, keeping his eye on Sam the whole time, wary of his prisoner trying something. His caution seemed more out of habit than any real expectation of being attacked, though, and there was genuine concern in his eyes as he took in Sam's condition.

He tutted. 'Don't eat too much; you might not be able to keep it down for a while.'

He walked out and closed the door after one last look at Sam. The key turned in the lock and there was the sound of his footsteps moving away down the hall outside, then silence.

Sam drank some water, sipping at it more to ease his throat than because he was thirsty and eyed the tray. The food was a hunk of bread with what looked like beef on it. After the Displacement Sam was definitely hungry, but he couldn't stand the thought of putting anything in his stomach just to have it come straight back up again. He had to replenish his energy or suffer the consequences, but thanks to James' discovery he had used far less than he usually did and he was hoping that he could afford to wait at least a few hours.

He put the cup to one side then blinked as another wave of dizziness came over him. He knew perfectly well that he should stay awake in his condition, with what was probably a concussion, but the Displacement, the adrenaline rush of the fight and the blow to his head proved to be too much and he fell into a deep sleep.

He woke once, very briefly, when someone shook him by the shoulder and shone a painfully bright light into his eyes. His fevered, barely conscious mind seemed to hear the voice of a young girl before he passed out once again.

When next he became conscious he was feeling much better. Not quite fully recovered, but refreshed and almost rested.

It was immediately obvious that he wasn't in the cell anymore and he opened his eyes to find that he was in a dimly lit room, lying on his back on a soft bed with bedding that smelled gently of flowers and wearing a long linen nightshirt.

He lifted his head to see a pretty young woman in a black and white uniform, a maid, moving quietly around the room. Even though she was obviously trying not to disturb him, it had been the soft rustling of her skirts that had woken him.

She felt his gaze and stopped what she was doing to bob in a small curtsy. 'Morning, sir! The master is at breakfast on the veranda if you are hungry.'

She smiled, then hurried over to the windows and threw them wide, letting in a stream of sunlight and the sounds of birds.

Sam squinted against the sudden light and winced at the pain that it caused behind his eyes, but it was nothing like the agony of before and when he sat up he found that he was no longer dizzy. He reached a hand up and gently explored the back of his head. The wound there had crusted over and it felt like there were a few stitches; a doctor must have seen him at some point.

When he finally adjusted to the light he caught sight of Table Mountain out of the window, a lot closer than it had been at the docks. He wasn't a prisoner anymore, but why? He couldn't have been unconscious for the weeks that the soldier had claimed he'd be locked up for, so what had changed? He supposed that he would find out soon enough at breakfast.

A quick glance showed him that there were clothes laying out for him on a chest of drawers beside the bed. They were the ones that he had turned up in the day before: a black Victorian-style suit of the same type that he had worn so often in London. They had been cleaned, thankfully, and there was no sign of blood or vomit on them.

He was still feeling very shaky, but the mention of food had awoken a sudden hunger in him and that urgent need far outweighed any lingering weakness. He swung out of bed, hastily tore the nightshirt over his head and reached for his clothes.

A little too late he remembered the maid.

She was watching him with wide eyes and an interested smile.

He coughed in embarrassment, but didn't try to cover himself as there was little point anymore. 'Please inform your master that I will be down shortly.'

'Are you sure you don't need any help dressing, sir? You look a bit unsteady on your legs, if you don't mind me saying.' She dropped her gaze from his eyes towards his lower body and her smile turned into a delighted grin.

Sam gave her as dignified a nod as he could. 'Thank you, it's a very kind offer, but I think I can manage.'

She laughed, a soft sound that was altogether more feminine and enticing than anything that Rachel could even dream of producing that it almost made him want to change his mind about accepting her help. 'Very well, sir!' There seemed to be genuine disappointment behind her mirth as the maid gave him another small curtsy and walked excessively slowly out of the room, looking at him over her shoulder the whole time.

The door clicked closed behind her and he sighed and started dressing.

Before he'd met Rachel he hadn't been naked in front of anyone except for in the showers at school after swimming or fencing and had never been completely comfortable. Now it seemed that he had gone to the other extreme; first bathing naked with Rachel in Okinawa, then spending almost two years with only a cloak to inadequately cover him in ancient Greece - he'd gotten so used to it just being normal that he hadn't even noticed that he'd been naked in front of the maid. He knew perfectly well that the vast majority of people weren't nearly as open-minded when it came to nudity, but he just couldn't quite get used to the fact that so many people thought that something that was so natural was so wrong.

Just as he was pulling on his jacket the maid reappeared and gave him another highly suggestive smile. 'If you'll follow me, sir, the master is expecting you.'

'Thank you.'

Sam followed the maid through the house. It was large, appeared to be constructed mostly from wood, and there were trophies of animals everywhere: the heads and hides of lions, tigers and antelope, the tusks of elephants and rhinos and the antlers of various unidentifiable beasts. To Sam's eye the waste of life was distasteful, but this was Africa back in a time when it was considered that there was nothing wrong with hunting for sport and indeed hunters were actually admired, especially in London's polite society, as being adventurous - they were almost as popular as detectives.

There were more trophies downstairs, but these were more human in origin: there were spears, shields, swords and guns of every kind hanging on every wall, some of which Sam recognised, like the hide-covered Zulu shield and crossed Assegai spears that he had seen in a Michael Caine film.

French windows at the back of the house opened out on a garden and that was where the maid left him, indicating for him to go out and giving him a cheeky wink before laughing gently and sauntering away.

Sam chuckled and watched her go appreciatively, before turning to step outside.

The terrace running along the length of the back of the house was covered with a wooden ceiling supported by carved pillars and it overlooked a huge walled-in garden filled with extremely colourful flowers. There were a couple of peacocks strutting across the lawn and it was their calls that he had heard from the bedroom.

The scene was so beautiful that it took him a few seconds to register that there was a large table covered with food to one side of the veranda. As he made his way over to it a sheepish-looking man stood up and came hurrying towards him with his hand extended. He was bald on top, but had massive, mutton-chop sideburns as if to compensate.

'Sir Sam, I'm Hercules Robinson, Governor of the Cape Colony.'

Sam shook the hand, automatically falling into English manners. 'Pleased to meet you, sir.'

'I must apologise for the way you were treated. If only we'd known you were coming...'

Sam instantly waved away the man's apology. Despite the fact that they had knocked him out and locked him in a cell, it was the English thing to do.

'Why have you released me? Surely a reply hasn't come from England so quickly.'

'Well, sir, you have my daughter, Eve, to thank for that.'

'Really?'

'Yes! She is an avid reader of The Illustrated London News and follows your cases with interest. When she heard that someone claiming to be the famous detective, Sir Sam Vives, had been arrested she begged me to let her see you. She recognised you from an engraving in an old issue and managed to convince me that it was in fact you. I so hope that you'll forgive me, but I must admit that I was still rather sceptical even so; you were rather unkempt, you see, and the engraving did depict you with much more of a moustache. However, my daughter can be quite persuasive and once we had you cleaned up it became obvious that you were indeed who you said you were.'

While the man spoke he led Sam to the table where a young girl was standing, shifting from foot to foot, excitedly waiting for them.

Sam smiled at her. She looked to be only a little bit older than Violeta, perhaps nine or ten, and the way she looked up at him with wide eyes reminded him sharply of his sister. He bowed to her. 'I am told I have you to thank for my freedom, Miss Eve.'

'Yes, sir.' She nodded enthusiastically, then picked up a newspaper from the table behind her and held it out to him.

He scanned it curiously. On the front page was a large headline proclaiming "Sir Sam Vives does it again!" Directly underneath was an engraving of what was clearly him, but looking much older and, curiously, with a large bushy moustache. It was a report on one of the cases that "he" had helped solve in Manchester - a series of robberies that had baffled the local police.

He handed it back to the girl. 'It's not a very good likeness, I don't know how you recognised me! It seems that you are a better detective than I.'

The girl smiled shyly, then slipped back into her place at the table to continue eating.

Sam turned back to Robinson, who smiled proudly and nodded in thanks at his kind words before gesturing at an empty seat. 'You must be starving, Sir Sam. Please, sit, eat.'

'Actually, I am.' Sam sat in the chair Robinson indicated and started piling food on his plate. 'How long have I been unconscious?'

'Two nights. And before you ask, let me assure you that I have not been sitting idle in that time. As soon as we found out who you were we started to investigate the activities of this man, Quentin Price, who you are pursuing.'

'Thank you.'

Robinson shrugged, giving him a wry smile. 'It was the least we could do.'

Sam chuckled, then stuffed almost an entire sausage into his mouth and began chewing as the man continued.

'We investigated the warehouses along by the docks, searching for the one which you told Watkins about. We located it without problem and found signs that it had been occupied for at least a couple of months, but the bandits were long gone, I'm afraid. However, we do have a fairly good idea of where they were heading; one of the two men they left dead in the warehouse was identified as Piet Kriel, the brother of Andries Kriel. Andries led one of the Boer commandos based near the Witwatersrand in the last war. I sent word for people to investigate and they found that many of the homesteads belonging to men who were in the Kriel Commando are deserted.

'It's obvious that something is up and that in itself would be enough for me to be concerned, even without your presence, and I have begun mobilising the army, but I am extremely hesitant to use them, unless absolutely necessary; we've only just gotten out of one war, we don't need another so soon.'

Sam nodded. 'Did Watkins give you the list I wrote for him? Have you taken steps to warn them?'

'He did, and we are working to do so, but there isn't much they can do on their own; they're miners, not fighters and won't be able to hold out against a determined force of Boers.'

Sam shook his head. 'I think their plan is more to intimidate rather than destroy; they want to force the companies to sell and then take over, they don't want to damage the infrastructure. And that includes the men working the mines.' He considered briefly. 'I would rather expect them to target the owners personally; that's more Price's style. If you can you should send guards to their homes rather than the mines themselves.'

Robinson nodded. 'That would make sense, I suppose, but if you're wrong and I leave the mines open for attack then it will be my head for the noose - Her Majesty gave me specific instructions that those gold mines are to be kept open at all costs; they are of utmost importance to the empire.'

'Then we should do all we can to protect them!' Sam punctuated his words with a slice of toast and smiled confidently at the man before spreading it thickly with jam and munching on it.

'Can you tell me more about this man you're chasing? Anything you know might help us stop him. For instance, why is he doing this? And who is this woman that Watkins said was with him?'

Sam frowned at the thought of Diana. He vaguely remembered her shouting out at the beginning of the fight and shooting her gun. He knew that she had hit one of the Boers, there was a dead man to testify to that, but he didn't know if she had been aiming at Rachel and missed, or whether she had shot him intentionally. It was in his nature, though, to give her the benefit of the doubt.

'The woman is Miss Diana Birch. She's not with him willingly, I know that much, but I have no idea what kind of hold he has over her. I would appreciate it if you tell your men to try not to harm her, if possible, but as for Quentin Price, they should do everything in their power to bring him down.'

Sam's heart was hard as he said those last words. A year ago, or even just a few months ago, he wouldn't have been able to condemn Quentin, despite all that he had done, but the look he had caught on his face just after he had shot the man he'd called Davis was too disturbing; he had *enjoyed* killing him. The glee had been quickly replaced by shock at his own actions, but it had been there nonetheless.

Robinson nodded again, this time more reluctantly. 'Very well, I will pass on that request, but obviously I can't promise anything about the girl; if she starts shooting at my men they will have to retaliate.'

'Understood. As for the man's motives, they are the usual: money and power. He is an evil man and a greedy one, and he will do whatever it takes to get what he wants.'

There was silence for a while as Robinson considered Sam's words.

Sam continued to eat ravenously and after a couple of minutes he looked up to find the young girl, Eve looking at him with wide eyes. He swallowed the huge mouthful of eggs and bacon that he had been chewing and smiled at her. 'I do apologise, madam, but I haven't had anything to eat in days.' He pretended to search the table. 'Could you pass the elephant, please?'

The girl tittered, then turned away shyly.

Sam went back to his food and winked at Robinson who smiled warmly at him.

He ate in silence for a few more minutes, then reluctantly pushed his plate away; it was time to talk seriously.

'You said you were mobilising the army, but that it would take some time to do so. How long are we talking about?'

'At least another two or three days, but as I said before, I am reluctant to send them north.' Robinson leaned forwards. 'You must understand, Sir Sam, that the gold mines do not exactly fall under my or even English jurisdiction; they fall under the control of the South African Republic. If I were to send troops in, then it would quite possibly constitute an act of war.'

'Can we talk to the government of the Republic? Will they step in?'

'I have sent messages to them, to President Kruger, but as yet I have received no reply; we are not exactly on the best of terms right now.'

'Then it seems that I must deal with Price myself.' Sam shrugged and grinned. 'It is what I have always done in the past, and has worked rather well so far!'

Robinson nodded. 'Very good, I will do what I can to help you, but unless you absolutely need them I will hold the army in reserve. I will move them to the border with the Republic, just north of Kimberley, but they will remain there unless I hear from you. I will, however, send a couple of men with you as guides; I wouldn't want you getting lost between Kimberley and Johannesburg!'

Sam frowned. 'Can't I just take a train all the way?'

Robinson laughed. 'My dear man! This isn't England! Be thankful that we have a line that will take you even half the way - a few years ago we didn't have that! No, I'm afraid the trains do not reach all the way to Johannesburg, you will have to ride from Kimberley. Which is why you'll need a guide.' He raised an eyebrow. 'I take it you can ride?'

'Um... Of course.' Sam actually wasn't too sure; Sam Vives had never been on a horse in his life, but he had to assume that Sir Sam Vives knew how to ride at least passably.

'Just as well, otherwise it would be very uncomfortable for you. I will have a horse and gear waiting for you in Kimberley, no need for you to take them with you from here.'

'Thank you, and I think it would be a good idea for Mr Watkins to come with me as well; he has information and resources that I need.'

'Watkins left for Johannesburg as soon as we'd finished questioning him, he should be well on his way there by now.'

Sam laughed. 'Really? From the impression I got, I thought he would be on a boat back to England by now!'

Robinson chuckled. 'From what I saw of the man, I wouldn't have been surprised either, however it seems that he has more of a backbone than both of us give him credit for. He mumbled something about a mission from London and caught the first train out. I have no idea how he was planning to get from Kimberley to Johannesburg or what he was going to do when he got there, but he seemed very determined.'

'Well, let us hope that he can accomplish something; I am going to have my work cut out for me and any assistance that I receive is more than welcome.'

Robinson nodded and pulled a silver watch from his pocket. 'Now, if I remember correctly, the next train leaves at ten, you have an hour and a half... Would you care for some more tea?'

'I'd love some, thank you.' Sam smiled and pulled his plate back towards himself.

CHAPTER 12
A PLEASANT RIDE IN THE COUNTRY

The train ride from Cape Town to Kimberley was a torturously slow journey of more than six hundred miles and took about a day. Sam barely noticed the time pass because he fell asleep the minute the train pulled out of the station - he hadn't actually been resting the last couple of days, he'd merely been recovering from being knocked unconscious and he was still exhausted.

He didn't sleep very well, though; the train was extremely basic in its design, not much more than a wooden box on wheels, without anything in the way of comfort, not even cushions on the seats, and the continual jostling and bumping as the unsprung carriage went over the uneven tracks woke him quite often.

During those brief moments, when he was jolted into wakefulness, he opened his eyes and looked out of the window. When he thought back to it later he compared his train journey to the one that Johnny Depp takes at the start of "Dead Man", where the countryside changes as he rides through it, but at the time it barely registered in his tired and still somewhat fevered mind - the scenery was beautiful, untouched and unspoiled as only the past could be, but it wasn't enough to keep him awake for more than a few seconds at a time.

Night came and went and it was mid-morning the next day when he was finally woken up by the conductor of the train, who shook him gently and told him that they had arrived at Kimberley.

Sam made his way off of the train with difficulty; his entire body had seized up and it felt like he'd had a four hour sparring session with Rachel - the consequence of not resting or eating soon enough after Displacing. He stood at the side of the track and looked around as he stretched, trying to restore some life to his muscles.

Kimberley station was large and fairly new and it looked like most of the passengers had gotten off there, which wasn't particularly surprising seeing as it was the end of the line and the farthest north that the train went; if anyone was heading to either the nearby diamond mines or the gold mines in Johannesburg, hoping to get rich, this was one of the quickest, and cheapest ways to get there.

Worryingly, though, there was no sign of the men that Robinson had promised would be waiting for him. There were a few rough-looking men carrying rifles among the passengers, but none of them even glanced at him, they just went about their business.

Sam waited until everybody had left the station, in case whoever was meeting him just couldn't see him in the press, but he was soon completely on his own, so he followed the crowd, thinking to find the town hall or someone who could point him to the army barracks.

However, he was barely out of the shadow of the station when a sweating young man in a black suit like his own, but much cheaper, came running up.

'Sir Sam? Excuse me, are you Sir Sam Vives?'

Sam nodded.

'I'm terribly sorry I'm late, I only found out a few minutes ago that you were expected.'

'And you are?'

'The name's Jessup, sir, I work in the mayor's office.'

Sam frowned and looked the man up and down. He didn't look like someone who was used to being very far from the city, or a desk for that matter. 'There was supposed to be a guide waiting for me. Is that you?'

'Oh, heavens, no; I'm just a clerk! I only liaise with the army, I don't do any of the rough stuff!' Jessup laughed nervously. 'Um, I'm sorry to have to be the bearer of bad tidings, but the army garrison, including your guide, was sent away on urgent business; there was a native attack on a village west of here and they have been called out to deal with it.'

'When will they be back?'

'Probably not for a couple of weeks.'

'Damn!' Despite the brave face he'd put on for the governor and his daughter, Sam was worried; he wasn't at all confident in his chances of stopping Quentin and this latest setback just served to make the likelihood of success even more remote.

Usually he went into his missions against Quentin fairly confidently; influencing a time-line required a very delicate touch and was incredibly difficult to do, which meant that it was very easy to disrupt - all Sam had to do was make sure that Quentin couldn't carry out his plan, he didn't have to make any changes himself. A prime example was the work he'd done previously as Sir Sam - he'd been able to enlist the help of Scotland Yard and the entire Metropolitan Police Force in looking for Quentin and Diana without having to worry about them remembering doing it after he left, in fact it was better that they didn't.

This mission was looking more and more impossible to carry out, though; he was lagging dangerously far behind Quentin, had been deprived of both Ralph and Rachel, couldn't count on the army, and now it seemed he had been left without the means of even getting to Johannesburg.

Fortunately he was presented with a solution to the last part at least.

'A horse and provisions have been made ready for you, though, sir. It's a fairly hard a ride to Johannesburg, about three hundred miles, but there is a clear road that the miners use.' Jessup frowned as he looked at Sam's black suit. 'If you think you're up to it.'

While it wasn't ideal, it was Sam's only chance and he seized it willingly. 'I should be able to handle it.'

The man smiled uncertainly. 'This way then, sir.'

An hour later Sam was dressed in a brand new khaki army uniform, complete with pith helmet and cavalry boots, which Jessup had bullied out of army stores for him, and was riding towards Johannesburg on a large black gelding. His gear turned out to include a rifle and a large pistol, as well as a bedroll and enough food for the week that it would take him to get to his destination, although he could always supplement it by hunting if he needed to. The road, little more than a track, followed a river, which meant that he didn't have to carry as much water as he normally would have done. The river was called the Vaal, according to the map the army had supplied him with, and it ran most of the way northeast from Kimberley to Johannesburg until it veered further east, making it very hard for him to get lost, at least for the first couple of hundred miles.

All in all it looked like things were picking up slightly and, in spite of the difficult task ahead of him, he was feeling moderately cheerful as he trotted along.

He passed a few people during the day and they called out greetings to him as they passed, but beyond that all he had to accompany him were the sounds of the nearby water and the wildlife. It was very pleasant indeed and he would have dearly loved to have shared the experience with Rachel.

It turned out that Sir Sam did in fact know how to ride, and quite well, but that didn't stop the bouncing up and down from doing awful things to his inner thighs and posterior and when he got off the horse that evening to make camp for the night he could hardly walk.

He found a flat piece of ground near a bend in the river where the bank sloped gently down to the water, allowing him to lead the horse down to it. After he had watered and fed it, he tied it to a tree and groomed it, then decided to take a bath to wash away the heat and the dust of the day.

He stripped and waded a few steps upriver then sat against the bank with his lower body in the water. He laid back and closed his eyes, letting the water soothe his aching muscles and cool the burning sensations in certain delicate places caused by the friction with the saddle.

The tranquillity of the day, the gentle burbling of the water and the hours of being on his own put him in a relaxed mood and he found himself dozing off.

The mood was broken and his eyes flew open when a twig broke with a sharp snap from close behind him.

He leapt up, simultaneously spinning and dropping into a fighting crouch so as to confront whoever it was, cursing himself for his lapse in judgement; he had completely forgotten the fact that there were enemies nearby and not only had he dropped his guard, but he had left all of his weapons in his camp - they were only five metres away, but that might as well have been miles for all the good they were going to do him.

'Well, that's one *hell* of a greeting.'

Diana was standing directly behind him. She threw away the twig that she had broken deliberately, then put her hands on her hips and looked him up and down with a huge, appraising grin.

She, like he himself, was naked.

She lifted her arms up and turned in place. 'As you can see I'm completely unarmed. You don't have to feel so threatened.'

Sam watched her warily as she rotated slowly, deliberately displaying herself to him, unnecessarily showing him a lack of weapons that had already been patently obvious.

When she was facing him again she dropped her arms. She raised an eyebrow and her mouth pulled sideways in a smirk as her eyes flickered downwards briefly.

Sam finally tore his eyes away from her and gazed into the dense trees, searching for other enemies that he knew had to be there somewhere.

'Mind if I join you?'

His attention was dragged back to her momentarily as she walked down the slope and into the river, but he quickly went back to scanning the nearby area for anyone else. He remained in alert as Diana sat down in the water next to him with a sigh.

'You don't think I'd take a bath like this if anybody else was watching, do you? I'm not that kind of girl.' She laughed gently.

Sam took a second to think about it. While he wouldn't put it past her or Quentin to use this as a tactic to distract him, they could just as easily have killed him while he was relaxing in the river, or waited until he was asleep. He slowly straightened from his crouch and turned, covering himself with his hands; unnoticed, his body had betrayed him somewhat and while nudity was one thing, *that* was quite another.

Diana propped herself up on her elbows, arching her back slightly to look up at him. She laughed again. 'Why so shy, Sam? Rachel said that you'd spent the last two years running around naked. I thought you'd be used to it.'

Sam tore his gaze away from her breasts and swallowed nervously. 'Rachel told you that?'

'Oh yes.' She winked. 'Rachel and I have spoken about you many times. Now, I don't suppose you have any shampoo, do you? My hair gets so frizzy in this climate...' She closed her eyes and settled back into the water.

Sam waded out into the river a bit so that he could stand in front of her, that way he could keep an eye on her and the tree line at the same time with the added benefit that his hips were below the water as well.

'What are you doing here, Diana?'

'Quentin told me to keep an eye on you.' Diana opened one of her eyes and looked up at him with a grin. 'I'm just obeying his orders. To the letter. I swear I'm on my own, there's nobody waiting to shoot you while your attention is, ahem, *elsewhere*. So why don't you just sit down and relax, while it's still warm enough to appreciate the water; the sun's going to be down soon and it gets pretty damn cold pretty quickly here.'

Eventually, Sam realised that there wasn't much he could do if she was lying to him; it wasn't as if he could stay awake for the whole week. He sat down a couple of metres away from her, but didn't lie back or close his eyes again. 'I'm not sure that this is exactly what Quentin meant.'

Diana smiled. 'I'm pretty sure that it isn't, but I didn't want to be shadowing you along the road for the next few days or so; it's much more fun to have a conversation. So, how have you been?'

'Small talk? Really?'

She gave him a frank look. 'Would you prefer to get straight down to it, then?'

Sam coloured and looked away.

She laughed. 'Oh, my, you really have only been with one woman, haven't you?'

Sam looked back at her and his face hardened, he'd had enough with her games. 'Yes. And that's the way it's going to stay.'

'That's a shame.' Diana sighed exaggeratedly. 'But it's not why I'm here.' She shifted and sat up in the water so she could look at him properly in the fading light. The playfulness disappeared from her face and was replaced by an earnest look. 'I want to help you.'

Sam blinked, surprised by her sudden change in mood.

Rachel had spoken to him about her last meeting with Diana before the woman had been called away to start working on this mission and told him how much she had changed, how there was another side to her that she hadn't expected. Sam hadn't quite believed it, but it seemed to be true after all.

The last time he had been face to face with Diana had been in Victorian London. He'd been her captive for days, been tortured and mistreated by the Twins while they waited for Quentin to arrive, then almost murdered by him. Admittedly, she'd been instrumental in saving his life and had been giving them as much information as she could to help them stop the Illuminati since, but he was still sceptical about the truth behind her supposed defection; he still half expected it to be some kind of trick, for there to be some kind of plan behind it that would lead to the destruction of the Displacers.

However, even though he was suspicious of her motives, he was in a desperate situation and needed all the help he could get. 'What do you want in return?'

He was surprised again when she looked away and spoke in a voice that he could barely hear over the gently gurgling water. 'I want your forgiveness.'

There was silence for a second and then Diana shivered. 'I'm cold.' She stood up and walked away from the river towards where she must have left her horse and clothes.

Sam couldn't help himself and watched her go. She really was a very good looking woman; her body was a lot softer than Rachel's, more rounded out in interesting places and her skin seemed to glow white in the fading light.

He immediately, and embarrassingly, found that he wasn't as acclimatised to nudity as he thought he was and gave himself thirty seconds to calm down before splashing out of the river and grabbing his clothing.

After dressing, he set about collecting wood to build a fire and soon had a good blaze going. The sun had gone down fully now and it had gotten dark surprisingly quickly. The temperature had dropped dramatically so he took the time to warm himself; he hadn't dried before dressing so his clothes were damp and the last thing he needed was to fall ill on top of everything else.

Diana appeared out of the night. She stopped on the edge of the glow of the firelight and spoke softly. 'Do you mind if I share your camp tonight?'

'Please.'

She tied her horse up and saw to its needs, then came over to the fire, bringing food and a pot with her. 'Shall I cook?'

'If you promise not to poison me.'

She laughed but didn't reply, just gave him a smile that was almost shy and went to fill the pot with water from the river.

Sam sat in silence and watched her cook. It looked like she had been doing it for years, instinctively knowing how to hang the pot over the fire and prepare the ingredients and in quick order she had dried beans and vegetables in the pot and there a few strips of meat sizzling on a stone in the fire.

'You're good at that.'

'Wait until you taste it before passing judgement!' She gave him a smile, then turned back to her work.

The smile gradually disappeared from her face as she stirred the pot, though. 'Quentin always relegates me to the rank of cook whenever we're on a mission; he prefers to do as much of the work as he can himself. He doesn't trust either me or my abilities.'

'I'm surprised he's let you out of his sight now, then.'

Diana shrugged. 'I don't think he had a choice. He thought that he was going to have a free run at this mission because of the ambush, but now he's having to do his own work as well as that of the Twins. Somebody had to keep an eye on you and he doesn't particularly want my help with the real mission, so this is as good a way as any of getting me out of his hair.'

'I'm actually glad he sent you.'

She looked up at him in surprise. 'Really?'

'Yes.' Sam grinned cheekily. 'I'm not a very good cook.'

Her face screwed up in mock hatred and she pointed her spoon at him. 'Don't make me use this.'

Sam laughed and, after a few seconds of mock scowling, Diana joined in.

It didn't take long for the meal to be ready and they ate in companionable silence.

Sam stole glances at her while he tucked into the surprising good food, still trying to reconcile the friendly woman with the one who had kept him prisoner, watched him beaten, then delivered him to Quentin. He got the feeling that if he scratched the surface of her emotions he would find the damaged little girl he'd uncovered when he'd tried to manipulate her during his captivity. However, the more he got to know her, the less he wanted to do that and the more he found he wanted to protect her.

She was in drab clothing, much like the Boers had been, but somehow she made the simple brown shirt and skirt seem almost elegant. Her deep red hair shone in the firelight and her green eyes twinkled every time she smiled. Despite himself, Sam found he was very attracted to her.

After they had eaten, Sam took the utensils down to the river and washed them. When he came back to the camp he found that Diana had laid out their bedrolls on opposite sides of the fire, as if she thought he wouldn't want to be near her and was already lying in hers, staring at the dying embers of the fire.

Sam put away the cooking things and then pulled his bedding closer to hers. He lay down in it facing her and neither of them said anything for a long while as they gazed at each other.

Eventually, Sam propped himself up on his elbow. 'If you had the opportunity, would you join us? Join the Displacers?'

She replied instantly, without any hesitation. 'Yes.'

Sam nodded and smiled, then laid back down, suddenly very tired. 'Goodnight, Diana.'

'Goodnight, Sam.'

As soon as it started to get light the next day they packed up the camp and loaded the horses. It took very little time and less than ten minutes after waking up they were on the road. Sam couldn't afford to waste any time; he had already lost a couple of days in Cape Town and was lagging further behind every minute - according to Diana, the Boers had organised changes of horses for Quentin, which meant that could push harder than Sam and would be in Johannesburg much quicker. All in all he would probably have close to a four day head start on his campaign against the mining companies.

The ride was agony for Sam from the first minute. He was still sore from the hours on the horse the day before and he shifted continually in the saddle, trying to find the position that was the least painful.

Diana saw his discomfort and laughed. 'I take it you haven't done much riding.'

He grimaced as he lifted his weight off the saddle again. 'No. Why, have you?'

She nodded. 'Quite a lot, actually; it's one of my hobbies and I have my own horse stabled just outside London. You should really take Rachel out riding sometime. There are some beautiful trails around Spain. It would be very romantic and I think she needs a bit more romance in her life - hitting her to prove you love her might have been enough for the cavemen, but we're in the twenty-first century now, Sam.'

She laughed as Sam blushed.

'I'll give you a few pointers today and hopefully it won't be as hard for you. And if you like I'll give you a nice rub down this evening to soothe away your pains.' She gave him a lascivious smile and leaned across the gap between the horses to pat him softly on the upper thigh.

She laughed again as Sam shifted in the saddle; suddenly uncomfortable in more ways than one, but then suddenly she turned serious. 'Sam, I'm not going to be able to ride with you for the entire way because the closer we get to Johannesburg the more likely it is that someone will see us, but if you don't mind I'll like to stay with you for at least a few days.'

'That's fine with me. Honestly, I'd be glad for the company.'

'Thank you.' Diana smiled gratefully, then something occurred to her. 'I keep meaning to ask; is Rachel alright? I saw the beating she took - it looked nasty and I know the Twins don't hold back when they're riled up.'

'Yeah, I found that out too...'

Diana hung her head in shame. 'I'm so sorry about that... I'm sorry about what I let them do to you.'

'You did your best to hold them back.'

'I should have done more. And I could have done more to stop what happened to Rachel.'

Sam shook his head. 'You did enough, believe me, and it's better for us if you don't blow your cover; it'll save more lives in the long run. And there's no need to worry about Rachel; she'll be fine. She got hurt worse than that in Sparta.' Sam realised that he was trying to convince himself as much as Diana and he swallowed before continuing, his voice catching slightly. 'I sent her home; there was no way she was going to be able to make this journey.'

'You sent her home?' Diana frowned. 'You should have left her in Cape Town to recover, that way there'd be less questions when you got home.'

Sam shook his head. 'She'll get much better care back in the present and besides, thanks to that guy who Quentin killed, we have to deal with Ralph's gunshot wound anyway. Who was he, by the way? Quentin called him Davis, right? I've never heard of him.'

'Grant Davis is, sorry, *was*, the leader of another of the Illuminati crews. The Master lumped us with him just for this mission, to keep an eye on Quentin.'

Sam smiled wryly. 'He didn't look like a very nice person.'

She laughed. 'You don't get to lead one of the Master's teams if you're nice, Sam and it says a lot about his character that he was the one chosen to keep tabs on our mission; the Master would never have sent someone who he didn't think could deal with Quentin, or make a tough decision if necessary. He was all smiles and niceties on the outside, but I could tell that deep down he was evil and he proved me right when he shot Quentin's father.'

'Why did Quentin get so angry about that? Wasn't he going to kill us all anyway?'

'He was only going to kill you and Rachel, he was going to leave his father alive. He said that he wasn't a threat, that he was an incompetent fool and that he was going to be an Elder soon anyway.'

'Ralph has a similarly low opinion of his son.'

'That won't change if he ever reads my reports on the girly fight that he had with Davis. I take it you didn't see much of it?'

'I caught the start of it, but I was a little bit busy after that.'

'That's a shame, because it's an image that I will enjoy replaying in my mind for many years.'

Sam laughed, but then looked sharply at her. 'I take it you didn't know about the ambush before you came here.'

The smile instantly disappeared from Diana's face and was replaced by something approaching alarm. 'No, of course not! I swear! It was a surprise to all of us when Quentin brought us to Cape Town months earlier than we'd planned instead of the village near Johannesburg.'

It was obvious that it meant a lot to her for him to believe her and he chose to do so; Rachel and James could make sure it was the truth later by questioning her thoroughly. 'So, was his not telling you about his plans another example of the micromanagement you were talking about? Or does Quentin suspect you?'

Diana smiled. 'Quentin has no idea that I'm in bed with the enemy.'

Sam raised his eyebrows at her terminology, but remained silent as she continued.

'I don't think he can even conceive of the idea of one of us betraying him; in his mind we are so subservient to his will that it would never occur to us to do anything beyond exactly what he says.'

Sam rode in silence for a while, taking in the information on his rival, the man he saw as his nemesis. He had known right from the start that there was something not quite right about Quentin, but the more he heard about him the more he realised the slim grasp that the man had on his sanity. And they had seen a glimpse of his true face in the warehouse, when he had killed Davis.

'Do you know if he's changed his plans at all, now that things are different?'

She shook her head. 'He left me behind as soon as he could, but I don't think he will; once he settles on a plan he tends to stick with it. He assumes that since he came up with it then there can't be any better alternative. One thing you can say about Quentin is that he doesn't lack in self-belief, which served him very well until you came along.'

Diana turned in the saddle to give Sam a warning look. 'No matter how many times you've defeated him, you mustn't underestimate him; there is a reason why he became the Master's top agent so quickly - he is smart, he is devious, he is ruthless and he is extremely dangerous. He will definitely kill you if he has the chance.'

'I kind of got that impression from the first time I met him, but I must admit I have lost a lot of my respect towards him. I'll try not to take him too lightly in future.'

'Good, because I really don't want anything to happen to you. Or Rachel.'

Diana said Rachel's name with such emotion that Sam was surprised. He glanced at her and for a second it seemed that there was something more behind her words than simply a desire not to see her get hurt, but anything beyond that was instantly gone as she gave him a wide smile.

'One thing that you do have in your favour is time; Quentin is in a hurry. He has a very tight schedule because of the limits imposed by our Leap, sorry, *Displacement* to Victorian London at Christmas, and that deadline is fast approaching.'

'So, another win condition for me could just be to delay him long enough.' Sam paused. He realised that there was a distinct hole in his knowledge. 'Um, what exactly happens when we get to the point where we already have a presence in the time-line?'

Unlike Rachel, who took every opportunity to tease him when he didn't know something that he should, Diana just gave him a serious answer. 'When that happens we just immediately get forced back home.'

'We don't have to do anything like travel to London so that we're there when our, um, previous presence is there, uh here...?' Sam trailed off; he was quickly getting into areas that were still confusing to him and for some reason he didn't want to make himself look like an idiot in front of Diana.

Again, though, she breezed past any ignorance he was showing. 'No, for some reason we don't have to worry about anything like that.'

'Oh, OK.'

They rode in silence for a while, enjoying the countryside and each other's company.

Sam racked his brain, trying to work out what he was going to do, but it didn't matter which angle he approached the problem from, he just got stuck. Eventually, he swallowed his pride and decided to ask for help.

'I have no idea how I'm going to beat Quentin. Every other time it's been more of a personal battle between us, even when he had the Bedouin in Egypt. But this time he's got a small army of Boers! Your message said twenty, right?'

Diana nodded. 'Give or take.'

'So, how the hell am I supposed to do anything about that? I can't fight them on my own and I won't have anything in the way of back up because the English army won't come in case they start another war. I don't know if there are any police, but they would probably sympathise with the Boers because of the political tensions in South

Africa right now and there's nothing I can do to get the Boers to abandon Quentin for the same reason.'

As much as he fought to stay calm, he knew that the frustration and worry was making its way into his voice. Not for the first time he wondered at the twist of fate that had put the job of saving the world in the hands of a teenage boy, who hadn't even been strong enough to stop himself being bullied.

Diana pulled her horse close so she could put her hand back on his leg and looked at him with concern. 'Sam, I just spent a month with your grandfather. We didn't spend all of that time just talking about me and the Illuminati - he spoke about *you* all the time; he gets quite talkative after a couple of fingers of whiskey in the evenings.'

Sam laughed gently. 'Yeah, it does seem to loosen his tongue a bit.'

'He knows how much pressure you are under and he is fully aware that it hasn't lessened at all, despite the Prophecy saying that you weren't the Changer, but only the Diviner.'

He looked at her, surprised; it really sounded like something that James would say, but he couldn't believe that he would say it to Diana and not to either him or Rachel.

'He's worried about you, Sam. He can see that you're taking all of the responsibility onto yourself and he wishes that he knew how to make you see that you don't have to; that you have friends and family there for you, who can help you and can take some of the weight from your shoulders.'

She lowered her voice until it could barely be heard over the sound of the horses. 'He also knows that you can't always win and he wishes he could tell you that it's OK to fail.'

Sam was struck speechless and he turned away from her to stare down at the horse's head bobbing up and down in front of him. If what she said was true, then why was he only now hearing this? And from someone who had been an enemy, who was *still* technically his enemy? Why hadn't James said anything? Or Andrew? Or Rachel? Had the Displacers become so desperate that they felt that they couldn't tell him it was alright for Quentin to beat him, for fear that somehow they would make it happen? Or of him not continuing to try his hardest to win?

Diana tapped his leg, dragging his attention back to her. 'That was what your grandfather said, but I have my own opinion to add - you are a remarkable man, Sam, and you have managed incredible things in the last year. You have succeeded where all others have failed and done things that nobody would have thought possible, but I don't think it's *only* due to your undeniable talent. I believe it's because of what's in here.' She put her hand on his chest. 'I believe it's because you care, Sam. You care, more than anybody else I know. Even when you were my captive and you were trying to manipulate me into releasing you, you still couldn't bring yourself to just destroy me emotionally.'

'You knew?'

'Of course I did!' She laughed at the shock on Sam's face. 'I'm not as naive as you think I am! I could tell you were holding back because you didn't want to hurt me and that's one of the things that makes me love you so much.'

Diana's mouth snapped shut and the smile instantly dropped from her face as she realised what she had just said.

Sam had no idea what to say and he just looked at her, reading the sudden pain in her face. He was only just coming to terms with his love for Rachel and what that meant to him and, while he realised that he did have feeling for this woman as well, he had no idea what they really were. He briefly toyed with the idea of stalling for time while he unravelled his feelings, or even trying to brush it off and pretend it had never happened, but quickly realised that he couldn't; the one thing he did know was that she deserved an honest answer from him and he would do his best to provide her with one, no matter how much it hurt her.

He was prevented from doing so, though, when Diana cried out in anguish and spurred her horse forwards, galloping ahead of him, mortified.

Sam cursed under his breath, not because he had to catch her and tell her that it was alright, but because he wasn't sure what the chase was going to do to his backside.

He kicked his gelding into action and went after her, but she was a much better rider than him and she soon disappeared into the distance among the trees. He persevered, though; not only because he didn't want to lose her completely, but also he didn't think she should be on her own.

After about ten minutes he caught a glimpse of her horse through the trees that had been thinning out as the road met up with the Vaal again and he reined in to investigate. There was no sign of Diana, but she wouldn't have gone very far without her mount and it was tied up, so she couldn't have had an accident.

He left his horse next to hers and made his way towards the river.

He found her just upstream, sitting on a rock with her arms wrapped around her knees, staring at the water.

She looked up as he walked over to her and smiled. She looked her normal happy self again, but he could tell that she wasn't.

During the brief gallop Sam had been too busy making sure he didn't fall off to organise his thoughts, but seeing her there he somehow knew what he had to say. He sat down next to her, reached out to take her hand in his and took a deep breath.

'Please, don't say it.' Her voice was soft, melodic and so full of sorrow that his heart almost broke for her.

'I'm sorry.'

'Don't be.' She squeezed his hand. 'I know that you love Rachel, I knew it before you did, I think; it was obvious, even back in London, whenever I saw you together - there's something special about you two, something that just felt *right* as soon as I saw it. So, yes, I know that I can never come between you, but I can't help how I feel.'

She looked at him, her eyes shining with tears. 'I love you, Sam, you're the best, kindest person I know and I need you to do me a favour.'

'What?'

Diana sniffed and wiped the tears from her cheeks as she stood up. 'I need you to forget I ever said such a stupid thing and get back on your horse; we have a madman to stop.'

She gave him one of her cheeky grins, the grins that were so much like the ones that Rachel gave him and yet so different, and he laughed. He let her pull him to his feet and together they went back to their horses.

'Oh, and one more thing, Sam.'

'What's that?'

'If you ever tell Rachel about me crying I will kill you.'

Neither of them mentioned the conversation again, although Sam did catch Diana watching him a few times when she thought he wasn't looking. They bathed in the river every night, whenever it was close enough to the road for them to camp beside it, doing so comfortably together and, to Sam's surprise, Diana managed to refrain from making any more lewd comments.

She supplemented their food stores by trapping small animals and finding edible plants. She even caught a couple of fish in a pool by tickling them, throwing them onto the bank with whoops of joy while Sam watched, amazed. He could have helped out; he'd learned how to fish in Okinawa, but he found that he was enjoying watching her too much. She was truly at home in the wild, something that astounded

Sam; she had always struck him as such a typical city dweller, but he now saw that there was a side to her that he hadn't suspected existed.

While Sam didn't feel the same bond with Diana as he did with Rachel, or ever quite manage to fully relax around her, he did find her to be good and fun company and the next four days passed quickly and pleasantly. He found himself wondering occasionally what might have happened if he'd met Diana first instead of Rachel, a train of thought that he quickly cut off each time it occurred to him.

On the fifth morning, Diana told him that it was getting too risky to stay together and that they had to split up - the closer they got to Johannesburg, the higher the possibility that there would be Boer scouts out looking for them.

Their goodbye wasn't emotional, it was just a parting of ways. Neither of them particularly wanted to make very much of it so they hugged, wished each other luck and then Sam got on his horse and rode away.

Diana remained where she was and watched him go, letting him go ahead so that she could trail him at a safe distance; it had to look as if she were really spying on him.

It took Sam three more days to get to Johannesburg.

He felt a lot less secure on his own and when he left the river behind it only got worse because he also left behind the comfort he hadn't known he had been drawing from its constant companionship.

He looked back over his shoulder many times during those days, but he never once caught a glimpse of Diana or anyone else trailing him, even when he got to the top of a hill and could see for miles behind him. Unless he'd lost her it was another demonstration of her competence and he resolved to ask her who she had learned her tracking and survival skills from.

As Sam neared Johannesburg, there were more and more signs of civilisation - the emptiness gave way to farmland and there were cattle, sheep and the occasional building down dirt paths leading from the road - until finally he reached what he assumed was the beginnings of Johannesburg itself.

With no plan and no real idea of what to do he decided to head to the centre of town, hoping that he would at least be able to find out what the current situation was.

He rode for a couple of hours through random scatterings of tents and shacks, then into a kind of suburb with rickety looking houses. It seemed that thousands of people had made their way there in order to make a living, and very few of them looked happy. Sam thought back to the pictures he'd seen of the slums and the history he'd read of the city before Displacing and wished he could do something to change it, but a city built on gold was one that was built on greed, with the powerful treading on the weak in order to build their wealth and, while there was still gold to mine, there was nothing to be done about it.

The centre turned out to be a market square that was home to milling cattle and horse-drawn wagons surrounded by a small collection of wooden buildings, which were only really distinguishable from any of the other shops or houses that the city was comprised of because they were slightly bigger and seemed more permanent. Johannesburg had only been founded a couple of years before and Sam had still been expecting something far more impressive after seeing the images of the modern day city. There were buildings in construction everywhere, though, and it was easy to see how it would eventually grow into the largest city in South Africa. However, at that point in time it had more of an air of a frontier town, nothing like Cape Town, which had been large and sprawling, or Kimberley, which had looked like something out of a silent movie with its grand stone buildings.

Sam tied his horse to a post outside the largest of the buildings, the town hall presumably, and was just about to make his way inside when a familiar voice called out.

'Sir Sam!'

He turned to find Watkins waving at him from across the street. The clerk came bounding over to Sam, a bounce in his step and a wide smile that was at odds with the image Sam had of the last time he had seen the man: quivering in fear and hiding behind the desk in his office. There was a sense of confidence and enthusiasm in him that hadn't been there before either.

Sam smiled and nodded in greeting. 'It seems that a ride in the country has agreed with you, Mr Watkins.'

'Indeed, I feel like a different man!'

Sam realised that he had completely forgotten about the clerk in the ten days since the ambush at the warehouse and he had disregarded the fact that he did indeed still have some support in the time-line; Ralph's preparations had at least given him this man. He just wasn't sure what use he would be able to make of him.

'What news do you have, Mr Watkins?'

'Well, you were right, Sir Sam; three of the companies on your list have sold their concessions and left. I don't know what kind of pressure your man is bringing to bear, but it seems to be highly effective.'

'Damn.' Sam was disappointed; he was too late to stop Quentin entirely, but only three mines lost to the man wasn't as bad as he'd feared it would be and there were a fair few left that he might still be able to do something about.

'Yes, well put, Sir Sam, "damn" indeed! I'm afraid I got here too late to put in a bid on the first two. However...'

Watkins pulled a large piece of paper from his ever-present briefcase and held it out to Sam with a grin. 'I did manage to outbid them for this - it's one of the richest claims in the field and I was very lucky to find the owner receptive to my explanations of who was behind the pressure and why he should sell to me and not Price.'

Sam laughed in delight as he scanned the document. Quentin had been so worried about what Sam was going to do that either missed or disregarded the countermeasures his father had put into motion the month before, the countermeasures that had been quietly working away behind the scenes to foil him all on their own.

Now he knew why Watkins was so cheerful; he was in his element, with all the wheeling and dealing that must happen after Quentin had applied his violently persuasive methods - he was very obviously a born administrator and Ralph had done a fantastic job of manoeuvring him to where he could best be used.

'Oh, well done, Mr Watkins! Very well done!' He handed the deed back to the clerk, who stashed it back in his case.

'Thank you, sir! And as for the rest of the targets, I have called a meeting with them this evening, if you'd care to attend? I am going to explain what had been happening and your presence would be a wonderful boost to both my own credibility and that of the threat. Many of them already know that something untoward is happening and have begun to take measures, although somewhat ineffectually, but with your aid I am confident that we can nip these intimidation tactics in the bud. Hopefully, that should serve to render your murderer quite harmless and then it will just be down to you to find and arrest the man!'

'It looks like you have everything well in hand, and this meeting of yours should just be the icing on the cake.' Sam chuckled and shook his head; he still had to deal with Quentin, but it seemed that his primary mission had been all but taken care of while he'd been enjoying himself on a pleasant ride with Diana and while the loss of two mines certainly hurt, it was compensated for by the gain of one - a satisfactory outcome considering the circumstances and it wasn't just logic telling him that; he could also feel it somehow.

'The meeting isn't for another few hours, sir. If you like we can get you a room in the hotel and you can freshen up after your long journey?'

'Well, thanks to your exemplary efforts it seems that I do indeed have time to put my feet up for a while! Lead on, Mr Watkins!'

Quentin looked up as Diana sauntered in.

'Well?'

'What kind of greeting is that?'

'The only one you're going to get. Make your report.'

'Sam Vives has just arrived in Johannesburg.'

'Good.' He nodded and looked back down at the maps spread out in front of him.

'You don't seem very happy. Has something gone wrong with your masterful plan?'

He glanced up at her from under eyebrows that creased in an annoyed frown.

She gave him a half smirk and watched him fume.

'Of course not, my intimidation tactics have been working perfectly.'

'Really?' She raised an eyebrow, feigning innocence.

'Yes, we already have two mines under the control of our agents.'

'That's interesting, because I heard a rumour that you had caused three mines to sell up, but that our enemies had managed to snatch one out from under you. I'm *very* glad to hear that isn't true.'

Quentin snarled and gave her a look of pure hatred, but made no further comment.

Diana sauntered over and glanced curiously at the maps that Quentin and the Boer leader, Andries Kriel, were poring over. There were half a dozen of them, but they were most interested in two in particular: one was of the centre of town, with the individual buildings surrounding the town square marked and labelled, and the other was the floor plan of a large building.

'What's all this?'

Quentin sighed and looked up at her again. He was irritated by her interruption, but nonetheless took the opportunity to expound on how brilliant he was, just as Diana had expected him to.

He opened his arms wide to encompass the papers on the table. 'This is the culmination of my plan. We may have had a small setback, but tonight all of that changes - the Displacers and their agents have done our work for us and are gathering the owners of all of the companies that we are targeting in the town hall. They think, rightly so, that if they get these people to band together, then we won't be able to intimidate them. We're not going to wait for them to join forces, we're going to attack them when they're all holed up tight, like fish in a barrel, then we'll hold them captive until they sign their concessions over to us.'

Diana turned her head to look at the Boer, who was scowling angry. 'You don't approve of the plan?'

'No, I don't like it one bit; it is one thing to threaten these people in their homes, where at most they have a couple of people with shotguns, it is quite another to storm the town hall in daylight.' He waved his hand at the list of men who would be attending the meeting. 'These people do not travel alone, they will be bringing guards with them. And we will most likely have to handle the local authorities as well.'

'It's nothing you can't handle and you have been more than compensated for any inconvenience.'

Quentin smirked at Diana as he responded to the man's doubts and she knew that he was fully expecting there to be casualties on both sides and he didn't care as long as he got the results he wanted.

The Boer hissed at him in anger. 'I have already lost my brother to this plan, do not think that there is any amount of money that can make up for that. The only reason that I am still helping you is because you are giving me the chance to kill Englishmen and take away the resources they need to make war on us.'

'And now you also have your chance to get revenge for your brother's death.'

Diana looked up at Quentin in alarm, did he know that it was her that had shot the Boer to stop him from killing Rachel?

Quentin didn't look at her, though, he just continued to impose his will on Kriel. 'The man who killed him will be at that meeting tonight: Sir Sam Vives is a prime example of the English aristocracy who have made your people suffer. He is yours to do with as you please - call it a bonus.'

Kriel nodded and Diana saw that he was convinced; vengeance was a powerful motivator and Quentin knew that very well.

As Kriel and Quentin turned back to their plans, ignoring her, she looked around the building that Quentin had chosen to run his campaign from. They were in a large, single-roomed wooden warehouse near the outskirts of the town, a couple of miles from the centre - it was another detail that Quentin had neglected to inform them of before they had Leapt and she had only found it because one of Kriel's men had met her half a day down the road and escorted her there. There were a couple of dozen rough-looking men scattered in small groups around the room. Some were talking in low voices, some of them were eating, but most were laughing quietly and confidently, while they cleaned their guns, displaying a casual competence and familiarity with their weapons that spoke volumes.

Diana swallowed, suddenly very worried for Sam; these men were killers. They had already won one war against the English and, while the attack that Quentin was proposing didn't follow the hit-and-run tactics that the Boer were used to, she knew that they would be more than capable of pulling it off.

She couldn't stay silent, she had to try to talk Quentin out of the plan, and failing that she needed to warn Sam. 'Why go to all this effort? Haven't we got enough with the two mines you've already secured us?'

Quentin sighed and looked up from his planning. 'Of course not!'

He picked up a fist-sized rock from the table. She had taken it for a paperweight, there just to hold down the maps in the slight breeze coming through the gaps in the building's poorly constructed walls, but when he held it up to the sunlight it glinted - it was a nugget of freshly mined gold.

Diana saw the greed in his eyes as he turned it back and forth - a new madness to add to the ones already churning in his brain and she shuddered.

He grinned. 'It's *never* enough.'

Diana nodded, then turned to leave, moving casually, trying not to call attention to herself; she had to get to Sam, to warn him. It was no use, though and she halted when he called out after her. 'And where do you think you're going?'

She turned back and forced a smile. 'I thought I'd take a look around, familiarise myself with the town. That way I won't be so useless when we carry out your plan.'

Quentin shook his head. 'You're not going anywhere; we're moving out in half an hour and I don't want to have to send someone to fetch you when you get lost. Find yourself something to eat, wash your hair, change your underwear, do whatever woman-stuff you need to do, just be ready to leave when I say so.'

Diana nodded and reluctantly went to where her gear had been stowed to start getting ready for an assault that she didn't want to happen.

CHAPTER 13
HAPPY RETURNS

The owners of the gold companies drifted in to the town hall one by one. They were each accompanied by at least one guard, although most brought whole packs, showing that they were already giving credence to the warnings they'd had from Watkins.

Sam was there early with the clerk so that he could greet them as they turned up and he answered the questions they immediately shot at him to the best of his ability, confirming the rumours about the murderer, Quentin Price, and his band of mercenaries.

When everybody had arrived, they made their way into the large well-appointed conference room on the ground floor that had been set aside for them and sat down in high-backed chairs with red velvet cushions around a large, highly polished hardwood table.

Every single person in the room, with the exception of Watkins and Sam, was dripping with gold, rings and pocket watches and dressed in an expensive suit. They smoked thick cigars and drank the whiskey that Watkins had thought to have provided for them.

Sam had decided to sit to one side and allow Watkins to take full control of the meeting; it was the man's area of expertise after all and it would also mean that any changes made in favour of the Displacers would stick. However, as the time passed, he found it harder and harder to stay silent; he found them all very distasteful; they represented the worst side of capitalism and if it weren't for the fact that they were being targeted by Quentin to the detriment of the time-line, he probably wouldn't have lifted a finger to help them.

The men were sceptical of what Watkins was telling them, suspecting a trick of some kind and were unwilling to take any measures that would reduce their profits and possibly weaken them against their Dutch South African competitors. They still didn't really believe it even when he produced a letter from one of their fellows who had been intimidated into selling his mine, laying down the tactics that had been used against him.

It wasn't until the shooting started that they were finally convinced.

Sam was able to piece together the events that he missed afterwards, using information from both the surviving bodyguards and Diana.

Apparently, many of the guards had been drinking heavily, despite being on duty, and when one of them wandered around the corner of the building to empty his bladder, he came face to face with eight Boers stacking crates outside the window of the conference room where the men were meeting, readying their assault.

He apparently fumbled with his rifle and it went off accidentally, blowing apart one of the crates, but not hurting anyone. This naturally caught the attention of the rest of the guards, the more sober of whom came running, guns levelled.

A gunfight broke out and the Boers hastily retreated into the cover of a nearby stable, forced to abandon their objective.

The direct assault on the conference room had been the linchpin of Quentin's plan and, fearing that he was quickly losing control of the situation, he ordered the rest of his men to attack the front of the building and brute force their way in. This had never been part of his original strategy and it caused chaos and indecision among the Boers, who were not prepared to go up against guards who were now ready and waiting for them.

After the first shot, Sam had made all of the men in the meeting room take cover, tilting over the heavy wooden table to create a shield for them to cower behind, then had pulled out his pistol and cautiously made his way to the door. It had taken a while for him to impress on the men the necessity of staying where they were instead of fleeing and by the time he peered out, the firefight had made its way inside. It was going badly for the guards; many of them were down, dead or wounded Sam couldn't tell, and the rest had retreated away from the entrance and taken cover wherever they could. They were liberally spraying bullets in the general direction of their enemy, hitting very little and mostly just wasting their reserves of ammunition.

The Boers had seized the advantage and pushed inside. They had tipped over desks to crouch behind and were taking shots whenever an opportunity presented itself. They were being far more effective than the guards in their efforts and were swiftly whittling down their opposition; finally they had precisely the kind of fight they were used to.

Sam remained in cover behind the door while he took in the situation. The conference room was half-way down the lobby area, so his position was between the two forces and he had clear firing lines at most of the Boers. However, he was reluctant to do anything, because he would draw their fire and put the company owners and Watkins in danger with him.

He spied Diana across the room. She had been one of the first to come in, most likely sent in the first group of attackers by Quentin out of complete disregard for her safety. She was behind a filing cabinet against the far wall, as safe as she could be under the circumstances, and Sam was relieved to see that she was uninjured. She held her rifle at the ready, but as far as he'd seen she hadn't fired a shot. He wondered if she would attempt to provide clandestine help to him if things became desperate, like she had in the warehouse, but quickly realised that he couldn't afford to pin his hopes to it.

The guards were steadily being picked off one by one by the efficient Boers and, despite his precarious position, Sam knew he couldn't wait any longer, he had to act before they either surrendered or fled, leaving the men they had been hired to protect defenceless. He took a deep breath and prepared to open fire, but before he could Quentin appeared.

The young man rushed in through the front door during a pause in the firing and dove awkwardly, although dramatically, behind an overturned desk, shoving aside the Boer who was already there and forcing him to scramble for alternative cover. He ducked down, cowering from the renewed gunfire that his appearance had provoked, safe behind the thick wood.

However, he evidently didn't realise that there was another, more deadly threat at his side.

Sam saw his chance. He could stop the attack and eliminate the danger to the time-line along with any future threat posed by Quentin by completely removing him from existence, all by simply pulling a trigger.

Rachel had always told him that if he was going to shoot at someone then he should aim for the body so as not to miss, but it was a very easy shot and Sam knew he could place the bullet anywhere he wanted, so he took aim at Quentin's head, wanting to be sure of a quick and painless kill.

It was at that moment that the man chose to look in his direction.

The Illuminati agent stopped dead as he met Sam's gaze, his eyes widening in terror as they flicked downwards and saw the pistol.

Their eyes locked again as he looked back up and the world seemed to fade away around Sam until he became oblivious to anything except the life that he held in his hand.

Sam hesitated; it seemed that the shot wasn't so easy after all.

The moment was broken as several Boers passed between the two of them and suddenly Quentin was gone.

Sam found out later that Kriel, the Boer leader had been shot. This broke the morale of the Boers and they retreated immediately, dragging their wounded leader with them.

Sam caught sight of Quentin again as he made his way out of the door and into the sunlight beyond, shooting at the guards and simultaneously berating the Boers as cowards. For a couple of seconds he had another clear shot, but he couldn't take it; it just wasn't in him and he lowered the gun to his side.

The guards, sensing victory in their grasp, surged forwards to chase the Boers.

Diana was slow to move, whether by accident or design, and was left behind in the lobby. She was quickly cut off from escape and surrounded. The guards pointed their weapons at her and, even though she left her gun on the floor when she stood and put her hands up, there was an anger in the men's faces and a desire for vengeance that made Sam panic.

He burst from behind the door and ran over to the guards, shouting for them to put down their weapons. They obeyed, some more reluctantly than others, and Sam grabbed Diana by the arm and led her away from them. He kept his hold on her, making sure she didn't go anywhere, as he watched the guards organising themselves, a couple of them going to make sure that the local authorities were on their way, a few checking on the wounded, and the rest going to make sure that the men in the conference room - the source of their paychecks - knew that they were safe due to their efforts.

Confident that they had everything well in hand, he turned to Diana, gritting his teeth in anger. 'It seems that once more I've been ambushed and you didn't bother to warn me about it.'

She quailed in his grasp and looked up at him with clear fear in her eyes.

With a start he came to his senses and let go of her, blanching slightly at the sight of the bruises he'd left on her arm. 'I'm sorry.'

'I... I... I couldn't get away to warn you, Quentin wouldn't let me.'

Sam took a deep breath to calm himself, then nodded. The death of so many of the guards and Boers hurt, but at least the attack had been foiled. 'Now that Quentin is beaten he'll go home, right? Please tell me this is over.'

Diana shook her head. 'No, it's not. He won't go home yet. Even though he's on his own he'll try to continue his mission.'

Sam sighed, knowing that the violence wasn't over. He pulled his pistol out of its holster and checked it quickly before shoving it back, angrily. 'OK, show me where his hideout is, please.'

Quentin furiously stomped around the room, throwing everything he could find and roaring at the top of his voice. Nothing had been safe from his wrath: the Boer's abandoned gear was broken and strewn in the corners, the maps were torn and trodden into the dirt, he'd even broken the table they had been on into pieces and was using one of its legs to smash the unlit lanterns hanging overhead like piñatas, spraying oil and glass everywhere.

He trampled everything into the ground in his rage, jumping up and down on it to grind it down further.

Sam stood in the doorway watching him.

The spectacle reminded him of the day Violeta had thrown a tantrum when he'd taken away one of her favourite teddy bears. She had been two at the time.

This was far more entertaining.

He could have enjoyed himself for much longer, but he was impatient to end this and get home. He coughed.

Quentin immediately spun around to face the door, squinting, trying to make out who it was, but Sam knew that all the man would see was a dark shadow against the bright light outside.

He slowly walked into the room, stepping carefully so as not to stumble on any of the debris.

The look on Quentin's face when he finally realised it was Sam was almost as amusing as the tantrum had been and he frantically looked around for his gun, but it had been one of the things he had been throwing around and it was on the other side of the room. He started to go for it, but Sam shot the floor in front of him and he skidded to a halt.

'Please don't move.'

Quentin smiled and turned slowly to face Sam. 'This is starting to become a bit of a recurring theme with us, isn't it? Although this is a permutation that we haven't tried yet. I'm interested to see how it turns out this time.'

'It turns out with you going home.'

'No. No, I don't think it does. I think I walk out that door and go on my way.'

Sam raised an eyebrow. 'Have you somehow missed the fact that I have a gun in my hand?'

'Of course not, but I know you won't kill me; you couldn't do it before and you're not going to do it now.'

'You're right.'

Quentin laughed in triumph.

Sam sighed, then smiled pleasantly. He twitched the gun a few millimetres to the side and fired.

Quentin screamed and spun in place, jerked around by the impact of the heavy bullet. He fell to the floor amid the shards of glass from the lanterns, clutching his left arm.

Sam closed the remaining distance to stand over his enemy, the gun now pointed directly at his head. 'Now, are you going to go home or do I have to shoot something else?'

Quentin grimaced in pain and growled up at him. 'I can't go like this! I'll never be able to concentrate.'

'I saw a cattle trough outside, I suggest you use it.'

Sam backed away as Quentin struggled to his feet. As well as the bullet hole in his left bicep he now had numerous scratches from the glass and one particularly large piece was sticking out of his cheek below his eye, a few inches beneath the scar that Sam had given him in Port Royal.

He staggered past Sam and out of the door.

Sam followed, never taking his eye off him or lowering the gun.

Quentin halted beside the trough and turned to snarl at him. 'You're going to regret not killing me, I'm...'

'Shut up, Quentin,' Sam interrupted him. 'And just bugger off already, will you? You're boring me.'

With a last growl Quentin leapt over the side of the wooden trough. There was a huge splash and water cascaded out onto the dirt, turning it to mud, which instantly turned back to dry dirt.

Cautiously, Sam approached the trough, pistol at the ready, but deflated when he saw that Quentin was indeed gone, the water still and stagnant as if it had never been disturbed.

The gun dropped from his grasp and he fell to his hands and knees. He felt sick.

The show of confidence and callousness he'd put on for Quentin had been just that: a show. Despite his threats he knew that he couldn't have killed Quentin and he doubted that he would have been able to shoot him a second time; it had taken the thought of Rachel's unconscious body to work up the courage to do so even once.

He flinched and scrabbled for the gun as a hand came down on his shoulder, but the tension flowed from him when he saw that it was Diana.

'Well, I enjoyed that quite a lot, but I can see that you didn't.'

'Not very much, no.' He struggled to his feet and holstered his pistol. He would have liked to have thrown it away, tossed it as far as he could, but he held onto it just in case.

'It's a shame, really; even though you forced him home he did succeed with his mission. The deeds for two of the gold mines are in the possession of our agents and on their way to London.' She sighed, exaggeratedly and shook her head. 'Unfortunately, the Master isn't going to have an excuse to punish him again.'

'Are you going to go home now?'

She shrugged. 'There's nothing to keep me here... unless you want to go for another ride in the country?' She smiled at him, hopefully.

'I should probably stay to fix the time-line, but now that it's over all I can think about is getting home to Rachel, sorry.'

'I understand.' She smiled sadly. 'So, will I see you in London? I'd love to have dinner with you and Rachel some time. It'll be my treat, we can pretend to be normal for a while.'

Sam looked into her eyes, there was so much hope there, so much longing. How could he possibly say no to her?

Reluctantly he shook his head. 'I'm not sure that would be a good idea. Not until you leave the Illuminati. Or I destroy them.'

Diana nodded, obviously disappointed, but hiding it well.

He tried to soften the blow a bit. 'I think I'm going to go back into town before I leave, just to make sure that everything is taken care of. Would you like to come?'

She saw straight through him, though, and laughed. 'Oh, Sam, you're far too nice.' Before he could react she grabbed the sides of his head and locked her lips to his.

While he didn't exactly kiss her back, he didn't push her away either and after what seemed like an age she gently pulled back and let go of him. 'Ah...' It was a soft sigh, less than a second long, but it managed to convey a world of emotion.

She smiled and looked up at him with beautiful, shining green eyes. 'Hold my hands while I leave? Please?'

Sam lifted his hands and she took them.

'See you soon, Sam Vives.'

'Safe journey, Diana.'

She closed her eyes and he felt her energy building. A minute later she was gone, as if she'd never been there.

Sam went to where they'd left their horses, Diana's mount was no longer there, of course, and he untied his and slowly rode back towards the centre of Johannesburg.

The town hall was in chaos still, the Illuminati's manipulation of the time-line intact. The bodies of the dead had been lined up on the steps of the building with blankets over them and the local authorities were busy getting statements from the surviving guards, while doctors tended the wounded and the few captured Boers were taken to the jail.

Sam walked through it all and into the hall itself. He found Watkins and the businessmen in the boardroom still. The table had been put back in place and they were all seated again, mopping their brows and sighing in relief as they spoke in hushed tones, sipping at the drinks that the clerk had organised to replace the ones that had been spilled in the excitement.

When Sam appeared, Watkins hurried over to him. He had a wide grin on his face and seemed excited. For a second Sam thought it was because he was glad to be alive, but it seemed that the man had been very busy in his absence.

'We did it, Sir Sam! They were so grateful we saved their lives that they spontaneously took a vote and gave us shares in their mines! Only a half a percent each, I'm afraid, but it's better than nothing. I have some men drawing up the papers right now; I want to get their signatures on contracts before they have a chance to change their minds.'

'Oh! That's wonderful news! Well done! I certainly hope you work on commission, Mr Watkins!'

Sam laughed, having meant it as a joke, but the man had a glint in his eye and smiled cheekily as he replied. 'Actually, sir, I do!'

Sam guffawed; Watkins stood to make a hell of a lot of money and his family would be rich for many generations to come.

'Right now they are discussing some kind of mutual assistance pact, so that if anyone does ever threaten them again they will present a unified front against them.'

'Then it seems I am no longer needed.'

'I think not. I can't thank you enough for your assistance, though, sir; I don't know what we would have done if you hadn't uncovered this plot against them in time.'

Sam was confused for a second, but recovered quickly - with Quentin gone, his reason for being there had changed and he was no longer hunting for a murderer. 'It was my pleasure.'

They shook hands and Watkins eagerly went back to the businessmen.

Sam realised that there really was nothing else he needed to be there for and he chuckled to himself, wishing that all his Displacements were as easy as this one had proven to be.

He closed his eyes, concentrated briefly and...

...woke up to James' urgent shout. 'Sam! Report! SAM!'

His eyes flew open as his thoughts shot back to the events of the week before and he kicked himself for not having prepared himself mentally before coming back.

'Rachel!' He ignored James' continuing shouts and leaped up, scrambling past Ralph to get to her. She was unconscious, still holding Ralph's hand, but the arm was now bent at a sickening angle and blood was steadily pouring out of her nose, soaking into her shirt, as her body in the present caught up with the injuries she had sustained in the past.

James jumped out of his armchair and flew across the room to Ralph, whose clothing was also rapidly becoming saturated with blood. 'Damn it, Sam, *tell me what happened!*'

Sam pulled Rachel into his arms and cradled her as he unlinked her hand from Ralph's. He was panicked and had no idea what to do, but James' shouts finally got through to him. 'It was an ambush, they were waiting for us.'

'Goddamn it...' James lifted his gaze from Ralph to look at Rachel. 'What's wrong with her?'

'The Twins beat her up pretty badly.'

The old man assessed her quickly, then growled. 'Then leave her, she'll be fine. Come here and help me with Ralph! NOW!'

Sam reluctantly lay Rachel back onto the sofa. He saw the logic in the old man's words; no matter how he felt for Rachel, she would live, but the same couldn't be said for Ralph.

'Help me get him onto the floor.'

Sam pushed the coffee table out of the way, knocking the tea on its tray flying.

He helped his grandfather lift Ralph down onto the rug and James ripped open the man's clothing to expose the wound. Blood was pumping from it.

'Give me your t-shirt.'

Sam took his school jumper off then pulled his t-shirt over his head.

James snatched it from his hands and folded it quickly. He pressed it into the wound and put Sam's hand over it. 'Keep pressure here while I ring for help.'

Sam did as he was told and James sat back against the sofa. His hands were bloody as he pulled out his phone and smears of it were all over him. The red stains spread to his face as he held his phone to his ear.

'This is James Hudson, serial TH2181, I have a code one at watcher's nest, repeat code one at watcher's nest. Ralph Price. Single gunshot to the abdomen. Rachel Evans, broken right humerus, nose and multiple contusions.'

He hung up, then came back to Ralph, throwing the phone on the floor next to him to free up his hands. 'Let me see.'

Sam let go of the t-shirt. It had been white before, but now it was a deep red. James pulled it gently away from the wound. 'Shit, it's bleeding too much, he won't make it at this rate. Help me roll him onto his side.'

Sam did as he was ordered and James reached underneath the man. 'There's no exit wound, the bullet's still inside. Well, at least we only have one hole to worry about. Put him back down.'

James refolded the t-shirt and put it back on the wound, pressing hard on it.

He was surprisingly calm, which in turn helped Sam to regain his composure and he glanced towards Rachel. She was still unconscious and blood was continuing to pour from her nose, but now that he had gotten over his initial panic he saw that she was breathing easily and there was colour in her cheeks below her blackened and swollen eyes. Her injuries were awful to look at, but in no way life-threatening and she would be fine with rest.

The phone rang and James reached for it. 'Sam, take over, please.'

James adjusted Sam's hands on the t-shirt, making sure he was pressing in the right place, then answered his phone.

'Yes? Yes... Yes... Understood.'

He hung up again. 'The ambulance will be here in a couple of minutes and so will the police. I'm going to have to go and let them in. *Do not* answer any questions about what happened, just act dumb. Understood?'

Sam nodded, but James persisted.

'Sam, this is very important. We have measures in place for exactly this kind of thing but the local authorities will be here first and will naturally ask questions. Our job now is to make sure our friends get treated, but stall the police out until the proper people get here to take care of the mess. Got it?'

'Yes.' His gaze wandered towards Rachel. That arm...

'Sam! Snap out of it!' James slapped him on the face. Hard.

Sam snarled and glared at the old man, but James didn't back down. *'Do you understand?'*

'Yes! I understand!'

The old gentleman smiled. 'Good. That's better; these two don't need you moping around feeling sorry for yourself. Hang onto that anger and use it to keep yourself alert.'

The doorbell rang and James struggled to his feet. 'Hold the fort, I'll be right back.'

Things happened very quickly after that.

Two pairs of medics rushed in, one pair lifted Rachel straight onto a gurney and took her away, while the others started pumping blood into Ralph before doing the same, accompanied by James. Sam desperately wanted to go with Rachel, but he was held back by two stern-looking policemen, big men who saw the bullet wound, made a call on their radios, then watched Sam suspiciously until another man arrived shortly afterwards, a swarthy detective in a cheap suit who made Sam sit in one of the armchairs and started shooting questions at him in Catalan.

He did his best to stall them, as James had said, but the detective was very persistent and he felt himself getting more and more nervous, quickly getting to the point where he would tell him anything, so that he could leave to be with Rachel.

It was at this point that the man in the black suit arrived. He was in his forties with short, almost military-cut hair, and he had a way of moving and standing that Sam recognised, having witnessed it in several of the men he'd seen fighting at Symposium, but most especially Harlon Kettle - the man was a killer.

The man pulled the detective into the hallway and dialled a number on his phone, then, when the call connected, he handed it over.

Sam watched as the policeman's posture and attitude changed in quick succession from suspicious, to angry, to alert, and finally to respectful. He nodded and spoke into the phone a few times, then went white and handed the phone back to the man before leaving in a hurry, the two uniformed policemen in tow.

The man spoke into the phone again for a few seconds, then hung up.

He came into the room and looked around, taking in the blood, dirty latex gloves, discarded clothing and broken tea cups with a single glance. 'Good afternoon, Mr Vives. Let's get you back to school, then I'll see about having this mess cleaned up.'

'What?!? No! I need to get to the hospital!' Sam had completely forgotten he was on his lunch break and had a whole afternoon of school left - it was the last thing he wanted to think about; now that the police had gone he could be with Rachel.

The man seemed mildly surprised that Sam was showing resistance. 'Mr Vives, you must go back to school and pretend that none of this is happening.'

'How am I supposed to do that with Rachel hurt?'

The man stared at him and Sam could see his mind working. Obviously this man knew that their work was unusual, even if he didn't know exactly what they did and he was probably wondering why Sam was being difficult rather than doing the logical thing, the thing Sam knew perfectly well what he should be doing, which was pretending to be a normal sixteen year-old boy.

Eventually his face softened and he smiled, the cool and professional mask slipping slightly.

'James told me you were special.'

Sam wasn't in the mood and he snapped back at him. 'Yes, I know, I don't know the rules, I have no idea what I'm doing, I never do what I'm supposed to...'

The man laughed. 'I don't know about any of that, I just know what James told me: that you often do what you believe is *right* rather than what you know you *should* be doing.'

'Is there something wrong with that?'

'No, of course not.' The smile disappeared and the cool, calm and commanding expression returned. 'But in certain situations it is not entirely necessary; Rachel Evans will be fine and she will be waiting for you when you can get away later. There is no need for you to ruin the life you still have with your family quite yet. She wouldn't want that, would she?'

Reluctantly Sam had to agree. 'I guess not.'

'Good. Now, there are clean clothes for you in the bathroom, go wash and change as quick as you can and then we'll see you back to school. Leave your dirty ones in the bath, they will be disposed of later.'

He stripped his blood spattered shoes and clothes off, dropped them into the corner of the room and showered quickly.

The clothes were sealed in a plastic bag that had "Vives School" written on it in black permanent marker. They turned out to be identical to the ones that he wore for school every day: the same school jumper, the same t-shirt and the same trousers, even down to identical trainers. They was all slightly worn, just as the clothes he had on were, and when he saw himself in the mirror he couldn't see any difference to how he'd looked that morning. The true test would be when he got home and his mother saw him, but the people at school would certainly be fooled. Sam was frankly astounded at the level of knowledge and preparation that the clothing betrayed, he was also not a little bit disturbed that the Displacers had known that such preparations would be necessary.

The man was waiting for him outside the door, typing into his phone, but he stopped when Sam appeared and tucked it into his pocket. He looked Sam up and down then nodded in approval. 'Good as new! Let's go, there's a car outside.'

'What about the flat?'

'As I said, it will be taken care of, no need for you to worry. Now, come on, we have to get a move on; lunch break is almost over. Your bag is by the door and there's a few sandwiches you can eat on the way.'

They made their way out onto the street where a huge black SUV with tinted windows and diplomatic number plates was sitting in the middle of the pavement, completely blocking it. Sam got in as quick as he could, fully conscious of the looks they were getting from neighbours and passers-by.

The man got into the back with him and the driver pulled away without needing to be told where they were going.

Sam tucked into the sandwiches, ravenously hungry after the Displacement. He was amused when the man looked away out of the window so as not to watch him eat; it was very much the kind of old-fashioned manners his grandfather had.

His school was close by and the ride took less than five minutes. They parked around the corner, out of sight of the school, legally this time.

The man got out with him and offered his hand. 'Good luck, Mr Vives.'

Sam shook his hand. 'Thank you, uh... I'm sorry, I don't know your name.'

The man smiled and nodded. 'It's better that way.' He got back into the car and it drove away, quickly disappearing around a corner.

Sam managed to sneak back onto school grounds easily enough, barely even needing to use the skills he'd gained in the past. He was still hungry; the sandwich hadn't been nearly enough, but there were only a few minutes of break left so he didn't have time to eat much else. He did manage to shove an entire chocolate bar into his face as he made his way to his next lesson after the bell went, though.

The afternoon was torture. Worse, it was maths.

He was unable to concentrate and was told off several times for constantly fidgeting. He spent the two hours watching the clock, praying for the time to go by.

When the bell finally went for the end of the day he was ready for it and sprinted straight home. He ran to his room, shouting at his mother that he wasn't hungry and that he was going for a run. He got changed as quickly as he could and left again before she could say anything or do anything to stop him.

He was running as soon as he hit the pavement outside his house and he headed straight for the hospital. It was only a couple of miles, but it was uphill all the way and, already tired from the Displacement, he arrived exhausted and out of breath. He stood in the queue for the information desk, gasping for air, but still nervously hopping back and forth from one foot to the other. He received several disapproving looks from a couple of old ladies in the queue in front of him that would usually have been enough for him to calm down and act appropriately, but right then he didn't care, in fact he barely noticed; his mind was on other, more important things than showing restraint in public.

Eventually he found out where Rachel was and ran for the stairs. He called out an apology to the nurse who shouted at him not to run, but didn't slow until he got to her room. He was going to burst straight in, but paused, finally coming to his senses enough to realise that it might be better for her not to make too much noise.

He leaned his head against the wall next to the door and fought to control his breath and his emotions; he wanted a clear head to deal with what he found. When he thought that he was calm enough to control himself, he knocked gently on the door and went in.

James was sitting in the chair by the bed, his head propped in his hand, staring at a motionless Rachel.

His grandfather was so lost in thought that he didn't notice Sam until he was at the foot of the bed.

The old man looked up and smiled. 'Hello, Sam.'

'Hi, Grandad. How is she?'

'She's fine. She still hasn't woken up, but the doctors say that's not unusual after so much trauma. And of course we both know that she's going to be exhausted after the Displacement, don't we?'

Sam nodded, but he was distracted, looking down at Rachel. He flinched when he saw the tubes sticking out of her, the wires attached to her chest under the hospital gown and the cast on her arm, but it was the bandage around her head and the swollen black mess that was what was left of her face that truly scared him.

He went to her side and put his hand around hers as best as he could with the tube sticking out of her veins, blinking as he felt the tears finally coming.

'It looks worse than it is, lad. No need to worry.'

'It's my fault she's like this, though; I froze, Grandad, not just in Andrew's flat when we got back, but during the ambush as well. If it hadn't been for Rachel we would have died there.'

'I think it's about time you gave me your report.'

Sam nodded, but didn't take his eyes from Rachel's face as he told James about the ambush. He told him how Davis had shot Ralph and then been killed by Quentin. He told him how he vaguely remembered Diana helping Rachel, saving her life. He told him, shamefully, how his rage at Rachel's injuries had almost driven him to kill Tessa and how the big woman had only been saved by Rachel's timely distraction.

He explained the rest of the Displacement in far fewer words, telling James no more than the bare facts, and then fell into silence.

James sat, taking it all in without comment, but then, instead of the sympathy that Sam was expecting from him, the sympathy that he always received when something bad happened, the old man's face turned hard, his voice holding a severe tone that Sam had never heard before.

'It sounds to me that you're finally waking up to the reality of your life as a Displacer and it's about bloody time.'

'Grandad? What...?'

He turned to stare at James, unbelieving, searching for the comfort he usually found in his grandfather's gentle eyes, but his expression stayed cold and unforgiving.

'Get over yourself, Sam. You need to *grow up,* boy! Rachel knew exactly what she was doing and deliberately put herself in harm's way for you. We would all do the same, even Ralph, though he would never admit it, because we all know that none of us can even dream of doing what you've been doing instinctively for the last year and a half.

'People die in our line of work, Sam, they die a lot, Rachel knows that, and she knows exactly how important you are to us, so she is desperately trying to make sure that *you're* not the one who dies next. She knows and, unlike you, she has *fully accepted* that *your* life is worth a *hell* of a lot more to us than hers.'

The old man stared at him, his eyes burning into Sam as he almost growled his next words. 'Now, knowing that, don't you think you owe it to her to stop feeling sorry for yourself and be a man for once?'

Sam flinched from the accusing gaze of the Elder, but refused to look away.

There were a few seconds of tense silence as the old man almost quivered in suppressed rage, but then James sighed and slumped in his chair. He suddenly looked exhausted, old, and that shook Sam far more than his cruel words had.

'I'm sorry, that was unfair. It's been a long day, please bear with me.' He took a deep breath and composed himself before continuing. 'Look, what we call the "Prophecy" is actually put together from fragments that we have collected from multiple sources all over the world. It encompasses a far wider range of sayings and writings than that tiny scrap of paper that you brought back from Egypt. Quite a few of the more obscure pieces talk of a *Protector,* a person whose whole purpose is to sacrifice themselves so that the one that is spoken about in the rest of the Prophecy can carry out their task. Rachel has been unknowingly fulfilling that role ever since she became one of us.

'We Elders recognised her obsession with martial arts straight away, we saw that *she* was this Protector, and we knew that it meant that the time of the Prophecy was upon us, that you would be following close on her heels. We knew that the two of you had to be together, that if you were "the one" then you would need her, so we made sure that you met as soon as we could. And then when you hit it off so well, and so quickly, it was just confirmation for us. Surely you must have felt the connection that you have to each other, something that goes far beyond mere physical attraction or feelings?'

'Of course.' Sam nodded. 'But why didn't you tell me about this? Does Rachel know?'

James shook his head. 'How could we tell you? Can you imagine what that knowledge would have done to you, to both of you, if you'd known that Rachel might be destined to die for you? We had to keep it from you so as not to influence any decisions you made; you would never let her be that for you, you would always find a way to keep her out of danger and you know it - it would have changed everything, jeopardised the success of your missions. You weren't ready, weren't mature enough to understand... But now, given recent events, I think it's about time you knew.'

The Elder struggled to his feet and hobbled over on stiff legs to stand at Rachel's bedside. He reached out to touch her shoulder gently, almost reverently.

'Everything that this poor girl has done since she joined us has been to give her the tools she needs to look after you. She's been training so that she can throw herself in front of a bullet for you if need be, and that's what she did in South Africa - she gave herself up so you could carry on the mission. And as for all the Displacements she has dragged you on, they were specifically tailored, *by her*, to give *you* the ability to survive when she can't be there. Or after she has given her life for yours.

'Whether she knows it or not and whether you *like* it or not, *this* is her purpose, and one day she might have to sacrifice everything for you. If that day ever comes, and I truly hope that it does not, then you cannot hesitate, you cannot freeze, you have to be ready to see her die for you, accept her *gift* to you, and finish your task.'

'I...' Sam shook his head, wanting to deny it, but the old man stopped him with a look.

'It is in your power to prevent that from ever happening, of course, but to do so you must make a choice - I know it will be hard for you, but one day, probably soon, it may come down to one moment, one split second, where you have to take another person's life, where you have to decide between killing or being killed, or more likely seeing Rachel killed when she tries to rectify your mistake.'

James' brow furrowed and his eyes closed as he lost himself in painful memories.

'It's not an easy decision to kill someone and it shouldn't be taken lightly. I know that only too well; I've had to make that choice far too many times in a life that has been far too long, but it is something you *have* to be ready to do, Sam, because it's a choice that you *will* have to make one day, whether you like it or not.

'You had a taste of what it means to make that decision when you attacked Tessa, but next time you may not be so lucky. You can't wait for that rage to build up inside of you before you act, you can't give them the chance to beat you, or Rachel, before you decide to retaliate. You mustn't hesitate like you did in Cape Town, because by then it might be too late. You know what our enemies will do if we let them, you've seen it first-hand now, so don't give them the chance - strike first, strike hard, show no mercy, and don't let them hurt you or yours.'

The old man's expression finally regained its familiar jovial half-smile and he turned to meet his grandson's eyes, his gaze piercing into Sam's soul.

'She loves you, that's obvious to everyone that sees the two of you together and she willingly makes this sacrifice for you - she does it because of that love, just as much as she does it because it's her duty or her destiny. You feeling sorry for yourself does not honour that sacrifice and you have to harden yourself to make difficult decisions.'

He put his hand on Sam's shoulder. 'Look, I'm sorry for being so harsh, but it's for your own good and having said all that, I truly believe that you have made the correct decisions up until now and as far as any of us can see there is nothing that you could have done better - you are doing a remarkable job, both of you, and I am so very proud of you.'

He patted Sam, wiped a tear from his eye and then smiled. 'Right, that's enough of that nonsense! You're probably starving so I'm going to rustle up some food for us, and I suppose I'm going to have to get myself a coffee, because I shudder at the thought of what they'll call tea in this place.'

He walked from the room, closing the door quietly behind him.

Sam looked down at Rachel, feeling suddenly cold.

He knew that he didn't want her getting hurt because of him, but he still wasn't sure that he could bring himself to kill someone.

However, he knew that if it was a choice between his principles and Rachel, he would choose her every time.

A couple of hours later Rachel still hadn't woken up and James made Sam go home to change and give his parents an excuse as to why he was going to be out all night.

The only excuse that Sam could come up with was that he was going to stay at Andrew's flat with Rachel. Thankfully, they didn't mind too much; it was Friday and they had nothing planned for the weekend, so the only reservations they had were the usual parent-type ones of a boy and girl spending time together alone. Fortunately, they were fairly easy-going and really liked Rachel, so they usually let him be with her as much as he liked.

He grabbed some food from the kitchen and a few things from his room, then ran back out the door, messing up Violeta's hair on the way past, not wanting to be away from Rachel for any longer than necessary.

He sat with James next to her bed in silence, trying to keep himself occupied by writing his report on the Displacement.

It was almost midnight when she finally woke up.

Sam immediately jumped up and went to her side as she blinked and looked up at him. She immediately recognised where she was and her brow creased. 'Why didn't you keep me in South Africa?' Immediately her eyes went wide in alarm. 'Did Ralph...? Is he...?'

Sam realised that he hadn't even asked about Ralph and he blushed and turned to James. The old man just laughed at his shameful look and came to stand by him. 'Ralph is fine, child. He lost a lot of blood, but the two of you got him home soon enough for no permanent damage to be done.'

Tears came to Rachel's eyes. 'James, I failed, I couldn't...'

'Shhh... Don't. Not now. Rest first, report later.' The old man patted Sam on the shoulder. 'I'm going to go check on Ralph. And I think I'll see if there's anywhere up in Intensive Care that I can stretch out for a bit.'

The Elder walked out, chuckling quietly to himself and muttering something about "kids these days".

Rachel gazed slowly, lethargically around the room, taking in the machines she was connected to and the tube sticking out of her hand. 'I don't know what they've got pumping into me, but I feel pretty good. How do I look?'

'Well, you've finally broken your nose. Congratulations!'

It was something they'd joked about many times before; how it was incredible that in all her years of training it hadn't ever been broken. She always maintained that nobody was a real fighter until they'd broken their nose at least once. They had always found it quite funny, but now that it had actually happened it suddenly wasn't.

She tried to reach up to touch it, but couldn't; while one hand was tangled with wires and the IV, the other arm was in plaster and immobilised. She frowned at the cast. 'Oh, right... I guess I forgot about that.'

'I'm so sorry, Rachel, this is my fault; you wouldn't have gotten hurt if I hadn't hesitated.'

She looked up at him and tutted. 'Don't be silly, Sam. I keep telling you: you're not the killing machine, I am. You did what you had to do, you got Ralph out and then came back to help - that was all anyone could have expected. So, how did it go anyway? You're still alive at least... which is nice.'

Sam laughed softly. 'Well, I guess you could call it a draw. Although I did get to shoot Quentin.'

'Nice! I'm looking forward to hearing all about that!' She yawned widely and forgetfully tried to lift her hand again, this time to cover her mouth. Her efforts got the wires tangled and she ineffectually shook her hand in an attempt to extricate herself until Sam took pity on her and reached over to help.

'Cheers.' She grinned up at him. 'I'm sorry to be such a wuss, Sam, but I think I'm going to need to go back to sleep.' Her words were slurred and her eyes were closing involuntarily as the exhaustion and the pain medications fought against her will to stay awake.

He bent over and kissed her gently on her bruised and broken lips. 'Rest well, my love, I'll be here when you wake up,' he whispered quietly, but she was already unconscious again and didn't hear him.

The nurses made a bed for Sam on the sofa in Rachel's room and he stayed there for the whole weekend as she drifted in and out of consciousness. He ate by her bedside and wrote his report then did his homework sitting in the armchair with a dinner tray on his lap - it wasn't exactly comfortable, but he refused to leave her.

James was hardly ever there, not because he didn't want to be, he just had too much to do in the aftermath of the trip to South Africa, including taking care of the Spanish authorities and temporarily rewriting Sam's report to take out any mention of Diana and the help she had provided.

On Sunday afternoon he returned, a worried look on his face. 'Sam, we're going to have to move Rachel to England today.'

'Why?'

'We can't keep her here; despite our best efforts the police are still asking too many questions. Ralph is going as well, as soon as he can be moved safely.' He gave Sam a sympathetic smile. 'I understand that you want to be with her, but it's Displacer policy; we like to keep our people as close as possible, and besides, their families are in England.'

'What about me? I'm Rachel's family!'

'I know, I know, but we have to do this.'

'Can't that man who showed up at the flat just arrange things? He seemed to be able to do anything.'

'I'm afraid not. He has access to power, but it's limited outside of Britain.'

'Who was he, anyway?'

'He's MI6, an agent in the consulate here in Barcelona.' James smiled at the surprise on Sam's face. 'You don't think we operate entirely autonomously do you? Many of our early members were highly placed in government and we have ties that we maintain. We receive certain privileges and protections in return for keeping the world safe.'

'The government knows about us?'

'No, not really, just bits and pieces. There is only one person who ever gets to know everything about us: the ruling monarch.'

'The ruling... You mean?'

James nodded.

Sam blinked, assimilating the information. 'Wow, so, uh, does she know... I mean, uh, has she heard of me?'

James laughed. 'Of course not! She just lets us get on with what we have to do.'

'Oh.' Sam was quite surprised to find he was disappointed. 'And what does the rest of the government know? What does MI6 know?'

'The Prime Minister and the Home Secretary are the only ones who know anything at all about us and the information they have is limited to the fact that we are an organisation that the Crown has endorsed and placed outside of the law. As for MI6, they are given dossiers on our agents around the world and have been told to ask no questions and smooth things over for us whenever we need it, which thankfully isn't very often.'

'So there's nothing any of them can do to keep Rachel here?'

'No, I'm afraid not.'

'Sam, it'll be alright.'

They both turned at the weak voice that came from the bed.

'You're awake!' Sam threw aside his school books and rushed to her side. He picked up her hand - now that she was out of danger she was no longer on the drip or the machines and there was nothing in the way anymore.

'Of course I'm awake, with all the bloody noise you two are making!'

'I don't want you to go.'

'Come on, Sam, I'll be fine; I've been through worse than this and I don't need you fussing over me all the time. Besides, I've got work to do in London - I can't be on holiday here in Barcelona all the time and you've still got school. You wouldn't be able to stay with me anyway.'

'Just six more months, then I'll leave school and we can be together all the time.'

Rachel smiled. 'We'll see. Now, I want to know what I missed before you have to go home.'

Sam smiled and pulled up a chair so that he could keep holding her hand while he spoke.

Neither of them noticed when James left the room; they only had eyes for each other.

All hell broke out as soon as Diana opened her eyes.

She took in the empty space beside her where Davis had been, before her attention was drawn by Tristan's bellow as he picked up his sister's motionless body and ran howling from the room, then finally her eyes swivelled to Quentin, who was writhing and groaning, clutching his arm, his eyes squeezed shut in agony, blood dripping on the floor from the bullet wound and the multiple cuts and scrapes he'd received.

Quentin's eyes shot open and he looked at her with hate-filled eyes. 'Well, don't just sit there gawking, bitch, help me! Ring a doctor.'

'Mr Price!'

The shout made both of them freeze and the madness slowly faded from Quentin's eyes as he turned to the laptop on the dining room table.

'Report, *please.*'

Quentin grimaced in pain as he replied. 'I'm a little busy, sir, can I call you...'

'By the look of you, you'll live long enough to give me your report. Miss Birch can see to your injuries while we talk, or had you forgotten that she has had medical training? I suggest you tell her where your medical supplies are - I assume you have had the foresight to keep stocks nearby?'

Quentin glanced sideways at Diana and hissed. 'In the kitchen, cupboard above the fridge.'

Diana stood and sauntered towards the kitchen, reluctantly leaving the rather enjoyable sight of Quentin squirming in pain behind her.

'Get a move on!' The pain-ridden shout followed her down the hallway and she stifled a laugh.

While she never liked seeing anyone suffer, it went against her code and her training as a nurse, if there was ever anyone that deserved to do so it was Quentin Price. She hurried her steps nonetheless; she didn't want to miss Quentin's report because he would probably try to lay the blame for something on either her or the Twins and she wanted to be there to refute him.

Surprisingly, the Master was actually very happy with the results of the mission and by the time Diana came back with the large medical kit, the Master was already busy confirming the truth of Quentin's claims by checking his bank accounts and the title deeds to the gold companies online.

While Quentin continued with his report Diana began the task of patching him up. The kit was remarkably comprehensive, going far beyond what was normal for household first aid and she knelt down beside Quentin to administer a shot of morphine for the pain before patching up his arm, then using a pair of long-nosed tweezers to begin picking the glass out of his face and hands.

'Well done, Mr Price. It's not quite as much as I was expecting, but I am satisfied.' There seemed to be glee in the electronically disguised voice.

Quentin had slumped in his seat after the injection, the drug taking firm hold on him, dulling his senses and his eyes were slightly defocused as he smiled inanely at the laptop. 'Thank you, sir.'

'And Mr Davis?'

'He died, I'm afraid.' He did his best to look regretful, but there was almost a smirk on Quentin's face as he nodded.

There was no regret in the Master's voice, though. 'Well, that is a shame, but sacrifices often have to be made for the greater good.'

Diana listened, horrified at the ease with which they dismissed the non-existence of one of their companions, a team leader no less. She'd felt insecure in the Illuminati before, but now she knew precisely how much the Master cared about his own and it was only the thought of what she could do for her friends that kept her there, kept her from running screaming from the room and disappearing forever.

She kept her back to the camera as much as possible as she continued to treat Quentin, trying to fade into the background so that they wouldn't notice her as much. She didn't particularly want to listen to them gloating over their costly victory, but she knew that this was a rare opportunity to be party to one of their private conversations and she was hoping that they might let slip something that she could give to Rachel.

The Master fell silent and Diana thought that he had finished, but after a few seconds he continued. 'Very well, Mr Price, you have restored at least *some* of my confidence in you. You may give me your full report at your leisure and in two months you will accompany me as I carry out my plan to destroy the Displacers once and for all.'

'Thank you, sir, I won't let you down.'

The call terminated and Quentin stood up, pushing her away from him in anger and knocking her to the floor, not caring that she hadn't removed all the glass from his face. He grabbed his phone from the table and placed a call as he staggered, almost drunkenly, out of the room. His voice slurred slightly when he was connected.

'Doctor? I need help immediately... No. I've been treated. Fairly incompetently, but I'll live until someone professional gets here...' He reached his bedroom and slammed the door shut, cutting Diana off from the rest of his conversation.

She was left alone, sitting on the floor, staring at the blank screen of the laptop in shock, the Master's final words echoing in her head.

CHAPTER 14
LOVE

Despite the necessity of moving Ralph back to England, he had to stay in Barcelona for a couple more days, until he was in a stable enough condition to be moved.

Thankfully, the bullet had been of an old design, no more than a simple piece of metal and, unlike many modern day ones, it hadn't been designed to break apart on impact to do as much damage as it could. Even so it had torn Ralph's liver and caused a massive amount of bleeding. He had almost died from blood loss in the ambulance on the way to the hospital and had gone into shock on the operating table and had to be resuscitated. Despite all that, he had been extremely lucky and was expected to make almost a full recovery in time.

Rachel, on the other hand, had been discharged from hospital the day after her transfer to London. Her injuries were all superficial; she had avoided any internal injuries by being in superb condition and by knowing how to angle her body so that the blows from the Twins hadn't done as much damage as they could have.

She couldn't go home to her mother's house because there would have been too many questions, so instead she moved into Displacer Headquarters. Among other things, this made it a lot easier for her to sneak out when she received a message from Diana, two weeks after the trip to South Africa, requesting a meeting with James.

Surprisingly, it was Diana who insisted that they take extreme precautions against being followed this time - it was a complicated and time consuming process and usually Diana was sceptical of its necessity, but she had been demanding in her message and Rachel knew enough about the Illuminati and their paranoia not to question her.

They arranged to meet at Charing Cross Train station. Rachel got there half an hour early and sat in a coffee shop overlooking the platforms. When Diana arrived on the appointed train, instead of joining up with her immediately, Rachel ignored her and let her walk out of the station. She remained where she was for a couple more minutes, watching the people who had gotten off the train with her, familiarising herself with their faces and clothing. When the last of them had gone past she stood and followed in Diana's footsteps across the road, past the Oscar Wilde sculpture towards Covent Garden.

Diana strolled through the quiet back streets, going slowly with her phone out as if she were texting someone, allowing Rachel to close the distance just enough to have her in sight. As they had discussed, when she got to Covent Garden, Diana put her phone away and started carrying out evasion tactics. She made several stops, going into shops, looking at a couple of things, before coming back out and changing direction. She went into a bookshop that had two entrances on two different streets, going in one way, browsing for a while so that Rachel could go around to the other end of the shop, then leaving out the other side where Rachel could inspect the people who came out after her. She walked through Covent Garden itself, going down the stairs in the south hall, looking in the toyshop window for a minute, then coming back up the other side, all while Rachel watched from above. They went through most of Rachel's bag of tricks, but the extreme precautions proved unnecessary and after an hour of wandering, seemingly aimlessly, Diana got into a taxi opposite Holborn tube station and Rachel quickly hopped in after her for the ten-minute ride to James' safe house.

They sat together in the back, each in a corner, and Diana swivelled in her seat to look Rachel up and down, taking in her injuries. The young Displacer was dressed in a huge, puffy jacket, not so much for the cold, but to conceal the broken arm that was still in a cast. She'd also been limping and she sat with her leg out in front of her, resting it. Her shoulder-length blonde hair was loose about her head and draped down over her face, unusual for her, but it put the yellowing bruises on her face into shadow and make-up hid the rest quite effectively.

'You're looking much better than last time I saw you. I'm glad you're alright. How is Ralph?'

'He's in bad shape, but he'll live... Sam told me about Davis. I'm sorry.'

Diana shrugged. 'I didn't know him very well, but after what he did to Ralph, I'm pretty sure he got what he deserved.'

Rachel shook her head. 'Nobody deserves that.'

'Maybe not, but if there was ever a candidate that wasn't Quentin...'

'Yeah, Quentin is *very* much a special case.'

Rachel smiled at the young woman. As always she was dressed elegantly, but with a slight lean towards a Victorian Gothic style, with a long dark green dress.

She was truly beautiful.

And that made Rachel's decision even easier.

She slid across the seat and then, to Diana's surprise, reached up and pulled the woman's head gently down towards her.

Their lips met and they kissed. It was long, lingering and tender, and so different to kissing Sam. Not worse, not better, just different.

When it was finished Diana raised an eyebrow and tilted her head in puzzlement. 'Not that I'm complaining, but what was that for?'

Rachel sighed and slid back to the other side of the seat. 'That was to thank you for saving my life. I saw what you did, I saw you shoot that man and I know how dangerous that was for you to do, that if Quentin had seen he would have killed you... And also because Sam said you were a good kisser and I wanted to find out for myself.'

Diana laughed. 'Thank god you're not the jealous type!'

'Oh, I am, and that's why I don't want you kissing Sam again.' Rachel smiled cheekily. 'Unless I'm there of course.'

She laughed as Diana's eyes widened in shock, then scooted forwards to pay the driver as they pulled up at their destination.

They walked to the door of the house and Rachel opened the door, then stood aside to let Diana go in.

The redhead paused as she was walking past and turned to smile at her. 'This is a conversation we must revisit at a later date.'

'I look forward to it.'

Diana brushed her hand against Rachel's, then went in.

Rachel closed the door and leaned against it. She exhaled the breath that she seemed to have been holding since the kiss and smiled; that had been a lot of fun and now it was time to tell Sam all about it on Skype.

She pushed away from the door and walked towards Headquarters with a huge grin on her face.

Sam hadn't been back to Andrew's flat since the Displacement, more than three weeks before; he hadn't wanted to deal with the memory of Rachel's unconscious body lying on the sofa, tantalisingly out of reach, while he'd been forced to help James with the bleeding Ralph. It had been torture for him to have her there, only feet away, and not be able to hold her or comfort her. He was only going back now because Andrew had called a meeting.

He let himself in, fully expecting it to be in the same state of chaos as he'd last seen it, but as he looked around he could find little sign that anything had ever happened.

The flat was as clean as it had ever been and there were no traces of the blood that had been smeared everywhere. The only difference he noticed was that Andrew had a new sofa and rug in his sitting room, which to Sam wasn't an unwelcome change, considering how old and worn both items had been.

He wandered along the corridor towards the study, automatically trying the door to the locked room as he went past, but as always it was securely bolted and padlocked. The police had asked him about the room, thinking that there was something hidden in there - the gun that had shot Ralph perhaps - and had been very suspicious when Sam had said he didn't know what the room contained. They had been contemplating breaking the door down when the MI6 agent from the consulate had arrived.

He started up the computer, turned on the screens, then flopped into the chair and connected to Skype.

'Morning, Sam!' Andrew was the only one connected and he was munching on a crumpet in his study at home as he waited for everyone else. He didn't tend to go into the Society on the weekends unless he had to; he liked to spend Saturdays relaxing, or "vegetating" as he liked to call it, which explained why he was still in his pyjamas.

'Hi! Long time no see.' He gave his uncle a pointed look.

Andrew swallowed before answering. 'Yeah, sorry about that. Been a bit busy my end. Good job in South Africa, by the way - you should see the size of my bank account!' He chuckled. 'Although, I will be using that money *exclusively* to aid the society, of course!'

Sam laughed. There was no reason to doubt the truth of Andrew's words; things like expensive holidays to exotic places weren't very attractive to Displacers when all they needed to do was close their eyes and concentrate once a month and they could be anywhere, at almost any time and for as long as they wanted. And besides, the Society already paid its members very well - Sam himself had a bank account in England that had been set up over Christmas and was accumulating a tidy sum every month.

In short order Rachel and James joined the conversation.

James was at home and, as always was having problems with his webcam - no matter how many times he was shown how to use it he could still manage to find a way to make it not work.

Rachel, however, was in Displacer Headquarters, but rather than use one of the Society's computers she had her own laptop and was sitting at a desk in the bedroom she had been assigned. Sam was very pleased to see several photos of him and her together sitting on the bedside table in the background.

James eventually sorted out his problems and began the meeting. 'If you'll permit me, I will dispense with the niceties and get straight down to business, except to say good morning and thank you all for coming. Diana has informed me of some kind of plan in the offing that the Master claims will destroy us. As yet she has no details to help us narrow down exactly what he intends to do, but obviously, we will want to stop it. However, we are also going to take the opportunity that their being distracted presents to carry out our own attack. To which end: as you know, a few months ago Andrew and I identified what we believe to be a weak point in the Illuminati that we can exploit. He has been working on that exclusively and in secret, which is why he has been so antisocial of late.'

The old man gave a nod and Andrew took over. 'John and I believe that we're now ready to carry out our plan. We've actually been ready for a while now, but we've been waiting for the best time to do it. Now, thanks to Diana, we think we've found the perfect time. According to her, the Master is going to go on this mission personally, accompanied by Quentin, so, as always, it will fall to Sam to detect their Displacement and he will be accompanied into the past by Rachel in their usual attempt to stop them. Meanwhile, John and I will be ready and when Sam tells us that the Illuminati are safely away on their mission we will strike at the exact same moment; that way hopefully they will have no chance to fight back.

'I don't think you need me to tell you what a unique opportunity this is for us; not only will we be able to find out exactly who the Master is, but John and I can also strike a massive blow at the Illuminati's finances. I'm not going to tell you exactly what we are doing because of James' compartmentalisation thingy, but it's *big* and if we can pull it off we're fairly sure that we're going to be able to take a large part of their riches for ourselves, perhaps more than half.'

Andrew grinned and rubbed his hands together, his eyes lighting up at the thought of what the Displacers could do if they had access to as much wealth as the Illuminati. 'Diana has given us an approximated date for next month, so Rachel needs to recover fully before then. So, this month I want you and Sam to go somewhere, a beach or a health spa or something, I don't care where you go, just *no bloody fighting*! OK? We have no idea what you're going to have to do to stop this big plan so you both need to be in optimal condition, mentally and physically, and prepared for anything.'

Sam and Rachel reluctantly nodded their heads in agreement; neither of them were quite sure that losing the opportunity to pick up new skills was the best way of going about things, but Andrew was the boss and he usually knew best.

'Alright. Well, I don't know about everybody else, but I'm fed up with always waiting around and reacting to whatever Quentin and the Illuminati decide to do; that's just setting us up for failure. So, we're going to take the initiative for once.'

Andrew fell silent and James spoke up again. 'Does anyone have anything they want to say?'

When nobody replied, he nodded. 'That is all for now, then. We'll finalise details closer to the time, but you two, do what Andrew says, please: no fighting! Also, Sam, you don't have to go up against this with just Rachel, let us know if you want some back up. We can send people with you this time - I know Anne and Lisa are available and probably a couple of others.'

Sam shook his head. 'If it's just Quentin and the Master then we should be fine. If Diana comes back and says that they're taking an army with them, then I'll probably change my mind, but for now I think it's best if we keep this as secret as possible, like you said, Grandad.'

James nodded. 'Fine, I'll leave the final decision in your hands.'

There was silence for a few seconds, then Andrew spoke up. 'Well, then, I've got relaxing to do. Good luck everybody and see you soon.'

Andrew's connection closed, but before James could leave as well, Sam called out to him. 'Grandad, can I have a word?'

'Yes, of course.'

'Um... Rachel, do you mind if I call you back in 5 minutes?'

Rachel looked surprised, but she didn't question him, instead she just nodded. 'Sure, Sam. I'll be here.'

'Thank you.'

When Rachel had disconnected, James looked at Sam quizzically, his brow creasing in worry. 'What's up, lad?'

James had been very busy since South Africa with Displacer business and meeting with Diana, this was the first chance that Sam had to speak to him since he'd gone back to England and there was something on his mind that he'd wanted to ask him about since the Displacement, that had been troubling him for a while. Even now he wasn't quite sure quite how to broach the subject, though, and in the end he decided to just be blunt and get to the point, like ripping off a plaster.

'Grandad... Um... Is there something about Displacing that makes us more attractive to women?'

James was silent for a second, but then he laughed and sat back, obviously relieved that it wasn't something more serious. 'What on earth makes you say that?'

'Well, it seems that everywhere I go there's a woman wanting to, well, you know. There were plenty of girls who wanted to dance with me at the celebration in Port Royal. Then I met Rachel of course. In South Africa I was getting all kinds of looks from a maid, and then there's Diana...'

That caught James' attention and he raised an eyebrow. 'Diana? Really?'

'Yes.' Sam coloured in embarrassment.

The old man shook his head and smiled wryly. 'Well, Diana is a different matter, but that's between you, her and Rachel.' He laughed out loud. 'You scoundrel!'

'It's not as if I'm looking for any of this, Grandad! It just seems to happen to me wherever I go! I... well, I just thought that we might give out some kind of aura or something... I don't know, like the energy we use to Displace might attract people.'

'No, lad, there's nothing like that, I wish there was; it would make our job a bit easier and a hell of a lot more fun, but no. Sorry. I think that it's probably more a symptom of who you are when you've Displaced in the past. Just think back to what you've been: a dashing ship's captain and Sir Sam Vives, a Knight of the British Empire and a famous detective to boot! Of course women are going to find you attractive! Not to mention that, as far as I'm a judge of things, you're not too bad looking.'

'But what should I do about it?'

James laughed again. 'Are you really asking what the rules are for Displacers maintaining sexual relations in the past?'

The old man seemed to be having the time of his life, while Sam just sank lower and lower into his chair in shame. 'I suppose so... Is there anything? Any guidelines that I should follow? I really don't want to do anything wrong.'

'Well... We can be injured, we can die, we can age, but we can't get or make anyone pregnant and we can't catch diseases... so I suggest you enjoy it while you can!' He winked. 'I know I did.'

Sam sat up in shock. 'Grandad!'

'What is it they're always saying in the movies these days? What happens in Vegas stays in Vegas? Is that it? Well, what happens on a Displacement...' He laughed. 'My grandson the Lothario! Wait until the boys hear about this one'

'Grandad, please don't...!'

It was too late, though, James had already gone, and his laughter seemed to echo in Sam's mind as he groaned and put his head in his hands.

In spite of his embarrassment, he was feeling somewhat relieved, though; he'd quite enjoyed the attention he'd been receiving from women since he'd joined the Displacers, especially Rachel, and he was glad that they had a choice in the matter, just like they would do with anyone else; he would hate to think that Rachel was only with him because of some side effect of Displacing.

He clicked the button to call Rachel and she immediately accepted the call. When she appeared she looked concerned. 'Hey! Is everything alright?'

'I guess so. I've just been thinking about Diana and you and all the, well, you know, kissing.'

Rachel raised an eyebrow and smirked. 'Really? You've been "thinking about it" have you? Tell me more!'

She laughed as Sam blushed. 'Not that way! Rachel, please! I'm trying to be serious!'

'I'm sorry, it was just too easy. OK, I'll be serious. Come on, tell me what's on your mind.'

'Well... I've been thinking a lot about the time I spent with Diana in South Africa - we spent a few days together and I got the impression that if I'd wanted to, she would have slept with me.'

'Of course she would have done! And you should have!'

Sam blinked; that wasn't the answer he'd been expecting. 'What? But, I'm with you! That would have been...'

'Oh, Sam.' Rachel shook her head. 'This is something else that you are going to have to learn, and I hope it doesn't break your heart before you do. We're *Displacers*, Sam, we live entire *lives* in the past. Do you really expect that people who spend five, ten, twenty, even *fifty* years in the past will do so without ever making "romantic attachments" so to speak?'

'I guess not... And have you, you know...?'

'I'm sorry to have to tell you this, Sam, but you weren't my first romance. You have to remember that when I met you I was almost thirty - that would have made me a *very* old virgin!'

'Oh...' It had been obvious that Rachel was more experienced than him when they'd made love for the first time in Okinawa, but having her confirm it made it real. And it hurt.

'But, you were my first in the present, in our real lives, and that's what really counts.'

'That's... I guess that's all I could really have expected.'

Rachel saw Sam's disappointment and smiled, speaking gently. 'Don't get me wrong, what you and I have is special and it's so intense that it hurts sometimes, but we can't force ourselves to hold back if we ever go on a long Displacement without each other.'

'Are you trying to tell me you want to see other people?'

Rachel laughed. 'No, dummy! I would be perfectly happy for us to spend hundreds of years Displacing with you, just the two of us, for the rest of our lives, but we both know that isn't likely to happen - not just because you can Displace twice as much as me, but because we have a job to do and will be given missions that we will have to go on separately. It wouldn't be fair for me to ask you not to do anything, just like I hope you wouldn't expect the same from me.'

'I suppose that makes sense.'

'You know it does, Sam; we are ourselves when we Displace, but we're someone else as well and yes, those lives disappear when we come home, but we must still live them as if they were really ours. You can't always be thinking about what is waiting for you when you return, because it will condition what you do in the past. You have to live in the moment, otherwise you won't be happy, which will lead to bitterness and grief, and it might well spoil what we have in real life.'

Sam sighed. 'Once again I prove just how little I know.'

'You know *nothing*, Sam Snow.'

'I what?'

'Seriously? You didn't get that? Jeez, I know what we're binge-watching over Easter... So, where shall we go next week? Any ideas?'

'Well, we could go somewhere in Spain for a change, like to Marbella in the sixties. You know: topless beaches...'

Rachel laughed and shook her head. 'Honestly! I think you're obsessed!'

Sam shrugged. 'Of course I am; I'm a teenage boy.'

They smiled at each other, taking a moment to look into each other's eyes, feeling their connection even though they were hundreds of miles away.

'Do you have any ideas, then?'

'Actually, I've got something *very* special I've been saving up.' Rachel leaned forwards to smile mysteriously into her camera. 'It's a bit unusual, but it will be good for us and I think you'll like it.'

'What is it?

'Why don't you let it be my surprise? Don't you trust me?'

Sam smiled. 'Of course I do.'

'Then I'll see you next week in Barcelona and we'll have a nice *quiet* Displacement together!'

CHAPTER 15
PEACE

When Sam opened his eyes he was sitting cross-legged in a sea of golden yellow.

Rachel was next to him and she immediately snatched her hand out of his. He opened his mouth to complain, but she gave him a warning look and turned away, closing her eyes again and folding her hands in her lap.

For an instant he felt a bit hurt, but then he looked around and belatedly realised why she was acting the way she was: the golden sea turned out to be the robes of the hundreds of Buddhist monks surrounding them, which were undulating softly in the breeze coming off the mountains that loomed high above the white walls of a curiously square white building. There was a chill and a distinct lack of oxygen in the air that was making it slightly difficult for him to breathe and while his geography and knowledge of Asia weren't very good, even he could recognise that they must be high up in the Himalayas, somewhere like Nepal or Tibet.

The monks were in neat lines, sitting with their eyes closed in a large courtyard. They were all identically shaven-headed and Sam only just managed to resist the temptation to reach up to check whether he had his own hair. He noticed that there weren't only men there; a few women were scattered around, wearing similar robes and, surprisingly, with the same severe haircut as the men.

His quick orientation done, he was about to close his eyes and join Rachel in the meditation when there was the sound of a gong and a disturbance at the front of the courtyard. He hurriedly followed suit as everybody around him opened their eyes and bowed low, although he kept his head raised slightly so that he could see what was going on.

A young man came through the door of the building. He waved to a couple of monks who were at the front of the courtyard and the gong rang again. In response, the monks all straightened in unison and went back to their meditation.

Sam continued to watch through slitted eyes as the man wandered among the monks. He was small, dressed exactly the same as everyone else and at first sight there was nothing to distinguish him from any of the other men or boys in the courtyard, however, there was just something about him that caught and held Sam's attention - a feeling of peace, but also, strangely, of power and he couldn't take his eyes off of him as he walked through the lines of monks, coming steadily closer. Eventually, Sam had to look away or risk being seen and he closed his eyes, forcing himself to relax, copying the posture and the breathing of the hundreds of men and women around him and trying to blend in.

Somehow he could still feel the man, though, and even with his eyes closed Sam could tell when he stopped beside him and could feel the monk's eyes upon him.

The man stood there, between him and Rachel, for long seconds, then with a soft rustle of his robes he moved on.

After about an hour the meditation session finished and everybody began to drift away.

Sam stood up, stretching his legs painfully, then shook his head and sighed. 'Well, this isn't quite what I was expecting.'

'Come on, don't tell me this isn't worth a week of suspense! Welcome to Tibet.' She turned in place, gesturing towards the spectacular view of the mountains all around them, then smiled and rolled the arm that she'd just used - any injury in the present wasn't brought into the past and her broken arm was as good as new.

'It is beautiful, yes... But where's the beach I wanted? And I certainly hope they have room service.'

Rachel chuckled, but contained herself; it somehow didn't feel respectful to make loud noises. 'We're in the Himalayas. There aren't many beaches around here, I'm afraid.'

'Damn.' Sam smiled. 'All joking aside, this is great and I think a few weeks of meditation will do us good.'

'That's what I thought. We both know the value of it; we saw what kind of things Master Hamato was capable of just with the power of his mind, so this could be just as useful to us as a few years training - let's contemplate our belly buttons for a while and try to work out how he did it.'

Sam nodded and breathed in the clean air with a contented sigh. 'Sounds good to me. I think I can manage to sit on my arse for a while; it'll be a nice change.'

Rachel laughed again.

Sam frowned as something occurred to him and looked over at the door where the young man had appeared from. 'Do you have any idea who that man was? And did you feel the energy coming off him? He's, I don't know... *special* somehow. Not a Displacer, but definitely *different.*'

'That was the Dalai Lama.'

'Really? He's been to Barcelona a few times, I even saw him once, a few years ago, from a distance.'

'This isn't *that* Dalai Lama, dummy, this is the eighth one, Jamphel Gyatso.' Rachel saw Sam's blank look and shook her head. 'Maybe I should have told you where we were going; you could have read up on some history.'

The courtyard had been steadily emptying while they'd been talking, with the monks and nuns making their way to the exits, but now they fell silent as a lone monk approached them. He was an old man, bent and half blind, leaning on a long stick, but he came up to them with a confidence that Sam recognised; he'd seen it before in one other person, his grandfather. He stood in front of them for long moments, peering at them through cloudy eyes as if he was looking for something, before finally nodding in satisfaction and motioning for them to follow him.

Rachel and Sam exchanged a disappointed look, they must have done something to stand out from the other monks and had been singled out as intruders.

'I'm sorry, it's my fault; I couldn't stop fidgeting.'

'It wasn't you, Sam, it was me; I should have warned you, given you time to prepare.'

They sighed and followed the old monk as he led them towards the huge building.

It looked like their trip might be coming to an abrupt end.

However, instead of just escorting them to the front gates, the old man led them deeper into the building.

They went up several flights of stairs and down multiple corridors, past rooms that were painted mostly in bright reds and golds and decorated with ornately carved wooden walls and columns, becoming more and more confused as they went on; unless the old man was planning to toss them from the roof, they weren't being thrown out as they had been expecting. They kept going up and up, until eventually they came to a halt in front of two plain wooden doors at what must have been close to the very top of the building. Their guide slid open one of the doors with a bow and indicated for them to go in.

They stepped inside the small room and immediately came to a halt at the sight of the young man waiting for them; the Dalai Lama.

He was standing in the middle of the room behind a low table, surrounded with cushions that had been laid directly on the wooden floor. The room was otherwise empty and panelled with unpainted and decorated wood, in stark contrast to the rest of the palace.

He smiled at them in welcome and gestured for them to sit on two of the cushions. They obeyed and he sat opposite them and poured tea from a large pot, handing them each a bowl when they were full.

Sam sipped at the man's nod of encouragement, tasting the hot yellow liquid. It was unusual, unlike any kind of tea he'd had before; it tasted of butter instead of milk, but he found it was a nice change from the stuff that he always seemed to get whenever he was doing anything involving the Displacers.

They drank under the watchful eyes of the monk, who didn't yet drink himself and when they put their bowls on the table, he immediately refilled them to the brim. He watched them for a few seconds, saw that they weren't going to drink any more, then filled his own bowl before putting aside the pot.

He sipped at his tea without taking his eyes from them, gazing at them over the rim of the bowl without blinking, but, instead of shifting uncomfortably as he normally would under such intense scrutiny, Sam found himself sitting motionless, mesmerised.

After a couple of minutes, the man smiled warmly, put his bowl to one side and finally broke the silence.

'I look at you, but I do not see. My eyes tell me one thing, but my mind and my heart tell me another. You do not belong here.'

Sam and Rachel exchanged a glance. They had heard reports of people being sensitive to the fact that a Displacer was not quite part of the time-line, but those individuals were usually insane or in some way involved with the Prophecy - the fortune teller Sam had met in Port Royal had been one of them. For someone who was neither of those things to see it so clearly was unheard of, yet the man seemed to be fully aware that they were not who they appeared to be.

That was surprising in itself, but what was even more shocking to Sam was Rachel's reaction; instead of protesting or trying to explain, she accepted the monk's words and bowed her head in shame - it was the first time he had ever seen anything other than confidence or bluster from her, even in the most difficult circumstances.

'We mean no disrespect, sir; we have come to learn.'

The man just nodded thoughtfully and looked from one of them to the other before his eyes finally settled on Rachel. 'You have power, but it is untempered, wild, barely within your control and tinged with darkness; there is *such* violence in you.' He shuddered. 'I can feel the energy radiating from you. You shine so beautifully...' he turned to Sam and his eyes widened in awe. 'But you... You are *incandescent*, and I can hardly look at you. There is such strength in you, but...' he blinked, frowning and tilting his head to one side. 'But that strength is fractured. You are frightened of it. You have doubts.'

He paused and looked at Sam, as if he were trying to figure out a puzzle.

'*What are you?*' It was almost a whisper, but the three words filled the small room, echoing far beyond when they should have been swallowed by silence.

Rachel took a deep breath and opened her mouth to answer, but he held up a hand to stop her and gave her an incredibly wide and joyful smile. 'Please, there are very few things that can surprise me. Let me try to work it out for myself!'

Rachel laughed gently and assented. 'Very well.'

The Dalai Lama gave her a small bow of thanks, his eyes twinkling in delight.

'You say you have come to study and that is good; I believe that here you can find the peace that both of you need so desperately. It will take many years, though. Can you afford the time away from what I sense is important work?'

They both nodded immediately and the man's eyes widened in interest as he again looked back and forth from one of them to the other. 'No hesitation. Interesting...' He looked at them again, as if he were searching their souls, and then smiled in triumph. 'Ah, of course.'

He picked up his bowl and took another sip of his drink, his eyes shining with amusement, and they both followed his lead.

Sam found that he was enjoying the tea. It was surprisingly filling, though, and he struggled to finish it, not wanting to appear impolite. He put the empty bowl back down, then watched in dismay as it was immediately filled back to the brim by the smiling man as he continued to speak.

'If you wish to stay, then you are most welcome. You cannot be ordained, of course, because I will not ask you to renounce the violence that I see in your future, but you can still be permitted to live amongst us. We are, as a rule, celibate, but I can see the connection between you is strong, so if you wish it you will be given special dispensation. I will however ask you to limit your interactions while in the company of my fellows; act as one of them, even if you are not, please.'

He looked from Sam to Rachel and received a nod from both.

'Thank you. Now, I am sorry, but I must attend to my work. I will call for you when I can, but I assure you that you will find what you seek not only from me, but from the entire congregation. Speak to them, learn from them, and, when my duties permit, we will talk over more tea.'

He grinned at them again, shaking his head as if he couldn't quite believe what he was seeing, then laughed and drained his bowl.

Rachel followed suit, but Sam hesitated, eyeing the rich yellow liquid reluctantly, not sure if he could or should try to drink it, however he felt the eyes of the Lama on him and he took a deep breath and downed it as quickly as he could.

Somehow the old man knew that their interview was over and the door slid open behind them. They stood and bowed to the Lama, not just out of respect, but because it felt like what they should do; that it was what he deserved, but he just laughed and waved them away, so they turned and left.

They followed the old monk to a nearby cell with two beds on the floor, where he left them with a bow and a toothless smile.

Sam put his hand to his stomach, suddenly quite queasy. 'Oh, god. What was that tea? It was nice and all, but...' He groaned.

'Butter tea. Oh yeah, I probably should have told you about the etiquette with Tibetan tea...'

'I think I've kind of worked it out for myself, thanks. Now, please tell me the toilet's not a bucket.'

At first the monks seemed to suspect that there was something different about them and treated them with some caution, but they were soon accepted as part of the Dalai Lama's retinue. As he'd said, he couldn't spend all his time with them, but he spared an hour or so whenever his duties as the spiritual leader of his people allowed him to and in the meantime they worked and studied alongside the rest of the monks and nuns, living the same simple lives as them, always searching for the peace that the young monk had told them they needed.

He never asked them any details of what or who they were, but just accepted them and taught them with an incredible patience and humour. They became his friends and accompanied him as he made occasional journeys from one sacred place to the next, watching him impart his wisdom to his people.

They studied for several years and found some sense of peace and tranquillity under the guidance of the monk and his teachers. It was a revelation for them, but far from being satisfied, it just made them see how much more they had left to learn - they had caught glimpses of a truth that was still there to be had, that was just beyond their reach, and somehow they knew that it would escape them forever if they left.

So they stayed.

Unfortunately, they weren't able to complete their studies; when he was only forty-six the Dalai Lama took ill and, despite the care and prayers of his people, he didn't recover. Sam and Rachel were called to his bedside one day, and were shocked to see the vital man, who they had come to know and love, grey and shivering. He still smiled when he saw them, though, and held his hand out to them in greeting.

They knelt by his bed and reached out to clasp his hand briefly before sitting back on their heels.

'I am sorry, my friends, but I cannot serve you tea.'

Sam smiled at him. 'That's fine, I never really cared much for your tea.'

'Sixteen years you drink it and *now* you tell me!' The man laughed, but the laugh turned into a cough and he turned his head away and covered his mouth with a cloth.

When he turned back to them there were flecks of blood on his lips.

'I will die today.' He searched their faces for confirmation and when neither Rachel or Sam denied it he nodded and sighed. 'It is of no matter.'

The beaming smile returned, but it was weaker than before as he began to slip away, the light in his eyes slowly fading. 'It's extraordinary: I have watched you grow and change, yet there you sit, exactly as you were. Older, wiser, but somehow also the same children you were when you arrived.' He chuckled. 'No matter how many times I look at you, it never gets boring!'

His eyelids drooped and he seemed to be about to fall asleep for a second, but then his eyes opened wide again with a start and he looked at them, suddenly as lucid and focussed as he'd always been, as if he'd tapped a last well of strength.

'You have done well, very well. You have fewer doubts, less pain, less anger than when you first came to me. That is good, but I have failed you; true peace still eludes you both.'

He waved a hand, silencing their protests.

His gaze fell on Sam. 'You, my boy, have one last lesson to learn and I feel it will be the hardest: you must learn that *everything* must come to an end. Until you accept that, you will *never* be at peace.'

'And you,' he turned his kind eyes to Rachel. 'You cannot be at peace until *he* is. *That* is the blessing and the curse of the bond between you.'

He coughed again, but far more weakly, the energy that he'd somehow found, expended. They watched impotently as he wheezed, struggling to breathe, and it was a long minute before he was able to speak again.

'You will need what you have learned here in the difficult days ahead, but never forget that you are stronger together.'

He looked from one to the other, seeing the understanding, the respect, and the love in their eyes.

He nodded, satisfied. 'It's almost time, I can feel it. So much left to do... Oh well, there will be time enough later.' He smiled up at them. 'I have one last favour to ask of you, if I may? Would you? Please?'

They knew what he was asking for and without saying a word they reached out to enclose the dry and cooling hand of their friend in theirs.

They shut their eyes and, after a few brief moments, disappeared.

The old man gasped in wonder. 'Magnificent!'

He let out one last shuddering breath, closed his eyes, and moved on.

'Well, neither of you have bruises or broken bones, so I'm assuming you had a good rest?'

James' voice intruded on their senses and they opened their eyes to find themselves back in Andrew's flat in Barcelona.

They sat for a second, neither of them moving or saying anything, trying to readjust to themselves; it had been a long Displacement, the longest either of them had ever been on, and it disorientating in the extreme.

Theoretically, it was possible to stay in the past much longer, coming back right before death after fifty or sixty years or more, but there was never usually any call for it and it wasn't advisable to stay that long, not just because of the increased risk of accidents, but also because, in extreme cases, it did things to the mind - occasionally Displacers would come back unsure of who they were and it would take some time, months, even years, for them to recover.

James leaned forward in his armchair, suddenly concerned. 'What's wrong? Are you alright?'

He looked back and forth from one of them to the other, taking in their calmness and stillness, reading the signs. 'Oh, god. How long?'

It was Rachel who replied. 'Sixteen years.'

'Sixteen...' James' face fell. He did some quick calculations, then looked at Sam, suddenly grief-stricken, his eyes welling. 'Oh, Sam, why? That makes you forty! You're as old as your parents now. I wanted to protect you...'

Sam cut him off with a smile and a shake of the head. 'Don't worry, Grandad. Believe me; it was just what I needed. What we needed.'

'Even so...'

'James.' It was Rachel who cut him off this time. 'Sam was there for exactly how long he had to be and so was I; we both had vital lessons to learn and now we'll be able to face what is to come a lot better prepared.'

James grumbled, but accepted what she said.

There was something that was bothering Sam, though - a strange feeling that he had never had before. An itching at the back of his mind that only one thing could scratch. A need. A craving that was preventing him from thinking about anything else. 'Uh, Grandad...'

'Yes, Sam?'

'I could murder a cup of tea.'

CHAPTER 16
LOOSE ENDS

Rachel and James had only been able to come for the weekend, because they had to be in London, on hand in case Diana had to meet urgently, and before Sam knew it they were gone and he was on his own again.

Somehow, for once it didn't seem so bad to be alone; both he and Rachel had come home from Tibet with a new outlook on life, brought about not only by the hours upon hours that they had spent meditating, but by the teachings of the monks and their leader, who had shown them how to live in the moment. They hadn't come back as Buddhists by any means, but they had certainly changed their way of looking at things and had come to the realisation that they had been living too quickly - they had been wishing for time in the present to pass by so that they could see each other again, or go on their next Displacement together, and consequently had been missing out on a lot of what their normal lives had to offer.

Another thing they had learned was compassion, and with that in mind Sam revisited his past feud with Rafa Sanchez.

He didn't confront the bully or even talk to him at first, he just watched him surreptitiously, learning about the youth who had spent so many years tormenting him and he quickly found that Rafa was an object of pity, rather than someone to fear.

He saw the bluster, saw the aggression, saw the distance at which he kept everyone except his small circle of bullies and he saw that those boys weren't really his friends, they were just there to stoke his ego and accompany him as he asserted his dominance at school.

He saw how difficult Rafa found his school work, and witnessed his frustration and his failure, even though he put in more effort than Sam had originally thought that he did.

He felt the loneliness in him as he watched him trudge home from school, alone.

Worst of all he saw the way his family lived; they were barely scraping by in the economic crisis - his parents were out of work, depressed and angry, and that naturally made Rafa the same.

Sam knew that there were different reasons why people became bullies and he quickly came to realise that with Rafa it hadn't only been because he liked hurting people.

He couldn't forgive him, but he could understand him, and he thought that if he helped then it might at least make a small part of his own world just that little bit better.

There wasn't much he could do about Rafa's home life, but he determined to help him at school.

He was patient, taking it slowly instead of just jumping straight in.

Where before he had always stayed as far away from Rafa as he could, now he started getting steadily closer during lunch and classes. He nodded at him when passing him in the halls and didn't go out of his way to avoid eye contact, using whatever opportunity naturally came his way to get Rafa used to seeing him around. At first all he received were angry comments like "what do you want?" or "bugger off Vives!", but he never replied or responded in any way, and after a week or so Rafa no longer made any snide remarks.

Sam kept it up for another few days and then started his offensive.

He began simply.

At lunch on Monday he sat at the same table as Rafa and pushed the remains of his crisps to him when he "couldn't finish them".

On Tuesday he made sure to partner with him in fencing class and complemented him on a technique.

Wednesday he handed Rafa a pen when his ran out of ink.

Predictably, it only took until Thursday morning for Rafa to completely lose his patience and he confronted Sam before school, cornering him by the lockers.

Sam wasn't surprised; he had been expecting it.

The bully leaned in to hiss at Sam, face inches from his, trying his old intimidation tactics. 'What do you think you're doing, Vives? Do you think you can play games with me now, just because you know how to fight?'

The old Sam would have seen the situation as a perfect excuse to teach Rafa a lesson and that was certainly what the watching students were expecting; the whole school knew about Sam's new-found martial talents and they were waiting in glee for Sam to humiliate the almost universally disliked Rafa.

That was the old Sam, though. The new Sam had found another way.

He didn't move, he didn't flinch and he didn't pull back. He remained impassive and just gazed up at the taller boy with no aggression, no hatred, and no fear in his eyes.

After a few seconds Rafa pulled back, looking almost ashamed, and walked away to class, pushing his way through the crowd.

There was general disappointment from the watchers and the hum of conversation started back up, but Sam ignored it as he watched Rafa walk away.

He smiled; that brief moment of shame had been the first positive emotion that he'd ever seen in the bully.

One of the things that Sam had noticed in his investigations was that Rafa always had a very basic packed lunch: no fruit, no desert, just some tap water and a sandwich that was little more than a hunk of bread with hardly any filling.

On Friday, the day after the confrontation, Sam asked his mother for an extra sandwich to take to school, then at lunch he went to stand next to Rafa and just placed it on the table in front of him.

Rafa looked at it, then looked up at Sam, who in turn just looked back at him, waiting, the same impassive expression on his face as the day before.

Rafa swallowed and his chin dropped onto his chest. He closed his eyes and took a deep breath. 'Would you like to sit down, Vives?'

Sam smiled to himself, but hid it quickly. 'Thank you, Rafa, and please, call me Sam.'

Rafa grabbed the sandwich and began tearing huge chunks off it with his teeth and swallowing them, almost without chewing, as if he were starving. However, after a few seconds he stopped suddenly and put it down as if coming to his senses, then turned to glare at Sam. 'Why are you doing this? Why are you playing with me like this? Are you having fun toying with someone less fortunate than you? Does it make you feel good?'

Sam looked him in the eyes, trying to convey as much honesty as he could. 'I'm not doing it for myself. I saw someone in need and it didn't matter that it was you.'

Rafa had no answer for that and he looked down at the table, unwilling to meet Sam's eyes. 'I don't want your charity.' His voice was suddenly quiet, but it had a force in it that spoke of an iron will and a fierce pride, emotions that had been easily twisted, under unfortunate circumstances, into arrogance and hatred.

'It's not charity; it's a bribe. I'm paying you off - I'll give you a sandwich every day and help you with your schoolwork *if* you agree not to bully anyone anymore.'

Rafa looked puzzled. 'But you've already stopped me from picking on anyone, you don't need to do this.'

'Yes, I do, because I'm not always going to be here and I want you to always remember my kindness to you.'

Sam didn't want to push too hard too quickly, so he stood up and left.

The next day he gave Rafa another sandwich and while they were eating, Sam gestured at Rafa's battered school bag, open on the table in front of them. 'So, what are you having trouble with?'

'Everything.' Rafa didn't bother swallowing before speaking, adding table manners to the list of things Sam could work on with him.

Sam laughed. 'OK, let's try to narrow it down a bit. We have double maths this afternoon, what about that?'

'Um... quadratic equations?'

'That's a good start; they're easy once you get the trick, you'll see.' Sam pulled his own maths book out of his bag. 'You just have to solve the equation, you know: "x equals minus b plus or minus the square root of b squared minus four a c over two a".'

Sam had the equation memorised, like most of the class, because it was essential for their exams at the end of the year and he had to work very hard not to laugh as Rafa's eyes almost crossed.

'Er...'

He smiled confidently at him, encouragingly. 'Let me show you. You'll soon see how simple they are, trust me.'

They met every day for lunch after that and at fencing class on Tuesday Rafa was one of the students who asked Sam for a private lesson.

The change was immediate in the bully, he was suddenly a whole other person, and Sam knew that all it had needed was someone to treat him with a decency and respect that he had never gotten, even from his parents.

They didn't exactly become friends, but they were no longer enemies, which was a very good start as far as Sam was concerned.

Easter arrived and with it the date that Diana said the Master was going to carry out his plan.

James had long since arranged for Sam's parents to let him to go to London during the school holidays and he flew into Gatwick and took the train to Victoria station, where he was met by Rachel.

They leapt into each other's arms as soon as Sam passed the ticket gates at the end of the platform and kissed, oblivious to the other passengers streaming by. It had only been a few weeks since they'd last seen each other, but every time they met up again it was like a missing piece had been slotted back into place.

The kiss turned into an embrace and still they stood there, neither of them wanting to let go, but eventually they had to and Rachel took Sam's hand to lead him away. 'Come on, we've got a table waiting for us at Richard's.'

The restaurant was only a short distance from the train station, and Sam didn't have much luggage, so they decided to walk in the unseasonably warm weather.

Richard's restaurant was in Westminster, near the Houses of Parliament, and was popular with both tourists and politicians, although the politicians tended to come in later in the day once the sitting was over in Parliament. It was lunchtime and it was busy, but Richard had reserved a table for them in the window, where they could watch the people going by on the street outside. He kept up to date menus at Headquarters, along with an open invitation for all members to stop by whenever they wanted and most of them took him up on the offer at least once a month, if not more. This was the first time that Sam and Rachel had been in on their own, though; the other couple of times they'd dined there had been with Andrew and James.

After they had ordered, Richard came out of the kitchen. He walked through the dining room, greeting a few regular customers as he passed, but making a beeline for them. 'Hello you two!'

He plonked a small carafe of red wine on the table with a wink. 'Don't tell James.'

Rachel laughed. 'We won't!'

'Did you have a good flight, Sam?'

'Yes, thank you, Richard.'

'I'm glad. You know, it's always good to have you back in London; it doesn't feel right having you so far away.'

'Really? Why?'

'Because we can sense it when you're not around. Hasn't anyone ever told you about this?'

Sam shook his head. 'No.'

Richard chuckled and patted Rachel on the shoulder. 'It's not only the lovely Rachel here who feels sad when you're gone; all of us can sense the energy that you put off, some more than others, but the Elders are a whole lot more sensitive to it.

'Every Displacer radiates energy, that's how we confirm if the people we find really have the talent. It's not very strong and normally you have to be pretty close to someone, but *you* we can feel from miles away. When you're near it's like the sun coming out, but then when you fly away back home it's like the clouds have rolled in - we know that the sun's still there somewhere, but it's covered, and we can no longer feel its warmth. It leaves a kind of emptiness in us.'

Something occurred to Sam and he paled. 'So, that probably means the Illuminati can feel me too, right?'

Richard nodded. 'I guess so.'

'So they'll know I'm here and they've probably worked out that I've come to stop their plans.'

Rachel sighed. 'There goes any surprise we thought we might have.'

They fell silent as they worked out the implications, but after a few seconds Sam laughed and they turned to him in surprise.

He grinned at them. 'Well, we weren't expecting things to be any different than usual, were we?'

The two Displacers shook their heads, obviously not finding it quite as funny as he did.

Richard looked at them earnestly, burning with curiosity. 'I'd heard rumours of an op Andrew's been planning for a while, and all the Elders have been feeling that there's something big on its way... Is that why you're here? Is that what's happening this weekend? Is it the Illuminati again? Or are you finally fighting back, Sam?'

Rachel shook her head and smiled. 'Sorry, Richard, we can't tell you.'

'Fair enough.' He shrugged, disappointed, but he obviously hadn't really been expecting any other answer. 'Well, I'm going to get your food ready, I'll be back to see you later.'

Sam smiled. 'Thank you. Oh, and Richard.'

Richard paused and looked back at him. 'Yes, Sam?'

'Thank you for having us.'

Richard blinked, genuinely surprised, and for a few seconds it seemed like he didn't know how to react. Finally he gave Sam a bemused smile. 'You know, you're the first Society member to thank me in about fifteen years.'

He walked away, chuckling to himself.

As ever, the food was incredible. Richard had learnt his craft with some of the top chefs in history and it showed; his restaurant had Michelin stars and featured in just about every guide book of London.

They took their time, savouring three delicious courses and it was late afternoon by the time they left and started making their way to Headquarters.

They were both feeling slightly tipsy because of the wine; they had of course drank alcohol while on Displacements, but their youthful bodies in the present weren't as accustomed to it as Sir Sam and Lady Rachel had been for instance. They wouldn't normally have drunk anything at all, but the wine at Richard's restaurant was as good as his cooking, so they had decided to treat themselves for once.

Neither of them noticed they were being stalked until a hand came down on each of their shoulders.

Usually it took a lot to sneak up on them, but the alcohol had dulled their senses and the feeling of being together again had overwhelmed any caution they had at walking around London, which was a home to the Illuminati just as much as it was to the Displacers and they were taken by surprise.

Sam was the first to react. Sobering up instantly, he spun in place to face the threat, his suitcase dropping to the floor with a clatter as his hands came up in defence, adrenaline pumping through his veins.

He froze in shock when he was confronted by the smiling face of Diana, who ignored his fierce expression and slipped between his raised fists to hug him and demurely plant a kiss on his cheek.

'Hi, Sam! Welcome back! It's so good to see you again!' She whispered in his ear, her hot breath raising goosebumps and making him shiver.

He relaxed and returned her hug awkwardly, not quite sure what to make either of it or the fact that she had turned up out of nowhere. 'How did you find us?'

'I told her where we'd be.' Rachel answered for Diana, smiling happily.

'Why?'

'Because we need to have a chat.' She turned to Diana. 'You took all the precautions I told you to?'

The woman gestured at her large sunglasses and the hat she had used to hide her distinctive hair. 'Of course! Come on, I've got a room waiting for us at a place nearby.'

"A place" turned out to be the luxurious Hotel 41 and "a room" was a large junior suite overlooking the gardens of Buckingham Palace.

'I only asked you to find somewhere we could talk!'

'I don't slum it, darling. And besides, it's worth it for this conversation.' Diana sat down on the large sofa under the panoramic window and waved her arms to indicate the huge, black and white room.

Rachel whistled as she looked around the room then out at the view. 'You'll get no argument from me.'

Sam had stopped dead just inside the door and he looked back and forth from one of them to the other. 'OK, why do I feel like I've been ambushed?'

'I have no idea, darling.' Rachel smiled and then went to sit down next to Diana.

They grinned at him, enjoying his discomfort.

'Er... Shouldn't we be getting to Headquarters? James is expecting us.'

'Actually, he's not; I told him you and I were going to get some privacy tonight.'

'Oh.'

He left his luggage by the door and went to perch on the end of the bed, facing them. He was curious to see what they had cooked up between them, so he waited for them to speak, unwilling to spoil the moment and afraid to sound stupid or over-eager at what he suspected and hoped might be happening.

The grin faded from Rachel's face and she sighed dramatically. 'Sam, we have a big mission sometime in the next few days, and there's a real possibility that one or both of us won't make it back - we need to sort things out between us before then...'

Sam laughed, interrupting her. 'Seriously? Your plan is to use the "let's enjoy tonight because tomorrow we might die" line?'

Diana put her hand on Rachel's knee, then trailed her fingertips slowly up her leg. 'Actually we were pretty sure we weren't going to need any line at all.'

Sam stared down at her hand as it continued its way up Rachel's leg. He found that he was chewing his bottom lip for some reason and he shifted position on the bed, feeling very uncomfortable all of a sudden.

He coughed and his voice squeaked slightly as he replied. 'I think you're right.'

He wasn't sure how he felt about what seemed to be happening: the teenage boy in him was obviously and predictably excited; the rational part of him looked at Diana as someone who was still working for their enemies; and the man in him saw Diana as the beautiful and desirable woman that she was.

It was confusing in the extreme and somehow seemed to be the very definition of his life as a Displacer.

Diana smiled at him reassuringly. 'You already know how I feel about you, Sam. I started to have feelings for you when you were my captive, funny though that seems, and then in South Africa I finally realised that I'd fallen in love with you. These last few months I've also come to find that I have pretty intense feelings for Rachel as well.'

Rachel smiled and put her arm around Diana's shoulders. 'The two of us have spoken about this a little bit, but we thought that it was only fair if we explored these feelings together with you.'

'So, you two haven't...'

Rachel laughed. 'Of course not, we only kissed that once - I would have told you if we'd done anything else, and I would have discussed it with you beforehand.'

Diana nodded 'We knew that the first time should be all of us together, *if* we decided to do anything.'

'If you wanted it too.'

Sam's mouth went dry; the situation was every boy's, every man's dream, and yet strangely he found that he was uncertain.

Rachel smiled, she saw his doubts, and she hadn't expected anything else from him. 'You and I have been together for twenty four years, Sam. You've only ever been with me and that's not fair on you, so I think it's time you lost a bit of that naivety, that innocence. It's charming and everything, but it could harm you on a Displacement.'

Diana smiled. 'In the end you don't need to be in love with someone to have sex with them. Obviously I'd like this to mean more, but it doesn't have to, it can be just that, sex.'

Sam swallowed; just hearing the word suddenly made it real, but he still wondered if this was the right thing to do; Rachel was the love of his life, he felt a connection to her that went beyond the purely physical, it went beyond love, there was even a prophecy about it! He never wanted to do anything to hurt her and he hadn't given in to temptation before, precisely because he thought it would hurt her. But now she was saying that it wouldn't hurt, that it was, in fact, what she wanted as well. And Diana was just so beautiful. She was so carnal, especially in the way she was looking at him.

There was almost no way he could refuse.

Rachel came and sat next to him on the bed. 'This is just an itch we need to scratch before it gets too distracting and begins to affect how we work and how we are together.'

Diana laughed from her place on the sofa. 'And besides, it'll be fun!'

Sam looked from one of them to the other. 'You know, when we had that conversation last month this wasn't quite what I imagined. Whose idea was this, anyway?'

He settled his gaze on Diana, fully expecting it to have been hers, but Rachel surprised him. 'It was mine. I thought it would be a good way of showing you that it's not a big deal, plus I just *really* want to do this.'

Diana stood up and walked across the room to join them on the bed, sitting on Sam's other side.

He had no idea where to look and if he'd been nervous before, he was terrified now that the girls were so close to him. His heart was beating so fast he thought it was going to explode.

He closed his eyes and took a deep breath before turning to gaze into Rachel's deep blue eyes. He took her hands in his. 'Of course I want this, how could I not? But only if you're sure it's truly what you want.'

'I'm sure.' Rachel smiled and leaned forward to kiss him. He closed his eyes, revelling in the feeling of her lips: firm, unyielding, strong. So familiar, so comforting.

He felt Diana's hands on his back and shoulders, stroking him as he began to lose himself in the kiss, but all too soon Rachel pulled back. He was about to protest, but she shushed him, took her hands from his and reached up to turn his head away from her.

He found himself looking into the calm green pools of Diana's eyes as she leaned in to him. Her lips were soft and voluptuous, so different to Rachel's, and the contrast made him shiver.

Four hands now roamed on his body and he lifted his own to caress Diana.

He didn't see it when the eyes of the women met around his head.

They shared a knowing look as Sam gave himself over to them; there was no need to say anything more.

Sam and Rachel slipped out of bed before dawn and dressed quickly. They kissed Diana goodbye and she hugged them, wished them good luck, then rolled over and went back to sleep.

They left the hotel to walk the short distance to Displacer Headquarters, Sam's suitcase clattering on the uneven pavement one of the few sounds competing with the birds so early in the morning.

Rachel smiled at him. 'That wasn't such a big deal, was it?'

Sam couldn't believe his ears. 'Are you kidding? Of course it was! It was a huge deal!'

'So you enjoyed yourself then?'

'What do you think?' He grinned at her, but was surprised when she sighed.

'Good. Because it can never happen again.'

'Oh.' He tried to keep the smile on his face, but it was hard; he hadn't expected what had happened the night before to become a regular thing, but the way they had all had so much fun, the way it had felt *so* right... he hadn't expected it to be a one time thing.

Suddenly, Rachel burst out laughing. 'The look on your face! I'm only joking - of course we can do it again; I want to and I'm pretty damn sure Diana does too!'

'You...' He growled playfully and grabbed at her with his free hand.

She skipped away from him. 'Careful! You have to be nice to me now; one word from me and poof! No more naughty rendezvous for you!'

He grinned and shook his head; life was never dull with Rachel.

They let themselves in the door of Displacer Headquarters and put their pegs on the wall. This early in the morning the only other people in were John, James, Andrew and, surprisingly, Anne.

They went downstairs and found all four of them having breakfast in the kitchen, yawning and talking in low voices. They looked up and fell silent as Sam and Rachel came down the stairs, but when they saw who it was they smiled and called out in greeting.

Andrew waved at them from the head of the table. 'Hey, you two. Grab yourselves some breakfast if you want it and then we'll get started. I know it's early, but we have no idea when Quentin's going to Displace and we need to be ready. '

They quickly filled trays with food and drink from the counter by the sink, then joined the rest of their colleagues at the table, digging into the food hungrily as Andrew brought the meeting to order.

'Before I lay out the plan, James wants to say something.'

James looked around the group, making sure everybody was paying attention. 'I bear a warning from the Elders...'

'Ooh! Ominous!' John laughed.

Andrew instantly turned on him. 'Shut it, John, this isn't the time.'

John held his hands up in mock surrender. 'Well, excuse me for trying to lighten up the dour mood in this dingy basement!' He pulled his fingers across his lips in a zipping motion, then folded his arms, a suitably contrite look on his face.

Andrew sighed. 'Sorry, John, I shouldn't have snapped at you - I haven't slept much for the last few months... James. Please continue.'

James took a moment to compose himself, waiting for everyone to settle down again before speaking. 'Obviously, I haven't told the rest of the council any of the details of what we're doing, but they know that something big is going to happen soon; we've been sensing an imminent change in the time-line for a while now, like we always do before the Illuminati carry out an important mission. However, and this is the bit that has us worried, it's not quite the same. Somehow the threat feels different; it feels less like an attack on the time-line itself and more, well, *personal* is the only word we've come up with that's come anywhere close to describing it. I'm not saying that we should second-guess ourselves or abandon the mission, just that we should be careful; this might not turn out the way we expect it to.'

There was silence as they puzzled over the information, each of them trying to work out what it might mean.

Eventually, Andrew rapped his knuckles on the table to catch everyone's attention.

'OK, let's leave the philosophising to the Elders, they can tell us what all that gobbledygook means when it's all over... Like they always do.'

He grinned at James who made a rather rude gesture in reply.

Andrew chuckled, but quickly turned serious again as he glanced around the table and he met the eyes of the group one by one as he spoke. 'Right, then, the plan is going to be a bit different than usual, not just because there are two separate missions, but because of how we are going to have to carry them out.'

His eyes fell briefly on Sam and Rachel and he addressed the next words to them. 'Neither of you have come across circumstances like this before, so you don't know this, but we don't usually have multiple groups of people Displacing at the same time to different places; if the groups are too close together the energy tends to interfere and everybody just ends up scattered willy-nilly around time. So, that means we're going to have to split up into two groups. You two will be going with James to his safe house, while we'll stay here at Headquarters and lock ourselves in the room we've been using to plan - that should be far enough apart. James and I have made sure there are enough provisions on hand in both places to last the weekend, just in case, and both groups will lock themselves in and we'll isolate ourselves from the outside world for as long as it takes to prevent any distractions. Got it so far?'

He looked around, receiving nods from everyone.

'Right. So, while Sam and Rachel are working to stop whatever the Master has in store for us, Anne, John and I will be carrying out our own plan. With James' help we have traced the roots of a large part of the Illuminati's power and money back to the Knights Templar and we're fairly sure that we can take that all away from them by changing the results of an election for a new master of the order and putting someone who isn't Illuminati controlled in place. As luck would have it, one of my ancestors is also a candidate to take the mantle, so we might even be lucky enough to add that money to our own coffers.'

He chuckled. 'Thanks to Sam and Rachel, I've already got a ton of money in my account, which feels *really* good, I can tell you, but I'm looking forward to adding a few more zeros while taking them away from Illuminati at the same time!'

Once more, there was a gleam in Andrew's eyes as he spoke that Sam really didn't like; the time that he and Rachel had spent in Tibet had taught them that the pursuit of wealth wasn't necessary, or healthy and was, in fact, the root of most of the world's worst problems. His uncle suddenly placing far more emphasis on the money side of things than he ever had was worrying, therefore, especially because it was an Illuminati trait, not a Displacer one. He didn't say anything though, because, despite everything, he knew exactly how important it was to take what they could away from the Illuminati, and it was equally important that the Displacers had sufficient funds to fight them - Andrew's newfound greed was a conversation that was going to have to wait for a later date and he put aside the unpleasant feeling that was blossoming in the pit of his stomach and listened to his uncle continue.

'I won't bore you with any more details except to say that John went to do the setup last month. He's already made sure that the plan is feasible and he'll be the one guiding us - he has the exact coordinates already, so there should be no errors and once we're in the Holy Land it should be a fairly simple matter for the three of us to bring enough influence to bear. And that's it: nothing we haven't already done many times before.'

His gaze settled on Sam. 'That's the easy part. The hard part is going to be timing everything; we want to Displace at the same time as the Master carries out his plan, so that the disturbance *they* cause covers any changes *we* are able to make. Hopefully that way any Elders they might possess will have no idea what we're doing until it's too late and I'm sorry Sam, but we're all relying on you for that - for the next few days you're going to have to be constantly keeping an eye out for signs of Quentin Displacing, which means not sleeping and not straying from the side of James and Rachel for too long, including shower and toilet breaks. I want someone outside the bathroom door if you're going to be more than five minutes.

Sam raised an eyebrow. 'Seriously?'

Rachel just sniggered while Andrew nodded. 'Seriously.'

James could barely contain himself. 'Don't worry Sam; I changed your nappies enough times, I think I can listen to you poo a couple of times.'

'Grandad...'

'Although, I will let Rachel step in to scrub your back in the shower; I draw the line at that.'

'Grandad!'

Andrew interrupted them with a sigh. 'Can we get back on topic please, James? Or do I have to send you to stand in the corner with John?'

James grinned at him. 'Sorry, boss.'

'Anyway... Sam, as soon as you feel something, you tell James and he will ring me. The three of us will start to Prepare and Displace as soon as we're ready. Because you're so much quicker than us, you'll give us exactly fifty-six seconds to do that before you Prepare and Displace yourself. That should mean we leave at as near to exactly the same time as possible.'

Sam frowned. 'Should I be writing this down?'

James laughed. 'Don't worry about it, lad; I'll be the one doing all the timing. All *you* have to worry about is concentrating on that bastard Quentin and not daydreaming about pirates or...' he pointedly looked at Rachel and winked. 'Harems in Arabia.'

She stuck her tongue out and crossed her eyes in response.

'Children, please!' Andrew was desperately trying to stay serious and in control of the meeting, but was failing dismally as James made gurning faces of his own back at Rachel.

He flung up his hands in exasperation. 'Oh, I give up. We've said enough, let's just go, already.' He stood up from the table and they all put their dirty crockery in the sink before following him upstairs.

John and Anne paused briefly in the hallway to bid Sam and Rachel good luck, then continued up towards the bedroom on the fourth floor to get settled, but Andrew lingered.

He pulled Sam to one side. 'Are you sure you don't want to take anyone else with you? It's not too late to bring in reinforcements; I panicked last night and roped Anne in at the last moment, so there's no shame in doing the same - I could give her to you, or we could get Lisa from the museum...'

Sam shook his head and smiled. 'I don't want to put anyone else in danger. If it's just the Master and Quentin like Diana says then we'll be fine, but if we're walking into another ambush, then having more people there won't make a difference and it will just mean we lose them too.'

Andrew looked at Sam in surprise. 'When did you become so mature?'

'When we have a moment I will tell you about our lord and saviour, Buddha.' Sam solemnly put his hands together in front of his head and gave his uncle a bow. 'Namaste.'

Andrew's eyes widened even further and he stared at Sam with his mouth open, completely lost for words.

After a few seconds Sam, Rachel and James broke out into laughter.

Andrew's face screwed up in annoyance. 'Oh, very funny.'

James came up and slapped him on the shoulder. 'That'll teach you to take things so seriously around these two! Come on boys and girls! Time for a stroll! See you later, Andrew!'

James walked out the door, followed by Rachel.

Sam turned back to his uncle and held out his hand. Andrew took it and Sam gripped it firmly. 'Be careful, Uncle. Please. I have a bad feeling about this.'

'We'll be OK. It's you two I'm worried about.'

Sam shook his head with a smile. 'No need.'

He gave Andrew's hand a last squeeze, then hurried after his grandfather.

CHAPTER 17
THE CALM BEFORE

The safe house was more than comfortable enough for a couple of days. It had been rented furnished and, as Andrew had said, the kitchen had been stocked up with enough food for an army. Most importantly there were enough tea bags for even James not to run out. James and Rachel had also taken enough clean clothes for a few days and, once Sam had put his luggage in the bedroom he would be sharing with Rachel, but wouldn't be allowed to sleep in, they all sat in the living room together. Rachel and Sam settled on the sofa while James took an armchair on the other side of the room, as far away as he could get so as to give them some semblance of privacy.

James had brought several books and Rachel had brought her laptop, loaded up with all of *Game of Thrones* for them to watch while they waited for Quentin to make his move. They set up and settled in for the long haul, but Sam couldn't relax; he still couldn't shake the feeling that something was wrong and he stopped Rachel before she could start the first episode.

She looked at him quizzically.

He leaned in to whisper to her, not sure if he wanted James to hear. 'You haven't heard anything else from Diana, have you?'

Rachel grinned and checked her phone. 'No, nothing new. Why? You missing her already?'

Sam shook his head. 'It's not that, I just think that there's something we're not seeing - I've got the same feeling I had before we went to South Africa, only this time it's a lot worse.

Rachel frowned. 'You told Ralph you thought that Quentin's plan was too simple, that there had to be more to it, but you never said anything about any feelings.'

'I know. I wasn't sure then, but I am now, and the warning James gave us from the Elders has just got my Spidey-sense tingling.'

'You shouldn't worry too much about it; I'm sure we'll be fine, we always are.' She leaned in and kissed him. 'I trust in you, Sam. You'll take us exactly where we need to be and you'll be able to get us out of any trouble we find ourselves in. You always do. And I'll be there with you.'

Although it was true that they were stronger together, Sam couldn't help thinking back to the conversation he'd had with James at Rachel's bedside in the hospital in Barcelona about how her fate was to sacrifice herself for him and he was troubled by how willing she seemed to be to do so. He pushed aside his doubts, though; there was nothing he could do about them at that moment, and forced a smile as he rested his forehead against hers.

They stayed like that for a few seconds, drawing comfort from each other, before Sam pulled back and waved at the laptop. 'Right then, let's see what the fuss is all about.'

Rachel grinned and reached out to press play.

James looked up from his book and gave them a scathing look as the theme music came on. 'Can you turn that down a bit?'

'Sorry!' Rachel mashed the volume button a few times and the music went down to a more appropriate level. She folded her legs underneath her and leant against Sam. He put his arm around her and they got comfortable.

James rolled his eyes and muttered under his breath as he went back to his reading. 'That tune's so damn boring and repetitive, I can't believe they paid someone good money to write it...'

Rachel and Sam shared a grin at his grumbling, but, as they got caught up in the TV show, neither of them noticed the worried look on his face, or the fact that he was just staring at the book, not turning any pages.

As expected, Quentin didn't make his move that day, but it didn't stop Andrew from phoning every hour on the hour to check in. The time passed pleasantly enough, though. They cooked and had lunch and dinner together as a kind of family, which Sam enjoyed immensely; it had been far too long since he'd spent so much time with his grandfather and while they ate James amused them with anecdotes from the war. James was a master storyteller, like many of the men and women they'd encountered at Symposium, and he had them in stitches with some of his tales; humour was a very British way of getting through difficult times and there had apparently been a lot of high jinks on the ships that he had served on. He'd often told Sam that somehow you never remembered the bad things, you just remembered the good times, and there were a surprising amount of them to recount.

Sam's favourite story had always been the one where his grandfather had been promoted to an officer... for all of five minutes. He'd put on his uniform immediately after receiving the confirmation and gone about his work.

The first officer he'd seen had been a bully, who always treated James and others badly, but who was now the same rank as him. The man had immediately made a "sarky comment", in James' words, that had something to do with "lower classes" and had gone on to express his opinion that James was "not officer material" in clear, colourful, and uncertain terms.

James had decked him, laying him out in one punch, applauded by everyone that had overheard them. He'd then gone straight back to his room and put his old uniform back on before turning himself in.

Far from being ashamed of the event and his loss of temper, the story was one of James' favourites and he was proud of it; like Sam he was a big champion of confronting bullies wherever possible.

Stories like that kept them entertained for hours and, although he would never say anything to Rachel, Sam vastly preferred listening to them than watching the series.

Night was tough. Sam stayed awake, following Andrew's orders, checking every so often to see whether Quentin had gone. He didn't think it was necessary; he was fairly sure that he'd wake up when something happened, but he did so anyway because he'd never be able forgive himself if they missed this opportunity because he'd dozed off.

They were fine until just after two in the morning; people in Spain generally stayed up until much later than people in England so Sam was used to it, but the activities and excitement of the night before eventually caught up with Rachel and Sam and they found it almost impossible to stay awake. Even a brief sparring session in the tiny back garden didn't help, especially because they had to hold back for fear of waking the neighbours and could barely work up a sweat.

In the end, at about four in the morning, James ordered Rachel to get some rest.

Sam fetched her a blanket and she lay on the sofa, instantly falling asleep. He kissed her on the forehead, then followed James into the kitchen.

He sat at the breakfast bar and watched James making coffee, yawning, his head propped in his hands.

While they were waiting for the coffee to percolate, James threw a large packet of chewing gum on the table in front of Sam. 'Best thing the Yanks ever brought over during the war that is, apart from the stockings of course; the women didn't half look good in those nylons, I can tell you!'

He grinned and Sam shook his head.

'Seriously, though, there's something about chewing that keeps you awake and we got into the habit of it during long night watches in the Atlantic. It beats smoking.'

Sam popped a piece in his mouth then put the rest in his pocket. 'Thank you.'

When it was done, James poured two mugs of coffee, topping them up with milk and plenty of sugar before handing one to Sam, who spat the gum out before taking a sip.

He grimaced; he didn't like coffee at the best of times, but having it taste of mint gum was a hell of a lot worse. He forced himself to gulp it down, though; he would try anything to keep awake.

He wrapped his hands around the mug and stared into the brown liquid.

'Penny for 'em?'

He frowned at James, meeting the old man's gentle eyes. 'Sorry, what?'

'What are you thinking, Sam?'

Sam shook his head. 'It doesn't matter.'

'Come on, spit it out. I can see that something's troubling you and it's not as if we haven't got any time on our hands. We don't often get a chance to talk like this, lad, so why don't you take advantage of it?'

Sam looked down at his coffee again. The last thing he wanted was to confront his grandfather at a time like this, but he had put off doing so for too long and there were questions that needed to be asked.

'Diana told me in South Africa that you'd said some things to her, one of which was that you don't expect me to win all the time and that it's alright for me to fail.'

'Ah,' James nodded. 'I was wondering when you were going to get around to that.'

'She told you?'

'Yes. She was quite upset with me that I hadn't spoken to you about it. She's got a lot of fire in her, that girl does. She's like Rachel, which is probably one of the reasons I like her.'

'And?'

'And what?'

'And why haven't you spoken to me about it?'

James took a sip of his coffee, sorting his thoughts before speaking. When he finally looked up at Sam there was sorrow, but also a determination in his eyes.

'I haven't spoken to you about it because it's not something you should ever hear, not from me, not from her, not from anyone and Diana overstepped her bounds by a long way by telling you. It was a mistake for me to ever talk to her about it, in fact, but I was feeling a bit down that day; it was after our visit to the tea shop in Barcelona - I guess it brought back some memories that I thought I'd gotten over and I suppose I was vulnerable. She was there, we got to chatting, I drank a bit too much and I said a bit too much as well. It wasn't ever meant for your ears.'

He sighed. 'With all the wins you've been handing us we can afford to take a loss. It'll hurt us, but it's not like it was a couple of years ago, so in that way it would be alright for you to lose. However, telling someone it's alright to fail is a terrible thing. I've seen what happens in battle when someone thinks they're going to lose, going to die, I've seen the will to fight and the will to live just leave them. It becomes a self-fulfilling prophecy; they believe they are going to die and they find a way to make it happen.

'That's why you should never have known - as I told you before, we're in a war with the Illuminati and just like those poor sods back then, you mustn't ever think that you're going to lose. You mustn't even think it's alright, because then you'll stop doing what you do best, you'll stop working angles that the rest of us can't even see and in this war it might not just mean a failed mission, it might cost you your life. Or your very existence.

'*That's* why I haven't spoken to you about this, and that's why I almost can't forgive Diana for telling you.'

'She thought she had my best interests at heart.'

'I know, and that's why I said "almost".' He grinned. 'She's too smart and good-looking to stay angry at for long. And most of all she cares about you deeply, almost as much as Rachel, I think. And that arse...'

'Grandad!'

James winked. 'I knew that would get you going. Now are you going to quit moping? Because tonight's going to be long enough as it is without you whingeing.'

'I don't whinge!'

'Whining, then.' James downed the rest of his coffee. 'Right! How about a game of scrabble? Now you can speak English properly, *at last*, maybe you'll actually come close to beating me.'

'How about we play in Spanish?'

'We can't; haven't got the accents, now, have we? Come on, pour us both another cup while I go get the board.' James slowly got out of his chair and stretched his back before making his way from the room.

Sam yawned and poured more thick black liquid into the mugs.

He had a feeling he was going to get very sick of coffee before the Easter holidays were over.

The previous time they were trying to react to the Illuminati, Andrew had instructed Sam to attempt to Displace every so often while concentrating on Quentin as a target. In the end, though, he had been able to sense when Quentin had gone into the past without trying.

This time was no different.

Halfway through the afternoon of the second day, Sam suddenly sat forward and slammed the laptop closed, cutting off screams of pain from some kind of bizarre wedding gone wrong.

'Grandad! NOW!'

James started, frightened half to death by Sam's sudden shout. His book fell to the floor and in his hurry to get to his phone he knocked it off the table and had to scramble on the floor for it. Still on his knees he brought up Andrew's number and called. He shouted into the phone for Andrew to begin, then hung up.

It would have been a comical scene if there hadn't been such urgency.

Sam turned to Rachel and took her hands in his. 'Are you ready?'

She smiled at him. 'Always, my love.'

He nodded and she closed her eyes to begin Preparing.

Sam looked over at James. His grandfather had his eyes glued to his watch, moving his mouth as he counted the seconds. At almost exactly the same moment that James looked up at him and mouthed *GO!* he felt the energy from Andrew, Anne and John as they Displaced, even from a mile away.

Sam suddenly felt a sense of calm and he smiled as he felt everything coming together perfectly. He closed his eyes and reached out for Quentin.

It took barely five seconds to find him and then...

...he opened his eyes to blinding sunlight.

Rachel's hand slipped out of his as she raised it to shade her eyes and they squinted against the glare and looked around, trying to orientate themselves.

They were standing on the beach with their backs to the water on a tiny island, in the middle of the ocean. It looked like one of the ones that was only supposed to exist in cartoons - only about a hundred metres across, with only a few scraggly palm trees in the middle and a clear view of the water on all sides.

The trees were the only signs of life, though; there was no sign of Quentin, no evidence that he had ever been there, nowhere for him to hide and no reason that Sam could see for him to be there, except to sunbathe or get away from everything. For one horrible moment he thought that maybe they were on one of the islands where they had done the atomic testing and at any second a bomb was going to go off and obliterate them, just like in the films he'd seen in history class.

But that wasn't possible; he knew that they were in the right place. He could still feel the energy from...

They spun as cruel laughter rang out behind them.

Quentin was standing knee deep in the water only a few metres away.

He was alone. There was no sign of the Master.

'Hi guys, thank you for coming so promptly!' He waved and gave them a huge smile, but there was an evil glint in his eye behind the humour that terrified Sam - he'd been expecting them, he'd planned for this, and he knew there was nothing they could do about it. They'd fallen into his trap, whatever it was.

'I think you'll agree I picked a nice spot for my little distraction. I'm afraid I can't stay to play with you, though; I forgot to bring any suntan lotion and besides, I have a party to go to. But please, feel free to enjoy yourselves while you're here: go for a swim, sunbathe, have rampant sex on the beach...'

He leered at Rachel and Sam found his hands involuntarily curling into fists - he wanted nothing more than to leap at Quentin, but it would be futile with him standing in the water already.

'Seriously, though, stay here for as long as you want. There's no point hurrying home anyway, because there's nothing you can do to help your friends; they should already be dead.' He waved cheerfully. 'See you around Vives. Oh, and by the way, the Master sends his love.'

He laughed once more, then leapt backwards into the ocean and instantly disappeared.

'No...'

Sam felt an icy chill run through him despite the sun beating down on his head. He grabbed Rachel by the arm and dragged her towards the water, breaking out into a run.

She hesitated, stumbling, still staring at where Quentin had been, not sure what was going on, so he released her and sprinted forwards without her.

Despite the fact that everyone would tell him it didn't matter how quickly he went home, that it didn't matter if they spent years on the island, that he would still get back at the *exact* same time, somehow Sam knew that every moment counted. Maybe it was that innocence that Rachel had accused him of having, maybe it was his instincts, or maybe there *was* something after all, some greater *power* that had put him there to do what needed to be done. Whatever it was, something was telling him that it wasn't too late.

There was still a chance.

He dived into the water and...

...opened his eyes.

'Sam? What's happening? What did he mean?' Rachel's eyes blinked open and she looked at him. Her face was screwed up in alarm, her panic evident, but there was also confusion on her face; she still hadn't realised what was happening.

There wasn't any time to answer her, though; he had to work fast.

He closed his eyes again and searched for Andrew as he tried to Prepare.

'Sam? Sam!' Rachel's voice faded, became fainter, further away as he sent his consciousness out...

Andrew was there, he could still feel him - there *was* time after all.

Sam could sense the energy within himself. Thanks to his grandfather's discovery there was still enough left.

But it didn't want to come.

It didn't matter, it *would* come; he would *force* it to.

He gritted his teeth.

All of the lessons about concentration and peace flew from him in an instant as he *tore* his way to where he needed to be with a mental scream.

The energy was coming now, finally, and he grabbed it, catching it in a stranglehold. It struggled to escape his grasp, but he tightened his grip on it and bent it to his will.

Just a few seconds more...

Somewhere at the back of his mind he became aware of James' phone ringing and he almost lost his focus in his panic. He wanted to shout at his grandfather: *don't answer! It's not fixed until you know! Don't answer it, please god DON'T! There's still a chance!* But he couldn't afford the time, he was almost...

ANDREW!!!

He grabbed at the bright light that was his uncle's presence in the past and sent his whole being...

'Hello?'

James' voice rang in Sam's head, clear and loud as a church bell, and he gasped, his eyes flying open, the connection with Andrew severed abruptly with a snap, sending an intense pain shooting through his chest and his soul.

He looked across the room and met James' eyes, saw the tears starting to come, saw the old man's mouth move as he struggled to speak.

Sam already knew what he was going to say.

EPILOGUE

The funeral took place in the small village church near the Price estate that had held the Symposium.

The Manor had long since been turned into a hotel and its gardens were now a golf course, but the Displacers had always been buried in the church grounds and that was never going to change.

Sam stood by the graveside after the service, staring down at the stone and the mound of fresh earth that marked the resting place of his uncle. There was another grave right next to it, that of his aunt, Susan, but of course there was only an empty casket in hers - the Displacers held funerals for all their members, whether they had existed or not, whether the body had been lost to the past or not.

He lifted his head and slowly gazed around the graveyard, taking in the neat rows of headstones. There were well over a hundred of them, all the same shape, all stamped with the same crest: the hourglass and scroll of the Honourable Society of Displacers.

Every Displacer who had ever been a member of the Society was buried there and only slightly more than half of them had died of old age, surrounded by their friends, family and fellows - the rest had been taken before their time. Like Andrew. Or *by* time, like Susan.

He fought to hold back the anger, the rage that had been building in him since James had spoken those three words, *Andrew is dead.* Now was not the time to let that fury out, though; he would keep it inside, build it, stoke the fires and make it white hot, and then he would use it to *burn* those who deserved it. This had gone on long enough - he would make them pay, he would make all of them pay.

With a sigh, he relaxed hands that had clenched into fists and looked up at the church and the people gathered there.

Anne was by the door, weeping.

Rachel was with her, trying to comfort her, while fighting back her own tears. She felt his gaze and looked over at him, anguish mixed with concern plain on her face, but he turned away from her, refusing to meet her eyes.

James was sitting on a bench under a tree, surrounded by his fellows. He looked older and more tired than Sam had ever seen him; the life had drained out of the old man, leaving him a mere shadow, an empty husk of what he had been.

The entire society had come to pay their respects to Andrew, including Elders and Displacers that Sam had never met.

Only one member was conspicuous by their absence - the spy, the traitor in their midst.

The Master.

John.

ABOUT THE AUTHOR

Simon Brading tried his hand at many things before it occurred to him that he might have a few stories to tell. As well as the odd novel he writes screenplays and also does some acting every so often.

www.simonbrading.co.uk

For news of special offers, upcoming releases, exclusive content, competitions and events, please follow me on social media.

Instagram - @sibrading
Facebook - Simon Brading Author
Tiktok - @SimonBradingAuthor

ALSO BY SIMON BRADING

The "Displacers" series - a young adult time travel adventure series for all ages.
The Time Traveller's Nephew
The Secret of the Ancients
The Whitechapel Plot
The Price of Greed
The Time for Vengeance

The "Misfit Squadron" Series - a Steampunk series set in an alternate World War 2.
The Battle Over Britain
The Russian Resistance
A Misfit Midwinter
The Lion and the Baron
The Maltese Defence
Tales from the Second Great War
The Siege of Gibraltar
The King's Mission
The Home Front
Taking to the Skies
The Invasion of Britain

The "Twin Ambitions" series - ballet books for children ages 7 and up.
Fight to Dance
Back to Basics

The "Ni Hon - The Two Books" Series - a young adult series set in a dystopian future Japan.
The Black Book

Others
Public Enemy
Empath
The Lifeboat at the End of the Universe